HE DIDN'T SAY ANYTHING

He just stepped into the room, kicked the door closed with his heel, drew her into his arms, and kissed her.

As always, she melted into him, her every thought, her every desire focused on Ronan, only Ronan. Desire flowed through her, warm and honey-sweet. Maybe tonight, she thought, maybe tonight he would carry her to bed and make love to her. She knew he wanted her. She could taste it in his kiss, feel it in the way his body quivered against hers.

She was breathless when he broke the kiss.

"I've been wanting to do that for hours," he said, his voice husky. "I keep telling myself that I'll bring you nothing but misery, but I can't leave you alone." He ran his knuckles lightly over her cheek. "I can't stay away."

She stared up at him, dazed by his kiss, mesmerized by the heat in his eyes. "I don't want you to stay away."

Books by Amanda Ashley

Dead Sexy

Desire After Dark

Night's Kiss

A Whisper of Eternity

After Sundown

Night's Touch

Published by Zebra Books

DEAD PERFECT

AMANDA ASHLEY

ZEBRA BOOKS
Kensington Publishing Corp.
www.kensingtonbooks.com

ZEBRA BOOKS are published by

Kensington Publishing Corp.
850 Third Avenue
New York, NY 10022

All Kensington titles, imprints, and distributed lines are available at special quantity discounts for bulk purchases for sales promotion, premiums, fund-raising, educational, or institutional use.

Special book excerpts or customized printings can also be created to fit specific needs. For details, write or phone the office of the Kensington Special Sales Manager: Attn. Special Sales Department. Kensington Publishing Corp., 850 Third Avenue, New York, NY 10022. Phone: 1-800-221-2647.

ISBN-13: 978-0-8217-8061-9
ISBN-10: 0-8217-8061-1

First Printing: February 2008
10 9 8 7 6 5 4 3 2 1

Printed in the United States of America

To Abbey Marie,
the newest member of our family.
Welcome, sweetie!

Chapter One

Shannah had followed him every night for the last four months. At first, she hadn't been sure why, other than the fact that she was dying and out of a job and had nothing better to do.

She remembered the first time she had seen him. She had been sitting by the back window in the Pot Pourri Café across the street from the town's only movie theater. She had been sipping a cup of hot chocolate when she saw him emerge from the theater. It had been late October, near Halloween, and the theater had been running classic vampire movies all month, showing a different film each night of the week. The old Bela Lugosi version of *Dracula* had been playing that night.

The stranger had been wearing a long black duster over snug black jeans and a black T-shirt. With his long black hair, her first thought was that he could have been a vampire himself except that his skin was a dusky brown instead of deathly pale. A wannabe vampire, obviously. She knew there was a whole cult of them in the city, men and women who frequented Goth clubs. They wore black clothes and capes. Some of them wore fake fangs and pretended to drink blood. She had heard that some didn't pretend, but actually drank blood. Others role-played on the Internet in vampire and Goth chat rooms.

Shannah had been sitting by the window in that same café when she saw the stranger the second time. He hadn't been coming out of the movie theater that night, merely strolling down the street, his hands thrust into the pockets of his jeans, which were black again. During the next few weeks, she saw him walking down the same street at about the same time almost every night, which she supposed wasn't really all that strange. After all, she went to the same café and sat at the same booth in the back at about the same time every night.

One evening, simply for something to do, she left the café and followed him, curious to see where he went. She followed him the next night, and the next. And suddenly it was a habit, a way to spend the long, lonely nights when she couldn't sleep. Sometimes he merely walked through the park across from City Hall. Sometimes he sat on one of the benches, as unmoving and silent as the bronze statue of the town's founding father that was located near the center of the park.

While following the man in the long black duster, she learned that he went to the movies every Wednesday evening and always sat in the last row. He wandered through the mall on Friday nights. He spent Saturday nights in the local pub, invariably sitting in the shadows in the far corner. He always ordered a glass of red wine, which he never finished. Other than the wine, she never saw him eat or drink anything. He never bought popcorn or candy at the movies. He never bought a soda or a cup of coffee or a hot dog in the mall.

When she followed him home, she learned that he lived in an old but elegant two-story house at the edge of town. The house had bars on the windows and a security screen door, and was surrounded by a block wall that must have been twelve feet high, complete with an impressive wrought-iron gate. She wondered what he was hiding in there, and spent untold hours pondering who and what he might be. A drug lord? An arms dealer? Some sort of international spy? A reclusive millionaire? A serial killer? A mad scientist? A terrorist? Her imagination knew no bounds.

The holidays came and went. He didn't go to visit family for Thanksgiving, and no one came to visit him. As far as she could see, he didn't celebrate Christmas. No tinsel-laden tree appeared in the large front window. No colorful lights adorned his house. He didn't go out to celebrate the New Year. But then, neither did she. As far as she knew, he didn't buy flowers or candy on Valentine's Day, nor did he go to visit a lady friend. He was a handsome man—tall, dark and handsome—which begged the question, why wasn't he married, or at least dating? Perhaps he was in mourning. Perhaps that was why he always wore black. Then again, maybe he wore it because it looked so good on him.

She camped out in the woods across from his house three or four times a week, weather permitting, but she never saw him emerge during the day. He took a daily newspaper, but he never picked it up until after the sun went down. The same with his mail. He never had any visitors. He never had pizza delivered. No repairmen ever came to call.

She wasn't sure when she started to think he really was a vampire, but the more she thought about it, the more convinced she became. He only came out at night. He lived alone. He didn't eat. He always wore black. He never had any visitors. She never saw him with anyone else because . . .

He was a vampire.

Vampires lived forever and were supposed to be able to pass immortality on to others.

Ergo, he was the only one who could help her.

All she needed now was the courage to approach him. But how? And when? And what would she say?

It was the first of March before she finally worked up enough courage to put intention into action. Tomorrow night, she decided resolutely. She would ask him tomorrow night.

But, just in case he refused her or she changed her mind at the last minute, she armed herself with a small bottle of holy water stolen from the Catholic church on the corner of Main Street, wondering, briefly, if stolen holy water would retain its effectiveness. She found a small gold crucifix and chain that had belonged to her favorite aunt. She fashioned a wooden stake out of the handle of an old broom. She filled the pockets of her coat and jeans with cloves of garlic.

That should do it, she thought, patting her coat pocket. If he was agreeable, by this time tomorrow night she would be Undead. If he decided to make a meal of her instead of transforming her, she would just be dead a few weeks earlier than the doctors had predicted.

Chapter Two

Ronan didn't have to glance over his shoulder to know that the slender girl with the long black hair and big blue eyes was following him again. She had drifted in his wake like a pale shadow for the last five months or so. She followed him to the park. She followed him to the movies, to the local pub, to the mall, to his post office box when he picked up his mail. She followed him home. Sometimes she spent the night in the wooded area across from his house.

He wondered when she slept.

He wondered why her complexion was so ashen.

He wondered who she was.

He wondered why in blue blazes she was following him.

One thing was certain. He didn't like her trailing after him one damn bit. He could have lost her easily enough. He could have destroyed her. He could have hypnotized her and made her forget he existed.

So, why hadn't he?

It was a question he had asked himself every night for the last five months.

It was a question for which he had no answer, and that annoyed the living hell out of him. But just now, he had other, more important things on his mind than a skinny mortal female.

Lifting his head, he caught the scent of prey on the evening breeze. With a thought, he vanished from her sight.

Shannah blinked and blinked again. Where had he gone? One minute he had been a few yards ahead of her and the next he was gone as if he had never been there at all.

Pausing, she rubbed her eyes. Had she started to imagine things? Maybe it was just one more symptom of her illness, like the fever that burned through her. Or maybe he really was a vampire. She giggled. Or the Invisible Man.

Feeling suddenly light-headed, she reached out, bracing one hand against the wall of a tall brick building. Her time was running out. She felt it in the deepest part of her being, knew it was only a matter of weeks, perhaps days, before she lapsed into a coma, never to awake again. And then what? The endless nothingness that she feared, or the heavenly paradise that her grandmother had promised awaited all those who believed?

Shannah took a deep breath. Before she left this world, she had to know if the man she had been following was truly a vampire.

On legs that wobbled with every step, she walked to the woods across from his house and settled down in her usual place to keep watch. It was quite cozy, all things considered. She had a couple of warm quilts, a small pillow, an ice chest filled with water and soft drinks, another chest filled with potato chips and her favorite candy bars. Not exactly a healthy diet, but what difference did it make now? It was only a matter of time as to which ran out first, the money her grandfather had left her, or her life. She giggled as she reached for a soda. At least she didn't have to worry about high cholesterol or getting fat. Or catching some horrible fatal disease, she thought with morbid amusement, since she already had one.

Tonight, she didn't have to wait long for the stranger to appear. He emerged out of the darkness a short time later and entered his house. The lights came on. Plumes of blue-gray smoke drifted from the chimney to be blown away by an itinerant breeze.

She had promised herself that she would approach him tonight but her courage suddenly deserted her. She would keep watch here again tonight, she decided, and knock on his door tomorrow afternoon. If he answered, she would know he wasn't a vampire. If he didn't . . . somehow she would have to work up the nerve to approach him after the sun went down.

But for now . . . her eyelids fluttered down. For now she needed sleep.

She woke late in the afternoon with the sun in her face and the usual cramping in her stomach. Sitting up, she folded her arms around her middle and rocked back and forth. When the worst of the pain was over, she drank some water, then splashed some on her face. Though she wasn't really hungry, she knew she needed to eat to keep her strength up and she forced herself to eat one of the bran muffins she had bought the day before, and to drink some orange juice.

Finally, with one hand propped against a tree, she gained her feet, her gaze moving to the house across the way. It looked like the kind of house you saw in movies, the kind inhabited by witches or haunted by unfriendly ghosts.

She had planned to approach the mysterious stranger that afternoon but now that the time had come, she found her courage failing her once more. Even though she was convinced he was the only answer to her problem, she wasn't sure she was ready to meet a vampire face to face.

"Oh, for goodness sakes, stop being such a coward," she muttered. "What have you got to lose? A few days at most."

Still, she wanted those days. In the last few months, she had learned that each new day, each hour of life, was a precious gift from God, a gift that was meant to be savored and cherished. She only wished she had realized that sooner.

She dusted off her jeans, straightened her T-shirt, ran her hands through the tangles in her hair. Glancing at her watch, she saw that it was a little after five. Too early for a vampire to be up and about. So, if he answered the door, that would prove he wasn't a vampire. And if he didn't answer, well if he didn't, it could mean one of two things. Either he had left the house while she slept, proving that he was just a man, or he was stretched out in his coffin somewhere, sleeping the sleep of the Undead.

Taking a deep breath, she squared her shoulders and marched resolutely across the grassy field and the road beyond. She pushed on the heavy gate, blew out a sigh of exasperation when it didn't open. She should have known that it would be locked.

Well, she wasn't going to let a little thing like a locked gate deter her now that she had finally found the courage to approach him. Turning to the left, she followed the block wall along the property line and there, at the back of the house, she found a tree with branches that extended over the wall.

Taking another deep breath, she reached for the

lowest branch. It had been years since she had climbed a tree and now she knew why. She hadn't worried about falling and breaking a leg, or, worse, her neck, when she'd been a little girl, but the possibility of either or both occurred to her now. And then she shrugged. A broken neck would be a quick, reasonably painless way to go.

Shaking the thought from her mind, she gained the top of the wall, swung her legs over the other side, and dropped to the ground in the backyard.

The house looked as forbidding from the back as it did from the front. The grounds were in dire need of attention. The lawn hadn't been mowed in weeks, perhaps months. There were weeds that needed pulling, trees that hadn't been pruned in a long time, a wrought-iron bench in need of paint. It was a big yard, one that could have been beautiful. It seemed a shame to let it get so overgrown. If she lived here, she would plant flowers along the walkway and rose bushes in the weed-infested gardens. She'd put a covered swing in the corner, maybe a gazebo near the gardens.

But it wasn't her house. With a shake of her head, she walked around to the front porch. Her palms were damp, her mouth as dry as the Sahara in mid-summer when she finally summoned the courage to knock on the door.

Minutes passed.

She knocked again, harder. And then once more.

So, was he sleeping in his coffin, or just not at home?

She was about to turn away when the door opened and she found herself staring up into the face of the man she had been following. She had never been close enough to see the color of his eyes. Now she saw that they were black. *As black as death.* The words whispered through the corridors of her mind even as she felt the warmth of the late afternoon sun on her back. Danger emanated from him like heat rising from summer-hot pavement.

He couldn't be a vampire.

He couldn't help her.

She was going to die.

Tears burned the backs of her eyes and dampened her cheeks. She didn't want to die, not now. She was only twenty-four. There was so much she wanted to do, so many places she wanted to go, so much of life she had yet to experience. And she was afraid. Afraid of the pain, afraid of dying.

His hooded gaze met hers, cool and direct. "What are you doing here?"

"Nothing. I'm sorry. I thought you were someone else."

"Who are you looking for?"

"It doesn't matter."

"Have you a name?"

"Shannah." She wiped her tear-damp cheeks with the back of her hand. "I'm sorry I bothered you. Good-bye."

She tried to turn away but her legs refused to obey. Caught in the dark web of his gaze, she could only stand there, her arms limp at her sides, staring up at him while hot tears trickled down her cheeks. She had never really noticed how handsome he was. Not in the way that the blond, bland young men in Hollywood were handsome, but in a dark, mysterious and forbidding sort of way. He had short thick eyelashes, a fine straight nose, a strong jaw line. He looked like a man who knew what he wanted in life and wouldn't hesitate to take it by fair means or foul.

"You've been following me for the last five months," he said brusquely. "Who did you think I was?" He glanced past her to the wrought-iron gate. "And how the hell did you get in here?"

She felt a rush of heat climb up the back of her neck as she searched her mind for a convincing lie but his gaze continued to hold hers captive and she suddenly lacked the will to lie to him.

"I thought you were a vampire," she said, thinking how foolish the words sounded when spoken out loud.

One dark brow lifted. "A vampire?" he murmured. "Indeed?"

She nodded, embarrassed now. "But it's still daylight, you know, and you're awake instead of closed up in your coffin so I guess I was wrong . . ." She bit down on her lower lip, aware that she was babbling like an idiot. "I'll be going now. I'm sorry I bothered you."

Shoulders drooping with discouragement, she turned away, took a few wobbly steps and with a small moan, tumbled down the porch stairs.

Ronan stared at the girl sprawled at the bottom of the steps, at the thin trickle of crimson oozing from a shallow cut in her forehead. He took a deep breath as the intoxicating scent of her blood was carried to him on an errant breeze. Was there anything in the world that smelled as sweet?

Muttering an oath, he turned on his heel and went back inside the house, only to emerge a moment later swathed in a heavy black hooded cloak that covered him from head to heel.

Bracing himself for the pain to come, he flew down the stairs, swept the girl into his arms, and darted back into the house, kicking the door shut behind him.

Eyes closed, he stood in the entryway for a moment, panting heavily, his skin tingling and tightening in a most unpleasant way. When the worst of the pain receded, he glanced down at the girl in his arms. She was unconscious, her breathing labored, her cheeks ashen. She was far too thin. Her skin was feverishly warm. There were dark purple shadows, like bruises, beneath her eyes, hollows in her pale cheeks. He could hear the beat of her heart, slow and heavy, smell the life-giving blood that flowed sluggishly through her veins and oozed in thick red drops from the shallow cut in her brow.

The crimson droplets beckoned him. His hold on her tightened. He licked his lips as the hunger stirred deep within, searing his insides, demanding to be fed.

Unable to resist either the pain of his hunger or the temptation of her blood, he lowered his head and licked the blood from the wound.

And tasted death.

Chapter Three

Shannah woke slowly. Her eyelids felt heavy and it was an effort to open her eyes. For a moment, she stared blankly at her surroundings. The walls were painted taupe with white trim. The ceiling was white. A fire burned in the hearth across from the canopied bed on which she lay. A thick white carpet covered the floor. Heavy draperies the same color as the walls covered the room's single window. The dresser against the far wall looked like an antique, as did the high-backed oak rocking chair in the corner. Large, expensive-looking paintings hung on the walls—one was of a stately park where people in eighteenth-century clothing strolled along tree-lined lanes; one was of a Paris cathedral; the third depicted a quiet lake beneath a full moon. The fourth painting was of a dark castle set upon a windswept hill.

Where was she?

Where was he?

Her head ached and when she touched her fingertips to her forehead, she made two discoveries—her fever was gone and there was a rather large bandage taped above her left eye. She didn't remember being injured. Frowning made her head hurt worse.

It wasn't until she slid her legs over the edge of the bed that she realized she wasn't wearing anything save for her bra, panties, and a dark blue velvet robe with a black satin collar.

When she stood, the robe's hem dragged on the floor and the sleeves fell past her hands. She glanced around the room, looking for her clothes, but they were nowhere in sight. She checked the closet and the chest of drawers. Both were empty.

She walked across the floor, her bare feet making no sound on the soft thick carpet. Putting her ear to the door, she listened for a moment before she opened it and stepped out into the hallway.

A glance up and down the narrow corridor showed several doors. None of them were open.

Clutching the collar of the robe in one hand, she tiptoed along the hallway, her footsteps muffled by the thick carpet beneath her feet.

She paused at the top of the landing, listening, and when she heard nothing, she padded quietly down the staircase.

At the bottom, she paused again.

Was she in *his* house? And if she was, where was he, and why were there no clothes in the closet? She had come here looking for a vampire. Now that her fever was gone and she was thinking more clearly, she knew how foolish that had been. Vampires were creatures of myth and legend.

But what if he was something even worse?

Where had he put her clothing? She could hardly walk back to her apartment in her bare feet, wearing nothing but a too large bathrobe, nice and comfy as it was.

Moving as quietly as she could, she made her way into the kitchen, thinking to fortify herself with a cup of strong black coffee.

No such luck. The cupboards were empty. The stove and the refrigerator looked new and unused. The fridge was empty. There was no table. Odd, that there was no food in the house but then, maybe he never ate at home. Still, it was mighty strange that he didn't at least have the basics. Or a few dishes.

She couldn't remember the last time she had been truly hungry. She rarely ate a full meal anymore. Doing so made her sick to her stomach and yet, for the first time in months, she was famished.

She was standing in the middle of the floor, her stomach growling, when there was a knock at the back door. She hesitated a moment before opening it.

A cute young man with curly brown hair stood at the door holding a large box of groceries. "Miss Shannah?"

"Yes?"

"Where do you want this?"

She glanced at the cardboard box in his hand. "I'm not sure. I didn't . . ."

"It was a phone order from Mr. Dark."

"Oh." Was that the stranger's name? Mr. Dark? She took a step backward. "Just put it on the counter, I guess."

The young man did as bidden. He handed her a receipt and a pen. "Just sign here."

She signed the receipt and handed the slip of paper and the pen back to the young man. "I'm afraid I don't have any cash for a tip."

"Don't worry about it," he said, grinning. "Mr. Dark took care of it. Have a good day, ma'am."

"Thank you."

She closed the door, then went to look through the box. It held a jar of instant coffee, a half-gallon of milk, a box of assorted individual servings of cereal, a small box of sugar, a loaf of bread, lunch meat and cheese, eggs, bacon, a box of pancake mix, syrup, a jar of peanut butter, another of jelly, a six-pack of soda, butter, salt and pepper, a small jar of mayonnaise, mustard, and ketchup, as well as paper plates and a package of plastic knives, forks, and spoons, some plastic cups, and a toothbrush and toothpaste. At the bottom of the box she found two frying pans and a toaster.

Her stomach growled loudly as she stared at the bounty before her. With a shake of her head, she put everything away, then set about making French toast and bacon for breakfast.

Mr. Dark, indeed, she mused. She didn't know if that was his real name or not, but it fit perfectly.

She carried her breakfast into the living room and sat on the sofa since there was no place to sit in the kitchen.

When she finished eating, she sat back, waiting for her stomach to cramp, for the food to come back up again, as it always did when she ate too much too fast. But nothing happened. Rising, she carried her dishes into the kitchen and put them in the sink. She would wash them later, she decided, for now she wanted to see the rest of the house.

The living room, done in shades of blue and gray, was roomy and comfortable, with a high-backed sofa, an overstuffed chair, a glass-topped coffee table, and a big screen plasma TV with surround sound. Heavy draperies covered the big picture window and the smaller windows located on either side of the front door.

The dining room was bare save for a large oil painting of a tall-masted ship adrift on a storm-tossed sea.

Continuing down the hallway, she looked in every room. There was a bathroom with a large shower, a marble sink, and a sunken tub. A large walk-in linen closet was located across from the bathroom. The bedroom next to the bathroom was decorated in shades of forest green and gold. The furniture was country oak. The walls were beige, all hung with large paintings—a stag in the midst of a sun-drenched meadow; a wolf posed on the edge of a craggy hill; a shepherd cradling a lamb to his chest; a herd of wild horses running across a moonlit prairie. He seemed to have a taste for art, she mused, moving on down the hallway. She was no expert, but all the paintings looked extremely expensive.

It was the last room that drew her inside. The walls on either side of the door were lined with floor-to-ceiling bookshelves; heavy wine-red velvet drapes covered a large window in the third wall. An enormous desk stood in front of the fourth wall. It held a computer, a large LCD flat screen monitor, a cordless mouse and keyboard, a combination printer/scanner/copier, and nothing else. She was tempted to turn on the computer but something held her back.

The bookshelves held a wide variety of books, everything from encyclopedias to mysteries to romance novels. One shelf held thirteen paperback books by the same author—Eva Black. Shannah had never read a romance novel in her life but the author's name sounded vaguely familiar.

Another shelf held mysteries written by Claire Ebon. Still another shelf held several hardback contemporary novels written by Stella Raven.

Shannah frowned. Black, Ebon, Raven. Odd, that they all had last names so similar in meaning. Odder still that her host's name was Mr. Dark. She puzzled over that for several minutes, then shrugged. It was probably just a coincidence.

Leaving the computer room, she went upstairs to explore the second floor. She wasn't surprised when she discovered that all the rooms except the one she had awakened in were empty. Bare floors, blank walls, all painted the same shade of off-white. Perhaps he had moved in recently, she thought. Maybe it was his first house. That would explain the lack of furniture, knick knacks, and the other odds and ends that people tended to collect when they had lived in the same house for a long time.

She should go home, she thought, before he came back from wherever he had gone. He hadn't been happy to see her on his doorstep. She was certain he wouldn't be happy to know she had been snooping around his house while he was away. She was surprised he had taken her in and let her spend the night.

Yes, she should go home, but not now. Feeling suddenly weary, she made her way back into the taupe bedroom and climbed up on the bed. Pulling the covers up to her chin, she closed her eyes. She was tired, so very, very tired. The doctors had warned her that she would feel that way when the end was near, though how they knew that was beyond her. They didn't even know what was wrong with her. At first, they had thought she had some rare form of leukemia, then they'd thought it might be some sexually transmitted disease similar to AIDS, only she didn't do drugs and she had never had sexual intercourse. Though the doctors couldn't decide what was wrong with her, they had all agreed on one thing. She was dying, and she didn't have much time left, perhaps six months. And now five of them were gone.

But she wouldn't think of that, not now. She would just close her eyes for a few minutes and then she would call for a cab and go home.

He rose at dusk, his nostrils assailed by the faint, lingering odors of eggs and milk and bacon. And over the stink of food he detected the tantalizing scent of the woman. So, she was still here. He had expected she would be long gone by now.

He moved through the house until he reached the bedroom, his senses quickening when he saw her lying in his bed, her hair spread across the white pillowcase like a splash of black ink. Her face was very nearly as pale as the pillowcase beneath her head. Her eyelashes lay like dark fans upon her cheeks.

She was dying. A rare disease of the blood, something so rare even her doctor wasn't sure what it was or what had caused it. Perhaps that explained why she had come looking for a vampire.

He had known many people in the course of his existence. Most came and went without making any noticeable impact on his life. Only a few had been memorable. She would be one of them, though he couldn't say why. He hardly knew her. If he were still capable of human feelings, he might have shed tears for her.

She moaned softly, her fingers worrying the covers. "No! No, I'm afraid. Oh, please, no . . ."

She began to thrash around under the covers. And then she screamed.

He had heard countless cries of terror throughout his long existence but this one cut through his heart and soul like a knife.

"Shannah." Murmuring her name, he sat on the edge of the mattress and drew her into his arms. "Wake up, child."

Her eyelids fluttered open. For a moment, she stared at him, her eyes wide and frightened. And then, with a strangled sob, she collapsed in his arms, her body trembling.

"It's all right, Shannah," he whispered. "There's nothing for you to be afraid of. You're safe here, with me."

It was a lie, of course, but she didn't know that.

When she continued to shiver, he pulled the blanket from the bed and draped it around her, and then he rocked her back and forth as if she were, indeed, a child.

Gradually, her trembling ceased and she lay quiet in his arms.

He brushed a lock of hair from her brow. "How do you feel?"

"I'm dying."

"Is that why you were looking for a vampire?"

She nodded. "I thought . . ."

"That I would bring you across?"

"Yes."

He smiled faintly. "You came well-armed." He had smelled the garlic she carried when he opened the door and saw her standing on the porch, had noted the cross she wore on a fine gold chain around her neck. When he put her to bed, he had been amused to find a crudely fashioned wooden stake tucked inside the waistband of her jeans, cloves of garlic and a small vial of holy water in the pockets of her jacket. He had disposed of all but the cross and chain. "And do you want to be a vampire?"

"No!" she exclaimed softly, and then, softer still, "but I don't want to die, either."

"Perhaps the doctors were wrong."

"They can't all be wrong," she said wearily. Pushing away from him, she sat up, her shoulders slumped, defeat evident in every line of her body. "I should go home."

"You should rest a little longer. Why don't you go back to sleep?"

"No." She had only a short time left; she didn't want to waste any of it by sleeping more than was absolutely necessary. She wanted to live every minute while she could. "Anyway," she said, throwing the covers aside, "I can't stay here."

He gazed deep into her eyes. "Of course you can." He tucked her under the covers once more, then stood beside the bed, looking down at her. "Go to sleep, Shannah. Everything will be better tomorrow."

"Yes," she said, yawning behind her hand. "Tomorrow." Her eyelids fluttered down. A moment later, she was asleep.

He watched her for a moment more, then knelt beside the bed. Brushing a lock of hair away from her neck, he ran his tongue lightly over her skin, felt his fangs lengthen in quick response to the scent of her blood, the pulse beating slow and regular in the hollow of her throat.

He closed his eyes as the hunger rose up within him, demanding to be fed. As gently as possible, he buried his fangs in the soft skin beneath her ear. In spite of the ravening hunger that clawed at him, he drank only a little. In spite of the impurity in her blood, it was sweet, sweeter than anything he had ever tasted.

Drawing away, he made a gash in his wrist with his teeth. Dark red blood bubbled from the ragged incision.

"Hear me, Shannah," he said, holding the bleeding wound to her lips, "you must open your mouth and drink."

Obediently, she opened her mouth and swallowed a few drops of his blood.

A flick of his tongue closed the wound in his wrist.

"Sleep now, my sweet Shannah," he murmured. "Sleep and dream of a long and healthy life."

Chapter Four

Shannah woke feeling better than she had in months. Flinging the covers aside, she practically flew out of bed. She didn't feel lethargic, as she usually did upon waking. She wasn't cold. She didn't have a headache. She was surprised when her stomach growled. She hadn't been truly hungry in months. Glancing at her watch, she saw that it was almost six o'clock. Good grief, she had been asleep almost twenty-four hours. No wonder she was hungry!

Going to the window, she drew back the curtains and stared out at the lowering clouds. Gathering the robe she still wore closer around her, she padded barefoot down the stairs, wondering where her mysterious host was.

She found him in the den, seated in front of the computer.

He looked up at her when she crossed the threshold. "Good evening, Shannah."

She smiled faintly, still feeling foolish for thinking he was a vampire. "Hi."

"How are you feeling?" he asked, though there was no need. The shadows were gone from her eyes, the hollows from her cheeks. Her eyes glowed as clear and blue as a summer sky. Her skin was radiant.

Her smile widened. "I feel wonderful. I don't understand it."

"Perhaps you just needed a good night's sleep," he suggested. "Make yourself at home, won't you? I'm not quite finished here."

"Thank you. Is it . . . would it be all right if I fix something to eat?"

"Of course."

"What would you like for dinner? I'm not a bad cook, if you don't want anything too fancy."

"Nothing for me, thank you. I've eaten."

"Already?"

He nodded.

She gestured at the monitor on the desk. "Are you working, or playing?" she asked, and then flushed. It was none of her business what he was doing.

"Working."

"Oh?" He heard the unspoken question in her voice.

"I'm a writer."

"Really? What do you write?"

"Books."

She glanced at the bookcase on the far wall. "Are any of these yours?"

"Yes, the ones written by Eva Black." He had written the ones by Ebon and Raven, as well, but they had been published before she was born.

"Wow, I've never met a real writer before. Could I read one?"

"If you like."

She moved to the bookcase, her gaze roaming over the shelves. "Why don't you use your own name?"

"I write mostly romances," he replied easily. "I thought

they would sell better if readers thought they had been written by a woman."

Even his editor didn't know he was a man. With his need to sleep during the day, and the differences in time between one coast and the other, it was virtually impossible for them to communicate by phone. Ronan had informed his editor and his agent that he slept days and wrote through the night, and since writers tended to be a little eccentric, they had accepted his excuse. All their correspondence had been by letter or email.

She nodded. "How long have you been writing?"

"I've been writing for a number of years," he said, "but my first book was published seven years ago." In truth, he had been writing for more than sixty years, but he had been Eva Black for a relatively short time. He often wondered what his editor would think if she knew that her publishing house had been selling his books under various pseudonyms since 1946.

Skimming the titles, Shannah ran her fingertips over the spines of the books. Pulling one from the shelf, she read the back cover blurb.

> *After a century of searching, he had found the woman of his dreams. Being a vampire had brought Paul Stark nothing but misery and loneliness until he met Lily Adams. It seemed a cruel trick of fate that Lily came from a long line of vampire hunters. Their attraction was mutual and immediate. Only two things stood between them—his lust for her blood, and her determination to kill every vampire she found.*

She looked at him over the top of the book. "This is about a vampire."

"Yes."

She stared at him speculatively, her eyes narrowed. He could see all her earlier suspicions roaring back to life.

"I write about pirates and unicorns, as well," he said, looking amused. "And doctors, lawyers, and Indian chiefs."

She felt a rush of heat flow into her cheeks. "I get the message," she muttered. Just because he wrote about vampires didn't make him one. "Could you tell me where my clothes are?"

"I sent them out to be cleaned. They'll be ready tomorrow."

"Tomorrow?" She glanced down at the robe she was still wearing. "Do you have a T-shirt or something that I could wear until then?"

"I think so." Heat pooled in his groin at the thought of her wearing one of his T-shirts and nothing more.

With a nod, she tucked the book under her arm and left the room.

Ronan leaned back in his chair, his elbows resting on the arms, his fingers steepled. Since Eva's last six books had made all the bestseller lists, including the prestigious *New York Times* list, his editor had been after him to let them put his photo in the backs of his novels. A couple of the talk shows wanted to interview him on early-morning radio and his agent had been pressuring him to do so. Thus far, he had refused for obvious reasons. But what if Shannah pretended to be Eva Black? He could send Shannah's photo to his editor. Shannah could do the interviews at the radio stations.

It was an intriguing idea. He could please his agent and his editor and get the publisher off his back all at the same time.

He turned back to the computer screen, his senses acutely aware of the woman in the kitchen. She was making spaghetti sauce. He could smell tomatoes, basil and oregano. But mostly, he could smell the woman. The scent of her blood was tantalizing, more so now that he had tasted her.

His hands curled over the edge of the desk. Why had he let her stay here? Did he really think he could keep his hunger under control when she was so close, so available? His grip on the edge of the desk tightened. The wood creaked under the strain.

Muttering an oath, he rose and began to pace the floor. Over the centuries, he had seen death in all its forms. None of them were pretty. Only a few mortals were lucky enough to expire peacefully in their sleep. She was dying, and she was far too young, and far too fair, to succumb to such a cruel fate. So he had given her a few drops of his blood to buy her a little more time, though he didn't know how much. A couple of days, a couple of weeks, perhaps a month or so, if she was lucky.

She didn't want to die.

He could arrange that. He knew how, though he had never bestowed the Dark Trick on anyone before. It was tempting, so tempting, but that would defeat his purpose for letting her stay. Aside from wanting photos and pestering him to do interviews and local book signings, his editor and his agent were both pressuring him to go on tour. It would be good publicity, they said. Readers liked to meet their favorite authors. It would be beneficial to meet the managers of some of the larger romance-friendly bookstores. It would be good for sales.

He had stalled as long as he could but he was running out of valid excuses.

Hence his need for Shannah. He could give her enough of his blood to form a link between them. He would be able to read her thoughts; if he wished it, she would be able to read his. They could go on tour together, with her pretending to be him when necessary. Through the link, he would be able to give her the answers to whatever questions readers or the news media might ask about his writing, at least after sundown. And if her health started to fail again, he had only to give her a little more of his blood.

It seemed an easy solution to the problem, and the more he thought about it, the more he liked it. Now, he had only to convince her. And if she refused . . . He smiled. She would agree, whether she wished it or not.

Going on tour would solve another problem, as well. He grimaced, annoyed with himself for choosing to quit the field rather than to simply stay and kill the vampire hunter who had come to town. He didn't know if the hunter was hunting him or if it was merely coincidence that the man had come to this place at this time. Ronan leaned against the edge of his desk, his fingertips drumming on the surface. He didn't want to kill the man if he didn't have to, but, should it become necessary, he wouldn't hesitate to do what had to be done.

Dropping back down into his chair, Ronan picked up the magazine he had bought a few days earlier. It was a national entertainment magazine, published weekly. An article touted on the front cover had caught his eye. The story "Vampires Among Us—Truth or Legend?" had been written by a freelance reporter named Carl Overstreet.

Ronan wondered if it had been the article that had brought the hunter to town. Propping his feet on the corner of his desk, he began to read:

Vampires. The very word makes your flesh crawl . . . with terror or titillation, depending on your point of view.

Vampires have been a subject of fascination and horror for countless centuries. Every culture and civilization throughout the known world, both past and present, have their own myths and legends about vampires, be they skeletal creatures who feast on human blood or psychic vampires who prey on the energy of their victims, leaving them exhausted in both body and spirit.

Thanks to the creative imagination of Bram Stoker, Count Dracula is probably the most famous bloodsucker of all time. Unlike the skeletal creature depicted in the silent movie, Nosferatu, the Count has been played as being suave and sensual by Frank Langella, witty and winsome by George Hamilton, sympathetic by Gary Oldman, downright scary by Christopher Lee in a series of Hammer films, as well as for laughs in Abbott and Costello Meet Frankenstein, *and by Leslie Nielsen in* Dracula: Dead and Loving It.

So, what do we really know about these creatures of the night? Popular fiction says they sleep by day and hunt by night. They can't be seen in mirrors, they are repelled by crosses, holy water and garlic. Some believe they must sleep in their coffins; others believe they must rest on the earth of their homeland. Some believe vampires are capable of flight, of transforming into bats or wolves and of changing their size and dimension. It is commonly believed that they are able to control animals and the weather, and hypnotize mortals to do their will.

But did vampires ever truly exist? Do they exist now? Do vampires walk among us, unseen and unknown? Every year, hundreds of people disappear without a trace, never to be heard from or seen again. Are vampires responsible? During the next few months I'll be traveling the country, digging deeper into the legend and mystique of vampires and other so-called creatures of the night.

Until next month, dear reader, watch your neck!

Muttering, "You'd better watch your own neck, you damn fool," Ronan tossed the magazine into the wastebasket beside his desk.

Shannah glanced over her shoulder. She hadn't heard him enter the room but she knew he was there, standing just inside the doorway like some huge bird of prey ready to swoop down and carry her away. She grinned inwardly. Since her illness, her imagination had gone into overdrive.

"Did you change your mind about dinner?" she asked.

"No." His gaze focused on the pulse beating in the hollow of her throat. He could hear the blood flowing through her veins, its music like a Siren's call to his ears. Though he had fed earlier, the hunger, ever-present, clawed at his vitals. His fangs pricked his tongue.

"Are you all right?" she asked, frowning.

Nodding, he looked away. By sheer force of will, he subdued the craving that burned through him, demanding to be satisfied.

"I'm going out for a while," he said. "I won't be gone long."

"Oh, well, I should probably be going home after I eat. If I don't see you again, I want to thank you now for your hospitality and everything . . ."

"I'd rather you stayed. Besides," he said, "you can't very well go out dressed like that."

He was right, of course. She had forgotten that she didn't have anything to wear, and she couldn't very well go home wearing nothing but his robe, no matter how nice it was. Maybe, when he returned, she could borrow one of his shirts and a pair of sweatpants, though his clothes were certain to be far too large. Still, it was better than what she had on now.

"All right," she said reluctantly. "I guess I can stay until tomorrow."

"That's not what I meant. I want you to stay here, with me, indefinitely."

She didn't like the sound of that one bit and she stared at him in sudden alarm, wondering if she had made a fatal mistake in coming here.

Sensing her inner turmoil, he said, "Shannah, I mean you no harm."

She didn't know why, but she believed him. Still, she couldn't stay. "I can't, really . . ."

"Of course you can."

"No. I have to go home. My apartment . . ." That was hardly a convincing argument. Her whole apartment would fit inside his living room. Of course, he didn't know that. She thought of her small place, and compared it to his house. There was nothing at home that she would miss. And whether it was the man or his mansion, she felt much better here than she had in months. That made no sense, of course, but then, these days, very little made sense. Still, she couldn't move in with this man. This stranger. She had been raised better than that.

She shook her head. "No," she said again, "I couldn't, but thanks again for your hospitality."

He smiled faintly. "When I get back, I'd like a chance to convince you to stay. I won't be gone long."

She watched him turn and walk away, heard the front door open and close as he left the house.

What a strange man he was. Why would he want her to stay here, with him? Perhaps because he *was* a strange man? The thought sent fear flooding through her. Maybe he really was some kind of homicidal maniac. Maybe the reason she suddenly felt so good was because he was a drug dealer and he had slipped her something last night. Maybe he planned to sell her on the white slave market.

Maybe she had better get the hell out of here while she still could!

She turned off the stove and ran out of the kitchen. She wasn't going to hang around to find out what kind of man he was, or just what plans he had in store for her. She was leaving this place right now, clothes or no clothes.

Chapter Five

Ronan stalked the ever-changing shadows of the night, a predator in search of prey, a hunter on the prowl. He loved the night, the taste of the wind on his tongue, the anticipation of the hunt. There had been times, in the beginning, when he had despised what he was, loathed what he had to do to survive, but those feelings hadn't lasted long. He had once been human, prey to what he had become. Now he was the predator; preying on mortals was natural to his kind. The memory of mortality and its inherent weaknesses were dim, overshadowed by the passing of time. The revulsion he had expected to feel the first time he satisfied his unnatural thirst had never materialized. One taste of the rich red elixir of life had driven all thought of repugnance from his mind. Nothing had ever tasted sweeter. Nothing had ever satisfied him more.

Now, he moved through the darkness with ease, his preternatural senses testing the evening breeze. Sounds and smells assailed him on every side as he sought for the one who would satisfy his hunger.

He bypassed a young couple holding hands, so caught

up in each other he doubted either of them would have noticed had he chosen one or both of them.

He moved past an old man sitting on the sidewalk in front of a seedy tavern, as well as several boisterous young men who reeked of booze and drugs.

Moving on, he passed a rookie cop walking a lonely beat.

And then he saw her, a middle-aged woman about to enter a single-story house at the end of a quiet street. Falling into step beside her, he mesmerized her with a glance and pulled her into the shadows beside the building. Taking her into his embrace, he took that which he needed to sustain his existence, and left her standing there, bewildered but unhurt, his memory erased from her mind.

With his thirst sated for the moment, he turned toward home, his thoughts on the woman who waited for him there. What would she think of his proposition? Dare he tell her the truth of what he was? In five hundred years, no one who had discovered the truth of his existence had lived to tell the tale. He remembered all too well the way his kind had been hunted in centuries past, hordes of frightened people storming through cemeteries, digging up the graves of suspected vampires, mutilating the corpses.

These days, people were generally too civilized to believe in the supernatural, although vampire hunters still plied their trade. He knew it would be a mistake to tell Shannah the truth. Why, then, did he feel compelled to do so? And why, of all the people he had known through the centuries, was he tempted to work the Dark Trick upon her? It was nothing to him whether she lived or died, yet the thought of her death filled him with an aching sadness he had not felt in hundreds of years.

Perhaps it was just that he had been alone for too

long. How often had he seen young lovers entwined and yearned for the closeness and the intimacy they shared? How often had he hungered, not for blood, but for the love of a woman? For one kiss, freely given?

Eager to see Shannah again, he quickened his pace, relishing the touch of the night air on his face.

Lights burned in the downstairs windows of the house. He grunted softly, thinking how odd it looked. Before Shannah, the house had always been dark when he returned. With his preternatural vision, he had no need for artificial lighting.

No one had ever left a light burning for him before. A smile curved his lips as he hurried up the long narrow drive. It faded as he opened the front door. He didn't have to enter the house to know that it was empty. To know that she had gone.

Pulling the door closed behind him, he went out into the night once more, his senses reaching out, his head lifting to sniff an errant breeze for her scent. He found it quickly, followed it easily, much like a hungry wolf on the trail of fresh blood.

It led him to a four-story red brick apartment building on the far side of town.

Sitting on the sofa clad in a pair of comfy old sweats and a pair of heavy socks, Shannah reached for the book she had stolen from Mr. Dark, if that was indeed his real name. Somehow, she doubted it. Not that it mattered, she thought as she opened the book.

She had fled his house as though pursued by demons. Keeping to the shadows, his robe clutched tightly around her, she had made her way home, praying that she would remain unobserved, especially by the police. It would have been difficult indeed to explain what she was doing running through the streets clad in nothing but a robe and her underwear. Thankfully, she hadn't seen anyone, and no one had seen her. She wondered now if she had overreacted. He had been nothing but kind to her since she showed up at his front door.

With a shake of her head, she turned her attention back to the book. There was a poem on the first page.

> *In the darkness, I dream of light*
> *Under Sol, I beg for night*
> *Each dawn I die, at dusk reborn*
> *Eternal shadow*
> *Alone*
> *Forlorn*

Though short, the aching loneliness inherent in the words touched a chord deep within her. Had he written the poem as well as the book? He didn't seem like the poetic type, she thought as she turned the page.

In minutes, she forgot everything but the story unfolding in front of her. Never before had she read anything that captured her attention so quickly. His writing was compelling, riveting, so visual she could see every scene unfolding in her mind as though she was there in the midst of the story, living each adventure with the vampire and his lady love.

She was so captivated that she was hardly aware of time passing. She was completely caught up in the plot. She was the heroine, in love with a man who was not a man at all, and her life was in danger . . .

She practically jumped out of her skin when someone knocked on the door. Frowning, she wondered who it could be. She wasn't expecting company; no one except her parents knew where she lived.

The knock came again, louder and more insistent.

Rising, the book clutched in one hand, she went to the door. "Who is it?"

She knew the answer even before she heard the deep timbre of his voice.

"Ronan."

"What do you want?" She glanced at the book in her hand. Was he here because she had taken it without permission?

"I want to see you, of course. Why else would I be here?"

Heart pounding, she stared at the door. Would he go away if she refused to let him in? Or would he break down the door? She could scream for help, but she knew no one would come.

"Shannah, open the damn door and let me in."

She wasn't sure she wanted to, but her hand seemed to move of its own volition and she found herself staring up into his face. Hearing the barely suppressed anger in his voice, she had expected him to barge in and . . . well, she wasn't sure just what she expected him to do. The one thing she hadn't expected was for him to ask her permission, but that was exactly what he did.

"May I come in?" he asked. He was dressed all in black again—shirt, pants, boots, duster.

She nodded, unable to speak past the lump in her throat. Retreating into the room, she sat down on the sofa again, the book clutched to her breast. If only she had a hero who would fly in and rescue her, like the one in the story!

He stepped into the room and closed the door behind him. His presence seemed to shrink her small apartment. She imagined she could feel it closing in around her. His gaze swept over her, the force of it almost tangible.

"Are you enjoying the book?" His voice was low, almost

hypnotic. It moved over her, a feather-light touch underscored with steel.

"Y-yes," she stammered. "V-very much." She held it out to him. "I was going to return it, and your robe, when I was through."

"Keep it. Why did you run away?"

She lifted her chin and squared her shoulders, all the while glancing around the room, searching for a weapon. The fireplace poker? The heavy glass vase on the coffee table? Could she reach either of them before he reached for her?

"I didn't run away," she lied. "I just came home."

"I asked you to stay. You said you would."

Her hands tightened on the book in her lap. "I'm a woman. I changed my mind."

"You're afraid of me," he mused, and she heard the puzzlement in his voice.

"Why . . . why would I be afraid of you?"

"I don't know. You tell me."

"I just wanted to come home."

"You're lying." He hunkered down on his heels until he was at eye level with her. "Why didn't you wait for me?"

"All right," she admitted defiantly. "I got scared and I left."

"I wasn't going to hurt you."

"No?"

"No."

"Why would you want me to stay there with you? You don't even know me."

"Had you stayed, I would have told you my reasons."

Curious in spite of her better judgment, she said, "So, tell me now."

Rising, he sat down on the sofa beside her, though he

was careful not to touch her for fear she might run screaming from the room.

She shivered at his nearness, uncertain if it was because he was so close or because of the sudden heat that flowed between them. He was a remarkably handsome man with his mesmerizing black eyes and dark good looks. Sometimes, when he looked at her, she felt as though he could see through her heart and straight into her soul, that he knew things about her that no one else knew. But that was impossible. Heart pounding with trepidation, she watched him reach for her hand, felt little frissons of awareness race up her arm as his fingers closed around hers. The book fell from her hand and slid off her lap onto the floor.

"What do you want from me?" She had intended it to sound like a demand; it came out as a breathless gasp.

"Nothing sinister, I assure you. I have an aversion to having my picture taken, to appearing in public and being subjected to interviews. My readers think I'm female and I should like to keep it that way. My agent and my publisher have been after me to go on tour for quite some time . . ."

She shook her head. "What does all that have to do with me?"

"I want you to pretend to be me."

She stared at him in open-mouthed astonishment. Of all the things he might have said, his answer caught her completely off guard. "But . . . how could I . . . ?"

"No one knows what I look like."

"I don't think I can . . ."

"I'll make it worth your while."

"But how could I possibly . . . people will ask me about your books . . ." She retrieved his book from the floor and held it up. "This is the only one I've read, and I haven't even finished it."

"When you've finished that one, I want you to read the ones I've published in the last year or so. I'll give you a complete list of all my books, along with a brief synopsis of each one for you to memorize. As for questions you might be asked, I'll help you with what to say."

"I just don't see how it could work."

"Trust me. We'll rehearse for a month or two, more if need be, until you feel comfortable. As I said, I'll make it worth your while."

"You're forgetting one thing. I don't have a couple of months."

"Let's not worry about that now."

"I was never very good at memorizing things."

"You'll be surprised at how easy it will come to you."

"And why will it be so easy now when it never was before?"

His smile warned her not to ask any more questions. "You'll also need to make an appointment to have your picture taken."

"I haven't said yes yet."

"You haven't said no."

"If I agree, will you tell me something?"

"Perhaps. What is it you wish to know?"

"Is Ronan your first name or your last?"

He smiled then. "It's both and neither," he said evasively.

"What does that mean?"

"It means it's the only name I use."

"Really? How do you get away with that?"

He shrugged. "It works for Cher and Madonna, why not me?"

She made a face at him. "Don't forget Bono. And the artist formerly known as Prince."

She was quick, he thought, pleased. "And so," he said,

his thumb drawing circles on the back of her hand. "What do you say?"

"Yes." She whispered the word, feeling as if it had been drawn out of her by his will and not her own. Once said, she realized it was what she wanted. Pretending to be an author might be fun, and it would give her something to think about besides her own imminent demise. "I'll do it," she said quietly. "For as long as I'm able. But I'm not giving up my apartment."

"It's foolish for you to pay rent here when you'll be living with me."

"I don't care. I need a place of my own. A place to come back to when . . . when I want to come home."

"All right. But I'll pay your rent as long as you're working for me."

"I can't ask you to do that!"

"You didn't ask me. Consider it part of your pay."

"You're going to pay me?"

"Of course." Rising, he tugged gently on her hand. "Let's go. We've got a lot of work to do, and only a short amount of time to do it."

She gathered her things together, then followed him outside where she glanced up and down the street. "Where's your car?"

"I walked."

"You walked all the way here?"

He shrugged. "It's not so far."

"Yes, it is. I don't know about you, but I'm driving back. You can come with me, or you can hoof it."

He agreed to ride with her. As soon as they were both in the car, with the doors closed, she wished she had chosen to walk. She drove a restored 1962 VW Bug. It was a small car, made smaller now by his presence.

Shannah started the engine, looked behind her, and pulled away from the curb. She was all too aware of the man sitting beside her. His shoulder was only inches from her own; once her hand brushed against his thigh as she reached for the gear shift. She could feel his gaze on her face. His scent tickled her nostrils. She tried to place it, but couldn't. It wasn't aftershave lotion, it wasn't cologne. Maybe it was just the man himself.

"What kind of car do you drive?" she asked, desperate to break the taut silence between them. "I mean, you do drive, don't you?"

"When I must."

She slid a glance at him. "So, what kind of car do you have?"

"An old Firebird."

"Black, I'll bet."

He turned to look at her, one brow raised.

She shrugged. "It wasn't that hard to figure out." She glanced pointedly at his attire. "You seem to like black."

He looked thoughtful a moment before replying, "It suits me."

When they neared the mall, he said, "Pull over. It's early yet. Maybe we can find you something appropriate to wear."

"Excuse me?"

"For the photo, Shannah. For the book cover, remember?"

"Oh, yeah." She pulled into the parking lot, found a place to park, and cut the engine.

It was Friday night and the mall was crowded. Ronan followed Shannah up the elevator to the second floor of Nordstrom's, trailed after her as she moved from rack to rack in the Women's Department, assiduously avoiding the mirrors that were virtually everywhere.

When a saleslady approached Shannah and asked if she could help, he told the woman they were looking for something suitable for a professional portrait. With a nod, the woman led them to another department and quickly picked out several outfits in Shannah's size.

"I want to see you in all of them," Ronan called as Shannah followed the saleslady toward the dressing rooms.

He waited for her near the entrance, his hunger aroused by the proximity of so many women, the sound of so many beating hearts.

Shannah emerged from the dressing room a few moments later clad in a mauve pantsuit.

He shook his head.

He rejected the next outfit, and the next, smiled when she appeared wearing a pair of navy blue slacks, a bright pink silk blouse, and a navy blue jacket with bright pink piping on the lapels. It made her look confident and successful.

"We'll take it," he said.

He bought her three other outfits for public appearances, pantyhose, shoes and matching handbags, as well as underwear, a nightgown, and a robe. He bought her several casual dresses with shoes to match, a couple pairs of jeans, sweaters and blouses. He also bought her a set of luggage and a day planner.

"This is too much," she said. "Really."

"You're supposed to be a successful author," he replied. "You need to look the part. Can you think of anything else?"

She shook her head as they left the last department store. "I don't know how we'll get all this into my car."

"We'll manage."

He was heading for the elevator when she stopped at the entrance to the food court. "I'm hungry."

"What do you want?"

"A corn dog and a root beer."

Nodding, he waited while she put her packages down,

then handed her a twenty-dollar bill. He was glad to see the line was thankfully short.

He felt his gorge rise at the myriad scents that assailed him, not only the smell of food and drink but the odor of the mall itself. But it was the scent of blood all around him that was the most unsettling. He could hear it pumping through a hundred hearts, smell it flowing, thick and rich and red, through the veins of the men and women closest to him. It aroused his thirst and with it, the urge to hunt. With an effort, he fought it down.

"Let's go," he said when she returned carrying a cardboard tray. "You can eat it in the car."

"Why are you in such a hurry?"

He shrugged. "I don't like crowds."

When she reached for the packages she had been carrying, he took them from her hand. "I've got them," he said, his voice gruff. "Let's go."

She frowned at him but knowing it was useless to argue, she followed him out of the mall to the car.

He loaded the packages into the back seat and the trunk. "I'll drive."

Again, she didn't argue, merely pulled her keys out of her pocket and dropped them into his outstretched hand.

He seemed tense, though she didn't know why.

She wolfed down the corn dog, surprised at how hungry she was and how good it tasted. The root beer, too, tasted better than any she'd had in a long time.

When they reached his house, he parked the car in front, slid from behind the wheel, walked around the front of the car and opened her door. When she reached for one of the packages in the back seat, he waved her off.

"I'll do it."

"At least let me help."

"Go to bed."

Shannah stared at him. "What?"

"I said go to bed." There was a strange glitter in his eyes; his voice was deep, a low growl that brooked no argument.

She didn't argue, didn't linger to ask what was wrong. Instead, she ran up the porch steps and into the house and didn't stop running until she was upstairs in the bedroom with the door locked behind her.

What had she gotten herself into?

Agitated and more than a little afraid, she paced the floor, then came to an abrupt halt. How had he found her apartment? She hadn't given him her address or her phone number. He didn't have her last name. She knew he hadn't followed her home when she ran away. She had glanced over her shoulder more than once to make sure he wasn't behind her.

So, how *had* he found her?

And how had he persuaded her to invite him inside? She'd had no intention of doing so. And how had he convinced her to participate in this charade? She'd had no intention of doing that, either. Yet here she was, sharing a house with a complete stranger, albeit a very handsome stranger, who had just bought her a wardrobe worth a small fortune and was willing to pay the rent on her apartment and a salary while she pretended to be him. It seemed too good to be true. As her mother had often said, anything that seemed too good to be true probably was.

What had she gotten herself into? He had scared her tonight when he'd told her to go to bed. There had been something in his eyes, his voice . . . She shivered at the memory. Maybe she should tell him she had reconsidered his proposal and changed her mind.

Sleep, she thought, she needed to get some sleep. Perhaps things would look clearer in the morning.

She changed into the nightgown he had bought for her, turned out the light, and slipped under the covers, only to lie there in the dark, wide awake, wondering if her decision to stay here was going to turn out to be the biggest mistake of her life.

With a sigh, she turned on the light and propped the pillows behind her back. Digging his book out of her bag, she began to read.

Chapter Six

Ronan listened to the sound of Shannah's footsteps as she paced the floor overhead. Her scent filled the house. He knew she was doubting her decision to stay here, knew she didn't trust him. Her agitation increased her heartbeat. He could smell the blood flowing through her veins. It called to his hunger, even as her fear aroused his instinctive urge to hunt.

He heard the faint creak of bedsprings as she got into bed, his mind instantly swarming with images of her lying there, her hair spread out on the pillow, her body relaxed as she waited for sleep.

Not trusting himself to stay under the same roof with her in his current condition, he fled the house.

Plagued by his unholy thirst, he stalked the dark streets until he found a woman leaving a café, unescorted. He followed her to her car and slid into the passenger seat.

She stared at him in alarm. "What do you think you're doing? Get out of . . ." The words died in her throat when she looked into his eyes. "No, please . . ."

He didn't blame her for being afraid and yet he felt his anger rise as she cowered back against the car door.

Perhaps he was being too harsh. Perhaps he shouldn't be irritated by her fear. He knew how he looked when the hunger was upon him. He had seen the same look on the faces of others of his kind.

She thrust her handbag at him. "Here, take it, take it all, but please don't hurt me."

Take it all. Did she have any idea what those words meant to one of his kind? To take it all, to drink it all, to revel in the power that came from drinking a mortal's life and memories? Of course, she was referring to something else entirely.

"What makes you think I want your money?" He hated himself as soon as the words left his lips. What was wrong with him? He never toyed with his prey, never frightened them. "I'm not going to hurt you," he said, his voice low and hypnotic.

She only stared at him, her body trembling uncontrollably.

"Listen to my voice," he said quietly. "There's nothing to be afraid of."

"Nothing to be afraid of." She repeated the words. There was no expression on her face, no emotion in her voice.

He drew her into his arms. "Relax, now. Close your eyes. You have nothing to fear from me."

She went limp in his embrace. Her head lolled back against his arm, exposing the long clean lines of her neck, and the frantic pulse beating in the hollow of her throat.

With a low growl, he bent his head and surrendered to the ravening beast within him.

Shannah woke with the sound of her own screams ringing in her ears. Sitting up, the blanket clutched to her chest, she turned on the light, her gaze darting around the room, lingering in the shadows in the corners.

Just a bad dream. That's all it had been. Just a bad dream. Expelling a shaky breath, she realized she had fallen asleep while reading Dark's vampire book. Just a bad dream. But it had seemed so real . . . glowing red eyes staring down at her, bared fangs only inches from her throat, a sudden sharp pain that quickly turned to sensual pleasure . . . So real.

She lifted a hand to her neck, her fingers probing the skin below her ear, relieved to feel nothing more than her own smooth skin.

She took one last look around the room, turned off the light, and slid under the covers once more.

"That settles it," she murmured. "No more books about vampires before bedtime."

Ronan spent the next few weeks coaching Shannah. He gave her a list of all his books and a brief synopsis for each one.

"I want you to read the books so you'll be familiar with them," he told her. "If you memorize the outlines for now, you'll be able to respond intelligently if someone asks you what a particular book is about."

He gave her answers for every possible question he thought she might be asked, questions like how much research she did for each book, and did she visit the different locales she wrote about, and why she had decided to write romance novels in general and paranormal romances in particular, and wasn't she afraid of giving her readers unrealistic expectations about love and happy endings.

Tonight, they were sitting on the sofa in the front

room, his books spread out between them. A fire burned in the hearth, adding a cheerful glow to the room.

"Another question interviewers might ask you is, don't you think that by writing romance novels, you're feeding into a dangerous fantasy."

"Well, aren't you?" Shannah asked.

"Honestly? I don't know. But you can't say that. If they ask you that question, just say that if that's the case, then you're in good company, since many of the classics, from *Cinderella* to *Jane Eyre*, are basically romances with happy endings."

"That may be all well and good for your books," she said glumly, "but there's no such thing as a happy ending in real life. Everybody knows that."

He was inclined to agree with her, but didn't say so.

"I mean, look at the statistics. Three out of five marriages end in divorce."

"Have you ever been in love, Shannah?"

"I thought I was once, but . . ." She shrugged as if it was of no importance. "It didn't work out."

She had been hurt, though she didn't say so. It saddened him to think that one so young should have been hurt so deeply.

"Another thing they'll ask you about is fan mail. I get quite a lot, although most of it comes as email these days."

"People actually write to you about your books?"

"Oh, yeah." Most of the letters were from women, of course, thanking him for giving them a brief respite from housework, or for helping them through a rough time in their lives, or for giving them a newfound love for reading. One letter he particularly cherished had come from a teenage girl who wrote that his books had saved her life. She had been contemplating suicide and whenever she felt that way, she went to her room and read his books. He also received mail from men from time to time, though most of them were inmates at various prisons and institutions.

"Do you write back?" she asked.

"Of course. Anyone who takes the time to sit down and write a letter deserves an answer."

"Could I read some of your fan mail?"

"If you like. But not now."

"What about my life?" she asked. "I mean, your life. What should I say if they ask about your past?"

"Tell them whatever you wish, as long as it's either true or can't be proven a lie. I'm sure someone will ask you how you started writing. My typical answer is that I started writing because I was bored with television."

"That's easy enough."

"Another question you're sure to be asked is how you do the research for your love scenes."

"You're not serious?"

"It's a very popular question."

"So, what do I say? That I take notes while I make love?"

He stared at her a moment, and then laughed. "That's a far better answer than anything I've ever come up with."

"I was kidding."

"If you say it in jest, it might be answer enough," he remarked, thinking he liked her more and more every day.

Shannah sat up straight and stretched her back and shoulders. "I'm hungry."

His gaze darted to the pulse beating in her throat. He was hungry, too, he thought.

Always hungry, whenever she was around.

She cocked her head to the side and regarded him through curious eyes. "Why don't you ever eat with me? I'm not that bad a cook, you know."

"I prefer to eat in private," he said. "It's a particular quirk of mine."

"That's really weird."

"I suppose so."

"If you like to eat in private, how come there wasn't any food in the kitchen when I got here?"

Damn the girl, why did she have to ask so many questions that were best left unanswered, at least for now?

"Weevils," he said, thinking quickly. "They were into everything, so I threw it all out."

She looked at him, her expression skeptical. "Even the dishes and the pots and pans?"

Bless the girl, she didn't miss a trick! "Why don't you go fix yourself something to eat?" he suggested. "I need to go out for a short time."

"You go out every night. Where do you go?"

"Maybe some day I'll tell you."

She made a face at him, then left the room.

He stared after her. She was far too bright and asked far too many questions for his liking. If he was smart, he would send her on her way and forget about the book tour. Staying home wouldn't hurt his career and he was certain he could mollify his editor and his agent. And if he couldn't, well, he could always change his name and find a new publisher. The only thing was, he liked having Shannah around. She had bloomed in the last few weeks. Where she had once been frail and sickly looking, she was now the picture of vibrant good health. Her skin glowed, her hair was thick and lustrous, her eyes bright and clear. She was a beautiful young woman in the prime of her life.

And he wanted her.

Shannah stood at the stove, stirring a pan of chicken noodle soup, her mind filled with questions, all of them about her mysterious host. She wondered where he slept, since she slept in the only bed in the house, and where he kept his clothes. She never saw him during the day. He didn't eat. She had noticed there were no mirrors in any of the rooms.

The word *vampire* whispered, unbidden, through the back corridors of her mind.

She dismissed it with a shake of her head. He had answered the door when the sun was still up. He couldn't be a vampire if he was active during the day, even though he looked like one.

She laughed out loud. Who knew what a vampire looked like? In books, they were often described as skeletal figures with hairy hands, long bony fingers, and glowing red eyes. In movies, they were often portrayed as funny and sexy, like George Hamilton, or handsome and sexy, like Frank Langella.

Ronan was definitely handsome and sexy. Maybe he *was* a vampire.

A vampire who wrote best-selling romance novels. Right.

She poured the soup into a bowl, pulled a box of saltines out of the cupboard, and sat down at the table. For weeks now, she had been able to eat anything she wanted without getting sick to her stomach. She felt wonderful. The small mirror she carried in her purse told her she looked better than she ever had in her whole life. Her skin practically glowed. Her hair was thicker than before. Was this a sign that death was imminent? Her doctor had said she might enjoy a burst of good health before the end.

Her doctor. She had an appointment with him tomorrow. She had been feeling so good the last few weeks, she had forgotten all about it until now; now she was tempted to skip it. If she was better, why bother going?

And if she wasn't? Why bother going when they couldn't do anything to help her?

She finished her soup, washed the dishes and put them away, then went into the living room. Ronan hadn't returned, so she picked up the book she had been reading. He really was a terrific writer. She had read three of his books so far and every one of them had been a keeper, a real page turner. She wondered where he got all his information about vampires, then shrugged. He had a computer. You could find anything you wanted to know on the Net. Plus he had hundreds of books. Some of them could be research books, she supposed, though she had never heard of vampire research books. But then, there were a lot of things she had never heard of.

Settling back on the sofa, she opened the book and lost herself in another world.

Ronan stood in the doorway, his gaze on the woman who was so engrossed in one of his books that she didn't even realize he was in the room. It pleased him to think she was so caught up in a world that he had created that she wasn't aware of her own surroundings. The thought made him smile. There was something deeply satisfying about knowing that others enjoyed his work. He had a dozen boxes filled with fan letters, as well as a number of files on his computer where he stored his email according to the year it had been received. But the fact that Shannah enjoyed his stories pleased him more than anything else.

She really was lovely, he mused, and then frowned. It occurred to him that she was quite young, probably too young to have written as many Eva Black books as he had. If asked, she would have to lie about her age. These days, with collagen injections, Botox, skin peels and plastic surgery, it was hard to judge a woman's true age. Of course, it wasn't unheard of for an author to turn out more than one book a year. He wrote two books a year, sometimes three. One author he knew of, who was much more famous than he was, wrote six books a year, but she was a law unto herself. He often wondered how she found time to do anything else.

Ronan took a step into the room. The movement caught Shannah's attention and she glanced in his direction.

He jerked his chin at the book in her lap. "Are you enjoying it?"

"Yes, very much, although I have to admit I was surprised when you killed off the housekeeper."

He laughed softly. "Always keep the reader guessing," he said, taking a place on the sofa. "If you kill off a major character, it keeps the reader wondering who else you might knock off before the end of the book."

"Ah. I'll have to remember that in case it comes up," she said, and then frowned. "There's so much to memorize, I know I'll never be able to remember it all."

"Sure you will."

"What if I forget something?"

"Then just fake it."

"What if my mind goes blank? What if I freeze up during one of the radio interviews?"

"Shannah, stop worrying. I wouldn't have asked you to do this if I didn't think you could handle it."

"But . . ."

"If it proves to be too much for you, or you really can't handle it, then we'll just cancel the tour and come home."

"Just like that?" she asked, snapping her fingers.

"Just like that."

"You're awfully kind."

Ronan stared at her. Kind? He had been called a lot of

things in five hundred years, but kind had not been one of them

His gaze moved over her, lingering on her lips. What would she do if he drew her into his arms and kissed her? Would she be shocked? Repelled? Or would she kiss him back?

As a vampire, there wasn't much he was afraid of, but he couldn't stand the thought of being rejected by this girl-woman with her tantalizing humanity and warm blue eyes.

"Ronan? Is something wrong?"

"Why do you ask?"

"I don't know. You look sort of . . . forlorn."

"Not to worry, Shannah. I'm fine."

"Good." She yawned behind her hand. "I think I'll go to bed. Good night, Ronan."

"Good night, Shannah."

He sat there long after she had gone upstairs, bemused by his growing affection for her. Funny, he hadn't realized how lonely he had been until she came into his life.

His writing took up a great deal of his waking hours. He was hooked on the card game Spider, and occasionally played poker on the Internet. He enjoyed reading, both for pleasure and research. He spent one night a week answering his fan mail. From time to time, when he was bored, he surfed some of the online vampire role-playing rooms. He often wondered what the others would think if they knew he wasn't playing a role.

Only now did he realize how boring and mundane his existence had become. In the beginning, he had wandered the four corners of the earth. He had explored cities, both ancient and modern. He had educated himself, gained an appreciation for art, learned foreign languages. In spite of all that, it had taken a slip of a girl like

Shannah to add a dash of excitement to his otherwise dreary existence.

Later that night, when he was certain she was asleep, he went to her bedside. Biting into his wrist, he watched the dark red blood ooze from the shallow gash. He commanded her to swallow a few drops before the wound healed and then, sitting beside her, he spoke to her mind, telling her more about the books he had written, his writing habits, the names of his agent, his publishing house and his editor, and anything else that he could think of that she might need to know when they went on the road.

He sat there until the sky grew rosy with the coming dawn, content to sit by her side and watch her sleep, to inhale the fragrance of her hair and skin, to listen to the slow, steady beat of her heart. To pretend that she was his, for now and for all time. He caressed her face, bent to brush a kiss across her lips.

As the sun grew higher, he sought his lair, his senses still filled with the sweet scent of her skin, the warmth of her cheek beneath his hand. With a sigh, he sank into the darkness of oblivion.

Chapter Seven

In the morning, after a quick breakfast of toast, juice and coffee, Shannah drove to her doctor's office. She had a standing weekly appointment, and she had missed the last three. She wasn't sure why she had decided to keep this appointment. What could the doctor tell her that she didn't already know?

"I've been worried about you," Doctor Harper said as he wrapped the blood pressure cuff around her arm. "I thought . . . well, no matter. You're looking quite well today."

"I feel wonderful."

Nodding, he watched the gauge, then removed the cuff from her arm.

"How is it?" she asked.

"Normal." He made a note on her chart. "I see you've even gained a little weight."

"Really?"

"Yes. How's your appetite been?"

"Better than usual. And I've been keeping everything down!"

"Indeed? Any headaches? Dizziness? Nausea?"

"No, no, and no."

He made more notes on her chart, listened to her

heart and lungs, jotted more notes on her chart. "I want you to go down to the lab so they can take some blood."

"All right." Needles, she thought. She hated them.

Leaving the lab twenty minutes later, she went to Baskin-Robbins and treated herself to a double hot fudge sundae with extra whipped crème, and then she went window shopping. She made one stop at the drug store where she bought a makeup mirror, a candy bar, and a pack of gum.

Walking back to her car, she thought again how amazing it was that she felt so well. She didn't feel the least bit tired. Eating didn't make her sick. She was sleeping better than ever. When she realized she was squinting, she put on her sunglasses, thinking how odd it was that the sun hurt her eyes when it never had before. Maybe it was just another symptom of her illness. She would have to ask the doctor about it next week.

Back at Ronan's house, she watched TV for a little while, then switched it off.

Going out into the backyard, she pulled weeds from the garden until her back ached, noting that, once the weeds were gone, there was nothing left.

Returning to the house, she filled a glass with ice and water and then, hoping she wasn't violating Ronan's trust in any way, she went into his office and booted up his computer.

Unable to restrain her curiosity, she opened a file named Fan Mail—January 2008. She whistled softly. There were over a thousand emails. Sitting back in the chair, she began to read.

Dear Miss Black—I love your books. I have them all and I've read each one of them over and over again. I don't know how you do it, but you always draw me into the story from page one. Your characters are so real, especially

*your vampires. If I didn't know it was impossible, I'd think
you were a vampire yourself. Just kidding. I can't wait for
your next book.*

Your number one fan. Sandy.

The letters were all basically the same, praising Eva
Black for her wonderful books, asking for autographs or
bookmarks or signed photos, or all three. Several were
from would-be writers asking for advice on how to get
published. A couple were from women who said they had
this really great idea for a book and if Miss Black would
just write it, they would be happy to split the royalties with
her. Shannah had to laugh out loud at their temerity.
Ronan would do all the work and they would split the royalties with him! A number of the emails were from readers asking for free books for themselves or donations for
fundraisers, or for a loved one who was sick or in prison.

Some of the readers thanked Eva profusely and sin-
cerely, relating how her books had helped them get
through a particularly rough time in their lives—the death
of a parent or a child, a divorce, a serious illness. Shannah
was moved by their gratitude. It must be humbling for an
author to receive such letters, she thought, to know that
your words had touched another's life so deeply.

One letter was from a woman who said she didn't like
Eva Black's last book, and that her husband hadn't liked
it, either.

Shannah laughed at that. It just proved that you
couldn't please all the people all the time.

She was amazed to find that the letters came from
both men and women, and that some of his readers were
as young as twelve and some were in their eighties. Apparently romances appealed to a wide range of people,
from schoolgirls to prison inmates.

Closing the fan mail file, she tried to open a document titled Work in Progress, only to discover she couldn't open the file without a password. Odd, that he lived alone but felt the need to have a password, and then she grinned. Not so odd, she thought. After all, she was here, trying to get a peek at something that was none of her business.

Frowning, she tried to think of what Ronan might use for a password. She tried his pen name and then she tried every word she could think of for black and for vampire, but none of them worked, either.

With a sigh of exasperation, she turned off the computer and went to fix something to eat.

Later, she wandered through the house, looking for something to do. Using a dish towel, she dusted the furniture, upstairs and down, but that didn't take long and she was again left with nothing to do.

Where was Ronan, she wondered. What did he do all day? If he was a writer, why wasn't he here, writing?

She had a lot of questions she wanted to ask him.

She asked the first one when she saw him that night. "Where do you go every day?"

"Hello to you, too." He sat down on the sofa, careful to leave a good amount of space between them though it didn't really help. With his preternatural senses, he was all too aware of her—the scent of her hair and perfume, the warmth of her skin, the ever-present allure of her blood. "You went to the doctor today. What did he say?"

"He said I'm doing well, and that I've gained some weight. Don't change the subject. I never see you until it's almost dark outside. Why? And how did you know I went to the doctor?"

"If you must know, I sleep days and work nights."

"Anyone would think you really are a vampire," she muttered. "Don't tell me you sleep in a coffin in the basement."

He laughed softly, but she noticed he didn't deny it.

She frowned. "I must be sleeping in your bed, so where do you sleep?"

"Shall we get busy?" he asked, hoping to distract her. "We still have a lot of work to do."

"How did you know I went to the doctor? I don't recall mentioning it to you."

"I can smell it on you."

"You cannot!"

He shrugged.

Shannah looked down at herself and sniffed. "What do you smell?"

"Disinfectant. Antibiotics. Alcohol." He frowned. "Dirt."

"You must have a nose like a bloodhound if you can smell all that!"

"Where did the dirt come from? Not your doctor's office, I hope."

"Of course not. I pulled some weeds in the backyard."

"There's no need for you to do that."

"I wanted to. Would you mind if I planted some flowers?"

"Do whatever you wish," he said impatiently. "Are you ready to get to work now? We still have a lot to do. I've made an appointment with a photographer for tomorrow night."

"So soon?"

He nodded. "I had an email from my editor. She needs the photo for the next book jacket as soon as possible."

Except for her high school photo, she had never had anyone take her picture professionally. "Will you come with me?"

"Of course. I told my agent that I would do signings in a few of the larger bookstores in Los Angeles and New York and a couple of radio interviews if they could set them up."

"Oh."

"Don't worry, you'll be fine. Just memorize the answers I've given you and stop worrying." He would be nearby for any night-time interviews or signings; during the day, she would be on her own, though he didn't think that would be a problem. He had implanted everything she needed to know in her mind while she slept. "I'm going to write for a few hours while you study."

She sighed. "All right. Um . . ."

"What?"

"My parents live in New York. Do you think we could visit them while we're there? I haven't seen them in over a year."

"Why didn't you go home when you got sick?"

"I did, for a little while, but they just . . ." She made a vague gesture with one hand. "They smothered me, you know? I mean, I know they love me and they're worried, but I couldn't breathe. Every time I turned around, they were hovering over me, telling me to eat something, telling me to rest, asking if I was feeling all right, if there was anything they could do. But now, well, since we're going to be so close . . ."

"I don't think it'll be a problem."

"Thank you, Ronan."

Nodding, he went into his office and closed the door. He knew immediately that she had been there earlier in the day. Her scent was heavy in the air.

Pulling up his current work in progress, he stared at the screen and then he began to write. His heroine changed from a rather plump blonde with green eyes to a slender young woman with inky black hair and sky blue eyes. Shannah. She had bewitched him with her smile and her innocence, with her quick intelligence and her rare flashes of wit.

For centuries, he had resisted the allure of some of the

most beautiful women in the world. How ironic, to find himself falling in love now, with a woman who would not even live a normal mortal life span.

No doubt the Fates were having a good laugh at his expense.

What would she say if he told her the truth?

He shook the thought from his mind. In spite of the fact that she had come to his house seeking a vampire, he feared she would run screaming from his presence if he told her she had actually found one. He knew that her coming to him had been an act of sheer desperation. Taking her blood had enabled him to divine her thoughts and he knew that, deep in her heart, the thought of becoming a vampire filled her with fear and revulsion. He knew, too, that had he offered her the Dark Gift the day she had knocked on his door, she would have refused. He dared not take a chance on revealing his true nature, not now, when he wasn't ready to let her go.

He glanced out the window. He wasn't ready to let her go, he thought, not now. Perhaps not ever.

Forcing himself to concentrate on the work at hand, he lost himself in a world of his own making, his fingers flying over the keyboard, his breathing growing erratic as he wrote the first love scene between his hero and heroine. Never before had he written a love scene so drawn out or so descriptive, and as he wrote it, he realized he was describing, in vivid detail, how he wanted to make love to Shannah.

"Wow, that is so hot! I'm surprised your computer doesn't go up in flames."

He glanced over his shoulder, shocked to find her standing behind him, stunned to realize he had been so caught up in what he was writing, thinking, that he hadn't even been aware of her presence in the room. Had she been a hunter, he thought dryly, no doubt there would be a stake through his heart.

"What are you doing in here?" he asked. "You're supposed to be memorizing your answers."

"I've been memorizing for over three hours," she retorted. "I don't know about you, but I need a break."

"Of course." He saved his work and exited the program. "Would you like to go for a walk?"

"Now? It's awfully late, don't you think?"

"Not at all. There's nothing for you to be afraid of," he said, sensing her thoughts. "I won't let the bogeyman get you." Little did she know that the man beside her was far more dangerous and scary than any childhood specter.

"All right."

They walked down the driveway and out the gate. It was a lovely night, cool and clear with just the faintest hint of a breeze. A quarter moon hung low in a velvet black sky dotted with twinkling silver stars.

Shannah walked beside Ronan, acutely aware of him beside her. He was so tall and strong and he exuded such power, it made her feel small and vulnerable. She had the feeling that if he took it into his head to do so, he could break her in two with his bare hands.

The thought sent a shiver down her spine even as she wondered where it had come from.

"Did you find anything interesting on my computer?" he asked.

The question startled her. How had he known? She hadn't moved anything except the mouse and she had been careful to put it back exactly the way she found it.

She stared up at him, trying to decide what to say.

"Well?" he coaxed.

"I . . . I read some of your fan mail," she blurted. "I hope you don't mind."

"Of course not. I said you could."

"You get so much of it, I don't know how you find time to read it all, and write, too."

He shrugged.

"I tried to read your work in progress," she said, sending him a sideways glance. As long as she was confessing, she might as well admit everything.

"Did you?"

She nodded.

"If you want to read it, I'll remove the password."

"You will? You don't mind?"

"You're supposed to be me," he said with a shrug. "The more you know about my writing, the better."

"You really are a good writer, you know."

"I'm glad you think so."

He smiled at her, and she smiled back.

They walked in silence for a time. When her hand brushed his, it sent a sizzle all the way up her arm. Unexpectedly, she recalled the love scene he had been writing earlier that night. It had been steamy without being graphic, descriptive without being lewd or vulgar. It had made her blush clear down to her toes when she imagined Ronan kissing her like that, making love to her like that. She shivered as she pictured his hands caressing her skin, his mouth on her bare flesh.

"Are you cold?" he asked.

She looked up at him. "What? Oh, no."

She stopped walking as his gaze met and held hers. His eyes were compelling, almost hypnotic.

"Do you want to go back?" he asked.

She shook her head.

"Shannah." She looked incredibly beautiful standing there looking up at him, her eyes wide and a little scared.

His hands folded over her shoulders as he drew her slowly toward him until their bodies were only a breath apart. Slowly, he lowered his head, until all she could see were his eyes and the desire that burned in their depths.

Helpless to resist, she tilted her head back and closed her eyes as his mouth covered hers.

Warmth. Heat. Pleasure.

She swayed toward him, her body drawn to his by a force she could neither understand nor ignore. She forgot everything else as his lips played over hers, now soft and exquisitely gentle, now firm and demanding. Nothing mattered, nothing but this man, this moment. If he kissed her like this until the end of time, it wouldn't be long enough. His tongue teased hers. Desire shot through her from the top of her head to the soles of her feet. Lordy, but the man could kiss!

She moaned softly, her fingers delving into the thick hair at his nape.

Ronan's hands slid down her back. Spreading his hands over her thighs, he drew her body closer to his. Too long, he thought, it had been too long since he had wanted a woman as desperately, as passionately, as he wanted this one. He had been a young vampire then, new in the life, unable to separate his hunger from his lust . . . and the girl had died because of it.

With a low groan, he put Shannah away from him, stood there, trembling, while she gazed up at him.

"Why did you stop?" she asked plaintively.

He drew in a deep breath. "This is hardly the time or the place."

Shannah looked around, only then realizing they were in the middle of the sidewalk and that cars were driving by. "I guess you're right."

"I know a place where we can be alone."

She looked up at him, her heart thundering in her chest. "Do you?" She wanted to sound playful, teasing. Instead, she sounded breathless.

"Indeed." Taking her by the hand, he led her back to his house.

Shannah shivered as they walked up the pathway to the door. The house looked spooky at night, the dark windows like blank eyes. Leaves rustled against the sides of the house, whispering secrets that she would never know. She let out a startled cry as a cat burst out of the shadows and disappeared around the corner of the house.

Ronan put his arm around her shoulders. He could feel her shivering. At first he thought it was from excitement, but then he realized her skin was cool, damp with sweat. Her heart was beating much too rapidly.

Swinging her into his arms, he carried her quickly into the house and placed her on the sofa. "Shannah?"

"I'm sorry, I . . . I felt so good this morning." She tried to smile. "The doctor said my vital signs were normal. I guess he was wrong."

"You'll be fine."

"No." Sadness welled in her eyes. "I'll never be well. These last few weeks were probably just a . . . I don't know. A reprieve." Her eyelids fluttered down, her body went limp.

Gathering her into his arms, Ronan sat down on the sofa, her body cradled against his chest. Biting his wrist, he held it to her lips.

"Drink, Shannah," he commanded. "Drink, and you'll feel better in the morning, I promise."

He stroked her throat to make her swallow, closed his eyes as she surrendered her will to his. It pleased him greatly to nourish her, to know that his blood would drive away her pain and extend her life a while longer.

He watched the color return to her cheeks, heard her heartbeat and breathing gradually return to normal. And then he lowered his head to her neck and drank.

Chapter Eight

In the morning, Shannah was surprised at how strong she felt, and how long she had slept. A glance at the clock showed it was almost two. She shrugged it off. Considering how she had felt last night, sleeping late didn't seem so strange. She blew out a sigh. Last night, she had been certain she was again at death's door. This morning, she felt like she could run the Boston Marathon and win. It was most confusing.

But it was too beautiful a day to fret about a future she couldn't change. She felt too wonderful to lay about any longer.

Bounding out of bed, she took a shower and brushed her teeth. Famished, she ate a big breakfast, then went out the front door to fetch the morning paper. After refilling her coffee cup, she headed out the back door, intending to sit outside, enjoy a second cup of coffee and get caught up on the latest news.

She frowned when she stepped into the sunlight. Squinting against the brightness, she went back into the house for her sunglasses. Funny, the sun had never bothered her before.

Sitting in the chaise lounge, she scanned the front

page of the paper. In all her life, she had never taken the time to read a newspaper from beginning to end.

"I could get used to this," she murmured as she turned the page.

The sun felt good against her skin. Laying the paper aside, she leaned back in the chaise lounge and closed her eyes.

Deep in the bowels of the house, Ronan stirred.

"Shannah." He murmured her name, heard it echo within the confines of his resting place.

She was sitting outside, dozing in the sun.

Lying there, drifting on the edge of oblivion, he felt what she felt, smelled what she smelled. He felt the touch of the sun caress his skin for the first time in over five hundred years. Here, safe in the darkness of his lair, it had no power to harm him. He was free to bask in its warmth vicariously, without pain or fear. An in-drawn breath brought him the scent of trees and grass and sun-warmed earth. Birdsong filled his ears, something he had not heard in centuries. He licked his lips and tasted the coffee she had been drinking, the bacon and eggs she had eaten for breakfast, tastes that he had forgotten long ago.

With a sigh and a faint smile, he surrendered to the darkness that dragged him down into oblivion.

It was late afternoon when Shannah woke. Returning to the house, she tossed her sunglasses on the table, then sat down and tried to study the list of possible questions Ronan thought she would be asked. It hit her all of a sudden that in just a few weeks, she would be in New York City or Los Angeles pretending to be a successful romance author. People would interview her. She would meet Ronan's readers. What if she said or did something to embarrass him or his agent or his publisher?

Why had she ever thought she could pull off such a charade? He needed someone with acting experience, someone outgoing and self-confident. She was shy around strangers, quiet even with her family. She would tell him that she'd changed her mind when she saw him tonight. A glance at the window showed that it was almost dark now. He would be there soon.

The thought of telling him "no" filled her with apprehension and she decided to put it off as long as possible. Hurrying up to her bedroom, she changed clothes and left the house, determined to eat dinner at a nice restaurant for a change.

She had just ordered and was sipping a glass of raspberry lemonade when Ronan slid into the chair across the table from her.

Shannah almost choked on her drink. "What are you doing here?"

"I thought you might like some company with your dinner."

"How did you know where I was?"

He shrugged. "Does it matter?"

"Yes, I think it does." She frowned at him. "And that reminds me, how did you find my apartment the other night?"

"I followed you home."

She shook her head. "No one followed me."

"Are you sure?"

"Yes. No . . ." She frowned. She had been certain that no one had followed her that night, but she could have been mistaken. But he hadn't followed her tonight. She was sure of that. He hadn't even been home when she left. "How did you . . . ?"

"Did you forget you have an appointment tonight?"

"What? Oh! I did!" she exclaimed. "Are we late?"

"You have time to have dinner."

"Are you sure? I need to change. What should I wear?"

He shrugged. "Whatever you think best."

The waitress brought her dinner a few moments later.

"Aren't you going to eat?" Shannah asked.

"No."

She ate quickly, aware of his presence across the table, of the way his dark eyes watched her, like a cat at a mouse hole. She should have told him she had changed her mind when he sat down, she thought, told him she couldn't pretend to be Eva Black, that there was no way she could remember everything, no way she would ever be able to convince his editor or his readers that she had written all those wonderful books.

She took a deep breath and let it out in a sigh. Maybe she would tell him later, at home. Yes, that might be better, since he was sure to be angry. Best not to cause a scene in a public place. She would tell him on the way to his house. She couldn't let him spend good money on photographs that would never be used.

A short time later, he paid the check and they left the restaurant. During the ride home, she tried to rehearse what she would say to him, but she couldn't seem to form her thoughts coherently, not when he was sitting so close, when she could feel his gaze like a physical caress on her face, when his presence made her heart beat fast.

Inside the house, she crossed her arms over her breasts and took a deep breath. "Ronan, I'm flattered that you think I could . . ."

"Shannah, we don't have time for that now." Putting his hands on her shoulders, he turned her toward the staircase. "We're going to be late as it is."

"But I can't . . . I'm not . . ."

"Later," he said.

With a sigh of exasperation, she hurried up the stairs. Fine, it wasn't her fault he wouldn't listen. As for the photographs, maybe she could buy one or two for her parents so the night wouldn't be a total waste of time. It might make a nice gift, a nice portrait for them to remember her by.

She decided on a navy blue knit dress and matching heels. It was dressy yet casual. She applied her makeup carefully, brushed her hair, took a last look in the mirror she had bought. And frowned. She hadn't really looked at herself lately; now she was surprised at how well she looked. Her skin had a healthy glow, her eyes sparkled, her hair was shiny. She had never looked better. A little beacon of hope flared inside her. Maybe she wasn't dying, after all. Doctors had made mistakes before.

Ronan nodded his approval when she went downstairs.

"Are you sure I look all right?"

He nodded. "Trust me. You look good enough to eat. Are you ready to go?"

She nodded, though she wasn't ready at all.

The photographer, Ed Dewhurst, was waiting for them when they arrived.

After welcoming the two of them, Dewhurst bade Shannah sit on a white wicker love seat. He arranged his camera, the lights, tilted her head at an angle, just so, and began taking pictures.

He shot her sitting up and reclining, smiling and looking pensive. He shot her in front of a variety of backdrops and colors. He draped a long white silk scarf around her neck and turned on a fan so that the ends of the scarf blew softly behind her.

Ronan stood out of the way, careful to avoid the large mirror that was set in the corner of the studio. He could see that Shannah was nervous and ill at ease. Her smile was tight, her whole demeanor declared she was uncomfortable in front of the camera.

Shannah tried to relax, but it was impossible. She felt silly posing this way and that way, and worse, she felt like a fraud. Finally, she glanced beseechingly at Ronan. His dark eyes were watching her every move. It should have made her more self-conscious; instead, she forgot all about the lights and the camera and the photographer. She posed for Ronan, her gaze on his face, her body yearning for his touch. She imagined his mouth on hers, his arms holding her close, closer.

"Perfect," Dewhurst said, quickly snapping one picture after another. "Beautiful. Yes, yes. That smile! Wonderful!"

A short time later, he put his camera down and turned off the lights. "That last roll," he said, nodding, "you'll be pleased with those, I'm sure."

"How soon can we see them?" Ronan asked.

"The proofs will be ready by next week."

"We don't have time for proofs," Ronan said. "I want to see finished pictures as soon as possible."

"That'll cost you extra."

"Just do it." Ronan shook Dewhurst's hand, then led Shannah out of the studio.

"I think it went well," he said as they walked to her car.

"Do you? I felt . . ."

He looked at her. "What did you feel?"

She shook her head. At first, she had felt silly, posing as if she were somebody, but then she had looked into Ronan's eyes and she had posed for him, wanted to look pretty for him. "Never mind."

"Tell me, Shannah. What did you feel?"

"Pretty," she said, ever so softly. "I felt pretty."

"And you were," he replied. "You are."

Looking into his eyes, she believed him.

But later that night, lying in bed, she found herself wondering yet again how he had found her apartment and how he had known where she was having dinner.

The next week flew by. The flowers she had hoped to plant in the garden were forgotten as she spent practically every minute memorizing possible questions and answers and reading Ronan's books. To her amazement, it grew easier and easier to memorize the answers. Even more amazing was the fact that she could recite long passages from all of his books. She wasn't sure why, but she had never gotten around to telling him she had changed her mind.

He removed the password from his current work in progress and she read it avidly not once but twice. Shannah was certain it was just her imagination, but the heroine seemed an awful lot like her, and not just her physical description.

Her dreams were filled with lusty images that could have been taken directly from his books. She had never had such dreams before. Dark dreams that left her restless and yearning for his touch, that made her wake in the middle of the night, his name on her lips, her hands reaching for him.

They went back to the studio to select a portrait. Shannah stared at the pictures spread before her, unable to believe that she was the woman in the photos. Did she really look like that?

She looked up at Ronan and shook her head. "This can't be me."

"Ah, but it is."

"But how . . . ?" Shannah looked at the pictures again. She looked cool and confident and sultry and beguiling all at the same time. She had never been cool or confident or sultry before. Why now?

She was still pondering that question when she looked into Ronan's eyes. He was the answer, she thought. He made her feel beautiful and sexy and desirable. And even as the thought crossed her mind, desire arced between them like chain lightning.

"We'll take this one," Ronan said. "And these two. And this one."

She felt her cheeks grow warm when she glanced at the photos he had chosen. She had been looking at him, thinking of him, when the photographer snapped the pictures.

"Do you think I could have one for my parents?" she asked.

"Certainly," he said. "Pick whichever one you want."

Ronan paid for the photographs and they left the studio.

"I thought you only needed one picture for the book jacket," she remarked as they walked to the car.

"We do," he said. "The other three are for me."

"Oh." She didn't know what else to say. It was incredible that he wanted her picture. Incredible and flattering.

She was getting into the car when she noticed that Ronan was still standing on the sidewalk, staring at something across the street.

Following his gaze, Shannah saw a blond-haired man standing on the opposite curb. He was staring at Ronan.

"Is that someone you know?" she asked when he finally got behind the wheel.

"In a manner of speaking."

"I take it he isn't a friend of yours."

Ronan grunted softly as he started the car and pulled away from the curb.

Shannah glanced out the back window. The man was still standing on the curb, staring after them.

"Who is he?"

"No one of importance. We'll be leaving for Los Angeles tomorrow night."

"So soon?"

He nodded.

"I've never been on a plane before."

"Are you afraid of flying?"

"I don't know." She grinned at him. "I guess we'll find out tomorrow night."

Chapter Nine

Shannah hadn't expected to be afraid of flying. After all, people did it every day. They had gotten through security all right, although she had thought taking off her shoes was a bit much. At any rate, they had made it safely through security and boarded the plane. She was surprised to find that Ronan had purchased a row of first-class seats for the two of them. He indicated she should sit by the window.

She hadn't been the least bit nervous during boarding but now that she was actually on the plane, in her seat, she was suddenly very, very scared.

Planes crashed all the time. And then there was the ever-constant threat of hijackers and terrorists. She knew she would never forget the sight of those two airplanes flying into the Twin Towers, or the nightmare images that had followed. She had been in bed, asleep, when her father called that morning. She had listened in stunned disbelief while he told her what was happening. Relieved that her parents were all right, she had turned on the television and watched, bewildered and horrified, as what was happening in New York City was played over and over again. It seemed as if the very fabric of time had been rewoven that day. There was the world before September 11th, and there was the world after. It was a day she knew she would never forget, a day when the impossible became possible and America realized it was no longer invulnerable.

Even now, years later, airport security was stringent. The lines had been long. By the time they made it through security, she felt more like a criminal going to prison than a passenger going cross-country. Most of the other travelers endured the hassle without grumbling too much. She didn't have any carry-on baggage other than a book, and neither did Ronan. While waiting in line, she had asked him if he had a photo ID, since she wasn't sure if vampires could be photographed, but apparently it was no problem, since he had a driver's license with his picture on it.

She glanced at the other people on board the plane. None of them looked like terrorists. None of them seemed particularly worried about the flight. People were chatting with their companions, adjusting their seats, reading, or simply staring out the window. Was she the only one wishing she were somewhere else?

"Shannah, is something wrong?"

"No, why?"

Ronan tapped one finger on the back of her hand. Looking down, she saw that her knuckles were white where she was gripping the edge of her seat.

"I guess I am a little nervous all of a sudden."

She quickly decided that nervous didn't begin to explain how she felt. She was excited by the prospect of flying, and terrified at the same time.

"There's nothing to be afraid of," Ronan said reassuringly.

"Except crashing."

"I won't let anything happen to you."

"Like you could stop it."

"Trust me, Shannah. Whatever happens, you'll be all right, I promise you."

She stared at him. How could he make such a promise? Sincere as he sounded, if the plane went down, there wasn't anything he could do to stop it.

Her heartbeat quickened when she heard the captain's voice saying they had been cleared for takeoff. She remembered reading somewhere that most plane crashes occurred during takeoffs or landings. This was it, she thought as the plane taxied down the runway. There was no turning back now. Fingers in a death grip on the armrest, she closed her eyes and prayed like she had never prayed before.

The plane picked up speed and suddenly it felt like she was floating.

"You can relax now," Ronan said. "We're in the air."

Opening her eyes, Shannah glanced out the window. The ground grew farther and farther away, the lights of the city faded into little yellow dots far below.

"Weren't you even a little scared?" she asked.

He chuckled softly. "Takes more than a plane lifting off to frighten me."

She regarded him curiously. "What does frighten you?"

He looked at her thoughtfully a moment, then shook his head. "Nothing."

"Nothing?" she asked skeptically. "Come on, everybody's afraid of something."

"I used to be afraid of a lot of things," he admitted. "But not anymore."

"Well, when you were afraid," she said, "what were you afraid of?"

"Being alone. Dying. Going to hell." He wondered briefly if the fires of hell could possibly be as painful as the touch of the sun's light on preternatural flesh. "The usual things mortals are afraid of."

"Mortals?" She lifted one brow. "As opposed to those who aren't mortal?"

"As opposed to dogs and cats," he answered smoothly.

"Sometimes I wonder about you," she muttered.

"What do you wonder?"

She made a vague gesture with her hand. "You never told me how you found my apartment. Sometimes it seems like you can read my mind. I never see you during the day. I've never seen you eat or drink anything. I mean, it's like . . ."

"Go on."

"Oh, I don't know what I'm trying to say. You're just weird, that's all."

He laughed softly. "Honey, you have no idea."

"Don't say that! It scares me. I can see the headlines now. Girl's body found in dumpster. Neighbors claim killer was such a nice quiet man, never caused any trouble."

He grunted softly. "Since you're the girl, I guess that makes me the killer."

He was smiling when he said it, but a chill went down Shannah's spine. There was something in his voice, a knife-like edge beneath the mildly spoken words.

She shook her head. "Don't mind me. I'm just nervous. It makes me say silly things."

"You have nothing to fear from me, Shannah. Believe that if you believe nothing else." He wasn't so sure he could guarantee the safety of the hundreds of other people on the plane. Every breath he took carried the scent of prey. Like a lion prowling the jungle, he could sense the weak in the herd, the weary, the ones who would welcome death. "Whatever happens, I'll keep you safe."

"I believe you." With a sigh, she rested her head against the back of the seat. "I think I'll take a nap."

"It'll have to be a short one," he said. "We'll be there in an hour or so."

But she didn't care. If the plane crashed, at least she wouldn't be awake when it happened.

She was almost asleep when she remembered she had missed her appointment with her doctor. No matter, she thought, she had never felt better. She would have to find time to call him when they reached Los Angeles. It was her last thought before sleep claimed her.

Ronan listened to the even sound of her breathing, watched the gentle rise and fall of her chest. She knew there was something not quite right about him. He wondered how long it would take her to figure out what it was, and what he would do when she did.

Looking at her, sleeping so innocently beside him, he feared he had done the unthinkable.

He had fallen in love with a mortal. And not just any mortal, but one who was dying. He stared out the window, his gaze piercing the distance of eternity. He could keep her from dying, he mused. That was why she had come to him in the first place. But once the deed was done, would she love him for it? Or spend eternity regretting the night a vampire gave her what she had come looking for?

Shannah was glad that it didn't take long to fly from Northern California to Los Angeles. It was a rather bumpy landing and it had Shannah gripping the edge of her seat again and praying the plane wouldn't sink in the Pacific Ocean or crash on the runway or land in someone's backyard.

She breathed an audible sigh of relief when the plane was safely on the ground.

They collected their bags and found a taxi. An hour

later, Shannah was drinking a Coke in her hotel room. She would have her first book signing tomorrow night at an exclusive bookstore in West Hollywood. It was a good thing Ronan would be there with her, she thought, because she knew she would be a nervous wreck without him. In spite of all his assurances to the contrary, she still wasn't sure she could carry this off.

She glanced in his direction. He stood at the window, gazing out into the darkness. She wondered what he was thinking about. Was he, too, having second thoughts about her ability?

"I can't believe we're really here," she remarked. "Have you been to Los Angeles before?"

"Once or twice." It hadn't been called Los Angeles then, and California hadn't been a state. It had been a beautiful place in those days, the air clean and sweet, the sky blue instead of brown with smog, wide dirt roads instead of clogged freeways. Progress wasn't always a good thing. "It's late," he said. "You should get some sleep."

She smothered a yawn. "I think you're right."

"I won't be here in the morning," he said, moving toward the door that connected his room to hers.

"Why not? Where are you going?"

"I've got some business to take care of."

"I'll go with you."

"No. Sleep late. Go sight-seeing if you like, or spend the day out by the pool."

"You'll be back in time for the signing?"

"Of course. And don't worry. You'll be fine."

She nodded, though she still had doubts.

Retracing his steps, he drew her into his arms and kissed the top of her head. "Sleep well, Shannah."

She smiled up at him. "Good night, Ronan."

"Good night, love."

She stared after him as he left the room. Love. He had

called her love. Warmth spread through her. Had he meant it? Or was it just a term of endearment, like "honey" and "sweetie" or any of a hundred other expressions of affection?

Love. Not long ago, she had been certain she would never fall in love again. It was too much trouble. Too time-consuming. Too painful when it was over. She had loved and lost and she had decided that, in the future, it would be better not to love at all. And then she had gotten sick and she didn't have the time or the energy to think about love or anything other than surviving from day to day.

But all that had been before she met Ronan. He was unlike any man she had ever known. She guessed he was probably in his mid-thirties, though he seemed older than his years. He was certainly older than any man she had ever dated . . .

Dated. The word made her giggle. They weren't dating, exactly, she thought. Mainly, he was teaching her how to be his alter ego. Still, there were those devastating, mind-boggling, soul-shattering kisses. It was for certain no one had ever kissed her like he did. Not even Billy Ray. Until Ronan kissed her, she would have said no man in the world kissed better than that swine, Billy Ray. Just proved how wrong a girl could be, she thought, grinning.

Just thinking about Ronan's kisses made her toes curl inside her shoes. Kicking off her heels, she went into the bathroom where she soaked in a hot bubble bath while her wicked imagination pictured Ronan in the tub with her, washing her back, nuzzling her neck . . .

With a shake of her head, she stepped out of the tub, dried off, and slipped into her nightgown. She was making far too much out of one endearment.

But she was still smiling when she fell asleep.

* * *

Ronan strolled along the dark streets, shielding his presence from those he passed along the way. It was relaxing, wandering through the city alone, especially after being confined inside an airplane. All those beating hearts. Warm bodies. Rivers of blood, each with a taste and texture of its own. The urge to feed, to gorge himself on the bounty before him, had been almost more than he could bear. He lived a solitary life most of the time. When he felt the need for company, he did what any man did, he went to one of the singles bars or one of the Goth hangouts and surrounded himself with music and people, and when he felt the need for feminine companionship, he found a woman who knew the score. His needs were few and simple. He had grown accustomed to his life and his lifestyle, had been content to live alone, until Shannah wandered up his driveway one afternoon and knocked on his door. Since the moment he had looked into her eyes, nothing in his life had been the same.

He walked the streets until the stars began to fade and then he found a deserted stretch of ground. He stood there, staring up at the sky, until a familiar tingle spread through his body, warning him of dawn's approach. With a sigh, he burrowed deep into the earth as the first hint of the sun's golden light heralded the dawn of a new day.

Chapter Ten

It was late afternoon when Shannah woke. She stayed in bed for several minutes, enjoying the luxury of having nothing to do. Luxury. It was something that had been sorely missing from her life until she met Ronan. Now it seemed as if her every wish had been granted. Her health was good. She had more clothes, and better clothes, than she had ever had before. She was in a posh room in a swanky hotel. She had cash in her wallet, given to her by a handsome man, and a whole day to do just as she pleased. It reminded her of the movie *Pretty Woman*. Ronan was Richard Gere and she was Julia Roberts.

Rising, she called room service and ordered breakfast. She took a long shower, washed her hair, then wrapped up in one of the fluffy hotel robes. She ate quickly, dressed, and called for a cab.

It was waiting for her when she went downstairs. Slipping on her sunglasses, she left the hotel.

She spent the day doing her best Julia Roberts impersonation. She went to an exclusive Beverly Hills salon and had a manicure and a facial, and then she spent several hours exploring the chic dress shops on Rodeo Drive. She bought two dresses, a gauzy white skirt and a peasant blouse, a gray cashmere sweater, and three pairs of shoes. Passing a men's shop, she went inside and bought a tie (black, of course) for Ronan. She didn't know him well enough, or have nerve enough, to be wearing nothing but the tie ala Julie Roberts's character when she saw him in the hotel that night, but it made her feel daring to buy it just the same.

The book signing was scheduled for eight p.m. At five, she returned to the hotel and ordered a lobster dinner with all the trimmings, only to find that she was too nervous to eat it.

She had just finished dressing when there was a knock on the connecting door.

She had tried it earlier, only to find it locked from Ronan's side. It opened now, revealing Ronan clad in a pair of black trousers, a white shirt open at the throat, and a black silk jacket.

"Lordy," she murmured, "you look good enough to eat."

His gaze moved over her. "As do you."

"Here," she said, handing him a long, narrow box, "I bought you a present."

He lifted one brow as he took the box from her hand and lifted the lid. A slow smile curved his lips as he withdrew the tie. It was black, with a tiny wolf's head embroidered in silver near the bottom.

"I don't know why, but it reminded me of you," she said. "Do you like it?"

"Very much."

"You don't have to wear it," she said as he slipped it around his neck. "I just wanted to buy you something."

"But I want to wear it." He couldn't remember the last time he had received a gift. The fact that it was from Shannah made it all the more special. "How does it look?"

"Perfect," she said. *Just like you.*

Drawing her into his arms, he kissed her cheek. "Thank you."

"You're welcome." She looked up at him. "I'm so nervous. I don't think I can do this. I've forgotten everything you told me, everything I memorized." She tapped her forehead with her fingertip. "Poof! Just like that, it's gone."

He laughed softly. "It will all come back to you, trust me."

"What if it doesn't?"

"You're not there to answer a lot of questions. Just to sign books."

"But people are sure to ask me . . ."

"Shannah." He placed his hands on her shoulders and gazed deeply into her eyes. "Relax, Shannah. You'll be fine. I'll be there with you. There's nothing to worry about. They're going to love you."

She stared up at him, mesmerized by the intensity of his gaze, calmed by the tone of his voice and his words of assurance. He was right, of course. She had nothing to worry about. She knew all the answers. She had read his books. She was ready.

"Shall we go?" he asked.

"Might as well," she said, grinning, "since we're all dressed up."

They took a taxi to the bookstore.

The manager came forward to greet them. "I'm Blanche DeVries," she said, offering her hand to Shannah. "And you must be Eva Black."

"Yes. And this is my . . . this is Ronan."

The manager's smile widened as she shook his hand. "I'm pleased to meet you, Mr. Ronan."

"The pleasure is mine," he said, bowing over her hand.

Blanche DeVries blushed to the roots of her dyed red hair. "If you'll follow me, we've set up a table back here."

Shannah followed the woman to a table that had been

set up in the middle of the store near the romance section. Ronan's latest novel was available, as well as several of his older books.

There was a small vase of flowers on a long cloth-covered table, as well as a water glass and bottle of Perrier. Stacks of his current book were arranged at the end of the table. Another, smaller table held soft drinks, a plate of cookies, a coffee urn, Styrofoam cups, and a bowl of mints.

"We're so happy you could make it," the manager said as Shannah took her seat. "Is there anything I can get for you?"

"No, thank you."

"Mr. Ronan, can I get you a chair or a cup of coffee, or anything?"

"No, thank you."

"Well, I think we're all set then," Blanche said. "If you need anything, just let me know."

"I will, thank you," Shannah replied. She watched the manager walk away, then looked at Ronan, one brow arched. "You just can't help yourself, can you?"

"What are you talking about?"

"You know what I mean. You had her eating out of your hand."

"Oh, that." He shrugged. "It's nothing."

Shannah grunted softly. She didn't know what *it* was, but it was definitely something!

At five minutes to seven, there were a dozen women lined up in front of the table, all waiting to get Eva Black's autograph.

It was a heady experience. Shannah signed new books, as well as older books that readers had brought with them in shopping bags. She listened as they praised her writing and her characters and gushed over her heroes. They asked when her next book would be coming out, begged her to tell them what it was about, or at least give them a hint. Was the hero from the last book in it? Did she plan to do a sequel sometime in the near future?

All the women, from the youngest to the oldest, wanted to know who Ronan was and when she replied that he was just a friend, they all smiled knowingly and asked if he was the model for her heroes.

"He does look just like a vampire, you know," one woman said, keeping her voice low as though she was afraid she might offend him.

"He does, doesn't he?" Shannah agreed.

As the evening wore on, she was amazed by the number of women who were willing to wait in line for an autograph. Twelve turned to twenty and then to thirty. Grandmothers and teens, young mothers with children in tow, even a few men showed up to get her autograph and praise her books. Many of the women lingered near the refreshment table, partaking of the cookies and coffee, chatting about their favorite authors, frequently stealing looks in Ronan's direction.

Ronan stood back, watching Shannah. She was a natural, he thought. She was warm and gracious, charming both old and young alike with her innocence and her ready smile. Knowing that she would be all right, he told her that he needed to go out for a few minutes.

Shannah stared up at him. "You're leaving me? Now? But . . ." She gestured at the people still waiting in line. "You can't go now."

"You're doing fine," he said, squeezing her shoulder. "I won't be gone long."

She didn't have time to wonder where he was going. The line of people waiting for her autograph now stretched from her table to the front door.

One man in particular stood out, though she wasn't sure why. He was average height, with blond hair and brown eyes. He wasn't especially good looking and yet there was something about him, something that made her think she had seen him before.

"Who should I make this out to?" Shannah asked when he reached the front of the line.

"Jim."

She signed the book and handed it to him with a smile, and then forgot all about him as more people crowded around her.

Ronan returned a few minutes later and resumed his place behind her.

A few of the women had brought cameras and asked if they could take her photograph, or have their photos taken with her. Feeling self-conscious, Shannah posed for them or with them, wondering what they would think if they knew she was a fraud and that the person who deserved their praise and adulation was standing quietly behind her. She couldn't understand why he shunned meeting the very people who had made him famous.

Several of the women wanted Ronan's photograph, also, but he politely declined.

Even Shannah couldn't convince him to pose.

"I just love your books," a teenage girl gushed. "They're so sexy! I wish my boyfriend was more like your heroes."

"Well, give him time," Shannah said with a wink, "or let him read one of my books. Maybe he'll get the hint."

"You're my favorite author," a middle-aged woman said, pulling several paperbacks from a plastic bag. "I'm so glad your books aren't full of bad language and sex. I never worry when I let my daughter read your books."

"Thank you," Shannah replied.

The lady leaned in closer. "I want to thank you for saving my marriage," she said, her voice hushed, "Before I read your books, I'd sort of lost interest in s-e-x. I mentioned it to my doctor and she suggested I read romance novels to help put me in the mood. And you know what?

They really helped!" She laughed softly. "My husband thanks you, too."

Feeling as though her cheeks were on fire, Shannah stammered, "I . . . I'm so glad."

"You don't write fast enough," another woman complained. "When I get your books, I can't put them down and then, when I'm done, I have to wait six months to a year for the next one!"

"I'm sorry," Shannah said, stifling the urge to laugh. "I'll try and write faster."

"You look too young to have written all those books," another woman remarked. "You must have started writing when you were twelve years old!"

Shannah and Ronan had discussed a number of answers she could give if someone mentioned her age. Smiling, she said, "I was thirteen, actually. Who shall I make this out to?"

She was amazed when the manager announced that it was nine o'clock and the store was closing. The time had flown by.

She signed a book for the manager and another for one of the clerks.

"I'd hoped to have some stock for you to sign," Blanche said, "but these are the last two copies."

"Good thing we didn't put them out," the clerk said, clutching her copy as if it was made of gold. "I can't remember when we've had a more successful signing."

"Yes," Blanche agreed. "I do hope you'll come again."

"I'd like that," Shannah replied. She thanked the manager again for her hospitality, then followed Ronan out of the store.

"I'm famished," she said. "Can we go get something to eat?"

"Sure."

They stopped at the first restaurant they came to and

went inside. "I don't suppose you're having anything," Shannah remarked.

"No," he said easily. "I grabbed a bite to eat earlier."

Shannah ordered a bacon, lettuce and tomato sandwich, fries, and a chocolate shake, then sat back and smiled at Ronan. "The book signing was fun. I can't imagine why you don't want to do them yourself."

He shook his head. "I'd rather remain out of the limelight."

"Did I do all right?"

"You did better than all right." He sat back in the booth, one arm resting along the edge of the seat. "So, what did you do this afternoon besides buy me a tie?"

"I bought clothes," she said, grinning. "Lots of clothes. Wait until you see the bills."

He smiled indulgently. "I'm glad you had a good time."

"What did you do today?" she asked.

He shrugged. "I slept late. Took a quick tour of the town. Enjoyed an early dinner. None of it was as gratifying as watching you this evening."

"Stop it, you're making me blush."

"And quite prettily, too."

"Ronan!" She pressed her hands to her heated cheeks.

"You charmed them all," he said, "just as I knew you would."

"I couldn't have done it if you hadn't been there with me."

"Of course you could."

She shook her head. "No way."

"Way," he said, grinning. "Trust me. Have you forgotten you're doing another signing tomorrow afternoon?"

"Oh! I did. I was so nervous about tonight, and then so relieved that nothing went wrong. You'll be there tomorrow, won't you?"

"No."

"No? Why not?"

"I have some other business to take care of while I'm in town. You'll do fine, Shannah. You proved it tonight."

"But . . ."

Leaning forward, he placed a finger over her lips, stifling her protests. "You'll be fine. I have every confidence in you. Now you need to have a little in yourself."

After dinner, they walked for a while, stopping now and then to look in this window or that, before catching a cab and returning to the hotel.

In her room, Shannah kicked off her heels and dropped into a chair. "I'm beat."

Coming up behind her, Ronan brushed her hair aside and began to massage her shoulders.

"Oh," she purred. "That feels wonderful."

He closed his eyes as his fingers kneaded her neck and shoulders. Her skin was soft and warm. His nostrils filled with the scent of her hair and skin. He could feel the heat of her blood rising from beneath her skin, hear it flowing through her veins. His fangs lengthened in response to the temptation she presented. He had fed earlier that evening but he was filled with a sudden urge to take her in his arms and feed again. He could easily wipe the memory from her mind . . .

With a shake of his head, he opened his eyes and stepped away from the chair.

"It's late," he said. "You should get some sleep."

She nodded, covering a yawn with her hand. "You're right, I am tired."

"Sleep well, Shannah."

"You, too."

She was extremely nervous when she entered the bookstore alone the next afternoon. She missed having

Ronan beside her. His presence gave her confidence, something she was sorely lacking on her own.

The store manager, a short, red-headed man named Fred Barton, led her to a table near the center aisle of the store. Again, there were flowers and refreshments and stacks of Ronan's latest novel.

Shannah sat down, wishing Ronan was there beside her, but she didn't have time to fret over his absence for long. Within minutes, she was surrounded by readers asking for her autograph or a photo or both. Most of the comments and questions were similar to the ones she had been asked the night before, readers wanting to know when her next book would be out, if she was planning a sequel to the last one.

During a lull, Shannah glanced around the store, startled to see the man who had introduced himself as Jim standing at a book rack a few feet away. Catching her gaze, he smiled and nodded at her.

Feeling a sudden sense of unease, Shannah nodded back. Was he following her, or was it just a coincidence that he happened to be there?

Her apprehension increased when he walked toward her, one hand reaching into his pocket. Good Lord, did he have a gun? But it was only a book, one of Ronan's older ones.

"Jim," he said, handing her the book. "Remember?"

"Yes. I'm surprised to see you here." She frowned inwardly, wishing she could remember why he looked familiar. She had seen him somewhere besides the signing the night before, but she couldn't remember where.

He shrugged. "I finished the book I bought last night. It was good, so I thought I'd try another."

"How did you know I was going to be here today?"

"It was in this morning's newspaper."

"Oh." She didn't know if it had been or not.

He glanced around. "Your friend didn't come with you today?"

"No, he had some personal business to take care of."

"Maybe I could take you out for a drink when you're through here."

"I don't think so."

"Come on," he coaxed with a smile. "There's a little pub right down the street. We can walk."

"I'm afraid not." She signed the book with a flourish and handed it to him. "Thank you for coming."

"My pleasure."

As it had last night, the two hours flew by. She thanked Mr. Barton for having her, signed the three backlist books that hadn't been sold, and was about to gather her things when a man stepped up to the table.

"Excuse me, Miss Black," he said. "I'm Carl Overstreet." Reaching into his coat pocket, he withdrew a business card. "I'm a freelance reporter. Would you mind answering a few questions?"

"I guess not." She glanced at the card, wishing Ronan was there to advise her.

"Thank you. This won't take long."

Shannah resumed her seat, her hands clenched in her lap. She wasn't sure she was up to a spur of the minute interview, then decided it might be good practice for the radio interview in New York.

Overstreet was right. It didn't take long. She thought it odd that he asked only a handful of questions, and most of those concerned Ronan and her relationship with him.

Rising, Overstreet shoved his notebook into his coat pocket, thanked her for her time, and left the store.

Shannah followed a few moments later.

Jim was waiting for her outside. He smiled affably, displaying a dimple in his left cheek. "I thought I'd wait around and see if I could change your mind about that drink."

She was about to say "no" and then she thought, why not? What harm could there be in a drink? "Just a quick one," she said. "I need to get home."

"Whatever you say."

Jim took her arm as they crossed the street. The pub was located on the next block.

The Pub O'Brien was a quaint little place, not too dark, not too crowded. Jim guided her to a table next to a window, held her chair for her, and then sat down. Moments later a pretty young woman wearing a white off-the-shoulder blouse and a short green and blue plaid skirt dropped a basket of peanuts on their table. Jim ordered a beer, Shannah asked for a 7-Up with a cherry.

"You're not much of a drinker, I guess," Jim remarked.

"Not really."

"You're the first romance writer I've ever met," Jim said. He leaned forward in his seat, his hands clasped, his forearms resting on the table.

She shrugged. "There are lots of us out there. Do you read many romances?"

"A few now and then."

"Most men don't."

He made a dismissive gesture. "Their loss, I guess. You write a good story, lots of action. Sometimes I find it hard to believe they're written by a woman."

"I'm not sure how you meant that, but I think I'll take it as a compliment."

"I hope so because that's how I meant it. So, the man who was with you. Anything serious going on there?"

Shannah hesitated, not sure how to answer that.

"Don't you know?" he asked with a grin.

"It could become serious," she replied, "but it's not

now." She smiled her thanks at the waitress who brought their drinks.

He grunted softly. "So, who is he? Your agent?"

"More like my publicist." Strange, she thought, that Jim and Overstreet both seemed more interested in Ronan than in her. "He arranged my tour."

"I see."

She frowned. "I'm not sure I like what you think you see."

"Hey, I didn't mean anything by it. Just trying to find out how involved you are with him."

"I really don't think that's any of your business."

"No, I guess not." He sat back in his seat. "I'm sorry if I came on too strong. It's just that I find you attractive and intriguing. And that's rare these days."

"Thank you." Sipping her drink, she gazed out the window. The sun was setting in the distance. She wondered if Ronan was back at the hotel.

"Any chance I could take you out to dinner tonight?"

"No, I don't think so." She took another sip of her drink, then set the glass aside. "I'd better go. He'll be waiting for me."

"All right." Jim quickly drained his glass and left some money on the table.

Shannah hurried toward the door, acutely conscious that he was behind her. She was suddenly uncomfortable without knowing why.

"Would you like me to drive you back to your hotel?" he asked.

"No, thank you. I'll get a cab."

"It's no trouble."

She shook her head. "No."

"All right, Miss Black. It was nice meeting you."

"Thank you for the drink. Good-bye."

She watched him walk back toward the bookstore, relieved to be alone.

Ronan was waiting for her when she reached her room at the hotel. "You're late," he said, his voice deceptively mild.

"Hello to you, too," she said, dropping her handbag on the table.

"Where have you been?"

"I went out for a drink when I left the bookstore. Is that all right with you?"

He took a deep breath, let it out in a long slow sigh. "I'm sorry, Shannah. How did the signing go?"

"It was good. Not quite as many people as last night, but they sold most of the books they had so . . ." She shrugged. "The manager asked me to sign the leftover stock."

Nodding, he closed the distance between them, his nostrils flaring. "Who were you with?"

"Lots of people."

"No." He inhaled deeply. "You were with two men."

Shannah felt a guilty flush heat her cheeks. "How do you know?"

"I know. Who were they?"

"One was a reporter. Carl something or other." Rummaging in her handbag, she pulled his card out and handed it to Ronan. "He asked a lot of questions about you."

Ronan glanced at the card, then dropped it on the coffee table. "What did he look like?"

Shannah shrugged. "Short, dumpy. Thick glasses. He wasn't Clark Kent, I can tell you that."

"And the other man?"

"He seemed nice enough. He took me out for a drink. I didn't see any harm in it."

"Who was he?"

She shrugged. "He said his name was Jim. Just another one of your many fans. He was at the signing last night, too."

Ronan's eyes narrowed ominously. "Describe him."

"He's a little taller than I am, with blond hair and . . . ." Shannah's eyes widened as she suddenly remembered where she had seen him before. "Of course! He was the man on the curb across from the photographer's studio. I thought he looked familiar!"

Hands clenching at his sides, Ronan swore a vile oath.

"You said he isn't a friend of yours, so who is he?" Shannah asked.

"It doesn't matter," Ronan replied curtly. Jim Hewitt was a vampire hunter. He hailed from Nevada, which begged the question—what the hell had he been doing in North Canyon Creek, and why was he now in Los Angeles? Ronan didn't like the answer that quickly came to mind. "Did you tell him where you're staying?"

"No."

"Did he follow you here?"

"I don't think so. It was just a drink. What's the big deal?"

"Nothing."

"Yeah, right. What's wrong? Who is this guy? Why are you so upset?"

"It's nothing for you to worry about. Have you had dinner?"

"Don't change the subject."

"He's someone I know. Someone I don't want to see. Someone I don't want you to see again."

"Well, since we're leaving town tomorrow night, that shouldn't be a problem. I'm going to order some dinner and take a bath. I don't suppose you want me to order anything for you?"

"I've already dined."

"Of course. I keep forgetting you like to eat in private." Sitting on the edge of the bed, she kicked off her shoes, then picked up the phone and ordered a shrimp dinner, a piece of lemon meringue pie, and a glass of iced tea.

Hanging up the phone, she looked at Ronan. "I'm going to take a bath now."

He nodded, then murmured, "Ah, I guess you want me to leave."

"Good guess. Maybe we can watch some TV later."

"Call me when you're ready."

"All right."

Drawing her into his arms, he kissed the top of her head. "I'm sorry for being such an ass. Forgive me?"

"I guess so," she said with a sigh. "But, geez, chill out, will ya?"

"Yes, ma'am," he said, laughing. "I'll chill out."

Still laughing, he went into his own room and shut the door. She really was too young for him, he thought, and in more ways than just her age, but she was still the most delightful creature he had ever known.

Chapter Eleven

Jim Hewitt stood at the end of the bar alone, one hand fisted around a glass of Irish whiskey. Maybe his luck was changing at last! He had gotten a tip from another hunter that Ronan was in a little town in Northern California. He had flown to North Canyon Creek as soon as he had finished his last job. He had spent a week and a half tracking the vampire, getting to know his habits and his hangouts.

Hewitt had followed the woman a couple of times, but he hadn't been able to find out much about her. The car she drove was registered to Scott Davis in Middletown, New York. The mail in her mailbox was addressed to Shannah Davis. Further investigation revealed that she was twenty-four years old and that she had lived in North Canyon Creek a little over a year. When he'd followed her and the vampire into the bookstore the night before, he'd had no idea she was a published author and concluded that Eva Black was a pseudonym. After leaving the bookstore, he'd done a little sleuthing into Eva Black's publishing history.

The first Eva Black book had been published seven years ago. Since then, she had published thirteen books, which meant that she either wrote at an alarmingly fast pace, or she had published her first book before she got out of high school, which seemed unlikely. Every instinct he possessed told him that she was a fraud, though what she hoped to gain by masquerading as Eva Black puzzled him. And when the real Eva Black got wind of it, there was sure to be a lawsuit . . . He shook his head. Nobody in their right mind would pass themselves off as a romance writer just for the fun of it. In the long run, there was nothing to be gained by it except perhaps a lot of embarrassment. So, for now, he would assume she was indeed Eva Black and that she was just very prolific. He knew of authors who wrote several books a year, and one young man who had published a book when he was only fifteen years old, and had that book made into a movie. In the long run, whether the woman was Eva Black or not was of little importance to him. What was important was her connection to the vampire. Was she under the vampire's thrall, or was she simply someone he had marked as prey? It was a mystery, but he liked mysteries, especially ones that came wrapped in packages as pretty as this one. And while it was the vampire he was after, he wasn't opposed to mixing a little pleasure with business if the opportunity presented itself.

Tonight, Hewitt had followed the lovely Miss Black back to her hotel. A little subtle sleuthing had uncovered the information that she and the vampire were checking out tomorrow night at six. And he would be right behind them.

Whistling softly, Jim finished his drink. He was about to leave the bar when a man moved up beside him.

"Can I buy you another?" the stranger asked.

"I don't think so."

"I think we could help each other."

"Is that right? What makes you think I need help?"

"You're after the vampire, right?"

Hewitt shrugged. "I don't know what you're talking about."

"The tall man hanging out with the author."

"I still don't know what you're talking about," Jim said, injecting a note of boredom into his voice. "Who the hell are you, anyway?"

"Carl Overstreet. I'm a freelance reporter. I've been working up in Northern California for the last few months, trying to get the real story on vampires."

"And you think Miss Black's companion is a vampire?"

"I know he is. And you're a hunter."

"What do you want?"

"I want an interview with the vampire before you take his head."

Hewitt laughed. "Right."

"I'll make it worth your while."

"You're out of your mind. What makes you think this guy's a vampire?"

"I saw him in action once, a few years ago."

"Where?"

"Some little town outside of Sacramento. I was in a bar, a little tanked, and went out the back door by mistake. It opened into an alley. And he was there, bent over some woman's neck. Scared the crap out of me when he looked up, his eyes red, his fangs dripping blood." Overstreet shuddered. "I ran back into the bar and out the front door like the devil was on my heels."

"So, how'd you know he was here, in L.A.?"

"I didn't. I came down to do a story on Spielberg's next blockbuster. It was just coincidence that I was in that bookstore in Hollywood the other night. I knew who he was the minute I saw him." Overstreet shuddered. "That's a face you don't forget."

Hewitt grunted softly. Ordering a glass of whiskey, he moved toward a table in the back of the pub.

"Come on," he called over his shoulder. "Let's talk."

Chapter Twelve

Shannah was a little less nervous as they boarded the plane for New York, but not much. This was a much longer flight than the last one. Once again, Ronan had managed to secure an entire row for their use, which meant they could really stretch out.

She gripped the arms of her seat as the plane took off and told herself there was nothing to be afraid of. Thousands of people flew across the country, across the world, every day. She closed her eyes and thought about how nice it would be to see her parents again, how surprised they would be to hear from her, how much fun it would be to see New York City again.

She breathed a little easier when they were airborne. Moments later, a flight attendant came by offering them food and drink. Shannah asked for a 7-Up, then sat back in her seat, watching the lights below gradually fade away into the distance.

"You all right?" Ronan asked.

She nodded. "What's our itinerary in New York?"

"You've got a book signing tomorrow night and a radio interview Friday morning."

"I hope I don't get tongue-tied."

"You'll be fine. Friday night we're going out to dinner with my agent and my editor."

"You'll be there, right?"

"I wouldn't miss it."

"Good."

He smiled at her, pleased beyond belief with how well she was doing. If he had searched for years, he couldn't have found anyone who could have done better at assuming the persona of Eva Black. Shannah was likeable and believable and totally charming. She would make just the right impression on his editor and his agent.

"You've got another book signing Saturday afternoon," he remarked. "Saturday night I've got tickets to see *Beauty and the Beast* if you want to go. We can leave for home any time after that."

"*Beauty and the Beast*! Oh, I've always wanted to see that!" She leaned over and kissed his cheek. "You're so good to me. How can I ever repay you?"

His gaze moved over her, slow and hot. "I'll think of something."

"Do you remember you said we could visit my parents while we're in New York?"

"I remember."

"Do you think we could go on Sunday?"

"Sure. Where do they live?"

"On Hillcrest Street in Middletown."

"Leave me the address and I'll meet you there around six."

"You're not coming with me?" she asked. "Never mind," she said before he could reply, "you've got business to attend to."

"Right. Is one day going to be enough, or would you like to stay longer?"

"I don't know. I'll have to play it by ear."

The flight was uneventful. It was a little after two a.m.

when they arrived at LaGuardia Airport, on the north shore of Queens. Ronan collected their bags and hailed a cab. Their driver was a handsome young man with a thick accent that made Shannah think of Jamaica.

Sitting in the back seat of the taxi, bouncing over an old bumpy highway, Shannah got her first look at Queens in over a year as they traveled toward the 59th Street Bridge which would take them into Manhattan. She smiled as they crossed the bridge. It always reminded her of the song made famous by the Simon & Garfunkel hit, "The Fifty-Ninth Street Bridge Song," more commonly known as "Feeling Groovy."

The scenery hadn't changed much, Shannah mused as they left the highway and drove through a neighborhood of warehouses, four-story buildings, garages, and the like. It was still less than scenic.

Eventually, they crossed the bridge, which was a gloomy, double-decker industrial bridge.

They reached Manhattan some thirty minutes later. The cab driver turned left onto Park Avenue. The two-way street was divided by a narrow island which held numerous pots of concrete planters filled with flowers, shrubs and low hedges. Hence the name Park Avenue, she supposed. The buildings that lined the street were old and elegant. There were several cute little shops she hoped to visit when she had the time—boutiques, flower shops, a small French bakery.

The cabby made a U-turn and pulled up in front of the Waldorf Astoria Hotel. While Ronan collected their bags, paid the fare and tipped the driver, Shannah took a good look at the hotel, unable to believe she was actually going to be staying there. She had seen it on numerous occasions but never been inside.

The Park Avenue lobby near took her breath away. It was beautiful. There were murals on the walls and a stunning mosaic floor. A gorgeous chandelier hung from the ceiling.

She waited while Ronan checked them in at the desk, more than ready for a long hot bath and eight hours' sleep. Even the elevator was elegant, she thought, as it whisked them up to the 29th floor. Once again, Ronan had reserved two suites adjoining.

"I could get used to this," Shannah murmured as she crossed the large foyer. The living room was elegant and well appointed. There was a wet bar and a television set, even a fireplace. Gold draperies covered the windows. A high-backed sofa, a comfortable overstuffed chair, and a couple of occasional tables formed a cozy conversation area. Fresh flowers decorated the tables, there were a number of pictures on the walls.

Leaving the living room, she went into the bedroom, which was done in rich tones of gold and red. The king-sized bed was covered with a white spread. There were table lamps on either side. There was a cozy armchair and ottoman covered in a pretty red print, and a glass-topped table. A separate boudoir offered a makeup mirror and dressing area. The marble bathroom was luxurious, with an oval tub, dual sinks, and a separate shower big enough for two.

Returning to the bedroom, she kicked off her sandals, then dug her bare toes into the luxurious carpet. "Wow," she murmured.

"It is nice, isn't it?" Ronan remarked, coming up behind her.

"Nice? My apartment is nice. This is . . ." She spread her arms wide and twirled around. "This is paradise." Moving to the window, she stared down at Park Avenue, then glanced at him over her shoulder. "I feel like a movie star."

He laughed softly. "I'm glad you like it." He took her

in his arms because she was vibrant and alive and he couldn't resist touching her, holding her, if only for a moment. "I'm sure you want to take a bath," he said, brushing a kiss across her brow, "so I'll leave you to it."

"What are you going to do?"

"I think I'll go stretch my legs while you soak in a hot tub."

"Will you come in and tell me good night before you go to bed?"

"Shall I tuck you in and tell you a bedtime story, too?"

She looked up at him, a smile curving her lips, her eyes filled with merriment. "I think I'd like that."

He smiled back at her, taking care that she didn't see the hunger in his eyes.

He wanted her more every time he saw her. Wanted her love, her laughter, her very essence. He wanted to possess her, body and soul, mind and spirit, wanted to make her his in every way possible. Not for the first time, he wondered what she would say, what she would think, if she knew what he was.

Fighting his hunger, he released her. "I'll see you before you go to bed."

Still smiling, she walked into the bathroom and closed the door.

He stared after her for a moment, then left the room, locking the door behind him.

He prowled the dark underbelly of the city, seeking sustenance among the homeless drifters. He fed, and then fed again, gorging himself until even his endless hunger was satisfied.

Sated, he returned to the lights of the city, strolling down the street until he came to a night club. Pausing at the door, he let his preternatural senses peruse the place before he stepped inside and sought a small table in the back.

Sitting with his back to the wall, he watched the patrons. Several couples were dancing to an old country song. Others were engaged in the age-old ritual of courting. He caught snippets of conversation; men wooing the girl of their choice with liquor and sweet words, women with their heads together while they debated the merits of this man or that. In all his years as a vampire, he had never contemplated marriage, never engaged in any long-term relationship with a woman. Not that he had lived his preternatural life as a monk. Undead or alive, he was still a man with a man's needs and a man's desires. And right now he desired Shannah above all else.

She was never far from his thoughts. Even now, he could hear the sound of her laughter in the back of his mind. It wasn't smart to fall in love with a mortal woman, nor was it wise to pursue any kind of relationship. In his experience, mortals could not be trusted. He knew of several vampires, both men and women, who had foolishly fallen in love. In every case, once they had revealed the truth, they had been deserted or destroyed. Ronan had no desire to end his existence. And no desire to continue on without Shannah. It was quite a dilemma and one for which he had no clear solution.

Fortunately, he still had time to decide what to do about Shannah. For now, he wanted to hold her in his arms. The thought was no sooner born than he was back at the hotel, knocking on her door.

Curled up in the cozy chair in the bedroom, Shannah glanced at her watch, wondering where Ronan had gone. He had told her he would come back and tell her good night, but it was almost morning.

She yawned, and yawned again, hoping he would

return soon because she didn't think she could stay awake much longer.

A soft knock at the door unleashed a million butter-flies in her stomach. She took a deep breath and then another as she made her way into the living room and opened the door.

He didn't say anything, just stepped into the room, kicked the door closed with his heel, drew her into his arms, and kissed her.

As always, she melted into him, her every thought, her every desire focused on Ronan, only Ronan. Desire flowed through her, warm and honey-sweet. Maybe tonight, she thought, maybe tonight he would carry her to bed and make love to her. She knew he wanted her. She could taste it in his kiss, feel it in the way his body quivered against hers.

She was breathless when he broke the kiss.

"I've been wanting to do that for hours," he said, his voice husky. "I keep telling myself that you're far too young for me, that I'll bring you nothing but misery, but I can't leave you alone." He ran his knuckles lightly over her cheek. "I can't stay away."

She stared up at him, dazed by his kiss, mesmerized by the heat in his eyes. "I don't want you to stay away. And I'm not too young."

"Then I'm too old for you."

She shook her head, her mind still reeling from the force of his declaration. "How old are you? Thirty? Thirty-five? That's not old."

He laughed softly. "I'm older than you are in more ways than just years, Shannah, love."

"I don't care. I want you."

"I know." His hand stroked her hair. "I know."

Lowering his head, he kissed her again.

Wanting more than kisses, Shannah backed slowly

toward the sofa. She dropped down on the cushions and he followed her, never taking his mouth from hers. He deepened the kiss, his hand sliding up and down her thigh, his thumb caressing the soft curve of her breast.

She shivered at his touch, and pressed herself wantonly against him. "Make love to me," she whispered.

"Have you ever been with a man before?" he asked, though he already knew the answer.

"What difference does that make?"

"Have you?"

"Of course. I'm twenty-four."

"Ah, Shannah, why don't I believe you?"

She pouted prettily. "I'm dying, Ronan. Don't let me die a virgin."

"You're not dying, love. I won't let you."

"You can't stop it." Sitting up, she wrapped her arms around her waist. "No one can. Even being out in the sun is starting to bother me now . . ."

"What do you mean?" he asked sharply.

"It hurts my eyes. Lately, I can't go outside during the day without wearing sunglasses."

"How long has this been going on?"

"Several weeks now. I first noticed it when I went to the doctor. It was right after I moved in with you. I should have mentioned it to him, I guess. Do you think it means I'm . . . that I'm getting worse?"

He grunted softly. Her sensitivity to the sun was more likely a side effect from his blood than any symptom of her illness, but he couldn't tell her that.

"Shannah." Sitting beside her, he drew her into his arms. "I promise you, you will not die for a long, long time."

She smiled faintly. "I almost believe you."

"Believe it."

"Have some sort of secret voodoo magic, do you?" she asked, forcing a smile. "Some kind of powerful mojo that will let me run faster than a speeding bullet and leap tall buildings in a single bound?"

"Something like that." He kissed the top of her head. "I'll take care of you, love. Everything will be all right."

Feeling suddenly weary, she rested her head against his shoulder. "Everything will be all right," she murmured. "I don't know why I believe you, but I do."

With a sigh, he eased her onto his lap, content to hold her and stroke her hair until he sensed the coming of dawn's first light.

Carrying her to bed, he tucked her in, then kissed her cheek.

She would make a beautiful vampire, he mused, gazing down at her. Perhaps he would discuss the possibility with her when they returned home.

Thursday night, Shannah sat at a table near the front of the bookstore. This store was bigger than the others had been and she felt like she really was somebody as she sat amid a mountain of books, smiling and signing autographs. Ronan stood behind her. No doubt people thought he was her bodyguard, the way he stood there, hardly moving, hardly blinking.

Shannah smiled as a pretty blonde handed her a book. "Who should I make this out to?"

"Melanie, please." The girl fidgeted with her handbag, then blurted, "Miss Black, I just have to tell you how much it means to me to meet you. When my mother got so sick that she couldn't read anymore, my sisters and I took turns reading your books to her. She loved them so much."

"Thank you for sharing that," Shannah said, touched by the woman's words. She glanced back at Ronan, wondering if he'd heard what the woman had to say. Did he think it was as wonderful as she did that his stories influenced people's lives in such heartfelt ways?

Shannah had been signing for about forty-five minutes when there was a brief lull. Glancing around, she thought she saw Jim lurking nearby, but that was ridiculous. It was one thing for him to follow her from one bookstore to another in Los Angeles, and quite another to think he had followed her all the way to New York City. She frowned when she saw the newspaper reporter, Carl Overstreet, in the next aisle.

A shiver ran down her spine. Jim plus Carl plus herself in New York in the same store at the same time was just way too much of a coincidence to be a coincidence.

"What's wrong, love?"

She looked up to see Ronan standing beside her. "Maybe nothing . . ."

"Tell me."

"That guy, Jim, is here. And so is the reporter I told you about."

"Where?"

She started to point them out, then frowned. Neither man was in view. "They were here just a minute ago."

"Sit tight. Smile. I'm going to have a look around."

She did as he said, smiling and signing, posing for pictures, and all the while a knot of tension was growing in her stomach. If Ronan was worried, then there must be something to worry about.

He returned a few minutes later. "They're gone," he said, for her ears alone.

She nodded and smiled. Thankfully, the rest of the time passed quickly.

After she signed some stock, she thanked the store manager, who shook her hand and asked her to please come again, then turned to shake Ronan's hand.

"I was wondering," Ronan said. "Is there a back way out of here?"

"Yes, of course. The service entrance," the manager replied, frowning. "Is there a problem?"

"There was a man here tonight who's been following Miss Black. We'd like to avoid him, if possible."

"Of course," the manager said. "This way."

Moments later, Shannah and Ronan were walking down a dark alley toward the sidewalk.

"Are you sure this is a good idea?" Shannah asked, glancing around. "I can't see my hand in front of my face."

"Just hold on to me," Ronan said.

"I think she should hold on to me."

The voice, low and raspy, slid out of the shadows to their left.

"I think you should mind your own business," Ronan replied, putting Shannah behind him. "And get out of here before you get hurt."

Malicious laughter echoed off the walls of the buildings. There was the unmistakable snick of a gun being cocked.

Shannah clutched Ronan's arm as stark terror raced down her spine. They were going to die, here, now, in this dirty alley.

She cried out in protest as Ronan removed her hand from her arm. There was the sound of scuffling, a harsh cry of pain, the sound of a gunshot, the acrid stink of gunpowder. And then silence.

She shrieked as a hand grabbed her forearm.

"Hush, love," Ronan said, "it's me."

She had to run to keep up with him as he hurried down the alley. "Wait! What happened?"

He dragged her out onto the sidewalk; then, taking her by the hand, he turned left and walked slowly down the street.

Shannah glanced over her shoulder. "What happened back there?"

"Nothing for you to worry about." Ronan couldn't help grinning as he recalled the look of stunned horror on the would-be mugger's face when he realized he was about to die. Panicked, he had fired his gun in a last ditch effort to cheat death, and missed. The stink of the man's fear had filled Ronan's nostrils and quickened his hunger. He had not soothed the man's fears before he buried his fangs in his neck. It had been years since he had taken a life in anger, or drained a man to the point of death. He had forgotten how exhilarating it could be when he released the predator within, when he shed the thin veneer of civility and unleashed the beast within him. But he couldn't tell Shannah that.

She looked up at him, her eyes wide. "Are you hurt? There's blood on your mouth."

"It's not mine." Grimacing, Ronan wiped his hand across his mouth. Not all blood tasted the same. Some, like Shannah's, was sweet. The would-be robber's had not been sweet but it had been satisfying just the same.

Ronan hailed a cab on the next block.

Shannah heard the sound of sirens as he closed the car door. Guilt pierced her. Had someone seen them leaving the alley and called the police?

Feeling suddenly light-headed, she sank back against the seat. "Did you . . . is he . . . ?"

A look silenced the question she had been about to ask.

The cab pulled up in front of the hotel a few minutes later. Ronan paid the cabby, took her by the hand, and led her into the hotel and up to her room.

She waited until they were inside and he had closed and locked the door. "Did you kill that man?"

He hesitated a moment, and then nodded.

"Oh." Feeling like a deflated balloon, she sank down on the edge of the sofa.

"Who was he?"

"I don't know. A pickpocket, a mugger." He shrugged. "What difference does it make?"

"But . . . you killed him. Shouldn't we have waited for the police?"

"No." Going to the window, he drew the curtains aside and peered into the darkness. "The last thing we need is to get involved with the police."

"But . . ."

"It's late." He turned away from the window, his gaze holding hers. "You're tired."

"Yes," she said, yawning. "I am tired."

Smiling faintly, he bent down and kissed her on the forehead. "Go to bed, love," he said quietly. "You've a busy day tomorrow."

And I've got something to dispose of tonight.

Chapter Thirteen

There was no mention of the dead man in the newspaper in the morning. Shannah looked on every page of every section. There was talk of the never-ending war in the Middle East, the latest sex scandal in Hollywood, a strike by the Teamsters, the suicide of a high profile lawyer, but not one word about the man in the alley. Shannah thought it odd, but then, this was New York City, not the small town where she had been raised. Maybe the death of a mugger in an alley was so commonplace these days that it didn't rate a story. For all she knew, the man's name could be among those listed in the obituaries.

A glance at the clock told her there was no time to ponder the matter. She had to wash and dry her hair, dress, and be at the radio station in an hour.

"How did the interview go?" Ronan asked later that night while she was changing her shoes.

"Fine, I guess. They said they would send me a copy of the tape so you could hear it."

He nodded. "Were you able to answer everything all right?"

"Yes, although I drew a blank when he asked me the name of your first manuscript. Fortunately, he had a stack of all your books on a table. When I saw the title, I remembered it was your first one."

"Quick thinking."

"Uh-huh. I wanted to hit him when he asked me how I researched my love scenes. Why does everyone ask that?"

He grinned at her. "Why do you think?"

"Well, I'm sure if you wrote murder mysteries, no one would ask me if I'd actually killed someone. He also asked me if I really believed in vampires and if I had ever let anyone drink my blood." She shook her head. "Can you believe that? Real vampires, indeed. Honestly . . ."

She felt a rush of heat flood her cheeks when she recalled that she had once thought Ronan was a vampire. Judging by the look in his eyes, he was remembering the same thing.

"And what did you say?" he asked, no longer grinning.

"I said I didn't believe in vampires, of course. You don't want your readers to think you're some kind of kook, do you?"

"Of course not," he replied, "but it might have added to my mystique if people thought I did."

"Well, next time someone asks me, I'll tell them that I believe in vampires and goblins and things that go bump in the night, and . . ." She looked down at her hands, her voice trailing off.

"And?" he prompted.

"I just remembered that man you killed." She wondered why the fact that Ronan had killed a man didn't bother her more than it did. Was it because she hadn't actually seen him do it, because she hadn't seen the body, or because she knew he had killed the man in self-defense? Whatever the reason, it bothered her that she wasn't more upset by what had happened. Had something like that happened a few weeks ago, she would probably have been in hysterics. What had happened to change her?

Ronan grunted softly. "He was of no consequence." And not very tasty, he recalled, but a free meal was a free meal. "Are you ready to go?"

She hesitated a moment but try as she might, she couldn't summon any regret over the man's fate. The man had had a gun. He might have robbed them, or worse, but for Ronan's swift intervention. Still . . .

"Shannah." His gaze caught and held hers. "It's over and done. Put it out of your mind."

She blinked at him, then shook her head. "How do I look?"

She pirouetted in front of him. The black cocktail dress was chic and flattering with its full skirt and bare back. The high heels did wonderful things for her legs.

"Good enough to eat, as always," he murmured. "Shall we go?"

Ronan's agent, Lorena Barbour, and his editor, Patricia Miliken, were waiting for them when they arrived at the restaurant. After introductions were made, the four of them went into the bar for drinks.

"I can't tell you how happy I am to meet you at last," Patricia said, smiling at Shannah. "I was beginning to think you were a recluse or something."

Lorena grinned. "My thoughts, exactly. I've been representing Eva for years and we've never met."

Shannah smiled. "I do tend to be a homebody. I don't like traveling, and I don't care for crowds."

"I understand," Patricia said, "and I promise not to ask you to do another tour for at least a year or two. But I must say, I think it's been worthwhile. We've been very pleased with the turnout at your signings."

"Thank you."

"Here," Patricia said, producing a manila envelope from her briefcase, "I thought you might want to see this. It's the cover for your next book."

Opening the envelope, Shannah withdrew a cover flat, making sure Ronan could see it, as well. It was a striking cover, done in blue and black, with a man and woman embracing under a full moon. It was subtle and seductive.

She looked at Ronan. "What do you think?"

"I like it."

"So do I," Shannah said, turning it over to read the back cover copy. "Oh, this is wonderful."

Patricia smiled, pleased. "I think the art department really outdid themselves this time. We'll take out the usual ads in the romance magazines."

Shannah nodded, thinking how exciting it would be if she were really a published author. She had never done anything noteworthy in her life. When she was gone, only a few people would remember she had ever existed. But Ronan's books, people would read them for years to come.

Dinner passed pleasantly. Most of the talk was about future projects. Patricia said they were looking into e-books and audio books, and that they had been approached by a major movie company that was interested in acquiring the rights to her last book. Details would be forthcoming at a later date.

Even though she was only pretending, Shannah couldn't hide her excitement at the thought of a movie being made out of one of Ronan's books.

"Wouldn't that be wonderful!" she exclaimed, smiling at him.

"Yes, indeed," he replied. "There might even be a part in it for you."

Patricia grinned. "I'm sure that could be arranged."

It was almost eleven when Shannah and Ronan left the restaurant amid hugs and handshakes.

"Did I do all right?" Shannah asked on the ride back to the hotel.

"You did fine."

Slipping off her heels, she wriggled her toes inside her nylons.

"One more signing and it's over," Ronan said.

"I can't say I'm sorry, although it was kind of fun, pretending to be somebody important."

Ronan took her hand in his and gave it a squeeze. "You are important, Shannah, don't ever think otherwise."

"I'm not," she said. "But you are." She looked at him, her eyes filled with admiration. "You've made something of yourself. You're a published author. People admire and respect you. They write you letters and send you presents and wait in line for your autograph. I mean, don't you think that's awesome?"

"I never gave it much thought," he admitted. "Mostly, I just write for myself, to pass the time."

"Well, it must be nice to get paid for doing something you like."

"Yeah," he said, grinning. "It is."

The taxi pulled up in front of the Waldorf a few minutes later. After paying the driver, Ronan picked up Shannah's shoes and stuck one in each pocket, and then he swung Shannah into his arms and carried her into the hotel.

"What are you doing?" she exclaimed.

"You don't want to ruin your stockings, do you?"

"No," she said, slipping her arms around his neck, "I guess not."

"I didn't think so."

Murmuring, "This is nice," she rested her head on his shoulder.

He carried her toward the elevator, heedless of the stares of the desk clerk and the people in the lobby.

"You must be very strong," she mused as they waited for the elevator.

He laughed softly. "Honey, I could carry you all night long."

"I believe you could." The thought bothered her on some deep dark level that she didn't quite understand.

The elevator arrived and he stepped inside.

The doors closed, and they were alone.

"You can put me down now," she said.

"No," he said, his voice low and husky, "I don't think so."

The look in his eyes made it suddenly hard for her to breathe. She murmured his name, her eyelids fluttering down as his mouth covered hers in a soul-shattering kiss. There was a roaring in her ears as his tongue slid along her lower lip, trailing fire.

She gasped and his tongue slid along the inside of her upper lip, tasting her.

She was melting, she thought, melting like chocolate on a hot day.

He put her on her feet, slowly, so that her body brushed intimately against his on the way down. With his mouth still on hers, he backed her up against the wall of the elevator, his body leaning into hers, letting her feel his heat, his desire. She put her arms around his neck and stood on her tiptoes, her only thought to be closer to him, to drown in his kisses.

She shivered as his hand slid up and down the length of her thigh.

"Ronan." She groaned his name as he deepened the

kiss, caught between the pleasure of his touch and the pain of wanting more, so much more.

"Hush, love." He rested his forehead against hers as he fought the searing hunger rising within him. He had fed earlier but his hunger rose again, fueled by his desire for the woman in his arms. He closed his eyes, afraid that this time his thirst would prevail and that Shannah would look up and see him for what he was.

"Ronan, please . . ."

The elevator came to a stop with a quiet shushing sound and the doors slid open.

He took a deep, shuddering breath.

"Ronan?"

Taking her by the hand, he stepped out of the elevator and walked her to her room. "Good night, Shannah."

She looked up at him, her eyes filled with confusion. "What's wrong?"

"Nothing, love."

"But . . . you . . . aren't we . . . aren't we going to sleep together?"

"I'd like nothing better, but it can't be tonight."

"Why not? I know you want me," she said, her voice barely audible. "I think you need me."

"Ah, Shannah, I need you more than you know, but this isn't the time."

"Why not?"

He looked at her, his eyes filled with anguish. "Because I'm afraid."

"Of what?"

"I'm afraid of hurting you or worse, scaring you. Good night."

Before she could ask for an explanation, he was gone.

She stared after him. Afraid of scaring her? What the heck did that mean? Was he into something kinky? She knew he was a dangerous man. She had sensed it on more than one occasion, but she had never worried that he might hurt her. She wondered now if she was being foolish, if she was putting her life at risk by trusting a man she knew very little about.

Frowning, she closed the door. She didn't have much time left, but what she had, she wanted to spend with Ronan.

Dissolving into mist, Ronan flowed out of the hotel and onto the sidewalk. Only when he was safe in the cover of darkness did he resume his own corporeal form.

Shannah. Her scent permeated his clothing, lingered on his skin, on his tongue. It filled his nostrils with every breath. He would never be rid of her, he thought. Even if he sent her away, even if he never saw her again after tonight, her image was indelibly imprinted in his memory.

He stalked the dark streets, his senses testing the wind for prey, and even as he closed in on his quarry, his thoughts were on Shannah, the taste of her lips, the warmth of her skin, the siren call of her heartbeat. Would his hunger for her lessen if he drank from her, or would it increase? If he dared drink from her, would he be able to stop before he took it all? And what of his desire? Would it ease if he made love to her? Or would it drive him over the edge? Would he take her blood and her life and leave nothing behind but a dry empty husk? It had happened once before and even though it had been centuries ago, he had never forgotten it, never forgiven himself.

He took his prey quickly and unawares, took what he needed to survive without remorse, and sent the woman on her way. And it wasn't enough. Though it assuaged his thirst, it didn't satisfy his need.

He was sorely afraid that only Shannah could do that, and that doing so would destroy her.

Shannah called her mother Saturday morning to let her know that she would be coming to visit Sunday afternoon and that a friend would be joining her later that evening.

"A male friend?" Verna Davis asked.

"Yes, Mom, but don't read any more into it than that."

"How are you feeling, dear?"

"I'm doing well, for now, and I don't want to talk about it."

Verna sighed. "Would you like anything special for dinner?"

"No, Mom, anything you want to fix is fine with me."

"What about your friend?"

"He probably won't be there in time for dinner."

"Oh, that's too bad. Well, no matter, I'll make your favorite chocolate cake for dessert."

"Sounds wonderful, Mom." There was no point in telling her mother that Ronan probably wouldn't eat the cake either. "I'll see you tomorrow."

Shannah looked at the clock. She had to be at the book signing in another hour. She wondered where Ronan was and what he was doing. It seemed odd that he was always busy elsewhere during the day. She wondered if he had a girlfriend who worked nights and could only see him during the day, but even if that was true, it didn't explain his absences here in New York. Of course, it was none of her business. They were just . . . what? Friends? Business partners who had the hots for each other?

She shook her head. What difference did it make? She didn't have time to get involved in any kind of relationship, romantic or otherwise. Doing so would only cause heartache for herself and anyone who was foolish enough to get emotionally or romantically involved with her.

After getting dressed, she took a cab to the bookstore, put on her happy face, and signed autographs and answered questions for the next two hours. But always, in the back of her mind, were thoughts of Ronan and the kisses they had shared in the elevator and the way he had left her at her door, as if he was scared to death of her.

It was a little after six when she returned to the hotel.

Ronan was in her room, waiting for her. Dressed in black slacks, a dark blue shirt, and a long black coat, he looked extremely handsome.

"How did the signing go?" he asked.

"It was good."

"Any sign of Overstreet or Hewitt?"

"No, at least I didn't see them."

"Good."

"I need to change my clothes and touch up my makeup before we leave for the theater," Shannah said. "Would you order me something to eat from room service?"

"Sure, what do you want?"

"A turkey sandwich and a small salad, please, and a glass of iced tea."

Nodding, he picked up the receiver while she went into the bedroom to change.

Her dinner arrived a few minutes before she emerged from the bedroom.

Ronan whistled softly. She seemed to grow more beautiful each time he saw her. Tonight, she was wearing a deep blue silk dress that outlined every delectable curve and made her eyes glow like sapphires. She wore a pair of navy high heels that did wonderful things for her legs.

She twirled in front of him. "Do you like it?" she asked. "It cost a small fortune."

"Believe me, it was worth that and more."

Smiling, she sat at the table and spread a napkin in her lap. "I guess you've eaten?"

He nodded. "I'll call for a cab so we won't have to wait."

Shannah ate quickly, her gaze darting to Ronan again and again. He couldn't be more perfect if he had been sculpted by Michelangelo. His shoulders were broad, his arms and legs long and well-muscled, his face the epitome of masculine strength and beauty. And his eyes . . . she had never seen eyes like his. They were deep and dark and expressive; sometimes they were shadowed with pain she didn't understand, at other times they were opaque, hiding secrets she wasn't sure she wanted to know.

He was pacing the floor in front of the windows. He moved with fluid grace, almost as if his feet weren't touching the floor. His long black coat flowed behind him like a dark cloud. Sometimes he looked . . . she frowned, searching for the right word. Otherworldly, she thought. That was it, as if he was a visitor from another time, another place. She grinned at the thought. She had obviously been reading too many of his books.

Finishing her dinner, she went into the bathroom to brush her teeth and apply fresh lipstick, and then she was ready to go.

She had never been to the theater before, and this one was beautiful. She wasn't surprised to find that they had seats in the front row orchestra. Ronan always managed to secure the best of everything.

"This is so exciting," she whispered as she thumbed through the program.

Ronan grinned at her. He probably thought she was acting like a tourist, but what the heck, she had never been to a Broadway show before. *Beauty and the Beast* had been her favorite fairy tale when she was a little girl, and it still was. She had seen both the French film and the Disney cartoon numerous times.

When the lights dimmed, Ronan's hand found hers and gave it a squeeze.

She was mesmerized from the moment the curtain went up and she heard the narrator's voice tell the tale of how the young prince had been cursed by an enchantress and doomed to live as a beast until he learned how to love. The settings, the actors, the songs, all held her spellbound. She loved Belle's enthusiasm, Gaston's arrogance, Lefou's clumsiness, Lumiere's humor, Cogsworth's gruffness that covered a soft heart, and Babette's coy manner. But mostly she loved the Beast. She felt his anger and his frustration, his sense of hopelessness at the fate that awaited him because she, too, had experienced those emotions and never more so than now, when her life was draining away and there was nothing anyone could do to stop it. She cried when he sang, "If I Can't Love Her." It was the most beautiful, heartbreakingly sad song she had ever heard.

They went out to the lobby during intermission. Shannah couldn't help noticing that practically every woman they passed slid a glance at Ronan and smiled.

He bought her a soft drink and a brownie and then they returned to their seats.

The second half of the show was as wonderful as the first. She cheered silently as the Beast saved Belle's life by fighting off a pack of wolves, smiled as Belle tended his wounds, felt her heart swell as Belle and the Beast danced to the title song. She loved the scene in the library when Belle read the story of King Arthur to the Beast because he didn't know how to read. She felt his pain and his loneliness when he let Belle go, watched in awe as the Beast was magically transformed into the

Prince right before her eyes at the end of the show. She wondered what was wrong with her that she liked him better as the Beast than the Prince.

She hated to see it end. She applauded until her hands hurt and left the theater singing "Be Our Guest."

She was still humming in the cab on the way back to the hotel.

"I take it you liked the show," Ronan remarked dryly.

"It was wonderful! The best play I've ever seen. Oh, I'd love to see it again some day. Thank you."

Leaning toward him, she kissed his cheek. The next thing she knew, she was on his lap, cradled in his arms while his mouth moved over hers.

Moaning softly, she wrapped her arms around his neck and held on for dear life as the world seemed to tilt on its axis, driving everything from her mind but the unmistakable evidence of his desire and the heat of his mouth on hers. As he deepened the kiss, images swirled through her mind, frightening images that made no sense. She saw Ronan moving swiftly through the night, his long black coat billowing behind him like the shadow of death. She saw him bending over a woman, his dark eyes blazing with an unholy light . . .

Startled, she drew away.

"Is something wrong?" he asked.

"I saw you," she said, her voice edged with disbelief. "You were with a woman. Who is she?"

"What are you talking about? What woman?"

"I saw you, in my mind. You were bending over a woman, and your eyes, they were . . . I don't know, red, glowing."

Ronan swore under his breath. He had never bonded with a mortal before, had no idea that giving Shannah his blood would give her access to his thoughts, his memories. He would have to block his thoughts from now on, he thought, lest she see other things she shouldn't.

"What does it mean?" she asked in alarm.

"That you've been reading too many vampire books?" he replied, his voice light.

She stared at him. Was that all it was? Just her imagination supplying images to go along with her night-time fantasies? That had to be it. What else could it be? She had to admit that when she read his books, she always pictured him as the hero, and his heroes were usually vampires.

She forced a smile. "I'm sure you're right," she agreed. But she wasn't sure at all.

Chapter Fourteen

Shannah stood on the sidewalk in front of her parents' house, an overnight bag in one hand. She hadn't been home in over a year and she was blown away by the changes her folks had made. The house, once a rather insipid shade of beige, was now a cheerful country blue with bright white trim and a red door. Shannah smiled as she walked up the red brick path to the porch. For as long as she could remember, her mother had been trying to convince her father to paint the house blue. After thirty-three years, her mother had finally prevailed.

"Shannah!" Verna Davis came through the doorway as if she had been shot out of a cannon. "You're here!"

"Hi, Mom."

Verna engulfed her daughter in a hug and held on tight.

"Mom. Mom, please don't cry."

"I can't help it," Verna said, sniffing. "I never thought I'd see you again."

"I'm doing fine, Mom." Shannah removed her sunglasses. Squinting against the sun, she dropped them into her pocket. "Really."

Verna stood back, her gaze moving over Shannah

from head to foot. "You look wonderful. Have they found a cure?" she asked hopefully.

"No, I'm afraid not."

"Then how . . . ?"

"I don't know. Maybe I'm in some kind of remission. All I know is I feel better than I ever have in my whole life." Shannah slipped her arm around her mother's waist. "You're looking good, too, Mom. You've lost some weight, haven't you?"

"Maybe a pound or two."

Shannah smiled. Her mother was a pretty woman, with light brown hair and dark brown eyes and a figure that, while a little plump, still made men turn and stare.

"Where's Dad?" Shannah asked as they walked up the porch stairs.

"Oh, he's out in the backyard puttering around."

Shannah dropped her bag inside the front door, her gaze moving around the living room. There was a new coat of pale green paint on the walls and a new flat screen TV, but other than that the place looked the same as always. Her father's well-used leather recliner stood in the corner, there was a bag of knitting beside her mother's favorite chair. Pictures of the family lined the mantel. A wooden rack held her mother's salt and pepper shaker collection, many of them older than Shannah.

"I'll just get some lemonade," Verna said. "Why don't you go out and say hi to your dad?"

"All right."

Shannah found her father working on one of the sprinkler heads in the backyard.

He looked up when he heard the back door open. "Hey, Stinky, you're home!"

Shannah grinned at the familiar nickname. "Hi, Dad."

Rising, Scott Davis wiped his hands on his jeans before

enfolding his daughter in a bear hug. "I'm glad to see you, girl," he said, his voice thick with emotion.

"I'm glad to see you, too."

Her father was a big man with black hair and blue eyes. As usual, he wore jeans, a plaid shirt, and work boots. He had been a construction foreman for over twenty years. As a child, she had loved stomping around the house wearing his big boots and hard hat.

He gave her another squeeze, then let her go. "You're looking well."

"I feel wonderful. I like what you've done to the house."

"Oh, that," he muttered. "She finally got her own way."

"It's about time, too," Shannah said, giving him a playful punch on the arm. "Admit it, it looks great."

"Yeah, but don't tell her I said so."

"Don't tell me what?" Verna asked, coming up behind them. Setting the tray she was carrying on a redwood table, she glanced between her husband and her daughter.

"Nothing," Shannah's father said, reaching for one of the glasses.

Verna looked at Shannah. "What's he hiding now?"

"Nothing, Mom. He just told me not to tell you how good the house looks."

"Oh, that!" Verna rolled her eyes. "Everybody thinks it looks a hundred percent better. I don't know why we didn't do it sooner."

Shannah sat down in one of the lawn chairs and her mother and father took seats on either side of her. Besides lemonade, Verna had brought out a plate of homemade chocolate chip cookies and some cheesecake.

Shannah glanced around the yard, remembering all the hours she had spent playing there as a child. Her old rope swing still hung from the big oak tree in the corner.

Someone had given her playhouse a fresh coat of yellow paint and patched the hole in the roof.

"So, Shanny," Verna said, passing the cookie plate around, "what brings you to New York?"

"Oh, Mom, you'll never believe this! I'm pretending to be a famous author."

Her mother stared at her, a cookie halfway to her mouth. "What? Why on earth would you do that?"

"I met this romance writer. He writes as Eva Black . . ."

"Eva Black!" Verna exclaimed. "I just bought one of her books . . . did you say *he*?"

Shannah nodded. "Eva Black is a pen name. His real name is Ronan. You'll meet him later."

"*He's* the friend you're bringing here? But we're just having pot roast . . . and the house is a mess, and . . ." Verna ran a hand over her hair. "Why didn't you tell me you were bringing a famous celebrity home? Oh, dear, I'm a bigger mess than the house."

"Mom, calm down. You've never looked better."

Rising, Verna headed for the back door. "I can't believe you didn't tell me Eva Black was coming to dinner."

"He probably won't eat anything," Shannah called, but it was too late. Her mother was already in the house.

"So," her father asked, "why are you pretending to be this guy?"

Shannah shrugged. "He doesn't want people to know who he is. He seems to think his readers will be disappointed or upset or something if they find out he's a man. Anyway, I've been doing book signings. Dad, you can't believe how much fun it is! I've even done a couple of radio interviews."

Scott shook his head. "Well, don't tell your mother. She'll be upset that she didn't know about it."

"They're going to give me copies of the tapes. I'll send them to you as soon as I get them."

Scott grinned. "Bless you, girl. Now I won't have to spend the next six months listening to your Mom complaining about how our only daughter was on the radio and she didn't get to hear her."

Shannah laughed. "I've been having a wonderful time. We're staying at the Waldorf, Dad, can you believe it? And last night Ronan took me to see *Beauty and the Beast.*"

"Sounds like you're living high on the hog, girl."

"Yes. I'm going to hate to see it end." She spoke without thinking. Too late, she realized her father would assume she was talking about her illness.

Leaning forward, he took her hands in his. "Honey, why don't you come home?"

"Dad, we've been over all this before. Besides, I didn't mean that. I meant I was going to hate it when the book tour was over. I've been having such a great time."

"Be that as it may, you belong here, with us. It's tearing your mother apart to think about you living alone when . . ." He cleared his throat. "We just think you should be here so we can look after you."

"I know, Dad." She didn't know why, but she just couldn't stand the thought of having her parents watch her waste away and die.

"I wish you'd reconsider, honey. You should be here, with the people who love you."

"I'll think about it, okay, but let's not talk about it now. Right now, I feel wonderful!" And she did, except her eyes were starting to burn. Reaching into her pocket, she pulled out her sunglasses and put them on.

Her mother rejoined them a short time later and the three of them spent the rest of the afternoon sitting outside, talking about old times. Shannah listened while her mother brought her up to date on the latest neighborhood gossip—who was getting married, who was getting divorced, who was expecting.

"How's Judy?" Shannah asked. In spite of the fact that Judy was two years older than Shannah, they had been best friends since grammar school.

"Oh, dear, that poor girl is pregnant again."

Shannah grinned. Since getting married, Judy seemed to be perpetually pregnant.

Later, Shannah helped her mother set the table for dinner, thinking how much she had missed sharing these simple tasks with her mom, remembering all the good times she'd had growing up in this house. Her parents had been terrific, supporting her in anything and everything she had wanted to do. They had cheered her on when she played soccer, attended recitals during a brief period when she thought she wanted to be a ballerina, spent a small fortune buying candy, Christmas wrapping paper, and magazine subscriptions so she could go to camp.

She sat in her usual place at the dinner table, her head bowed while her father asked a blessing on the food. Tears filled her eyes when he asked the good Lord to bless his daughter with health and strength.

Too choked up to speak, she concentrated on the food on her plate until her emotions were under control again.

"Mom, you're still the world's best cook," she said, smiling.

Verna beamed with pleasure. She was the kind of mother that had been popular in the fifties, when women were happy to stay home and look after their families. She had always been there when Shannah got home from school, eager to hear about her day over milk and cookies.

When the meal was over, Shannah found herself looking at the door, listening for Ronan's knock, wondering where he was and what her parents would think of him.

And then he was there, looking as suave and handsome as always. Verna invited him inside with a smile, obviously a little star-struck at having a published author in her home. Scott Davis was cordial though more reserved. Shannah hid a smile, remembering that her father had treated her dates the same way when she was in high school.

"So," Verna said when they were all seated in the living room, "however did you start writing romances?"

Forty-five minutes later, Verna was still asking questions.

"I think that's enough, Mother," Scott said. "I'm going outside to smoke my pipe. Why don't you come along and keep me company?"

"Maybe later, dear."

"Now, Mother," Scott said. "I think Shannah and her guest might like a little time alone."

"Oh, yes, of course." Rising, Verna followed her husband out the back door.

"I'm sorry about that," Shannah said. "She's never met anyone famous before."

Ronan shrugged. "She's delightful."

"I think so."

"Why don't we take a walk?"

"All right. Let me get my coat and tell my folks we're going."

Moments later, they left the house.

"Did you want to walk any place in particular?" Shannah asked.

"No." He pulled her off the sidewalk and into the shadows. "Your father was right. I just wanted to get you alone."

She looked up at him, startled, but before she could say anything, he was kissing her, kissing her with such fervor that there was no longer any doubt in her mind about their relationship.

They were definitely more than just friends.

Heat and excitement flowed through her, honey-sweet, intoxicating, addicting. She wanted his hands on her body, his mouth on hers. She wanted to run her hands over his body, to explore the hard wall of his chest, the long line of his back. She wanted to drag him deeper into the shadows and beg him to make love to her, there, on the ground, with only the moon and stars to keep their secret.

And she might have done all those things if her legs hadn't suddenly gone weak, not from his kisses, but from a familiar light-headedness that left her feeling faint and a little dizzy.

"Ronan . . ." She looked up at him, blinking, as his face swam in and out of focus.

"Shannah!"

Sweeping her into his arms, he carried her swiftly down the street until he came to a small park. He followed a narrow winding path until he was well out of sight of anyone who might happen by and then he lowered her to the ground. She was pale and unconscious, her breathing shallow and labored. It was startling, how swiftly the illness struck, how quickly it left her incapacitated.

Lifting his arm, he bit into a vein in his wrist, then held the bleeding wound to her lips.

"Drink." He spoke to her mind, the word a command she could not ignore. "Drink, love, and then forget what you have done."

He watched anxiously as the color returned to her cheeks and her breathing grew regular. He would have to watch her more closely in the future. Had this occurred when he wasn't with her . . . he shuddered to think what might have happened.

When she stirred, he drew his arm away and licked the wound in his arm, closing it. Wiping the blood from her mouth, he sat on the ground, then lifted her onto his lap and cradled her to his chest.

"Shannah?"

Her eyelids fluttered open and she stared up at him, her gaze unfocused. "What happened?"

"You fainted."

"I did?"

"How do you feel now?"

"Fine." She frowned. "Why do I feel fine?"

"I'm sure it was just a passing weakness."

"Maybe. I never used to recover so quickly though, at least not until I met you. Are you sure you're not a miracle worker?"

"I'm sure," he said dryly.

She licked her lips. "There's a funny taste in my mouth. Did you give me something to drink?"

"No." Still holding her, he rose effortlessly and set her on her feet. "Are you sure you're all right?"

"I think so."

"Are you sure?"

"I'll race you back to the house," she said, grinning. "That's how all right I feel."

"I think we'd better walk."

"Suit yourself." Shannah glanced around. "How did we get here? I don't remember being in the park."

"I couldn't leave you on the street."

"So you brought me here? Why didn't you take me home? Never mind, forget I said that. My Mom would have freaked out."

"That's what I thought," Ronan said, taking her by the hand. "Are you ready to go?"

"Sure."

Her parents were waiting for them in the living room when they returned to the house.

"Everything all right?" her father asked.

Shannah grinned inwardly. Like all fathers, he worried when his daughter was out with a new young man, even when that man was a famous author.

"Fine, Daddy," Shannah said. "I was just . . . just showing Ronan around."

"We'll be saying good night, then," Verna said, putting her knitting aside. "Shanny, I made up the guest room for Ronan. Why don't you show him where it is?"

"All right, Mom, thanks."

"Sweet dreams, dear," Verna said, kissing Shannah on the cheek. "Good night, Ronan. I hope you'll be comfortable. Shanny will show you where everything is."

"Thank you, Mrs. Davis."

Shannah's father kissed her on the cheek, shook Ronan's hand, then followed his wife down the hall to their bedroom.

"The guest room's upstairs," Shannah said, "across from my room."

Ronan lifted one brow. "Is that an invitation?"

"If you want it to be."

He laughed softly. "You don't think I'm going to deflower you under your father's roof, do you?"

"A girl can hope," Shannah muttered, her cheeks growing hot. "Come on."

With a shake of his head, he followed her up the stairs, unabashedly admiring the sway of her hips as he did so.

"This is your room," she said, stopping in front of a closed door. She gestured across the hall. "And that's my room, in case you change your mind in the middle of the night."

Ronan grinned at her, amused by her persistence and her audacity. "Good night, love."

He watched her go into her room and shut the door before going into his own.

She didn't know who she was asking to make love to her, he thought, or what she was asking for. Hopefully, she would never know.

Sitting on the edge of her bed, Shannah replayed everything that had happened from the time she and Ronan had left the house. They had gone for a walk. He had pulled her into the shadows and kissed her. She remembered feeling suddenly weak, and then nothing after that until she woke on the ground, looking up into Ronan's worried face.

Going into the bathroom, she poured some mouthwash into a paper cup and rinsed out her mouth, hoping to dispel the strange taste that lingered there. It was an oddly familiar taste, but she couldn't quite place it.

She took a quick shower, put on her nightgown, brushed out her hair, and climbed into bed, only to lie there, wide awake. Was Ronan in bed? Was he asleep? Or was he lying there, staring up at the ceiling, unable to sleep for thinking of her? Wanting her the way she wanted him?

Ronan, in bed. She frowned thoughtfully. What did he wear to sleep in? He hadn't brought any luggage with him. Was he sleeping in his underwear, or in nothing at all?

Impulsively, she slid out of bed and padded across the hallway. She pressed her ear to the door, listening for some sound that would indicate he was still awake. Hearing nothing, she turned the knob. The door opened on silent hinges and she stepped inside, closing the door behind her before she tiptoed toward the bed.

Even in the dark, she could see that it was empty.

Frowning, she turned on the light and glanced around the room. There was no sign of Ronan.

Chapter Fifteen

Ronan walked the dark streets of Middletown. Tall trees lined the sidewalks like dark sentinels. A full moon hung low in the midnight sky. It was still hours until dawn and he was reluctant to seek his rest so early. Noting the deserted streets and dark houses, it was obvious that few residents of the town shared his love of the night. Sad, he thought, for there was a beauty and a serenity in the night that few took the time to notice.

Leaving the residential area, he found a singles bar on the edge of town. The place was doing a brisk business and he ducked inside and found an empty booth in the back. His senses were quickly overcome with the myriad scents and sounds that filled the air.

A waitress appeared at his table and he asked for a glass of red wine, then sat back and watched the mortals at play. But he had little interest in their comings and goings. It made no difference in his existence if they found what were looking for, whether it was forgetfulness in a bottle, or a warm body with whom to share the night. All he could think of was Shannah. Her scent clung to his clothing. His wrist still tingled from where her mouth had drawn nourishment. The taste of her kisses lingered on his lips, his body remembered the heat and the softness of each lush curve, his arms ached to hold her again. He yearned to lie beside her, to bury himself in her sweetness and pretend, if only for a little while, that she was a healthy woman and he was a mortal man, and that there was nothing on earth or in heaven to keep them apart.

He sipped the wine the waitress had brought him, amused by his maudlin thoughts. He had been content with his life until he met Shannah, but a few months in her company had him yearning for things he thought he had put behind him forever.

Things like marriage . . . He grunted softly. He must be losing his mind, to sit there and contemplate marriage to a mortal. A mortal who was dying. But she didn't have to die. With luck, his blood would keep her alive for years to come, or he could bring her across and keep her with him forever. He swore softly. He knew how to bestow the Dark Trick on a mortal, but he had never done it. What if he tried and failed? There wasn't much he was afraid of, but the thought of trying to bring Shannah across, and failing, filled him with dread.

Would she accept the Dark Gift if he offered it to her? She had come to him looking for a vampire but he had known she didn't really believe vampires existed, that it had been fear and desperation that had sent her to his door. How would she feel if she knew that he was indeed a vampire? Would she still want the Dark Gift if she knew obtaining it was a very real possibility?

He sat in the bar until it closed and then he went out into the darkness once more, enjoying the beauty and the quiet of the night.

A patrol car slowed, keeping pace with him for half a block or so before going on.

A dog barked at his passing.

A cat hissed at his approach and then scurried up a tree.

He walked by Shannah's house, pausing in the shadows to listen to the even sound of her breathing. Assured that she was sleeping soundly, he returned to the park where he had taken her earlier and sought shelter in the cool loving arms of the earth.

In the morning, Shannah wasn't surprised to find that Ronan was nowhere in the house. She made some excuse to her mother about his having an early appointment with his agent in the city, then spent the rest of the day wondering where he was and what he was doing and why she was surprised that he wasn't there in the first place. He was never around in the morning. Still, he might have told her he would be gone.

She had breakfast with her parents, then helped her mother tidy up the house. Later that afternoon, she and her mother drove into the city. They had lunch at Shannah's favorite restaurant, and then did a little more shopping.

They were leaving one of the department stores when someone called Shannah's name. Turning, she saw her friend, Judy Kingston, hurrying toward her. Judy had blue eyes, red hair, and a pixy nose dusted with freckles. Shannah felt a twinge of guilt for leaving Middletown without telling Judy good-bye.

"Shannah, I don't believe it!" Judy gave her a hug. "You don't know how I've missed you!"

"Oh, Judy," Shannah said, returning her friend's hug. "I've missed you, too!"

Judy smiled at Verna. "Hi, Mrs. Davis."

"Hello, Judy. If you girls will excuse me, I'll just run into the drug store while you chat. I need to pick up a few things."

"Sure, Mom," Shannah said.

"Shan, where have you been for the last eighteen months?" Judy asked. "Your parents wouldn't say much, except that you'd moved to California, of all places."

Shannah shrugged. "I just needed to get away, you know? Look at you!" she exclaimed, hoping to change the subject. "Mom told me you were pregnant again!"

Judy placed one hand over her swollen belly. "Aren't I always?"

Shannah laughed. Judy had two boys and twin girls. They were, Shannah thought, four of the cutest red-headed kids she had ever seen.

"I think this is going to be our last one," Judy said. "Or should I say the last two."

"Twins again?" Shannah exclaimed. "Oh, Judy, how exciting! I think."

"Shannah, I'm twenty-six years old and I have four kids under the age of six and two more on the way. Believe me, I'm past being excited."

Shannah nodded, though it was hard to feel sympathetic when Judy had everything Shannah wanted and would never have.

"How are the other kids doing?"

"They're all fine. My mom's home with them, God bless her. I love my kids dearly but if I couldn't get out of the house once in a while, I swear I'd have a nervous breakdown."

"Well, you look terrific."

"I look fat, but you look great." Judy sighed dramatically. "I don't think I'll ever be skinny again."

"Listen, do you want to go have a cup of coffee?"

"I'd love to, but I can't. I'm already overdue at home. My mom's great about watching the kids every week or so, but I feel like I'm taking advantage of her if I'm gone for more than a couple of hours. It was great seeing you again, Shan. Call me soonest." She gave Shannah a hug. "Oh, and tell your mom good-bye for me."

"I will. And you give your mom my best."

With a nod and a wave, Judy hurried down the street.

Shannah stared after her friend. She and Judy had been practically inseparable all through school, but then Judy met Alex and the next thing Shannah knew, Judy had graduated and married Alex. Since then, it seemed as though Judy was constantly pregnant. Shannah felt a sudden wave of envy for her friend. Judy didn't know how lucky she was. She had a wonderful husband, happy, healthy kids, a nice house and, God willing, years to enjoy it all.

With a sigh, she went into the drug store to look for her mother. She found her at the cash register paying for her purchases.

"Did you and Judy have a nice chat?" Verna asked as they walked toward the car.

"Yes. I sure have missed her."

"She's missed you, too. I know she'd love it if you moved back home. Of course, your father and I would like nothing better."

"I don't know, Mom," Shannah said evasively. "We'll see."

It was a little after four-thirty when Shannah pulled into the driveway of her parents' home. Switching off the ignition, Shannah noticed there was a late model Honda parked in front of the house. Though there was nothing ominous about the car's appearance, she hurried up the walk to the front door and into the house.

"Is anything wrong?" her mother asked, hurrying into the house behind her.

"No, nothing," Shannah assured her mother, and then almost jumped out of her skin when the doorbell rang.

"I'll get it," Verna said.

"No!" Shannah said, "I'll get it." Taking a deep breath,

she opened the front door, felt her heart jump into her throat when she saw Jim Hewitt and Carl Overstreet standing on the porch.

"Afternoon, Miss Black," Hewitt said.

"What are you doing here?"

"Forgive the inconvenience," Hewitt said. "We were hoping to get an interview."

Shannah glanced at Overstreet, then back at Hewitt. "Don't tell me you're a reporter, too."

Hewitt nodded.

"And you came here together? Why? Do you work for the same paper?"

"No," Hewitt said smoothly. "We're more like friendly rivals and since we both wanted a story, we thought we'd save some money and rent a car together. Talking to the two of us will save you time, you know?"

"Who is it, dear?" Verna asked, coming up behind Shannah.

"Reporters, Mom. They want to do an interview with me."

"Oh, that's very nice, I'm sure, but wouldn't they rather talk to . . ."

"I'll take care of this, Mom. Would you make us some coffee, please?"

"Of course." With a little huff of annoyance at being summarily dismissed, Verna disappeared into the house.

"So," Hewitt said, "what do you say? We won't take up too much of your time."

Shannah considered for a minute. Would they think it was odd if she said no? If she were really an author, wouldn't she welcome any publicity she could get? Darn Ronan, where was he when she needed him?

"I guess I have time to answer a few questions," she decided.

Hewitt smiled. "Good."

"Let's sit out here," Shannah said, "on the porch."

"Whatever you say."

She sat on the swing and Hewitt and Overstreet pulled up two chairs and sat facing her.

Overstreet withdrew a small spiral notebook and the stub of a pencil from his shirt pocket. "How's the tour been going?"

"Very well, I think," Shannah replied. "The store managers have all seemed pleased with the sales and the turnout."

"Will you be returning home soon?" Hewitt asked.

"Yes, I think so. Why didn't you tell me you were a reporter?"

He shrugged. "I didn't want you to think that was why I was interested in you."

"Oh."

"Now that you know," he said with a wink, " I'm still interested."

"Knock it off," Overstreet said irritably. "We're not here to get you a date."

Hewitt shrugged. "Can't blame a guy for trying."

Overstreet scowled at him, then looked back at Shannah. "How long have you known your publicist?"

"Not long, why?"

"Readers are interested in that kind of thing," Overstreet said.

"Has he gone back to California?" Hewitt asked.

"No." Feeling oddly uncomfortable, she looked from one man to the other.

Eyes narrowed, Overstreet slid a glance at the house and then he leaned forward, reminding her of a wolf on the scent of blood. "Is he here?"

"No, he . . . uh, went into the city on business."

"So," Hewitt said, "will you be doing any more signings or interviews while you're here?"

"No, I won't." She frowned at Overstreet. "How did you two find me?"

Hewitt and Overstreet exchanged glances.

"We've been following you," Hewitt admitted with a sheepish grin. "Hoping for a scoop."

Shannah was trying to think of a suitable reply when her mother stepped out onto the porch.

"Here, let me help you with that," Hewitt said. Rising, he took the tray from Verna's hands and placed it on the table between the two chairs. "Will you join us?"

"Thank you." Verna poured coffee for the two men, a cup for Shannah, and one for herself, then she sat down on the swing next to Shannah. "So, you're reporters?"

"Yes, ma'am. Your daughter's a remarkable author. You must be very proud of her."

Verna glanced uncertainly at Shannah.

"Of course she is," Shannah said quickly. "You know how mothers are."

"Of course," Hewitt said, smiling at Verna. "So, what do you think of your daughter's books?"

"I . . . uh, well, naturally, I think they're wonderful," Verna said, warming to the subject. "But Shannah doesn't really . . ."

"Mom, could I have a refill?"

"What? Oh, of course, dear."

"I'm sorry your publicist isn't here," Hewitt said. "I was hoping to ask him a few questions."

"What publicist?" Verna asked.

"The man traveling with your daughter," Overstreet said.

"Oh, you mean Ronan," Verna said, laughing. "He's not . . ."

"Mom, maybe Mr. Hewitt and Mr. Overstreet would like some of that cake you made last night."

"Of course, why didn't I think of that?" Verna smiled

at the two men. "I'll just be a minute." Rising, she hurried into the house.

"Excuse me," Shannah said, "I'll be right back."

She found her mother in the kitchen pulling dishes out of the cupboard. "Mom, they don't know that I'm not Eva Black. It's a secret."

"It is?"

"Yes, didn't I tell you?"

"I don't think so, dear," Verna exclaimed. "I hope I didn't say anything out of line."

"No." Shannah smiled. "Let me take the cake out and get rid of them."

"All right, dear. I'm sorry if I spoke out of turn."

"I don't think any harm was done."

Taking the two plates, Shannah returned to the front porch.

"Here you go. My mom's a great cook."

She handed each of the men a plate, then resumed her seat on the swing.

"Any other questions?"

"How long have you had a publicist?" Overstreet asked.

"Not long."

"Does a good job, does he?" Hewitt asked.

"Yes, he does."

Hewitt grunted softly. "I notice he only accompanies you at night."

"He likes to play the role of bodyguard, too," Shannah said coolly. "He doesn't think I should travel alone after dark."

"I can't argue with that," Overstreet said. "Will he be here tonight?"

It occurred to Shannah that they seemed far more interested in Ronan than they were in her. Did they suspect that she was simply playing a role and that Ronan was the famous Eva Black? That would explain why they were following her, why they were asking so many questions about him, although she couldn't imagine it would make a very interesting story. Then again, maybe it would be of interest, at least to the men and women who had come to the signings. What would Ronan's fans think if they discovered she was an imposter? What if she had broken the law?

"I'm not sure of his plans," she said. "And now, if you'll excuse me, I really must get back to work."

"Do you think . . . ?"

"As I said, I have to go." She rose, indicating the interview was over.

"Of course." Hewitt's smile didn't reach his eyes. "Thank you for your time."

"Yes," Overstreet said, rising, "thank you."

She watched the two men descend the stairs and get into the Honda parked at the curb. She wished suddenly that Ronan had been there. He would have known what to do. Nothing ever seemed to bother him, but doubts assailed her. Had she said something wrong? Did they know she was a fraud? Would they reveal it to the whole world? What would Ronan do if Hewitt and Overstreet splashed the truth on the front pages of their respective newspapers? And did it really matter? She didn't understand why he wanted to remain anonymous, or why he had arranged such an elaborate charade.

Well, there was no sense worrying about the consequences now. It was over and done and whatever happened now, she'd had a wonderful time in New York. She'd had a chance to experience life as a celebrity, and she liked it. She had been wined and dined by Ronan's editor and agent, and she had liked that, too. And she'd had the opportunity to see a play on a New York stage. Humming the *Beauty and the Beast* theme song, she picked up the cake plates and went into the house to help her mother with dinner.

Ronan appeared just as her mother was serving dessert later that night.

"I'm beginning to think you're afraid to try my cooking," Verna said with a pout. "You've missed every meal since you got here, but you're not getting away without trying my Dutch apple pie. Now you just sit down and try this and tell me if it isn't the best apple pie you've ever tasted."

Ronan sat down beside Shannah and forced a smile. "I don't eat many sweets, so I'm really not much of a judge."

"Go on with you now, I've never met a man yet who didn't love my apple pie."

Ronan glanced at Shannah, but no help was forthcoming in that direction.

"Mom really does make the best apple pie," she said, her voice filled with pride and affection. "I think you'll like it."

"She won't stop nagging until you try it," Mr. Davis said with an affectionate glance at his wife. "But you won't be sorry. She does make the world's best pie."

Ronan nodded helplessly. He hadn't eaten solid food in centuries, but there was no way to avoid it now without hurting Verna's feelings. Still, the very thought of ingesting mortal cuisine made him cringe.

"We missed you today," Shannah was saying, unaware of his growing unease. "Where did you go?"

"I had some business to take care of," Ronan replied. But he wasn't looking at Shannah. He was watching her mother as she cut a huge slice of apple pie.

"Do you want some vanilla ice cream with that?" Verna asked.

He shook his head, his nostrils filling with the scent of

apples and cinnamon, sugar and flour. His stomach clenched.

"A slice of cheese, perhaps?" Verna asked.

"No, thank you."

Verna set the plate before him, then stood beside his chair, her arms crossed over her chest. "Just try that," she said, "and tell me it isn't the best pie you've ever tasted."

Feeling like a man about to knowingly swallow poison, Ronan picked up a fork and took a small bite. He chewed the disgusting mess and forced himself to swallow. It was all he could do not to gag.

"Well?" Verna asked expectantly.

"It's . . ." He swallowed again. "It's very good."

Verna cut a slice for Scott, one for Shannah, and one for herself. "Would you like a glass of milk or a cup of coffee, Ronan?"

"No," he said, his voice sounding oddly strangled. "Thank you."

"Shannah?"

"Milk, thanks."

"Coffee for me," Scott said.

"Ronan, we had company today," Shannah said.

"Oh?" Feeling Verna's expectant gaze, Ronan choked down another bite of pie.

"Jim Hewitt and Carl Overstreet came to see me."

Ronan coughed into his napkin. "What did they want?"

"I'm not sure. Mostly, they asked about you."

"Me?" He was going to die, now, tonight, he thought ruefully. He had survived for centuries, only to be done in by a slice of homemade apple pie.

Shannah nodded, thinking that he looked rather odd. "They wanted to know where you were and when we were going back home."

"What did you tell them?"

"That you were in the city on business. You don't think they suspect that I'm a fraud, do you?"

"You're not a fraud," he said, his voice tight. He took another bite of pie, then pushed away from the table. "Excuse me," he said, and fled the room, and the house.

"Oh, dear," Verna said, "I hope he isn't sick. You don't think it was the pie, do you?"

Scott shrugged. "I don't think so, Mother. This is my second piece and it tastes fine to me."

"I'll just go make sure he's all right," Shannah said. Leaving the table, she went in search of Ronan.

She found him in the furthest corner of the backyard on his hands and knees being violently ill. Chewing on her lower lip, she waited until his nausea subsided, then handed him a couple of tissues she found in her pocket.

"Are you all right?" she asked.

Sitting back on his heels, Ronan wiped his mouth. Unless he missed his guess, he had just discovered a new method for destroying vampires, one that was right up there with sunlight and beheading. Instead of driving a wooden stake through his heart, all you had to do was stuff him with homemade apple pie.

"Ronan?"

"I'll be all right," he said, but it was a lie. It felt like a thousand piranhas were eating away at his insides.

"Was it the pie?" she asked. "Are you allergic to apples or cinnamon or something?"

"Yes, something." He closed his eyes. He hadn't eaten solid food in five hundred years, though he had wondered, from time to time, what it would be like. Now he knew.

"You shouldn't have eaten it then."

"Your mother didn't give me much choice," he said glumly. "Besides, I didn't want to hurt her feelings."

Shannah laughed softly. "That was mighty sweet of you."

"Yeah, sweet," he muttered, "that's me."

"Are you ready to go back inside?"

"I don't think so."

"Well, come on," she said, offering him her hand, "we can sit in the swing until you feel better. You'll be more comfortable there."

He grunted softly, certain that he would never feel better again.

The next evening, at dusk, Shannah and Ronan bade her parents good-bye.

With tears shining in her eyes, Verna begged Shannah to move back home. Her father, too, tried to persuade her that it was for the best.

"Maybe later," Shannah said, "but Ronan needs me right now. Isn't that right, Ronan?"

"Yes, of course."

Shannah hugged her mother and her father. "I'll call you soon," she promised.

She was quiet on the way back to the Waldorf. She loved her parents and she knew she would miss them, but she couldn't stay, didn't want them to watch her get weaker and weaker, couldn't abide the thought of seeing the sadness in their eyes, didn't want them to feel guilty because they couldn't kiss her hurt and make it better.

When they reached the hotel, they packed their bags, then took a cab to the airport, and now they were on board the plane. Shannah glanced out the window, knowing she would never see her parents again. Earlier in the day, she had gone to see Judy. It had been a bitter-sweet visit. But her good-byes had all been said.

"So," she said, turning away from the window to look at Ronan, "where were you this afternoon? Never mind, don't answer that," she said irritably. "I know what your answer will be. You went into the city on business, right?"

He looked at her, his expression mildly amused. It only served to annoy her more.

"Just what kind of business were you taking care of? It can't be book business, since you don't want anyone to know who you are."

Ronan lifted one brow. "Feeling a little testy this evening, are we?"

"I'm just tired of being kept in the dark, that's all."

Kept in the dark. He had to laugh at that. If she only knew.

The plane hit some turbulence. Shannah's hands grasped the arm rests, her knuckles white.

"Take it easy," he said. "There's nothing to worry about."

She nodded, but she didn't look convinced. And she didn't relax her grip on the seat.

"Your folks wanted you to stay with them," he said, hoping to distract her.

"I know, but nothing's changed. They worry about me too much, you know? I can't stand to see the hurt in their eyes, or the pity. Or the guilt. I know they feel like it's their fault that I'm sick."

"What do you want to do when we get home?"

"I don't know. I guess I should go back to my place . . ."

"I'd rather you didn't."

"Well, I really don't want to, but I can't go on living with you."

"Why not? You've been doing it for the last few months."

"I know, but . . . well, you needed me to be there, you know, so you could coach me, and now . . ."

"I still need you there."

She stared at him, her eyes wide. "You do?"

"I've lived alone most of my life. I don't want to do it anymore."

"But . . ."

"Get rid of your apartment and move in with me."

It was so very tempting. And so very wrong. It had been one thing when it was business, but to move in with him now, just because he wanted her to . . . What would her parents say? Nowadays, a woman moving in with a man was no big deal to most people, but her parents were old-fashioned in some respects. They still believed in honesty and fidelity and chastity before marriage. And they had instilled those values in their daughter.

"I'm not asking for anything more than your company," Ronan said. "Anything beyond that will be up to you." He took one of her hands in his. "Say yes, love."

It was an offer she couldn't refuse. "If I say yes, will you tell me where you go during the day?"

"I will, when you need to know."

"You promise?"

"I promise."

"Then my answer is yes, love . . . oh!" She shrieked as the plane shuddered.

She wasn't the only one. Several other women screamed as the plane began to lose altitude.

A flight attendant appeared, her voice quivering as she assured them that everything was all right, and then instructed them to fasten their seat belts.

Shannah clutched Ronan's arm. "We're going to crash, aren't we?"

"I don't know. Shannah, look at me."

"What?"

"Shannah, whatever happens, I promise I'll keep you safe."

"Yeah, right. I don't want to die now, not like this!"

"Shannah, listen to me, you'll be all right." His gaze

caught and held hers. "Whatever happens, you'll be all right. Trust me, love, there's nothing to fear. I won't let anything hurt you. Do you understand?"

She stared at him, her eyes unfocused. "Nothing to fear," she murmured.

"You will sleep now," he said quietly, "and you'll stay asleep until I tell you to awake."

"Sleep." Her eyelids fluttered down. The tension left her body and she slumped down in her seat.

Slipping his arm around her waist, Ronan lifted her onto his lap and held her tight while the plane plummeted toward the ground.

Chapter Sixteen

Ronan cradled Shannah to his chest, speaking softly to her mind while pandemonium erupted all around him. Cries of alarm and screams of panic were underscored by a tremulous voice murmuring the Lord's Prayer.

Feeling an unexpected sense of regret that he couldn't save them all, Ronan summoned his preternatural powers and transported himself and Shannah out of the plane and onto the ground, well away from the airplane's trajectory.

Standing there in the dark, holding Shannah in his arms, he watched the nose of the plane hit the ground. It balanced there for a moment and then, as if it was moving in slow motion, the aircraft flipped over and broke in half. Even before it burst into flames, he knew there would be no survivors.

He glanced at Shannah, still spellbound in his arms, and wondered how he would explain the fact that they had survived the crash when no one else had. And then he shrugged. There were countless stories of people who had made miraculous escapes from accidents where no one should have survived.

He glanced at the night sky. No doubt the pilot had sent out a call for help before the plane crashed. How long would it take for rescuers to arrive on the scene? And what should he do until then? Should he wait here for help to arrive, or should he transport himself and Shannah home to California? If he left the scene now, there was a distinct possibility that it could cause questions that might be hard to answer later. For instance, if asked, how would Shannah explain leaving the crash site and getting home? They were miles from the nearest city. Damn! It would be an easy thing to transport them to his house but it seemed wiser to stay. He hadn't survived this long by drawing attention to himself.

Carrying Shannah further away from the wreck, he found a cleared grassy area. He would wait with her as long as he could, and then he would have to seek shelter from the sun.

Sitting down, he stroked Shannah's hair while he spoke quietly to her mind. "Shannah, listen to me. The plane crashed. We managed to get out just before it caught fire and ran to safety. Do you understand?"

She nodded.

"If they ask you any questions, you don't remember anything else. If I'm not here when you wake up, you're to tell anyone who asks that I went looking for help. Is that clear?"

"We got out of the plane before it caught fire," she said, her voice flat. "If you're not here when I wake up, I'm to tell anyone who asks that you went looking for help."

He kissed her cheek. "Good girl."

Reaching into his pocket, he withdrew all the cash he had and stuffed it into the pocket of her slacks.

For a time, he stared at the flames, his thoughts filled with death. He had seen much of it in his time, most of it needless. Mankind was a violent race. He had seen wars, large and small. He had seen mighty kings and rulers rise and fall. He had seen fathers and sons turn against one another, arguing over a scrap of land or a difference in politics or religion. He had seen men ride off to war, certain of victory, seen those same men lying dead on the field of battle. Death. The world was full of it.

He held Shannah in his arms, content to do so until he sensed the coming of dawn. Though he hated to leave her out there, alone, he had no other choice.

He trailed his fingertips over her cheek. "Shannah," he murmured, "you will sleep until someone awakens you. You will not be afraid to get on another plane for the trip home. If I don't find you before you get home, I'll meet you there. Do you understand?"

She nodded.

"Dammit, I don't want to leave you out here alone!"

Even as he said the words, he felt the first rays of the sun on his back, heard the whirring of a helicopter overhead.

Dropping a quick kiss on Shannah's brow, he dissolved into mist and disappeared into the deep shadows of the woods.

Shannah woke feeling groggy and bewildered, with no memory of what had happened between the time the plane started going down and a uniformed police officer woke her up.

The area around the crash site was crawling with people and they all asked her questions, questions for which she had no answers.

"All I remember is running away from the plane. I don't remember anything after that." If she said it once, she said it a hundred times. But did she really remember running away from the crash? Even though she had said it dozens of times, she had no clear memory of running from the plane, no lingering sense of fear at coming so close to a fiery death.

Finally, an ambulance drove her to a hospital in La Porte City where a doctor checked her over from head to toe, declared, in amazement, that she didn't have a scratch on her, and released her. The airlines put her up in a hotel and gave her a ticket home that was good any time she felt like using it.

When she reached her room in the hotel, she went straight to bed, only to lie there wondering where Ronan was. Why had he left her alone and gone for help when there was no need? Where had he gone? And where was he now?

She rolled onto her side and closed her eyes. Why had the two of them survived when everyone else on board had perished? She wasn't anxious to die, but it seemed unfair that she should survive when she was dying anyway. Suddenly overcome with guilt, she burst into tears. She wept for all the people who had died, wept for her own life, which would end all too soon, wept for the husband and the children she would never have, wept for the pain her death would bring her parents, wept until she had no tears left.

When she woke several hours later, the sun had set and Ronan was sitting on the foot of the bed, watching her.

"Ronan! How did you get here? How did you find me? Where have you been?"

"So many questions." Rising, he moved to the side of the bed and sat down beside her. "Are you all right, love?"

Sitting up, she brushed a wisp of hair from her face. "Yes, but . . ."

"Are you ready to go home?"

"Yes, but . . ."

"No questions now."

But she couldn't wait. "Why didn't we die with everyone else? Why didn't I die? It doesn't make sense . . . I should have died, too."

"Shannah, hush, love."

"I can't help it. I feel so guilty for being alive when everyone else was killed. Why me? Why us?"

"Perhaps we had the most to live for?"

She shook her head. "No! I'm dying. There were people on that plane who had long lives ahead of them! Young mothers, children. It isn't right . . ."

"Ah, Shannah." He drew her into his arms and held her tight. "There are no answers to questions like that. It's normal to feel guilty when you survive something like this, but there's no need. It isn't your fault the others died. It isn't your fault that you survived. It's just Fate. The luck of the draw, the turn of the wheel." He smiled down at her. "Just be glad that you're still alive, love, and make the most of whatever time you have left."

She nodded.

"Why don't you take a shower?" he suggested. "I'll go down to the gift shop and see if I can find you something to wear."

"All right."

She thought about what Ronan had said while she showered. His words made sense. They even made her feel a little bit better. And yet she couldn't help feeling that she was forgetting something that had happened just before the crash, something important that remained just out of her reach. Something to do with Ronan . . .

With a shake of her head, she turned off the water in the shower, dried off, and wrapped herself in a towel.

A moment later, there was a knock on the bathroom

door. She opened it a crack to see Ronan on the other side, a large plastic shopping bag in his hand.

He handed her the sack. "I think you'll find everything you need inside."

"Thank you."

After closing the door, she delved into the bag, removing a pair of jeans, a T-shirt and a sweatshirt, a black bra and a pair of matching panties, a pair of low-heeled sandals, a nightgown, a comb, a brush, a toothbrush and toothpaste.

She dressed quickly, combed out her hair, stepped into the sandals, and went into the other room.

Ronan turned away from the window when she entered the room.

"I can't believe you found all this in the gift shop," Shannah remarked.

"I didn't." His gaze moved over her. "Everything fit all right?"

She felt a flush burn her cheeks. "Yes," she said, "everything."

"Are you feeling any better?"

"A little," she admitted, frowning. "But there's something bothering me and I can't quite put my finger on it. Something I should remember. It seems important . . ."

"I'm sure it will come to you, in time, if it's important."

"I guess so," she said doubtfully.

"Would you like to go out for a while?" he asked.

She nodded, thinking some fresh air and a walk might do her some good.

"Have you had dinner?" he asked.

"No, I'm not hungry."

"You need to eat."

"Not now." The very thought of food make her sick to her stomach.

He didn't argue.

After leaving the hotel, they walked in silence for a while. Shannah felt numb inside, as if a part of her had died in the crash. Maybe she should have died, she thought glumly. At least it would have been quickly over. The doctors didn't know what was wrong with her. What if it took her months and months to die? She didn't want to suffer for a long time, to lie in a hospital bed and slowly waste away.

"Hey," Ronan said, "why so quiet?"

She shrugged. "I was just thinking about . . ." Her eyes narrowed and she turned to look at him. "On the plane, you promised me that whatever happened, you'd keep me safe."

He shrugged. "What did you want me to say? I was trying to make you feel better."

"But there was more . . . why can't I remember?"

Taking her by the hand, he said, "Come on, let's get a drink."

They found a quiet night club on the next block. Shannah ordered a virgin strawberry daiquiri and Ronan ordered a glass of red wine.

He studied her over the rim of his glass, wondering what he would say if she suddenly remembered everything that had happened before the crash. He told himself there was nothing to worry about and yet he wasn't so sure. No one else had ever recalled being hypnotized by him. Perhaps it was the result of the blood he had given her. Perhaps it had weakened his power over her and, at the same time, strengthened her will to resist his telepathic suggestions. If she remembered everything he had said on the plane before the crash and after, it would require a great deal of explanation.

* * *

Jim Hewitt looked up at the small television set that was located on a shelf in a corner of the bar.

"Hey, Overstreet," he called, "look at this. Bartender, can you turn up the sound?"

"What's going on?" Carl Overstreet looked up at the screen where a television reporter was standing in front of the smoldering wreckage of a plane.

"Remember when we followed Black and her publicist to the airport? Didn't they leave on Flight 271?"

Overstreet snorted. "If he's her publicist, I'm Jane Pauley."

Hewitt jerked his chin toward the TV. "That's Flight 271. Good thing we couldn't get tickets."

"Yeah," Overstreet muttered, his eyes narrowing. "Good thing."

Hewitt grunted. It hadn't seemed like a good thing at the time. Once Eva Black had boarded the plane, she had been lost to them, at least temporarily. Now it looked like she was gone for good, and with her their only link to her companion.

"Do you think he was killed?" Overstreet asked.

Hewitt shrugged, his gaze intent on the screen. "I don't know. Vampires are susceptible to fire, just like anyone else. Maybe more so."

"Yeah, but . . . wait a minute," Overstreet said. "Listen to this."

" . . . .Miss Eva Black and her companion, Mr. Dark, were the sole survivors when the plane's engine malfunctioned and crashed in this barren stretch of Iowa countryside. Neither Miss Black, a well-known author who resides in Northern California, nor her companion, Mr. Dark, were available for comment. In other news . . ."

Hewitt grinned. He'd bet his last dollar that Mr. Dark was none other than Ronan.

"What's so funny?" Overstreet asked.

"Just thinking that this is our lucky day. So, what do you say, Carl, you up for another trip to sunny California?"

"Sure, I've got nothing else to do." With a shrug, the reporter tossed off his drink. "But how do we find him when we get there?"

"As it happens, I know how to find him."

Using the ticket the airlines had given her, Shannah booked a flight home for the next night. Ronan was able to get a seat on the same flight. He watched her carefully as they boarded the plane, but she did so without fear.

The flight was uneventful. When they arrived at the airport, Ronan hailed a cab.

Shannah sat beside him, silently staring out the window.

It was after midnight when they reached Ronan's house. Shannah felt a sense of homecoming unlike anything she had ever felt before as she stepped across the threshold.

Funny, that this big old house that wasn't even hers felt more like home than her own apartment.

She waited for Ronan to lock the door and switch on the lights. "Do you still want me to live here, with you?" she asked.

"Yes. Why? You haven't changed your mind, have you?"

"No."

Murmuring her name, he drew her into his arms. The plane crash had reminded him anew of how fragile human life was, how quickly it could be snuffed out. He wanted to spend every moment possible with the woman in his arms. He wanted her with him forever.

Shannah leaned against him, her head pillowed on his chest, her eyes closed. The sound of his heartbeat soothed her. His arms were strong around her, protective, comforting. She was safe here, with him. Nothing could hurt her while he was there . . .

Trust me, love, there's nothing to fear. I won't let anything hurt you.

The words echoed so loudly in her mind she looked up to see if he had spoken.

"Did you say something?"

"No, why?"

"I thought . . . never mind. It's late," she said, smothering a yawn. "I think I'll go to bed."

"All right."

"Will you sit with me until I fall asleep?"

"If you wish."

"Give me a few minutes, okay?"

Nodding, he watched her climb the stairs until she was out of sight, and then he began to pace the floor. Had he made a mistake in asking her to move in? It would be harder to keep his secret, harder to explain his continued absences during the day. And yet he could not abide the thought of letting her go. She was too fragile to live alone. He needed to have her nearby, where he could keep watch over her, where he could come to her aid should she need it. He was not entirely helpless during the day. If she needed him when he was at rest, he could, with a great deal of effort, rise to meet her needs, so long as she was inside the house.

He waited fifteen minutes and then he went up the stairs to her bedroom. She was already in bed, her hair spread around her shoulders in waves of black silk. She looked up at him through eyes shadowed with remorse and he wondered how long it would take her to get over feeling guilty because she had survived, and be grateful that she was still alive. He knew he could wipe the guilt from her memory, but he was reluctant to mess with her mind too often.

Wordlessly, he drew her into his arms, one hand stroking her back. "I'm glad you survived," he murmured. "My existence wouldn't be the same without you."

"Your existence?"

"My life," he amended easily.

"Do I really mean that much to you?"

"That much and more," he said fervently. "Until you came into my life, I was lost and I didn't even know it."

"I think that's the sweetest thing anyone has ever said to me."

"I want to make you happy, love. If there's anything you want, you have only to name it. Do whatever you want in the house, buy whatever you wish, whatever you need."

"That's very generous of you."

"Not really. I'm just being selfish."

"It doesn't sound selfish to me."

"Ah, but it is, don't you see? Making you happy makes me happy."

She smiled up at him. "Maybe that's why I was spared," she remarked. "To spend my last few days making you happy."

"Perhaps. Let's not question fate, let's just enjoy the time we have."

"I love you, Ronan."

"Shannah!"

"Do you love me?"

"More than you can imagine."

With a sigh, she snuggled against him, her arms around his waist.

He held her until she fell asleep, held her until the hunger gnawing at his insides could no longer be ignored.

Brushing a kiss across her brow, he settled her under the covers, and then he went out into the night to search the drifting shadows for prey.

Chapter Seventeen

After five hundred and thirteen years as a vampire, it didn't take Ronan long to find that which he sought, that which he needed. He fed quickly, neatly, and went on his way.

Five hundred and thirteen years. It didn't seem possible that so many centuries had passed, or that he had changed in so many ways and yet remained ever the same.

He had been born in the summer of 1459 in a small town off the English coast, a town that no longer existed. He had grown up on a farm, the youngest child in a family of four girls and five boys. His brothers and sisters had all married and left home by the time he was seventeen and he alone had remained to help his father work the farm. At the age of twenty-four, he had married the girl on the neighboring farm. It hadn't been a love match, though Verity had been a sweet girl, biddable and kind-hearted. Though he had married her to please his parents, he hadn't been completely unhappy with his bride. She had been a pretty thing, with expressive brown eyes and a shy smile. Their marriage had been amicable if not exciting. In time, Verity had grown to love him and he had learned to care and appreciate her for the good woman she was. They had been married eight years and had long since given up any hope of having children when Verity told him she was pregnant. Seven months later, she had died in childbirth and the babe with her. He had mourned her death and the loss of his child, mourned the fact that he had never loved her.

He had immersed himself in work after the death of his wife and child. His mother and father had assured him that the grief would pass, that he would marry again. He never knew if they were right or wrong. Three years after Verity's death, Rosalyn had come to town and changed his life forever.

She had been a wild, wanton woman, the perfect anti-dote for the lethargy that had plagued him. She had teased and flirted shamelessly, and one night under a dark moon she had taken him into the shadows beyond the town and seduced him. When he had offered to marry her, she laughed in his face.

"You are so young," she had exclaimed. "And so tasty." She had kissed him again, arousing him to fever pitch once more, and then she sank her fangs into his throat.

Though he was taller and broader and outweighed her by a good sixty pounds, he had been helpless to resist her. He had felt himself growing weak, weaker, knew he was on the brink of death. When she lifted her head and looked down at him, her lips had been stained with his blood.

"Why?" he asked, his voice little more than a whisper.

She shrugged, and then, to his astonishment, she slit her wrist with a fingernail. Drops of dark red bubbled from the wound. He recoiled when she offered him her arm.

"I have drained you to the point of death," she said. "Now you must drink or die. The choice is yours."

Feeling as though he might float away on the next breeze, he shook his head. "No."

"Drink," she coaxed. "Someday you will thank me."

As he grew weaker, his fear of dying overcame his revulsion. With a low growl, he grabbed her arm.

"I'll never thank you," he vowed, "not if I live to be a hundred."

She laughed softly as he pressed her wrist to his lips.

He drank like a man who had been denied nourishment for days, drank until she had jerked her wrist away. And then, to his amazement, she lifted him into her arms as if he weighed no more than a child, carried him deep into a cave, and then vanished from his sight. Confused and afraid of what had happened between them, he struggled to his feet. He had only taken a few steps when pain ripped through his body. Certain she had left him in the cave to die, he curled into a ball, moaning softly as the world around him went dark, sucking him down into the blackness of oblivion.

When he woke the following night, he was a newly made vampire with the whole of the world and eternity stretching before him. They were exciting times. Sir Francis Drake sailed around the world, John Smith founded Jamestown, Gutenberg invented a printing press with movable type, the Pilgrims came to America. And he came with them, a new vampire in a new world.

He had enjoyed his existence but never more so than now. After all these years, years that he owed to Rosalyn, he had fallen in love. And for that, he would ever be grateful.

Looking up at the starry sky, he murmured, "You were right, Rosalyn. Wherever you are, I thank you."

And then he returned to the house that was now a home because Shannah was waiting for him there.

Chapter Eighteen

Shannah woke at dusk to find Ronan standing in front of her bedroom window, looking out. Sitting up, she admired the width of his shoulders, his tight buns, the snug fit of his jeans, the long line of his legs. He really was a perfect specimen, the kind of man that graced the covers of magazines like *GQ* and appeared on posters in clothing stores.

His soft chuckle filled the silence. "Do you like what you see?"

"How did you know I was looking?"

"I can feel your gaze on my back." He turned to face her, his arms crossed over his chest. "And other places."

"Oh." She knew she was blushing but she couldn't help it. Drat the man, she had blushed more since she met him than she had in her whole life.

"So," he said, "now that you're officially moved in, what would you think about keeping the same hours I do?"

"I don't suppose you could write during the day?"

"No. I'm afraid I'm too old and set in my ways to change now."

She could understand that, she supposed. After all, he

was a successful author, and as such, he was entitled to his quirks.

"Shannah?"

"I'm willing to try."

"You won't mind sleeping during the day?"

"I don't know. I guess not." Truth be told, she had been going to bed later and getting up later since the first night she came here.

Sitting up, she stretched her arms over her head. Still, it would be odd, getting up when the sun went to bed, sleeping while the sun was up, but it would be worth it if it meant spending more time with Ronan.

"So, what hours do you keep, exactly?"

"I usually get up an hour or two before sundown and stay up until dawn."

"You sleep all day?"

"Writing takes a lot out of me." He grinned at her. "Of course, since you came along, I haven't done a whole lot of writing."

Shannah chewed on her thumbnail. His hours didn't sound so bad, although she wasn't sure she could sleep that long. Of course, she wouldn't have to keep his exact hours.

"You don't have to adjust your schedule to mine if you'd rather not," he said. "We can go on as we are."

"No, that's okay. We can try it for a while and see how it works out," she said. "Since we'll be keeping the same hours, does that mean we'll be eating our meals together now?"

Damn, why hadn't he thought of that? He could always sit across from her and plant the idea in her mind that he had shared the meal with her. It would probably be the easiest solution.

"I usually only eat one meal a day," he said.

"And you like to eat alone," she said. "I know."

He nodded.

"Well, we'll work something out," she said brightly. "So, what hours do you write?"

"Until you came along, I usually wrote most of the night."

"Oh. Well, I don't want to interfere with your work . . ."

"Ah, but I want you to. Writing is a lonely business."

"But you have to keep writing. Think of all those fans waiting for your next book! I'll just read or watch TV when you're working." Of course, that wouldn't give them much time together.

Crossing the floor, he took her by the hand and drew her out of bed and into his arms. "Good evening, love."

She smiled up at him, then closed her eyes as he lowered his head and claimed a kiss.

Yes, she thought dreamily, she could get used to this.

"Why don't you get dressed and have dinner," he suggested, "and then, if you like, we can go out."

"All right."

"Where would you like to go?"

"The movies? I haven't been in ages."

"The movies it is." He kissed the tip of her nose. "I'll even buy you a box of popcorn."

They left for the theater at 6:30. It was odd, Ronan thought, sitting with a girl at the movies, holding hands like any other mortal couple. He tried to shut out the cacophony of beating hearts, the myriad odors that rose from the people around him, the smell of popcorn, soda, candy, nachos and cheese, the whispers and giggles, the scent of lust emanating from the teenage boy in the next row, his own growing desire for the woman beside him.

With so many distractions, it was little wonder that he paid scant attention to what was happening on the screen. He was relieved when the movie was over. Outside, he drew in a deep breath. Due to his preternatural senses, he was ever aware of the hundreds of scents and sounds that surrounded him, but out here, in the open, they were less intense.

"I need to check my post office box," he remarked as they walked across the street to the parking lot. "I haven't picked up my mail in weeks."

"I used to follow you there sometimes," she confessed.

"I know."

"I don't believe you! How could you know? I was always careful to stay out of sight."

"Sorry to disappoint you, love, but you weren't nearly as sneaky as you thought."

"Well," she muttered with mock despair, "so much for my James Bond impersonation."

Ronan laughed, thinking how good it felt. Laughter was something that had been missing from his life for a long time.

They pulled up in front of the post office a few minutes later. "Do you want to wait in the car," he asked, "or come in with me?"

Shannah glanced out the window. The post office was located next to the Department of Motor Vehicles. They were the only two buildings on the block, and both were dark. "I'll go with you."

He opened the door for her, then took her hand and they walked into the building together. Her footsteps echoed on the cement floor. Ronan walked without making a sound.

"It's spooky in here," she remarked.

"Is it?"

"Don't you think so?"

"No, but then I've never been afraid of the dark."

It wasn't entirely dark inside the building but it

seemed eerie somehow, to be wandering around inside when the main part of the post office was closed.

She followed him to his box, waited while he opened it and withdrew a handful of letters and a package.

"Anything good?" she asked curiously.

"A few letters," he replied, thumbing through the envelopes. "The usual junk mail."

"What's in the package?"

He glanced at the return address. "Probably my latest book. Nellie Brown always pre-orders a copy and sends it to me so I can autograph it for her."

"I hope no one ever compares your autograph with mine," Shannah said.

He grunted softly. "I hadn't thought of that." He tossed the junk mail in one of the trash containers; then, taking Shannah by the hand again, he left the building.

He paused outside, his hand tightening on hers as he glanced up and down the sidewalk.

"What's wrong?" Shannah asked.

Lifting his head, he sniffed the wind, then moved to the curb and looked up and down the street.

"Ronan?"

"It's nothing," he replied after a moment. "Let's go."

"You're scaring me."

"Get in the car."

She quickly did as she was told. Ronan slid behind the wheel and pulled out of the parking lot. She noticed he glanced in the rear-view mirror several times and that he took the long way home.

"What was that all about?" she asked when they pulled into the driveway.

He shrugged. "I guess I was being paranoid."

"Is there another James Bond trailing you?"

"I think so."

"You're not serious?"

"'Fraid so."

"Who?"

"Your friend, Hewitt."

Shannah stared at him. "I don't believe you. How could he find me? He doesn't even know my real name."

"You said he bought one of my books. My post office box is in the back." He swore softly. "I knew putting my address in there would come back to haunt me one of these days."

Shannah glanced out the back window as Ronan cut the engine. "Do you think he followed us here?"

Ronan shook his head. Hewitt didn't have to follow them. He already knew where to find them.

"I guess that book tour wasn't such a good idea," Shannah remarked, and then she frowned. "Why would he follow me?"

Ronan shrugged, content, for the moment, to let her think she was the one Hewitt was looking for even though he knew better. Hewitt wasn't looking for Shannah. He was hunting a vampire.

They started their new life together the following evening. Ronan woke an hour or so before sundown. Though legend and lore had it that vampires were helpless until the sun went down, he had found that he could rise before sunset so long as he stayed inside, out of the reach of the sun, hence the heavy draperies that covered all the windows in the house.

He slept in a large room located in the basement. The door, made of stone, had no handle and was virtually invisible to the human eye. A heavy iron bar on the inside of the door ensured that, should an intruder inadvertently discover the entrance, he wouldn't be able to gain access. The walls were also made of stone, as was the floor, which was covered with a thick gray carpet. There was an easy chair in one corner, a couple of tables, a large armoire where he kept his clothing, a small sink and a shower behind a hand-painted screen, and the bed in which he slept. He had no need for lights.

Rising, he showered and dressed and then went upstairs.

He found Shannah still sleeping. She looked incredibly young and vulnerable lying there, her cheek pillowed on her hand, her hair spread over her shoulders.

Hunger surged through him, and with it the urge to slip under the covers, to draw her into his arms and satisfy both of his cravings.

In the future, he would have to feed before he sought her out. He was about to go in search of prey when she stirred. A sigh whispered past her lips. Her eyelids fluttered open.

"Ronan. Good morn . . ." She laughed softly. "I guess I should say good evening."

He nodded. "Why don't you shower and dress? I'll meet you downstairs."

"All right. What time is it?"

"A little after seven." He hated daylight savings time, when the days were longer and the nights shorter.

Approaching the bed, he brushed a kiss across her brow. It was a mistake. He could hear the slow, steady beat of her heart, smell the blood flowing in her veins. Her skin was soft and warm beneath his lips. The taste of her, the very nearness of her, only increased his desire to hold her, to taste her, to possess her fully and completely as only a vampire could.

"I'll see you downstairs," he said, his voice thick, and then he fled the room before his hunger for her blood and his desire for her flesh overcame his will power.

It took only moments to find his prey—a young woman

waiting for a downtown bus. He mesmerized her with a look and led her away from the bus stop toward a movie theater on the next block. He bought two tickets and led her inside to a seat in the back row. Putting his arm around her shoulders, he drew her close, taking what he needed while she stared, spellbound, at the screen.

Speaking to her mind, he told her to forget what had happened and remember only that she had, on impulse, gone to the movies.

He returned home quickly and was sitting on the sofa when Shannah descended the stairs.

She was lovely, as always. Her hair fell down her back in waves of black silk, her eyes were bright, her smile warm. She wore a pair of white jeans that clung to her like a second skin and a green sweater that flattered every feminine curve.

"I'm going to fix something to eat," she said. "Are you sure you won't join me . . . oh, I keep forgetting." She frowned at him. "Why do you eat alone? Are your table manners that bad?"

He laughed softly. "What are you going to fix, breakfast or dinner?"

She frowned. "Well, since this is now going to be my morning, I guess I'll fix breakfast. Most important meal of the day, you know. Are you sure you won't change your mind?"

"Not tonight. I think I'll write for a while," he said. "We can go out later, if you like."

"I'd rather stay home. I'm feeling a little tired."

He looked at her sharply, wondering if it was time to give her a little more of his blood.

"I'm all right," she said. "It's just going to take a little while to get used to these hours."

With a nod, he left the room and went down the hall to his office. Sitting at his desk, he fired up the computer and pulled up his latest work in progress, then he sat back in his chair and stared at the screen, wondering how long he could keep her from finding out who and what he was, and what she would do when she discovered the truth.

And then there was Jim Hewitt, vampire hunter, to consider. It was obvious the man was hunting him. Sooner or later, he would have to confront Hewitt. Most likely, he would have to kill him.

With a shake of his head, he put everything else from his mind and tried to focus on his story, but to no avail. He was all too aware of the woman in the kitchen. Her presence filled his senses. Each breath he took carried the scent of her hair, her skin, her blood, the light flowery fragrance of her perfume, the strawberry scent of her shampoo.

His heart beat in time with hers. His fangs pricked his tongue. His hunger, so recently fed, stirred to life once more. She was here, under his roof.

She was mortal.

She was prey.

He listened to her footsteps as she moved around the kitchen, the swish of cloth against her skin, the clink of dishes as she set the table, the sound of running water, the sizzle of bacon frying in a pan.

And his hunger grew.

Cursing softly, he rose and shut the door, hoping that would help, but to no avail. Had he been blind and deaf, he could have found her in the bottom of a well at midnight. He had taken her blood and given her his. There was a bond between them that could not be broken so long as she lived, a bond that called to him relentlessly, urging him to drink deeply, to drink it all and then give it back to her. To do so would heal her once and for all.

It would make her what he was, a creature of the night. Undead. A vampire.

Once again, he reminded himself that she had come to him seeking just such a thing.

As he had so often, he wondered if she would want the Dark Trick if she knew that he could give it to her.

Pushing all thoughts of Shannah from his mind, he forced himself to concentrate on the task at hand, frowning as the words that flowed across his computer screen echoed his own internal struggle.

He had been writing for several hours when her knock came at the door.

"Come on in," he called.

She opened the door and peeked inside. "Am I interrupting?"

"Yes, but it's a welcome one. I was just about to quit for the night."

"Good. There's a movie on TV I've been wanting to see. Do you want to watch it with me?"

"Sure." He saved his work and switched off his computer, then followed her into the living room.

She curled up on the sofa and he sat beside her, scarcely aware of the story being enacted on the screen. His whole being was centered on the woman beside him, each breath she took, each movement she made, each beat of her heart, the way the lamplight shone in her hair, the curve of her cheek, the smooth line of her neck, the pulse that beat in the hollow of her throat. She laughed at something on the screen and the sound wrapped around his heart like a mother's love surrounds her child.

He had it bad, he thought ruefully. After more than five hundred years, he was hopelessly, helplessly, in love.

As though feeling his scrutiny, she turned to face him, and he was lost. In five hundred years, he had never

wanted a woman as badly as he wanted the fragile creature sitting beside him. He wanted to hold her, protect
her, shower her with his love. He intended to do whatever necessary to make her happy. He would grant her
anything she wanted, anything she needed, if she would
only stay with him as long as she lived. In exchange, he
would give her his blood as needed. With him, she
would want for nothing.

"Ronan?"

"Hmm?"

"Why are you looking at me like that?"

"Like what?"

"Like I'm Little Red Riding Hood and you're the Big
Bad Wolf."

"Perhaps because I'd like to devour you."

She blinked at him, her expression making it obvious
that she didn't know if he was kidding her or not.

"You must know I want you," he said quietly.

Her eyes grew wide. "Y . . . yes."

"And you want me."

She nodded.

"Tell me what you want."

Shannah licked her lips, then shook her head. She
didn't know what she wanted.

When he was holding her, kissing her, she was certain
she wanted him to take her to bed and make love to her
all night long. But now, with his dark gaze holding hers,
she wasn't sure. She didn't think he would hurt her.
Quite the opposite. She was sure he would be a gentle
lover, tender and thoughtful, but . . . she knew it was
wrong. It went against everything she had been taught
while growing up, both by her parents and her church.
And yet, it didn't seem fair. She was dying and, right or
wrong, she didn't want to die a virgin. Still, did she want
to die with the sin of fornication on her conscience?

"Shannah?"

She shook her head. "I don't know." Why didn't he just sweep her into his arms and seduce her? Kiss her until all thought of right or wrong was forgotten? Coward, she thought. If he seduced her, she could secretly revel in his touch and still tell herself it wasn't her fault . . .

She looked into his eyes, those deep dark eyes that seemed to hold all the secrets of the universe, and knew if she stayed another minute, she would be lost.

"I think I'll go get something to drink," she said, scrambling off the sofa. "Can I get you anything?"

He shook his head, his expression telling her clearly that he was well aware of what she was doing, and why.

"I think I'll go write for another hour or two," he said. "Will you be all right?"

Blinking back her tears, she went into the kitchen, wondering if he was sorry he had asked her to stay.

Chapter Nineteen

Shannah woke to the sound of someone leaning on the doorbell. Rolling over, she stared blearily at the clock on the bedside table. It was a little after ten a.m. Who could possibly be coming to call at this hour? Or any hour? She didn't have any friends in North Canyon Creek, and as far as she knew, Ronan never had visitors. Deciding it was probably a solicitor of some kind, she closed her eyes and pulled the covers over her head. Whoever it was, they could come back later.

The doorbell rang again, louder and more insistent.

Shannah pounded on her pillow. Why didn't they go away? Grabbing her robe, she pulled it on as she padded down the stairs to the front door.

"Who is it?" she called irritably.

"Jim Hewitt."

Suddenly wide awake, Shannah stared at the door as if it was a snake that might bite her. Hewitt! What on earth was he doing here? "What do you want?"

"I need to talk to you, Miss Black."

"So talk."

"It's important, Eva. It's about Ronan."

Shannah felt her heart skip a beat. "What about him?"

"This isn't something I can discuss out here on the front porch."

"I'm sorry, I'm not in the habit of inviting strangers into the house."

She couldn't be sure, but she thought she heard him swear.

"There's a coffee shop in town," he said. "The Pot Pourri. Do you know it?"

"Yes." It was the coffee shop where she used to spend her evenings, the one where she had been the first time she saw Ronan walking down the street.

"I'll meet you there in, what, half an hour?"

"How did you get through the gate?"

"Does it matter?"

She wondered if Hewitt had climbed over the back wall, the way she had. She would have to tell Ronan his security fence wasn't as safe as he thought.

"Miss Black?"

"Yes, all right, I'll be there."

Going upstairs, she dressed quickly, brushed her hair and her teeth, grabbed her handbag and the keys to Ronan's car, and headed for town, determined to find out how Jim Hewitt knew where she lived, and why he had followed her to North Canyon Creek.

Shannah entered the Pot Pourri a little over thirty minutes later. Jim Hewitt was sitting at a booth near the door. He wore a white shirt open at the throat and a brown sports jacket. He rose when he saw her.

Taking a deep breath, she walked toward him. As she neared the curved booth, she saw that he wasn't alone.

Carl Overstreet nodded at her. "Hey, Miss Black. It's good to see you again."

She nodded at the newspaperman, then sat down.

Hewitt slid in beside her, sandwiching her in between the two men. She didn't like it. It made her feel trapped. And more than a little uneasy. She assured herself there was nothing to worry about. It was broad daylight. They were in a public place. The café was crowded, and there was a cop sitting at the counter.

She glanced from one man to the other. "So, what's this all about?"

"How long have you known Ronan?" Hewitt asked.

"A few months, not that it's any of your business."

"How well do you know him?"

She shrugged. "As well as you can know anyone in a couple of months." She glanced from Hewitt to Overstreet. "Either tell me what this is about, or I'm leaving."

"What does he do during the day?" Overstreet asked.

"I don't know. Why don't you ask him?" She looked at Hewitt. "Get out of my way. I'm leaving."

"Please," Hewitt said, "this is important."

As tempted as she was to tell him to go to hell, her curiosity won out. "Go on."

"Have you ever seen him in the middle of the afternoon?" Hewitt asked.

Feeling suddenly cold, she stared at Hewitt. "No."

"Have you ever seen him eat?"

"No," she said, and then frowned. "I mean, I did, once," she said, remembering her mother's apple pie and Ronan's reaction to it.

"You actually saw him eat something?"

"Yes, but . . ."

"But what?"

"It made him sick. He said he was allergic to it."

"Allergic!" Hewitt slammed his hand on the table. "That's a good one. Do you know why he doesn't eat?"

"No, but I'm sure you're going to tell me."

Carl Overstreet leaned forward. "What do you know about vampires?"

The chill in Shannah's blood turned to ice. "Only that they don't exist, except in books and movies."

Now Hewitt leaned forward, his expression intense. "What if I told you they do exist?"

"I wouldn't believe you."

"He's one of them."

She stared at Hewitt, and then she laughed. "No, he isn't. I've seen him during the day."

"Yeah?" Overstreet said. "What time?"

"I don't know. I guess it was around five or six, but the sun was still up, so he can't be a vampire."

"Older vampires can rise before sundown."

Shannah stared at Hewitt. Ronan, a vampire? Had she been right all along?

"What does all this have to do with me?"

"I want to know where he takes his rest," Hewitt said.

"I want to interview him for my magazine," Overstreet said.

Shannah looked at the two men, and then she burst out laughing. "You're crazy," she said, wiping tears from her eyes. "Both of you. I don't know where he sleeps, and I wouldn't tell you if I did. And as for doing an interview, I can assure you that he won't."

"Listen," Hewitt said, "as long as you stay with him, your life is in danger. Do you understand that?"

"Believe me, I'm perfectly safe there."

"What can I say to convince you?" Hewitt asked.

"Nothing. He's not a vampire and I'm not in any danger. Now, if you'll excuse me, I'm going home."

Hewitt reached into his jacket pocket and withdrew a business card. "Call my cell phone if you change your mind," he said, handing her the card. "I don't know what he's told you, but I can assure you that he is a vampire. A very old vampire. I'd hate for you to be his next victim."

Shannah slipped the card into the pocket of her jeans, then looked pointedly at Hewitt, who slid out of the booth so that she could leave.

She didn't look back, but she could feel both of the men watching her as she left the café. She thought about what Hewitt and Overstreet had said as she drove home. What if they were right? What if Ronan was a vampire? Was she in danger?

She shook the thought away. If he had wanted to do her harm, he'd had plenty of opportunity. She had been at Ronan's mercy since the day she met him. If he was a vampire, he could have taken her blood or killed her at any time. Instead, he had taken her in and cared for her.

She frowned. Why had he done that? He hadn't known anything about her at the time.

Pulling into the driveway, she parked the car in front of the house, then sat there for a moment, one finger tapping nervously on the steering wheel. What should she do now? Go inside and pretend nothing unusual had happened today? Confront him? Pack up and leave? But she had no place to stay, now that she had given up her apartment, no place to go except home to her parents. Home. Maybe that was the answer. Maybe that had always been the answer.

Why did Jim Hewitt want to know where Ronan slept? The answer popped into her mind immediately. Thinking him to be a vampire, Hewitt and Overstreet undoubtedly wanted to destroy him, and after reading Ronan's books, she knew that such a thing was best done in the middle of the day, when the sun was high in the sky and the vampire was trapped in sleep, helpless to defend himself.

Did Ronan sleep in a coffin?

Was it somewhere in the house?

Exiting the car, she went up the steps and into the house, careful to lock the door behind her in case Hewitt and Overstreet decided to show up again. Unlike vampires, who had to have an invitation to enter a person's home, Hewitt and Overstreet could burst in un-invited and unannounced. She remembered the night Ronan had shown up at her apartment. He had knocked on the door, demanding that she let him in. She had ex-pected him to storm inside when she unlocked the door, but he had stood in the hallway and asked if he could come inside.

She shook her head, not knowing what to think, what to believe. She had come to his house looking for a vam-pire, not really believing that she would find one. But what if she had?

Shannah glanced at the clock. It was only eleven-thirty. Ronan never made an appearance this early in the day.

She stood in the middle of the floor, wondering if she was making a mistake by staying. Was she being foolish, like those silly girls in horror movies who went into the basement when there was a monster in the house?

Was there a monster in this house? Wise or foolish, she couldn't leave until she knew the truth, heard it from Ronan's own lips.

Too nervous to sit still, too agitated to go back to bed, Shannah found a cloth and a bottle of furniture polish and began to dust. Moving from room to room, she told her-self she was just trying to pass the hours until dusk, but she checked each room carefully, rapping on the walls, check-ing inside closets and cupboards, looking for hidden doors or passages, running her hands over books and door frames and wall sconces in hopes of finding a lever that would lead to some hidden hideaway, but to no avail.

Moving upstairs, she made a similar search of all the

empty rooms, again with no success. Going into the bedroom where she slept, she checked the walls and the
closet, looked behind the furniture and the doors, exploring every nook and cranny, but she didn't find anything. No hidden doors or passageways, nothing the
least bit suspicious.

Discouraged but relieved, she went downstairs and
fixed herself a glass of iced tea, grabbed her sunglasses
and a magazine, and went outside to sit in the sun.

Leaning back in the chaise lounge, her eyes closed,
she murmured, "Ronan, where are you?" and almost
spilled tea in her lap when his image leaped into her
mind.

He was lying in a sleek black coffin in a dark room. She
wondered briefly how she could see anything at all when
there was no light in the room, but she could see him
clearly. His eyes were closed, his arms folded across his
chest. He wore a black T-shirt and a pair of black sweatpants. His feet were bare. A distant part of her mind
found that incredibly endearing.

Gasping, she opened her eyes and the image vanished.
It was true, she thought, he really was a vampire.

She spent the rest of the afternoon trying to decide
what to do. One minute she was certain that she should
not only leave his house but leave the state as fast as possible, the next she was remembering the soul-stirring
passion of his kisses, the fervor in his voice when he said
he needed her. He made her feel whole, complete.
Loved.

When the sun began to set, she went into the house
intending to fix something to eat, only to find she had
no appetite.

She was sitting on the sofa, still trying to decide what
she should do, when he entered the room.

She looked at him through narrowed eyes, as if seeing

him for the first time. He didn't look like a vampire. He looked like a perfectly normal, healthy male in his late twenties or early thirties.

He smiled as he walked toward her. There was no hint of fang in his smile, though his teeth were remarkably straight and white.

"I was hoping to find you in bed and kiss you awake." His voice was deep, filled with the promise of dark delights.

She forced a smile, suddenly unable to speak for the cold knot of fear that sat in her belly like a block of ice.

"Is something wrong?" he asked.

She shook her head, her heart pounding as he sat down on the sofa beside her, making her acutely aware of how big he was. His shoulders were broad, his arms long and well-muscled, his hands large and strong.

"Something's troubling you," he said. "You might as well tell me what it is."

"Jim Hewitt and Carl Overstreet came to see me today."

His eyes narrowed; one hand clenched into a tight fist. "Indeed?"

"All this time, I thought Hewitt was following me, but I was wrong. It's you he's after, isn't it?"

"Why would he be after me?"

"I don't know, but I'm sure that you do."

"What did he tell you?"

"He said . . ." She took a deep breath. Her last, perhaps? "He said that you're a vampire."

She waited for him to laugh, waited for him to deny it, to say something, anything, to prove that Hewitt was out of his mind. Instead, he simply stared at her for several taut moments during which time she could scarcely breathe.

"You came looking for one of the Undead," he said

at last. "What are you going to do, now that you've found one?"

His words struck her like a blast of icy wind, leaving her momentarily numb. She knew, in that moment, that she had never truly believed he was a vampire. Even when she had come knocking on his door, she hadn't really believed he was a vampire. Now, looking back, she realized that, due to her illness, she hadn't been thinking clearly. Still, it was strange that she had felt so much better since coming to stay with him. But if he was a vampire, why hadn't he drained her dry, or made her what he was?

"I . . . I don't believe you." She couldn't believe it. It was simply too frightening to contemplate, too bizarre to be real.

"It's true nonetheless."

She lifted a trembling hand to her neck. "Why haven't you bitten me, then? Isn't that what vampires do?"

He nodded, his gaze never leaving her face.

Her eyes grew wide. "Have you . . . did you bite me?" Her eyes grew wider still. "Am I going to turn into a vampire?"

"No, Shannah. But I have tasted your blood, and given you mine."

She stared at him in stunned disbelief. And then shook her head. "No! I don't believe you! I'd never forget something so . . . so vile."

"You would, if I didn't want you to remember."

"So, now you're a hypnotist as well as a vampire?"

He didn't say anything, just continued to watch her, like a hungry wolf watching a lamb.

She frowned, her thoughts chasing themselves like mice in a maze. Her mind cleared suddenly, as if someone had lifted a veil from her memories. It was true. He had given her his blood on several occasions. "That's why I feel better, isn't it?"

He nodded again, his gaze still on her face.

"Oh, Lord," she murmured, "Hewitt was right." She laughed out loud as hysteria threatened to overcome her. "I was right! You are a vampire."

"Shannah, calm down. There's nothing for you to be afraid of."

"Nothing? You're a vampire!" She recalled the vision she'd had of him earlier, asleep in his coffin. That, more than anything else, convinced her that it was true. Scrambling off the sofa, she ran for the front door.

And plowed into the very man she was trying to escape.

She looked up at him, her eyes wide and scared. She glanced back at the sofa, where he had been sitting only moments before.

"How . . . how did you . . . ?" Her voice trailed off as black spots danced before her eyes and then she was falling, pitching headlong into a sea of darkness.

Chapter Twenty

When she woke, she was in bed and Ronan was standing beside her. She looked up at him. He didn't look like a vampire. Maybe she had dreamed the whole thing.

"No," he said, "it wasn't a dream."

She blinked at him, startled. "How do you know what I was thinking?"

"I can read your thoughts."

She shook her head. "That's impossible!"

"Is it?"

"What am I thinking now?"

"You're wondering what I'm going to do with you."

She swallowed. It was exactly what she had been thinking. "What are you going to do?"

She flinched when he sat on the edge of the bed.

"Shannah, why are you suddenly afraid of me? Have I ever done anything to hurt you?"

"No."

"You came to me looking for a vampire," he reminded her again. "I can give you what you came looking for, if that's what you truly want."

She looked at him, speechless, the fear inside of her growing even as she told herself that no matter what he said, vampires didn't exist. It was impossible. A myth. And yet the signs had been there all the time. He didn't eat. She never saw him until it was almost dark. There were no mirrors in the house.

He had taken her blood.

"Is it what you want?" he asked. "To be a vampire?"

"No." She shuddered at the mere idea. "Vampires kill people. They drink blood."

He didn't deny it.

She sat up, clutching the covers with both hands as if they could protect her. "Have you killed people?" It was a silly question. She had been there when he killed that man in New York City.

"I'm a vampire."

"What kind of answer is that?" she asked irritably.

He shrugged. "An honest one."

"That man in New York, did you . . . did you drink from him?"

He nodded.

"I read in a book once that vampires could survive on the blood of animals. Is that true?"

"Yes." When necessary, he had dined on the blood of beasts. It provided sustenance, but no pleasure.

"The plane crash . . ." Her brows rushed together in a frown as she tried to remember something important, something elusive. Trying to recall it made her head ache. One thing she did remember was his promise that no matter what happened, he would keep her safe. At the time, she had wondered how he could make such a promise. "I would have died in the crash if not for you, wouldn't I? It wasn't fate that saved me, it was you."

He nodded.

She thought of all the people on the flight, especially the children, who had died. "Couldn't you have saved everyone?"

"No."

"Would you, if you could have?"

"Yes, but once the plane started going down, there was nothing I could do to stop it. I had only a few minutes to get the two of us out of there."

She pondered that a moment, thinking there was no longer any reason for her feel guilty. It hadn't been some random quirk of fate that had saved her, she thought. Then again, maybe it was. Maybe it had been the hand of Providence that had led her to Ronan's door in the first place.

"Does it hurt, becoming a vampire, I mean."

He thought about it a moment, trying to remember. There had been a certain amount of discomfort as his mortal body died, but it had been brief and quickly forgotten as preternatural power flowed through him. He had fallen into a lethargic state with the rising of the sun. When darkness had fallen, he had risen as a new creature, every sense magnified, his body humming with vitality and power and a hellish thirst.

"Ronan?"

"There is a little pain, but nothing as bad as what you're suffering now."

"Can you feel what I'm feeling, too?"

"I know you're hurting." She was needing his blood more and more often, no doubt a sign that the disease was growing worse, and that her time was growing shorter.

Her fingers kneaded the edge of the blanket. "I don't know what to do. I don't want to make a decision I'll be sorry for later."

He nodded, his dark eyes filled with understanding. "It was not a life I would have chosen," he remarked. "It was thrust upon me, and yet . . ." He paused a moment, looking inward. "I do not regret it now."

"How long have you been a vampire?"

"Five hundred and thirteen years."

"Five hundred and thirteen years!" she exclaimed. "Oh, my."

"A long time," he remarked, as if realizing it for the first time.

"No kidding." Five hundred years. Shannah could scarcely imagine such a thing. She studied him carefully. Who would ever believe he had been born five centuries ago? She was certainly having trouble believing it! "To live so long," she murmured. It was incredible. "The things you must have seen, but . . . five hundred years."

He grunted softly. It seemed like an eternity, the way she said it. Of course, it was a long time for anyone to live, man or vampire. Strange, how quickly the years and centuries had gone by. Time was something he rarely thought of these days except in terms of book deadlines. He had roamed the world, never in a hurry. What he didn't see this year would still be there the next year or the next. In his travels, he had seen the Great Pyramids of Giza. The pyramid had been built by the Egyptian pharaoh, Khufu, of the Fourth Dynasty around the year 2560 BC to serve as his tomb when he died. An Arab proverb stated that, "Man fears time, time fears the pyramids."

He had seen the Taj Mahal in India, built by Shah Jehan who had ordered the building of the Taj Mahal in honor of his wife, who had borne him fourteen children in eighteen years and died in childbirth.

He had walked among the stones at Stonehenge in England, prowled the ruins of Machu Picchu in the mountains of Peru, strolled in the shadow of the Great Wall of China, stared in wonder at the Coliseum in Rome.

And all of it alone. What would it be like to see it all anew through Shannah's eyes?

Shannah. She was regarding him curiously, her head cocked to one side.

"Is there something else you want to know?" he asked.

"Why don't you just read my mind?" she muttered, somewhat flippantly.

"Sometimes conversation is pleasant. What's troubling you?"

"I was just thinking . . . you've lived for over five hundred years . . ."

"Go on."

"You must have known a lot of women in that time."

"Do I detect a note of jealousy in your voice?"

She shrugged. "I guess you've been married several times."

"No. Just once, when I was still a mortal man."

"Really?" She couldn't hide her shock. "Why? Haven't you been awfully lonely?"

"At times."

"Surely you've . . . I mean, in five hundred years, you must have . . ." She felt her cheeks grow hot as a new thought occurred to her. Maybe vampires couldn't make love. Maybe they were impotent. But no, she had felt the telltale evidence of his desire for her on several occasions.

"I haven't lived like a monk, if that's what you're wondering," he said dryly. "I may be a vampire, but I'm still a man."

"Do the women know what you are when you make love to them?"

"What do you think?"

"I guess not." She frowned. "Is that why you always stopped when we were . . . you know?"

He nodded. "The lust for flesh and the lust for blood are tightly interwoven and you, my sweet, are far too tempting."

The thought repulsed and fascinated her at the same time. "So, what's it like, being a vampire?"

"In many ways, it's no different from being mortal. Except for the obvious, of course."

"Of course. And you don't miss the sun, or food and stuff like that?"

"Not anymore."

She pondered that a moment, then sighed. "This is all so confusing and unbelievable. I'm sure I'll wake up tomorrow and find this whole conversation was just some sort of fever dream."

He took her hand in his and kissed her palm. The touch of his lips, the heat of his tongue on her skin, sent shivers of delight racing up her arm.

"It's not a dream, Shannah, and it's not a nightmare, unless you want it to be."

"What do you mean?"

"I can take you home to your parents and make you forget I ever existed," he said quietly. "I can make you forget you ever came here, that we ever met."

"You can?"

"If that's what you want."

She thought about it a moment, then shook her head. "No, I don't want to forget."

"What do you want?"

"You don't look like a vampire."

"No?" He stared at the pulse throbbing in the hollow of her throat, let his hunger rise within him, felt his fangs lengthen.

He knew when his eyes burned red by the sudden look of horror on her face. He ran his tongue over the tips of his fangs, then asked, "Is this what you wanted to see?"

For a moment, he feared she would faint again, and then she leaned forward. "Does it hurt, when they come out?" she asked, pointing at his fangs.

He laughed softly. Once again, she had surprised him. "No, it doesn't hurt."

"Could you change back to Ronan now?"

He took a deep breath, felt his fangs retract as the force of his will overcame the urge to feed.

"Thank you." She shook her head. "No one will ever believe any of this."

"You can't tell anyone, Shannah. You must know that."

"Carl Overstreet will be very disappointed to hear that."

"Overstreet! What's he got to do with anything?"

"He wants to interview you."

"Interview with a vampire?" Ronan muttered wryly. "I think that's already been done."

Shannah laughed, then turned serious once more. "Who is Jim Hewitt? You said you knew him. He told me he was a reporter, but he isn't, is he?"

"No, he's a vampire hunter, and not a particularly good one, or he would have been dead long ago."

Her eyes widened. "You wouldn't . . ."

"I would."

She nibbled on her lower lip, then nodded. "I guess it would be self-defense, in a way."

"It's the first law of the jungle," he said flatly. "Preservation of one's own life."

"I guess so . . ." She closed her eyes, suddenly weary.

"Shannah?"

"Hmm?"

"Are you all right?"

"I don't know. I feel so sleepy all of a sudden."

"Yes," he said, "you're tired. Very tired. You're going to go to sleep now and dream only wonderful, happy dreams."

"Happy dreams," she murmured.

"I'm going to give you something to drink, and it's going to taste good."

"Good . . ."

"But you won't remember drinking it tomorrow."

"I won't remember . . ."

"Sleep now."

He waited until her breathing was slow and regular before he bit into his wrist and pressed it to her lips.

Chapter Twenty-One

"So," Overstreet said, "what do we do now?"

Hewitt shrugged. "Wait, I guess."

"What do you think she'll do?"

"I'm not sure. I guess she'll either pack up and head for the hills or she'll confront him with what we told her."

"That could be dangerous," Overstreet remarked. "What if he decides to dispose of her to shut her up?"

"It's a possibility, but it was a chance we had to take."

"Yeah, well, I'd hate for anything to happen to the girl," Overstreet said, "but I'm more worried about my own neck right now."

Hewitt nodded. "At least we know that he's in the house, or somewhere nearby. If she won't tell us where he sleeps, we'll just have to go in and have a look around."

"How do you plan to do that?"

"I'm working on it."

"Well, work faster. My next column is due soon."

Hewitt nodded. "I need to get a few things together before we go hunting."

Overstreet laughed. "Gonna hit the local Vampires R Us store?"

"Something like that," Hewitt said, grinning. "And then we'll pay Miss Black another visit."

Carl Overstreet grinned as he read over what he had written.

Well, dear reader, just a quick update on my search to discover if vampires do, indeed, exist. I know, I know, a lot of you are skeptical, but I can tell you, with absolute certainty, that vampires are real and that they dwell among us. I met a woman who knows one. I, myself, have seen this creature and I can tell you that our vampire is not gaunt and pale. His palms aren't hairy. Far from it. He looks like any other normal male. My partner in this endeavor is a professional vampire hunter, one who has destroyed vampires in many cities across the land. Vampires exist, dear reader, never doubt it.

For the real skinny, be sure to read my article next month.

In the meantime, here are a few pertinent facts. If you find disturbed earth or constant mists at a gravesite, disturbed coffins, holes in the ground, footsteps leading away from the grave, or hear a groaning from under the earth, you might want to make sure that the deceased is truly deceased.

Should you find a vampire, a stake through the heart is the most common way to dispose of the creature. Beheading is also recommended, though a bit messy. Sunlight may or may not work, as some ancient vampires are immune. Cremation is effective; the ashes should be scattered.

There are numerous ways said to be effective in protecting yourself against a vampire. They include hanging garlic around the windows and doors and around your neck. Holy water will burn them; it can also effectively be sprinkled around windows and doors and over thresholds. Staying in after dark might be the best defense of all, as the Undead can't enter a dwelling place without an invitation.

Until next time, dear reader, watch your neck!

Chapter Twenty-Two

Shannah woke late the next morning feeling bright-eyed and bushy-tailed. Sitting up, she stretched her arms over her head and smiled. Slipping out of bed, she pulled on her robe and went downstairs, noting, as she did so, that she felt strong again. Odd, how one day she felt as if she was at death's door and the next she felt like she could run a marathon. She paused on the steps as a sudden recollection of the bizarre conversation she'd had with Ronan the night before jumped to the forefront of her mind.

He was a five hundred year old vampire.

She frowned as she continued on down the stairs. There was something else, something he had told her that she couldn't quite recall. It suddenly seemed important that she remember what it was.

Going into the kitchen, she turned on the coffeemaker, then sat down at the table, her chin cradled in her palm. What was it that she couldn't remember? She closed her eyes, her fingertips drumming on the tabletop. They had been talking about what it was like to be a vampire when a sudden weariness had overtaken her. She had told Ronan she was sleepy and the next thing she remembered was waking up in her bed. Why couldn't she remember what happened between last night and this morning?

Rising, she poured herself a cup of coffee, then put a couple of slices of bread into the toaster. When it was done, she opened the refrigerator to get the butter, and saw a bottle of tomato juice. The contents were red. As red as blood . . .

And she remembered. He had given her his blood last night. And he had told her that he had given her his blood on other occasions as well, given it to her and then wiped the memory of having done so from her memory. She could hear his voice now, in the back of her mind.

I'm going to give you something to drink, he had said, his voice low and seductive, *and it's going to taste good. But you won't remember drinking it tomorrow.*

Frowning, she closed the refrigerator door. Why could she remember what he had said today when she had forgotten it all those other times? How could she ever have forgotten something as gross as drinking someone else's blood? And a vampire's blood, at that. She picked up a slice of toast only to find that her appetite was gone. With a shake of her head, she dropped it down the garbage disposal.

A glance at the clock showed it was only a little after eleven. So much for keeping his hours, she thought.

Leaving the kitchen, she wandered through the house, the word "vampire" repeating in her mind over and over again.

After a time, she went into the kitchen for another cup of coffee. She sat at the table, wondering where his lair was. He didn't seem to have any trouble finding her. He had found her at her apartment. He had found her at the restaurant. He had found her at a hotel after the plane crash. Why couldn't she find him?

Sitting there, she formed a mental image of Ronan— long black hair, dark eyes, strong masculine features and physique. She imagined a fine wire stretched from her thoughts to his, and then frowned. If he was sleeping the sleep of the dead, or the Undead, he wouldn't be having any thoughts, would he? She would have to try something else. He had taken her blood and given her his. According to the books he wrote, books she knew now were based on fact, a blood exchange was supposed to form some kind of supernatural bond between the vampire and the one he had shared blood with.

She finished her coffee and put the cup aside, then stood in the middle of the room, her eyes closed, and concentrated on Ronan. She lost track of time as she stood there, waiting, though she wasn't sure exactly what it was she was waiting for.

Gradually, into her mind came the same image she'd had before, of Ronan lying in a casket. When nothing happened, she conjured a mental image of blood, a deep red river of blood, flowing between them, and as she did so, she felt herself being drawn toward the door in the kitchen that led into the basement.

Opening the door, she turned on the light and went down the stairs, her feet carrying her toward the far wall. She ran her hands over the wall, searching for a secret lever, a break in the stone, something. Anything. But there was nothing there.

With a shake of her head, she was about to turn away when something urged her to try again. Taking a deep breath, all her energy focused on Ronan, she placed her hands against the wall once again. She gasped as something like an electric shock ran up her arms. He was on the other side of the wall. She knew it as surely as she knew he would rise with the setting of the sun.

He was in there, and she would be out here, waiting for him when he awoke.

* * *

Ronan came awake as the sun began to set. One minute he was lost in the oblivion of his kind, the next he was awake and aware of everything around him.

Aware that Shannah was waiting for him on the other side of the door.

Rising, he ran a hand through his hair, wondering how she had found him and how long she had been waiting in the basement.

He considered changing his clothes; then, figuring she had waited long enough, he took a deep breath, lifted the heavy iron bar and opened the door.

She was pacing the floor, her back toward him.

"Good evening, Shannah."

She jumped, startled by the sound of his voice, then whirled around to face him. She started to speak, but the words stuck in her throat when she glanced through the open doorway and saw the coffin beyond.

"It's true," she murmured, her face going pale. "It's all true, isn't it?"

"I thought we had established that last night." He frowned. "You're not going to faint on me, are you?"

"I don't know."

He took a cautious step toward her and when she didn't back away, he slipped his arm around her waist to steady her.

"I don't know what's wrong with me. I knew it was true, that you were really a vampire," she said, her gaze riveted on the casket. "At least I thought I did . . ."

"It's just a bed, Shannah."

She laughed humorlessly. "A bed with a lid."

"How did you find me?"

"What?" She looked up at him, her eyes wide and scared.

"Are you afraid of me, now?"

She glanced through the open doorway again, then lifted her gaze to his. "I don't know. Does it matter?"

"It matters to me."

She searched her heart and then shook her head. "No, I'm not afraid, not of you."

"Of what I am?"

"Yes," she murmured, staring at the casket again. "A little."

He grasped her chin between his thumb and forefinger and lifted her face toward him. "How did you find me?"

"I'm not sure. But you always seemed to be able to find me, so I thought . . . I just focused on you . . . I'd seen you in my mind once before, you know. Anyway, I focused on you and on the blood we had shared, and it drew me down here and . . . you're not going to believe this, but when I touched the wall, I knew you were on the other side."

"Shannah, calm down. Take a deep breath. That's right. Nothing's changed. I'm the same as I've always been."

"I know, I know, but . . ." She pointed toward the open door and the casket beyond. "It's just so . . . I don't know." She looked up at him, her eyes swimming with tears. "I don't want to die!"

"You don't have to."

She shook her head. "I don't want to be what you are. I don't want to sleep in a . . . in one of those. I don't want to die every time the sun goes down! I'm afraid, Ronan, I'm so afraid."

"Shh. There now, love, there's nothing to fear. Hush, now." Taking her hand in his, he led her up the stairs and into the kitchen. Closing the door behind him, he took her into the living room. Sitting on the sofa, he drew her onto his lap, one hand slowly stroking her back and her hair. "Don't cry, love, I won't let you die."

"I don't . . ."

"My blood will keep you alive, Shannah, just the way it

has been since you first came here. If you can't accept it, I'll wipe the memory from your mind each time, just as I have before."

She sniffed. "But it doesn't work."

"What doesn't work?"

"Erasing the memory from my mind. Last night, you told me I wouldn't remember . . ." She shuddered. "You told me I wouldn't remember drinking your blood, but I did."

He swore softly. That changed things. "Shannah, look at me. Can you read my mind?"

"No, of course not," she said, then frowned. "You're thinking that things have changed. You're wondering why your suggestions aren't working anymore." Her eyes widened. "Why can I read your mind?"

"The bond between us must be stronger than I thought." He erected a mental barrier between them. "Try again."

She concentrated for several moments, then shook her head. "What did you do?"

"I wanted to see if I could block you."

"Why? Don't you want me to know what you're thinking?"

"It was just a test, love. This is new to me, too."

"Is it?"

He nodded. "I've never bonded with anyone else."

She didn't know what to say. Didn't know what to do except rest her head on his shoulder and trust that he would take care of her.

He held her in his arms until she fell asleep and then he carried her up the stairs and put her to bed. He sat beside her, watching her sleep until night gradually turned to day.

As the first faint streaks of light began to steal the darkness from the sky, he brushed a lock of hair away from her brow, acknowledging once again that he was hopelessly, helplessly in love with her.

Chapter Twenty-Three

"I have an idea," Ronan remarked thoughtfully.

Shannah glanced at him. "What kind of an idea?"

They were sitting in the living room in front of the fireplace. Shannah had finished her dinner and Ronan had just returned from the hunt. Neither had mentioned where he had been or what they had discussed the night before.

"I want to introduce you to some others of my kind."

"What? Why?" Her expression made it clear she wasn't at all keen on the idea of meeting other vampires.

He took her hand in his and gave it a squeeze. "Because even I can't keep you alive forever."

"Ronan . . ."

"I want you to get a taste of what it's like to live as a vampire, to see that, except for the obvious differences, they live like everyone else."

"I can see that just by living here, with you."

"No. In the last seventy years or so, I've lived like a hermit, staying in this house most of the time, content to concentrate on my books and my writing. It wasn't until you came along that I realized how much I've been missing, how cut off I've been from the rest of the world and everything in it."

"Where are these other vampires?" she asked suspiciously.

"Everywhere, love."

"Are there more of them here, in North Canyon Creek?"

"No. This is a relatively small town. But in larger cities you'll find many of them. There are thousands of us throughout the world."

"And no one knows?" she asked incredulously. "How is that possible?"

"Some know but refuse to believe. Others, like Hewitt, hunt us."

"He wants to kill you, doesn't he?"

"He wants to destroy me. There's a difference."

"These other vampires you want me to meet, are they your friends?"

"Yes, in a manner of speaking."

"What does that mean?"

"It means we're acquainted, but that we're always cautious around each other. Vampires are not very trusting, not even of their own kind."

"So you don't have any friends?"

"Only a very few. I think you'll like them."

"Will they be there? Will I get to meet them?"

"Yes. So, what do you say?"

"Will I be safe among them?"

"Yes, love."

She glanced at their joined hands and then looked at him intently. "Am I, Ronan?"

"Are you what?"

"Your love."

"Do you doubt it?"

"You've never said it."

"No, I never have." He drew her gently into his arms and brushed a kiss across her lips. "I've never said it to any woman, but I love you, Shannah, more than you can imagine."

"And I love you," she replied fervently. "So very much."

"I can't imagine why."

"How can I help it, when you've been so kind to me, when I . . ."

"Go on."

"When I melt every time you kiss me."

"Do you?"

She nodded, and then she blushed.

Smiling, he stroked her cheek with the back of his hand, loving the softness of her skin, the way her breath caught in her throat at his touch, the sudden quickening of her heartbeat.

"So," he said, his voice husky. "What do you say?"

"I'd go anywhere with you," she said, and then frowned. "We don't have to fly, do we?"

"Not this time," he said with a grin. "How soon can you be ready to leave?"

Since they weren't flying, Shannah had assumed they would be traveling by car.

She packed a bag and her overnight case and was waiting for Ronan when he appeared shortly before dusk the following evening. As usual, he was clad all in black. As usual, she couldn't help noticing how well the color suited him, and how handsome he was. He smiled when he saw her.

"Ready?" he asked.

She nodded, and he put his arm around her.

"Wait," she said, "I need my luggage."

"Forget it. I'll buy you a new wardrobe when we get there."

"Where is there?"

"Las Vegas."

Her eyes widened. "Las Vegas?"

"My friend is a dealer in one of the casinos." He flashed her a smile. "He works nights, of course."

"Of course."

"Hang on," Ronan said. "We'll be there in no time at all."

She wanted to ask how they were going to get there if they weren't flying and they weren't driving, but there was a sudden rushing sound in her ears, the sense of movement though she couldn't see anything, a feeling of weightlessness.

Some time later, hours or minutes, she couldn't tell, she found herself standing on the sidewalk beside Ronan in the heart of Las Vegas. She stared at the lights that were so bright, it was almost like daylight even though night had fallen. People crowded the sidewalks, some dressed up for an evening out on the town, some in jeans and T-shirts. The street was an ocean of automobiles and taxis, and they were all in a hurry.

She looked up at Ronan. "How did we get here?" she asked, breathless.

"Vampire transportation. Faster than flying," he said with a grin. "And safer, too."

"But how . . . ?"

"I'm not sure how to explain it. I just think of where I want to go, and I'm there."

"I'm not sure I like it," she muttered, "but you're right, it's better than flying."

"Come on." Taking her by the hand, he led her to the entrance of the Diamondback Casino.

It, too, was crowded with people. Ronan spoke to

someone at the desk, who gave him a room key and asked how long they would be staying.

"I'm not sure," Ronan replied with a shrug. "A day or two, perhaps a week or two."

"Very well, sir," the clerk said. "Enjoy your stay."

With a nod, Ronan tucked the key into his pocket. "So," he said, "what's your pleasure?"

"What do you mean?"

"Have you ever been to Vegas before?"

"No."

He grunted softly. "Well, there are all kinds of games of chance. Poker, blackjack, dice, Keno, the slots, video poker, the wheel of fortune, you name it, they've got it. Come on."

Taking her by the hand, he led her down a short flight of stairs onto the casino floor. More lights. More people. More noise. Bells and whistles rang out, mingling with the sound of laughter and excited voices.

"It's just like the movie *Ocean's Eleven*," she murmured.

Ronan laughed. "Come on, love, let's try our hand at the slots to begin with."

He exchanged a fifty dollar bill for fifty dollars' worth of quarters and led her to a row of slot machines located along the back wall. They found two unoccupied machines that were side by side and sat down.

Shannah dropped four quarters into the slot and pulled the handle, squealed in delight when she hit a jackpot.

That fast, she was hooked.

Ronan fed quarters into his own machine, but it was Shannah who held his attention. Her cheeks were flushed, her eyes glowed with the same excitement whether she won two dollars or twenty.

An hour later, she had won over three hundred dollars and she was ready to try her hand at something else.

Ronan glanced at his watch. "Let's hit the blackjack table," he suggested. "My friend deals at one of them."

Shannah cashed her winnings in, then followed Ronan toward the blackjack table where Ronan's friend worked. Three men and an elderly woman were seated at the table.

Ronan sat down and Shannah stood behind him, one hand on his shoulder.

"Hey, Ronan," the dealer said. "Long time no see."

"Pete. How's it going?"

The man's teeth flashed in a bright smile. "Same as always."

Ronan placed a five dollar bill on the table in front of him.

Pete dealt a round of cards to the players, face down, and then dealt a card to himself, also face down.

Ronan lifted a corner of his card and Shannah saw that he had a ten of hearts.

She watched as the dealer dealt another round of cards. Ronan's second card was the ace of spades. Two of the other men at the table won, the other man and the elderly woman lost.

It was a fast game. Ronan played several hands and won most of them.

"I've got a break coming up in a few minutes," Pete said, shuffling the deck. "You gonna be around?"

Ronan nodded. Collecting his winnings, he put the chips in his pants' pocket. "We'll wait for you in the coffee shop."

"Right."

Shannah ordered a cup of coffee and a slice of lemon meringue pie. Ronan also ordered a cup of coffee.

"For appearance's sake," he explained when she looked at him curiously.

Pete arrived a few minutes later. He slid into the booth beside Ronan. "So," he said, "who's this pretty lady?"

"Pete, this is Shannah Davis. Shannah, this is Pete Sandoval."

"Pleased to meet you," she murmured automatically. She tried not to stare at him. Though she knew he was a vampire, he looked perfectly normal. But then, so did Ronan.

Grinning, Pete leaned forward and whispered, "Wanna see my fangs?"

Shannah's cheeks grew hot. "I'm sorry, I didn't mean to stare."

"I wanted Shannah to meet a few of us," Ronan said.

Pete sat back, one arm stretched across the top of the booth. "Any particular reason?"

"I'm trying to convince her to become one of us."

"No sh . . . I mean, is that right?"

Ronan nodded.

"So," Sandoval said, looking at Shannah, "what's holding you back?"

"Several things," she replied.

"Well, it is a big decision," Sandoval remarked. "Most of the vampires I know were brought across against their will."

"Were you?"

"Oh, yeah." He shrugged. "I'm not sorry now, but it was a big adjustment in the beginning." He laughed softly. "My folks had given me to the church. I was supposed to become a priest. One night and one bite put an end to all that."

"I'm so sorry," Shannah murmured.

"Hey, it was a long time ago. So, Ronan, my man, how long will you be here?"

"We haven't decided yet."

"Well, I'll probably see you again before you leave. I've got to get back." Sandoval smiled at Shannah. "A pleasure to meet you."

"Thank you."

Shannah watched Sandoval leave the coffee shop before asking, "How long has he been a vampire?"

"About six hundred years, I think."

"And I thought you were old," Shannah muttered dryly.

Ronan laughed. "Come on, let's get out of here."

"Where are we going now?"

"To get a cab. There's a club a few miles from here."

"What kind of club?"

"A vampire club."

She looked at him in disbelief. "You have your own club?"

"Come and see."

The Sarcophagus—she thought it was a horrid name—was located on a dimly lit street in an older part of the city. Graffiti adorned the walls of the building. There were iron bars on the windows and the door. Were the bars to keep mortals out, she wondered morbidly, or to keep them from leaving if they accidentally strayed inside?

A man wearing black slacks, a black T-shirt and a long black cape lined in red satin answered Ronan's knock. "Is she expecting you?" the man asked.

"No," Ronan said, "but she'll be glad to see me."

"Wait here."

The door closed in their faces. Moments later, it opened again.

"Come in," the man said. "She's waiting for you in her private booth."

Muttering, "Thanks," Ronan took Shannah by the hand and walked through the door. They went down a narrow entryway and passed through a curtain of black beads.

It was dark inside the club, so dark that Shannah could scarcely see Ronan even though he was right beside her. Candles provided what little light there was in the room. Several couples were dancing to slow, sultry music provided by a three-piece band. Other couples and singles sat at a long, curved bar, some with drinks in their hands. She wondered, morbidly, if they were drinking blood. Like Ronan and the man who had answered the door, just about everyone in the room wore black.

Still holding Shannah's hand, Ronan skirted the dance floor until he came to a curtained booth in the back corner of the room.

A softly feminine voice bid them enter.

Shannah wondered how the occupant of the booth had known they were there. Her heart was pounding as Ronan parted the red velvet curtains and ushered her inside.

A young woman sat in the booth. The seat was black leather, the table looked like black marble. But it was the girl who held Shannah's attention. She was young, no more than fifteen or sixteen, with long yellow hair and dark brown eyes. Her skin was smooth and clear, almost luminous. She wore a tight-fitting red spandex top. Several gold bracelets glittered on her wrists.

"Please, sit down," the young woman invited.

Shannah slid into the booth.

"Ronan," the girl said. "It is good to see you here."

"Valerie, it's good to see you again."

The girl held out a slender, well-manicured hand. "It has been far too long since your last visit to my city."

Taking Valerie's hand in his, Ronan made a courtly bow, then turned her hand over and kissed her palm.

Valerie smiled, displaying even white teeth. "And who is this?" she asked, glancing in Shannah's direction.

"Valerie, this is Shannah. She's a friend of mine," he said, sliding into the seat beside her.

Valerie inclined her head in Shannah's direction. "Welcome to the Sarcophagus, friend of Ronan."

"Thank you." Shannah clasped her hands in her lap, unnerved by the woman's unblinking gaze and the unmistakable aura of power that surrounded her.

"So," Valerie said, turning her gaze on Ronan once more, "what brings you here after such a long absence?"

"A yearning to be among those of my own kind," he replied easily.

Valerie glanced at Shannah again. "I see. Have you forgotten that mortals are not welcome in this place?"

"No, but Shannah is curious about the way we live."

"Indeed?" Valerie looked at Shannah more sharply. "And why is that?"

Shannah shrank back against the seat, unable to speak under the weight of the vampire's gaze. She had no doubt that Valerie could crush her with a thought.

"Valerie, let her alone," Ronan said.

The young woman waved a graceful hand. "Very well, friend of Ronan, you may stay with my blessing. And you," she said, speaking to Ronan, "I will expect you to come and see me again before you leave the city."

With a curt nod, Ronan slid out of the booth, reached for Shannah's hand, and helped her to her feet.

Skirting the dance floor, he found an empty table and they sat down.

"Who is she?" Shannah asked.

"Valerie? I guess you could say she's the reigning vampire queen of Las Vegas."

"But she . . . she's just a girl. She can't be more than what, sixteen?"

"Valerie looks young because she was only fourteen or fifteen when she was brought across, but that was over a thousand years ago."

A thousand years! It was beyond incredible, Shannah

thought. What would it be like to live that long? What did one do to pass the time? Surely, in a thousand years, a person would have seen and done everything there was to see and do. She tried to imagine what it would be like to be a teenager for a thousand years, then shook her head. What would it be like to be twenty-four forever, to never change? To never grow old. To never die . . .

"Don't let her youthful appearance fool you," Ronan said. "She's a powerful vampire, perhaps the most powerful one in existence. So powerful that the sun no longer has the power to destroy her. This is her city. No vampire is allowed to remain here without her permission."

"She seems to like you."

"We've shared a few good times in the past."

"What does that mean?"

"Just what I said."

Shannah stared at him, afraid to ask what "vampire good times" might be.

A short time later, Ronan led her over to the bar where he introduced her to several men and women. He hadn't told her they were vampires, but if what Valerie had said was true, they must be. She forced a smile and tried not to stare, stood quietly while Ronan talked to one of the men for a few minutes. She noticed that the vampires were all beautiful. Their skin was clear, their hair thick and lustrous, their teeth very white.

"Do you know all of these . . . people?" she asked as they moved away from the bar.

"No, not all of them."

"Valerie said mortals aren't welcome here. Does that mean everyone in here is a vampire, except me?"

He nodded. "Scared?"

She glanced around the room, noticing that more than one vampire was watching her intently. She hoped it was only curiosity, although she couldn't help feeling that they were looking at her as if wondering what she would taste like. "Do you blame me?"

"I guess not," he said with a wry grin. "Would you like to dance?"

She glanced at the couples on the dance floor. Most of them were dancing so close together it was hard to tell where one person ended and the other began. The music was dark and erotic, the low beat of the drum echoing in the room like the beating of a heart. "I don't think so."

"Come on," he urged, taking her by the hand. "I promise not to let anyone take a bite out of you. Except me."

"Very funny," Shannah muttered as she followed him onto the dance floor.

She felt terribly self-conscious as Ronan turned and drew her into his arms. But she soon forgot they were surrounded by vampires, forgot everything but the thrill of being near him.

He held her close, his body brushing against hers, making every nerve ending tingle with awareness. The arm around her waist was strong and sure. His breath was warm on her cheek, his hand moved up and down her back in long, lazy strokes.

She rested her cheek against his shoulder and hoped the dance would never end. She had never thought of herself as much of a dancer but she had no trouble following Ronan's lead. He moved with a slow sensuality and her body followed his lead as though they had danced together for years.

She looked up, her gaze meeting his. There was no mistaking the heat in his eyes. She didn't have to read his mind to know what he was thinking, or feeling. His touch, his gaze, the very air that sizzled between them was so charged, she was surprised she didn't melt right there on the dance floor.

He didn't let her go when the song ended, only held her close until another one began. She was breathless by then, her heart pounding, every nerve and cell in her body aware of his hand holding hers, his arm around her waist. Tension hummed between them, vibrant and alive. Dancing with Ronan was more than dancing, it was like making love to music.

They danced until the band took a break. As Ronan led her from the dance floor, Shannah had an almost overpowering urge to laugh. Who would have thought that vampires danced, or dealt blackjack in Vegas, or played musical instruments? Or wrote romance novels . . .

Or told bad jokes. She couldn't help grinning as they passed a table where three men and two women were sitting.

"I heard this one from my sister's little girl," one of the men was saying. "Where do vampires keep their money?" He glanced around the table. "Give up? In a blood bank."

Shannah frowned. His sister's kid? She couldn't help wondering if the sister knew that her brother was a vampire. At the same time, it suddenly made vampires seem more human, somehow. He had a sister and a niece, which meant he wasn't a very old vampire, unless his sister and her family were vampires, too. Did his family know what he was? And if they didn't know, how did he manage to keep it a secret?

"Are you ready to go?" Ronan asked.

"Yes," she said, smothering a yawn. "I'm a little tired."

Leaving the club, Ronan hailed a cab. Once inside, he drew Shannah into the circle of his arms and held her close. Brushing a kiss across the top of her head, he considered how much his lifestyle had changed since she had shown up on his front porch. His existence, which had been simple and blissfully free of complications for hundreds of years, had turned upside down, and all because of this one frail mortal female.

He knew she had been ill at ease in the club, but she hadn't seemed repulsed, or worse, frightened. He didn't want to force the Dark Trick on her, but he wasn't sure he could accept her decision if she refused. Would she hate him if he brought her across against her will, or thank him once it was done? His one fear was that she would despise him for doing it, despise herself for what she had become, and destroy herself. That was the one thing he knew he could never live with.

Chapter Twenty-Four

Jim Hewitt paced the floor of his hotel room. "Dammit, where the devil are they?"

With a shrug, Carl Overstreet sat back in the room's only chair. "Beats the heck out of me. Maybe he left town and took her with him. Maybe he killed her."

Hewitt swore. They had staked out the vampire's lair day and night. For the last week, there had been no visible sign of activity in the house. Alarmed, Hewitt had gone to the house and knocked on the door and when there was no answer, he had tried looking in the windows. Yesterday morning, he had broken a back window and gone inside, afraid of what he might find. But the house was empty. There was no sign of foul play. No sign of the vampire at all. He had found a small suitcase containing women's clothes, and an overnight bag in the living room. He had found more clothing in the bedroom closet, which had him hoping that she was still alive and would be returning to the house sooner or later. On the other hand, he had known vampires to quit their current residence at a moment's notice and never return.

He swore again. If anything had happened to the woman, it would be his fault. He had bungled this hunt from the beginning. He just hoped that Eva Black wasn't paying for it. He had seen a number of vampire kills in his time. Bodies drained of blood, some with their throats torn away, some who appeared to be sleeping, until you realized their skin was the color of paper. Either way, it was never a pretty sight.

Killing a vampire was never easy, or pretty for that matter, he mused ruefully. Whether they were dispatched while resting in their coffins or they were awake and defending themselves, it was never easy and always messy.

"I'm going to go out and check the house again," he said, caressing the hawthorn stake he had made earlier that day. "Maybe this time I'll get lucky."

"Okay, see ya," Overstreet said.

Powering up his laptop, he began to write his next article.

So, dear reader, we come together again. Our subject this week is vampire hunters. I see your eyebrows going up, your smirk, your disbelief. Vampire hunters, indeed, you're thinking. Poppycock! Well, I didn't think these wielders of holy water existed either, until I met one. To preserve his anonymity, I'm going to call him Steve.

Steve is thirty-five years old and he's been hunting vampires for eighteen years. When I asked him how he came to such a profession, he shrugged and said, "It's what my family does." Apparently vampire hunters are born, not made.

Vampire hunting, it turns out, is a pretty lucrative business, which is a good thing, since cleaning bills and new clothes for hunters are probably astronomical, given all the blood involved in lopping off heads and ripping out hearts.

But I digress. I can see that many of you are skeptical and think I'm making this up. Be assured that I'm quite serious. If you're smart, you won't wander outside after dark, or invite strangers into your house. If you're a believer, buy yourself a good sturdy crucifix and keep it with you at all times. A word of caution, a cross is only as effective as your faith.

Until next time, watch your neck!

Chapter Twenty-Five

During the next several nights, Ronan introduced Shannah to a number of vampires, both male and female. Xavier and Tonio worked at the Aladdin, Michal worked at the Bellagio. Francine, who was tall and willowy with long blond hair and incredible green eyes, was a dancer in one of the night clubs on the Strip; Cleo was a standup comedienne, Domini was a cocktail waitress at the Diamondback.

Shannah found them all to be rather charming, especially Pete Sandoval. She hadn't expected to like Ronan's friends, and she hadn't expected them to like her, either. After all, they were vampires, predators, and she was prey. It was all so strange. Looking at them, she never would have guessed they were vampires. Of course, Ronan didn't look like one of the Undead, either, most of the time. Except for Pete Sandoval, all the vampires Ronan had introduced her to were young in the life. Of course, vampires considered anyone under two hundred years old to be young.

She watched them all, noting that they laughed at each other's jokes, most of which Shannah found rather macabre. When they weren't working, they went out on the town, going to the shows, trying their luck at the gaming tables, or just wandering along the city streets like the rest of the tourists, peering in shop windows, marveling at the lights and the fountains. She hadn't expected vampires to have a sense of humor, or to enjoy shopping and movies. Ronan had been right. The Undead were pretty much like the living, all things considered.

Shannah enjoyed their company. But she enjoyed being alone with Ronan most of all. He took her to the best restaurants in the city and kept her company while she ate. He took her shopping at the most exclusive stores, insisting that she buy whatever she liked no matter what the cost. Until she met Ronan, she had never had the pleasure or the luxury of buying new clothes without worrying about the price. Her parents hadn't been poor by any means, but they weren't rich, either, at least not in the way Ronan was rich.

The only time she was ill at ease was when he left her at the hotel while he went in search of prey. She knew now where he had gone all those nights back home when he'd had to go out. She tried to accept it, to tell herself that it was normal for him, a part of his existence, and that he would die without it. She reminded herself that he wasn't really hurting the people he preyed upon, that, unlike movie vampires, he wasn't a ravening monster who ripped out people's throats. But the thought of what he did to survive, what his friends did, sickened her just the same.

He had given her his blood on numerous occasions.

It was the reason for her renewed health and strength. If it wasn't for Ronan's blood, she knew she would be dead now. How could she condemn him for drinking blood to stay alive when she had done the same thing, and for the same reason?

He was out hunting now. Rather than wait in their

room, Shannah had gone down to the casino. There was something exciting about the lights and the noise, though she tired of it all rather quickly. She glanced at her watch, wondering how much longer he would be, wondering what the tourists would think if they knew that the dealer at the blackjack table and the pretty waitress serving drinks were vampires.

Shannah was absently feeding quarters into her favorite slot machine when Ronan found her twenty minutes later.

"Come on," he said with a grin, "we don't want to be late."

"Late?" she asked, smiling. "Late for what?"

"Pete and Francine are getting married."

Shannah blinked at him. "Married?" Vampires getting married. It was something she had never contemplated.

Ronan nodded, his expression rueful. "I can't believe it, either, but they want us to be their witnesses."

"Do a lot of vampires get married?"

"Not often, but it happens."

"Do they always marry other vampires?"

His gaze rested on her face. "Not always."

Shannah frowned. Ronan had been a vampire for over five hundred years. What if he married a vampire and they lived another five hundred years? Could any relationship possibly survive that long? Talk about being in love forever! She shook her head. Could any marriage, even the most sublime, endure for five centuries?

"Come on, love."

Laughing, she dropped her winnings into her purse and followed Ronan out of the casino. Taking her by the hand, he led the way down the street to a small white chapel.

Pete and Francine were waiting inside, along with Xavier, Domini, and Cleo. Pete wore a black tuxedo with a red bow tie and a matching cummerbund, Francine wore a slinky red dress that was slit up the sides, matching stiletto heels, and a red hat with a short veil.

"I'm glad you two could make it," Pete said as they entered the foyer. "Tonio and Michal had to work the late shift tonight."

"This is kind of sudden, isn't it?" Ronan asked, shaking the groom's hand.

"We had the night off and nothing to do," Pete said with a shrug. "I've never been married before and neither has Francine, so we thought, hey, why not give it a try for a hundred years or so and see how it works out."

A hundred years or so, Shannah thought. Most people didn't even live that long, yet Pete and Francine were going to spend a century or so seeing how they liked being married because it was their night off and they had nothing better to do.

Xavier snorted softly. "You will probably be tired of each other after the first fifty years."

Shannah stared at the vampires, thinking that they were making a mockery of something that was sacred. Her great grandparents had been married for sixty-two years. She had always hoped to have a marriage as strong and lasting as theirs had been, but that wouldn't happen now.

She stood beside Ronan, her hand in his, while Pete and Francine were united in marriage by a red-haired man wearing a gold Elvis Presley jumpsuit.

"I now pronounce you man and wife," the minister said in a strong, obviously fake Southern drawl. "You can kiss her now, son, she's all yours."

Pete kissed Francine, then swept her into his arms. "We'll celebrate tomorrow night," he said, addressing his guests. "Right now, I want to be alone with my bride until the sun comes up."

Cleo laughed. Xavier patted Pete on the back.

Ronan wished Pete and Francine well, bade Cleo, Domini, and Xavier good night, and then took Shannah by the hand and gave it a squeeze. "Let's go, love," he said quietly.

Hand in hand, they walked back toward the bright lights of the casino.

"Something's troubling you," Ronan remarked while they waited for the street light to change. "Do you want to talk about it?"

She raised one shoulder and let it fall. "It's just that, well, I always thought marriage was special. I know it doesn't seem to mean much anymore. Celebrities change husbands like they change their underwear. Some of their marriages don't even last a day! And Pete and Francine . . ." She shook her head. "They're getting married because they didn't have anything else to do tonight. It should mean more than that. People should be in love when they get married. It should mean something, a lifetime commitment. They talk about trying it out for a hundred years. I . . ." She blinked lest he see her tears. "I'm sorry. I didn't mean to run on like that."

"No harm done, love."

"I wish . . ."

"What?"

"Nothing."

Stepping into the darkness between two buildings, Ronan pulled her into his arms.

"What are you doing?" she asked.

"Holding you."

She stared up at him and then she leaned into him, her cheek resting on his chest.

"I always wanted a big wedding," she whispered. "I used to cut out pictures of wedding dresses when I was a little girl and I had a collection of bride dolls . . . and now . . ." There would be no long white dress, no honeymoon, no children. She sniffed back her tears. Crying wouldn't change anything.

Ronan held her close while she cried, one hand stroking her back. He felt her pain and her anger, sensed the illness that was lying in wait to steal her away from him.

She would need his blood before the night was through.

He waited until she was in bed, asleep, before he went in to her. Sitting on the edge of the mattress, he spoke softly to her mind. When he held his wrist to her lips, she roused enough to take what she needed before sleep claimed her once more.

Feeling restless, he went out into the night. He hadn't gone far when Valerie materialized beside him.

"Do you mind if I walk with you?" she asked.

"Of course not."

"You have been here a week," she said, slipping her arm through his, "and you have not yet come to see me again."

"I'm sorry. I've been busy."

"With your little mortal?"

"Uh-huh."

"She hasn't long to live, has she?"

He shook his head. None of the other vampires had detected Shannah's illness but nothing got by Valerie.

She ran her fingernails lightly over his forearm. "Are you going to bring her across?"

"I don't know."

"Have you discussed it with her?"

"She's against it. The funny thing is, I met her because she wanted to be a vampire, or she thought she did. Once she found out it was possible, she changed her mind."

"Mortals," Valerie said disdainfully. "I'm surprised they've survived as long as they have."

He laughed softly. Like many ancient vampires, Valerie had conveniently forgotten that she had once been mortal herself.

"It's a good thing for us that they have," Ronan replied dryly.

"So true," Valerie said with a grin. "You care deeply for this girl, don't you?"

"Yeah."

Valerie looked up at him, her gaze probing his. "You're in love with her." It wasn't a question but a statement of fact.

"I'm afraid so."

"I warned you years ago not to get involved with mortals," Valerie said. "No good ever comes of it. If you turn her into a vampire, she'll tire of you sooner or later and strike out on her own. If you don't bring her across, she'll die. Either way, you'll lose her."

"You're right," he said. "I know you're right."

"But it doesn't change anything, does it?"

"No," Ronan said with a bitter laugh. "It doesn't change a thing."

"I'm going out for a midnight snack," Valerie said. "Will you join me?"

"Maybe another time."

"As you wish," she said, and vanished from his sight.

Returning to the hotel, Ronan went up to Shannah's room. Sitting on the edge of the bed, he stroked the curve of her cheek, reveling in the warmth and softness of her skin. He ran his fingers through the rich fall of her hair, breathed in the all too human scent of her. She was lovely, more lovely than any woman he had ever known. But it wasn't her appearance that enthralled him. It was the sweetness of her spirit, the warmth of her smile, her trust.

He sat at her side until dawn's first light brightened the sky, and then he went in search of his own resting place, impatient for the coming night when he could see her again.

It was late afternoon when Shannah woke. Yawning, she sat up, squinting against the sunlight pouring into the room. Rising, she drew the drapes across the window, shutting out the light.

Ronan couldn't abide the sun. Was she becoming a vampire? Was that why the sun's light hurt her eyes, why she slept so late? Was he turning her into what he was against her will?

He had given her his blood last night. She didn't know how she knew it, but she did. How much longer would he be able to keep her alive? She felt good this morning, yet she lacked the abundance of energy she usually felt after she had taken his blood. Did that mean it was losing its effectiveness, or that the end was near and nothing could stop it? She shivered, suddenly cold all over.

Sooner or later, his blood would stop being effective.

Sooner or later she would have to decide between being what he was, or not being at all.

Shaking off her dismal thoughts, she wondered how the newlyweds were doing and then wondered, with a morbid grin, where they were spending the day. Did they have a double casket? Were they sharing the same one? Or had they just pushed their old ones close together, like twin beds? The thought gave her the creeps.

Feeling tired in spite of the fact that she had just gotten out of bed, she called room service and ordered something to eat.

After breakfast, she combed her hair and brushed her teeth and then decided she just didn't have the energy or the desire to get dressed and go out.

Still wearing her nightgown, she curled up in a chair.

She read one of Ronan's books for a while, then turned on the TV, flipping through the channels until she found a movie she wanted to watch.

Ronan found her curled up in the chair when he entered the room shortly before sundown. Her nightgown was black; long and flowing, it kept her modesty intact and managed to be sexy at the same time.

He started to wake her, then changed his mind, deciding she probably needed the rest.

Sitting on the sofa, he thought about what Valerie had said the night before. Most vampires shunned any contact with mortals other than what was necessary for their survival. Until he met Shannah, it had been a rule that he had followed as well.

Was Valerie right? Was he destined to lose Shannah no matter what he did? Tonio had brought a mortal woman across thirty or forty years ago. They had lived together for about ten years before the woman decided she wanted to "see the world on her own." To Ronan's knowledge, Tonio hadn't seen or heard from the woman since.

Ronan stared at the TV screen, hardly aware of what he was watching. If he brought Shannah across, would she tire of him after a few years? Would he tire of her? He honestly didn't know, but it was a chance he was willing to take.

He sat by her side all that night, hoping she would awake. When she didn't, he carried her to bed and tucked her in. Brushing a kiss across her brow, he went to seek his own rest.

As usual, Shannah slept late the following day. On waking, she was surprised to find herself in bed instead of in the chair where she had fallen asleep. She felt a moment of regret that she had slept through the night.

What had Ronan done after he put her to bed? She didn't like the idea of his wandering through the casinos alone. He was too handsome, too appealing.

Rising, she ordered breakfast from room service, then dressed and went downstairs. She wandered into the casino, which didn't seem nearly as glamorous or exciting in the afternoon as it did at night. She noticed it wasn't as crowded, either.

She played blackjack for twenty minutes or so, but it wasn't as much fun without Ronan. She tried her hand at the slots and at video poker and then left the hotel.

Putting on her sunglasses, she strolled up the street, looking in windows, watching the people who passed by. She meandered through a couple of the other casinos, stopping to play a slot machine here and there without any luck.

Maybe she just wasn't a gambler, she mused as she left another casino behind. It was fun for a few minutes but she quickly lost interest in the games, even when she was winning. If she was going to spend money, she would much rather shop than gamble.

She didn't know about Ronan, but she was ready to go home.

She went into a café for a late lunch, then decided to take in a movie.

It was dark when she left the theater, or at least as dark as it got in Vegas.

Shannah was crossing the street when a tall man wearing a hat and a long coat fell into step beside her. She darted a glance in his direction, felt a shiver go down her spine when she saw the predatory gleam in his eye.

She quickened her step, one hand clutching her purse. She breathed a sigh of relief when she left him behind, only to gasp when she realized he was again at her side, matching her step for step.

She glanced around, looking for help, wondering if anyone would come to her aid if she screamed even though, as yet, he hadn't done anything.

Panic made her heart beat faster. She was about to break into a run, deciding it was better to look foolish than get mugged, when his hand closed around her upper arm in a vice-like grip and he dragged her into the shadows of a side street.

When she would have screamed, he slapped his hand across her mouth. Leaning close, he whispered, "You don't want to do that."

She stared at him, her heart pounding with fear, and then with dread when his eyes took on a fiendish red glow. His top lip curled back, exposing his fangs. This was the vampire of legend, the kind of vampire who drained his victims dry and left them lying on the ground, a dry empty shell.

She stared into his face, her insides turning cold as she saw death in his eyes. Her death.

Ronan! Ronan, help me, oh, please, help me! The words screamed in her mind as the vampire grasped a handful of her hair and jerked her head back, exposing her throat.

This couldn't be happening, she thought. She didn't want to die like this. Her stomach clenched with horror as the vampire lowered his head toward her neck. With a cry, she began to struggle in his grasp. Her nails raked his face with no effect. When she tried to knee him, he slapped her, hard, twice, then dragged her body up against his, his arm like iron around her waist. She screamed when she felt the scrape of his fangs against her skin.

She closed her eyes, only to snap them open when the vampire suddenly released her. She staggered backward, her head striking the wall of a building. Moaning softly, she slid down the wall. Dazed, she shook her head to clear it, then stared at the two figures that were slowly circling each other. It took her a moment to realize that the second figure was Ronan.

It was a scene straight out of a nightmare. Eyes blazing red as hellfire, their fangs bared and their hands like claws, the two vampires circled each other.

Shannah stared at them, unable to move, as they suddenly lunged at each other in what she knew would be a battle to the death. It was brutal and ugly, a ballet of blood fought in silence.

She watched Ronan as if seeing him for the first time. Always, he had been gentle, restrained, in control. Now she saw the predator that lurked within him. His power sizzled through the night air, raising the hair along her nape. The sharp coppery tang of blood stung her nostrils.

She wanted to cover her eyes, to run away and hide, but she could only crouch there, her gaze fixed on Ronan as the battle raged on. And then, suddenly, it was over and Ronan stood alone. He stared at something in his hand, something that left drops of what looked like dark water on the pavement at his feet.

His eyes blazed with triumph and the heat of battle. When his gaze met hers, he turned away with a low growl.

Feeling as though she had been freed from a sorcerer's spell, Shannah scrambled to her feet and ran out of the alley.

Eyes closed, Ronan listened to the sound of her retreating footsteps. She had seen him at his worst now, seen the ugliness he had tried to spare her. Would she look at him differently now? Would she see him as nothing but a monster instead of a man?

Muttering an oath, he lifted the body of the vampire onto his shoulder. Moving with preternatural speed, he left the city behind, searching for a deserted place where no one would find the body before dawn. When he found a ravine, he dropped the body inside and tossed the heart in after it. Come morning, the sun would destroy the remains.

He only hoped he hadn't destroyed his relationship with Shannah.

He found a place to wash up before returning to the hotel, then stood in the hallway outside her door, suddenly reluctant to face her. He could hear her pacing the floor inside, smell the residue of fear that clung to her as she tried to erase what she had seen from her mind.

Would she want to see him now, he wondered, or should he leave her be for what remained of the night? Deciding time and distance might be to his advantage, he was about to turn away when the muffled sound of her sobs reached his ears. The thought of her in her room, crying and alone, was more than he could bear, especially when he was the cause of her tears.

Lifting his hand, he knocked on the door.

"Who's there?" she called, her voice shaky and uncertain.

"It's me. Are you all right?"

Footsteps, and then the door opened and Shannah stood there, her eyes wide, one hand pressed to her heart.

"Are you all right?" he repeated.

"I'm not hurt, if that's what you mean. I'm not sure I'll ever be all right again."

He blew out a sigh. "I'm sorry you had to see that."

Her gaze moved over him. "Are you okay?"

He nodded. "As always. Do you want me to go?"

"No." Taking him by the arm, she pulled him inside, then closed the door.

Crossing her arms under her breasts, she looked up at him.

For once, he couldn't read her expression and so he stood there, waiting.

"He would have killed me, wouldn't he?"

Ronan nodded, once, curtly.

"You saved my life," she said quietly. "Again."

"But now you've seen me as I really am, and you no longer like what you see."

She frowned thoughtfully, then shook her head. "How can you think that? I'd be dead if it wasn't for you."

"You wouldn't have been here in the first place if it wasn't for me."

She couldn't argue with that and she didn't try.

"You should have run away," he said, his voice tinged with anger. Had he lost the fight, she would have been at the mercy of the other vampire.

"I did run away."

"Yes," he said dryly, "when it was over. He could have destroyed me, you know. What would you have done then?"

She hadn't considered for a moment that Ronan wouldn't win. He had always seemed so strong, so invincible, she couldn't imagine anyone defeating him. Placing her hand on his chest, she said, "You were magnificent."

He lifted one brow. "Magnificent? Is that why you ran away?"

"No. I'm not sure why I ran. I guess . . ." She shrugged. "I don't know."

"Perhaps it was your good sense asserting itself, albeit too late."

"Thank you for rescuing me."

"You're not afraid of me, then? You're not repulsed by what you saw?"

"A little. It was ugly and I was scared, but . . ." She looked up at him, her eyes shining with unshed tears. "I don't want to think about it anymore. I just want you to hold me."

He drew her gently into his arms, thinking again what a remarkable creature she was, grateful that in spite of everything she had seen, she hadn't run screaming from his presence.

Chapter Twenty-Six

She dreamed of dying. Floating above her body, she watched the doctors who were gathered around her, trying in vain to revive her.

She heard the hum and whine of the life support system, the voices of the doctors, sharp with urgency, and then a resigned voice saying, "It's over, we've lost her."

She heard her mother's hoarse cry of denial when the doctor called to deliver the sad news, saw the grief on the faces of her mother and father as they laid her to rest. Sealed inside a white coffin, she heard the dirt clods falling on the lid. She screamed in fear when she was unable to lift the lid. Sobbing, she begged them to let her out before it was too late, before she really was dead. She screamed until her throat ached, pounded on the lid of the casket until her hands bled, broke her fingernails in a vain effort to claw her way out. Heard her own scream of terror as she realized she was going to suffocate . . .

"Shannah! Shannah, wake up!"

"No! No! Let me out!" She lashed out at the dark figure bending over her, her nails drawing blood as they raked his cheek. "Let me out! Oh, please, let me out! I'm not dead!"

Ronan caught both of her hands in one of his. "Shannah, calm down. You've had a nightmare."

She collapsed against him, sobbing uncontrollably.

"Shh, love, it's all right." He held her tight, one hand stroking her back, her hair. "It was just a bad dream."

"It was so real." Shivering, she huddled against him. "I w-want to . . . to go home."

He let out a sigh, thinking that he was losing her far sooner than he had planned. But he couldn't keep her with him against her will, not anymore. He could refuse her nothing that he had the power to give, and if she wanted to go home, he would take her there.

"All right, love," he said quietly. "Do you want to call your parents and tell them you're coming?"

She looked up at him, her brow furrowed. "Oh," she said, sniffling. "I didn't mean my parents' home. I meant your home."

Her words plucked a thorn of despair from his heart. "I'll take good care of you," he promised.

"I know."

He handed her a handkerchief when she sniffed again. Sitting up, she blew her nose and wiped her eyes.

"That must have been some nightmare," he said. "Do you want to talk about it?"

"I dreamed that I died and that my parents . . . they buried me. But I wasn't dead and I couldn't get out!" She looked at him, her eyes wide with horror. "Do you think they ever bury people who aren't dead?"

"Not anymore," he said reassuringly. In the old days, it had been a common occurrence to bury someone thinking they were deceased. There had been occasions when a coffin was exhumed and when it was opened, scratches had been found on the inside of the lid, indicating that the deceased hadn't been deceased at all. In time, a string was tied to one of the deceased's hands, with the other end of the string being attached to a bell above ground. Should the one interred suddenly regain consciousness and begin to thrash about, the movement caused the bell to ring. It was believed that it was that ancient custom that had spawned the term "dead ringer."

Shannah blew out a sigh. "It was the worst nightmare I've ever had."

"I'm sure it was."

She touched his bloodied cheek. "Did I do that?"

"It's nothing."

"I'm sorry." She dabbed at his cheek with his handkerchief but there was no need. The shallow scratches were already healing.

"Believe me," he said with a wry grin, "I've been hurt much worse."

"Can we leave tonight?"

"If that's what you want."

"It is. I don't like it here."

"All right, love. Gather your things while I go and tell Valerie we're leaving."

"Thank you, Ronan."

He kissed the tip of her nose. "I won't be long."

Ronan found Valerie at the club, sitting at her usual booth. A young vampire with long brown hair and pale green eyes sat beside her, his expression one of rapt adoration.

Valerie smiled warmly when Ronan sat down across from her. "I didn't expect to see you again so soon," she said, "yet you are always welcome."

"I've come to say good-bye."

"I had hoped you would stay a while longer so that we might reminisce about times past."

"I would have liked that," he said, meaning it, "but Shannah wishes to go home."

"Ah. And have you decided what you're going to do with your little mortal?"

"It's up to her."

Valerie nodded. "I wish you all the best in whatever you decide."

"Thanks." Taking her hand in his, he kissed her palm, aware, as he did so, of the young vampire's jealous gaze. Releasing Valerie's hand, Ronan winked at the young man. "Don't worry, kid, she's all yours."

Valerie laughed softly. "Ah, Ronan, you've got it wrong," she said, stroking the young vampire's cheek. "He is all mine."

Grinning, Ronan left the club.

Shannah was dressed and sitting on the edge of the bed when he returned to the hotel. He noticed at once how pale she looked. The disease was escalating, he thought bleakly. He would have to give her his blood more often if he hoped to keep her alive.

"Are you ready?" he asked.

She nodded.

Tucking her belongings under one arm, he drew her close against him and closed his eyes, focusing his will and his energy on going home. It still amazed him that a single thought could propel him across great distances. It had taken him a while to perfect the art but it had come in handy more than once, especially back in the old days, when vampire hunters had been far more numerous, and far more tenacious.

The familiar weightlessness engulfed him and with it the sense of moving at incredible speed. It was a rather startling sensation that at first had left him feeling light-headed and slightly disoriented. But, like every other aspect of his preternatural life, he had grown accustomed to it.

Moments later, they were standing in the middle of

the living room. A wave of his hand kindled a fire in the hearth and turned on the lights.

He glanced at Shannah. One look at her face, and he dropped her belongings on the floor and carried her swiftly up the stairs to her room. Flinging the covers on the bed aside, he placed her gently on the mattress, ripped open the skin on his wrist, and held his arm to her lips.

"Drink, Shannah."

She stared up at him, her face deathly pale, her eyes unfocused. "No . . ."

"You must drink!"

She shook her head. "Call my . . . mom and dad . . . tell them . . . I'm sorry."

"Dammit, Shannah, you will drink!"

She shook her head weakly. "No. It's too late . . . just . . . let me go."

It was the one thing he could not do. Sitting on the edge of the bed, he took her face in his hands and gazed deep into her eyes, heedless of the blood trickling down his arm, dripping onto the sheets. "You must drink, Shannah. You want to drink. The taste will be sweet and you will not stop until I tell you."

"Please don't make me . . ."

He could not, would not let her go. He called on his preternatural powers, felt them come to the fore as he gazed deeper into her eyes, capturing her will with his. "Shannah, listen to my voice. You must do as I say. Please, love, I cannot let you go."

This time, when he pressed his wrist to her lips, she did not resist.

Jim Hewitt sat in his car, his fingers drumming impatiently on the steering wheel. He was getting almighty tired of spending his nights sitting in his car on the off-chance that Ronan and the girl would . . .

He sat up straight, his eyes narrowing as lights came on in the house. Picking up his cell phone, he punched in Overstreet's number. "Carl?"

"Yeah," Overstreet said crossly, "whaddya want?"

"They're back."

"You've seen them?"

"No, but the lights just came on in the house." Hewitt glanced at his watch. "It's a little after midnight. Get some sleep. I'll stay here until six, and then it's your turn."

"What's the point of watching during the day?"

"We need to know if she's with him."

"Oh, yeah, right."

"You'll get that story yet," Hewitt said, and ended the call.

He sat in his car a moment more, then got out and made his way up to the front gate. He had expected it to be locked, was surprised when it swung open at his touch. Making his way around to the side of the house, he peeked in the first window he came to. He held his breath as he watched the vampire sweep an apparently unconscious Eva Black into his arms and carry her out of sight. Damn! Was he too late?

Muttering an oath, he went around to the front door, swore again when it refused to open. Damn and double damn! Was she already dead or was that filthy blood-sucker draining her dry while he stood out here on the porch, helpless?

He smacked his fist against the side of the house. Helpless, was he? Not by a long shot. Yanking his cell phone out of his pocket, he called the police.

Ronan had changed the bloody sheet, tucked Shannah into bed, and was making his way downstairs when he noticed red lights flashing outside. He was about to go out and see what was going on when someone knocked on his front door.

Frowning, he opened it to find two uniformed police officers standing on the porch. Their name tags identified them as Officer Burton and Officer Lincoln.

"Is something wrong, Officer?" He addressed his question to Burton, who was the taller and the older of the two.

"We had a report that there was a dead woman in the house."

Ronan glanced past the cops to the street. A familiar car was parked behind the police vehicle. The car was empty but he imagined Hewitt was lurking somewhere close by.

"Do you mind if we come in?" The second officer looked like he was fresh out of the Academy. Young and green, he was filled with the arrogance and confidence of youth.

Ronan stepped back. "Not at all."

"Is there anyone else in the house?" Burton asked, glancing around.

"My girlfriend. She's asleep upstairs."

"Mind if we take a look?" the young officer asked. His brusque tone made it sound more like a demand than a request.

Ronan shrugged. "Help yourself."

Officer Burton went upstairs. The other cop remained near Ronan, one hand resting on his holstered revolver.

Ronan listened to Burton's footsteps as he went from room to room, pausing only when he entered Shannah's bedroom. With his preternatural powers, Ronan had no trouble tracing the man's progress.

A short time later, Officer Burton returned to the living room. "It's like he said, Linc. There's a girl sleeping upstairs. No signs of a struggle. Nothing out of the ordinary that I could see."

The young officer nodded, obviously disappointed that they weren't going to see any action. "Must have been a crank call."

Burton nodded, then turned to Ronan. "Sorry to have bothered you, sir."

"No problem, Officer," Ronan replied.

He followed the two men to the door and watched them get into their squad car, noting, as he did so, that Hewitt's car was gone.

Ronan swore softly as he closed and locked the door. The man was becoming quite a nuisance. Something would have to be done about him sooner or later.

Overstreet looked up as Hewitt slammed into the room. "Something wrong?"

Hewitt dropped into a chair. "No. They're both there."

Overstreet studied the hunter's face. "So, what's got your shorts in a knot?"

Hewitt made a dismissive gesture with his hand. "I looked in the window and saw him carrying the woman upstairs. She looked dead. Face the color of chalk. I couldn't get into the house without his knowing it, so I called the cops. You know, anonymous tip. They checked it out. I guess they didn't find anything out of line."

"So, she's still alive?"

"Either that or he hid the body." Hewitt dragged a hand across his jaw. Somehow, the two of them would search the house again, and they would keep looking until they found the vampire's resting place. It was somewhere inside the house. Hewitt was sure of it. They would find it tomorrow if they had to rip the place apart, brick by brick and board by board!

Chapter Twenty-Seven

"Shannah, why are you resisting this?" Ronan blew out a breath of exasperation. "I'm offering you what you came looking for."

"I know, but I wasn't thinking clearly at the time. Ronan, I don't want to be a vampire. I can't drink blood, or sleep in a . . . a . . . where you sleep. I just can't!"

"Shannah, love, you're already a blood drinker. Trust me, being a vampire isn't as bad as you think. Come out with me now, tonight. Let me show you what it's really like."

"You mean, go with you when you . . . ?"

"Hunt," he supplied.

She shuddered at the images that single word brought to mind. Images of wolves stalking buffalo calves, lions attacking young gazelles, tigers dragging their prey into the treetops.

She shook her head. "I don't think I can do that."

"Of course you can." He held out his hand. "Trust me, Shannah, just one more time."

After a moment's hesitation, she laced her fingers with his and let him lead her out into the shadows of the night.

She clung to Ronan's hand as he walked down the

street. Why had she agreed to do this? She knew what he did to survive, what he had to do, but she didn't like to think about it. Even knowing it was necessary didn't make it any easier to accept.

Why had she agreed to accompany him? Out of curiosity? Or was she actually, on some deep level, contemplating a future as a vampire? No, that was out of the question. It was against everything she believed in. Yet here she was, taking one more step into a world that few knew existed.

They walked through the town until they reached a dimly lit street not far from the café where she had first seen him so many months ago.

Ronan stopped at the corner and she stopped beside him.

"What are we doing?" she asked after a couple of minutes.

"Waiting."

She glanced around. There were three small specialty stores and a Chinese restaurant near where they stood. All were closed at this time of night. Music floated through the open door of a night club down the street.

"What are we waiting for?" she asked.

"Her." Ronan pointed at a dark-haired woman emerging from the bar down the street. "Wait here."

Shannah wrapped her arms around her waist as she watched Ronan approach the brunette. He spoke to her for a moment and then he took the woman's hand in his and led her to where Shannah waited.

Shannah stared at the woman. She was tall and slim, perhaps thirty years old. If she was married, she didn't wear a ring. Under Ronan's spell, the woman's expression was blank, as if all her emotions had been erased.

Shannah trailed behind as Ronan led the woman into

a nearby alley. He spoke to the woman once again, and then he drew her into his arms.

The woman didn't resist.

Shannah looked at the two of them, speechless, her heart racing. She didn't want to see this.

Ronan looked at Shannah over the brunette's head. His eyes were glowing strangely. He smiled, revealing sharp white fangs.

And then he bent his head over the woman's neck.

Shannah stared at the scene before her. It was like something out of a horror movie, or a nightmare. Though she couldn't actually see what he was doing, she knew what was happening, knew that his fangs had pierced the woman's flesh, that he was feeding off her life's blood.

The woman stood motionless in Ronan's embrace, her eyes closed, her head canted to one side.

Shannah looked at Ronan again and her mind filled with his thoughts, his feelings. Chief among them was a sensation of intense pleasure and relief as the woman's life force flowed into him, quieting his hunger, filling him with warmth. She was surprised to discover that he felt compassion for the woman, compassion and gratitude.

Lifting his head, Ronan looked at Shannah, his expression shuttered.

She stared back at him, wondering what he read in her eyes.

Bending down, he ran his tongue over the woman's neck; then, taking her by the hand, Ronan led her out of the alley. He spoke briefly to the brunette, who nodded and walked away.

Ronan remained where he was, waiting for Shannah to emerge from the alley. "And so," he said, "you have seen me for what I am. Does it disgust you? Frighten you?"

She shook her head. She wasn't afraid. Searching her feelings, she realized she wasn't even repulsed by what he had done. There had been nothing cruel about it. He had treated the woman kindly, even with respect. And though she couldn't deny that he had taken something precious from the woman, the woman didn't seem to be any the worse off because of it.

"Shannah?" He closed the short distance between them, his steps tentative, his expression guarded. Did he expect her to run away, screaming? "Does this change anything between us?"

"No."

His relief was palpable.

"But I still don't think I can do it. To drink a stranger's blood, to have to do it every night . . ." She shook her head. "No."

"In the beginning I had misgivings, as well, but all the things that you think are so important now soon become irrelevant, just as those things you view as repugnant now soon become second nature."

"I don't know . . . what of my family? My friends? Will they all become irrelevant, too?"

"No, Shannah. I was speaking of more mundane things."

"I just don't know." She looked up at him, her eyes filled with doubts and a shadow of fear that he had seen there far too often of late. Fear of death.

"You needn't decide now."

But she couldn't wait too long. Her time was running out. He knew it, and so did she.

Shannah turned away from the answering machine. There were four messages from her doctor. She should have called him, she thought. She had intended to when they were in New York but she had been feeling so good and having such a wonderful time she had put it off, and then there had been the plane crash, and she had forgotten all about it. She knew she should go see him, but she didn't want to hear what he had to say. She knew she was getting worse; he would know it, too, and she didn't want to spend whatever time she had left in the hospital with doctors and nurses poking and prodding and smiling their bright, false smiles as they assured her everything would be all right.

She called her parents and spent an hour on the phone, assuring them time and again that she was fine.

When she hung up, she sat at Ronan's desk and wrote letters of good-bye to her mom and dad, telling them that she loved them and that Ronan had taken good care of her. She wrote a letter to Judy, telling her how much she had appreciated her friendship through the years, assuring her that Ronan had made her last days easy to bear.

When she was done, she sealed the letters and put them in her dresser drawer, underneath her nightgowns.

Going downstairs, she went into the kitchen. She was standing in front of the refrigerator, trying to decide what to fix for dinner, when she heard a knock at the front door.

She peeked out the window, groaned softly when she saw Carl Overstreet and Jim Hewitt standing on the porch. What did they want now?

She darted back before they could see her, then stood there wondering if she should open the door or let them think she wasn't home.

One of them knocked on the door, loudly, and then rang the doorbell again.

Shannah held her breath, waiting for them to go away.

She heard shuffling footsteps and muffled voices, the scraping sound of metal against metal, and suddenly the door swung open.

"What do you think you're doing?" Shannah exclaimed, more angry than afraid. "Get the hell out of here!"

"I told you she was home," Hewitt said dryly.

"Yeah, yeah," Overstreet muttered. "Get on with it."

"How did you get in here?" Shannah demanded.

"There are ways," Hewitt said, slipping something into his pocket.

Shannah grimaced. How they had gotten in didn't matter. They were here now. And they had to leave before Ronan arrived.

"So," Overstreet said, "did you find out where he sleeps?"

"No." As if she would ever tell them.

The reporter's eyes narrowed ominously. "This would be a lot easier on everybody if you'd just cooperate with us."

"Knock it off, Overstreet," Hewitt said sharply.

"We're wasting our time," the reporter said, his eyes darting around the room. "She lives with the guy. She must know where he sleeps."

Shannah fisted her hands on her hips and lifted her chin defiantly. "Well, I don't."

"Did you ask him if he was a vampire?" Hewitt asked.

"Of course."

"What did he say?" Both men leaned forward expectantly.

"Do you mean before or after he stopped laughing?"

"She's lying," Overstreet said. "He's here. All we have to do is find him."

Hewitt nodded. "I'm sorry about this, Miss Black," he said.

Shannah thought he meant breaking into the house until he pulled a pair of handcuffs out of his coat pocket. Before she could protest, he pulled her toward the staircase and handcuffed her left wrist to the banister.

"What are you doing?" she cried, tugging on the cuff.
"Let me go this instant!"

"Just sit tight, sister," Overstreet said.

Shannah stared at Hewitt. "I'll have you arrested for
this!"

"I doubt it."

Furious tears filled her eyes as she watched the two men
split up to search the house. She tugged on the handcuff
again. What if one of the men found Ronan while he
slept, she thought frantically. But surely they wouldn't find
his hiding place. She never would have found it save for
the blood bond they shared. Hewitt and Overstreet had
no such bond. But Hewitt was a vampire hunter. He would
know where to look and what to look for.

Leaning against the banister, she tracked their movements through the house by listening to their footsteps
and the sounds of doors being opened and closed.
Taking a deep breath, she forced herself to relax. As long
as they were upstairs, there was nothing to worry about.

The two men searched for what must have been an
hour before they returned to where they had left her.

"I told you he wasn't here," she said icily. "Now will you
let me go?"

Overstreet glanced at the window. "It'll be dark soon.
Let's get out of here while we can."

Hewitt nodded. "I think you're right."

He removed the cuff from Shannah's wrist. She
rubbed it, then let out a shriek when Hewitt grabbed her
arm and pulled her toward the front door.

"Let me go!"

"I think you'd better come with us," Hewitt said, haul-
ing her along behind him. "You're not safe here."

"You're the ones who won't be safe if you don't let
me go!"

"Uh, just where are we going?" Overstreet asked, hurrying outside after the two of them.

"I'm not sure," Hewitt said. "We need a place with a powerful threshold." He frowned as he opened his car door and pushed Shannah into the passenger seat. He grabbed hold of her ankle when she lunged toward the driver's side door.

"My aunt's got a place not far from here," Overstreet said, glancing anxiously over his shoulder. "It's been in the family for years. We can stay there."

"Good," Hewitt said. "Get in and let's get the hell out of here."

Trapped between Overstreet and Hewitt, Shannah stared out the front window, her heart pounding. She told herself there was nothing to be afraid of. Ronan had always found her before. He would find her this time, too.

She repeated that over and over again as the city fell behind and darkness spread her cloak over the land.

The house that belonged to Carl Overstreet's aunt was located at the end of a long dirt road. It appeared old and weather-beaten, the paint faded in some places and peeling in others. Shutters that had once been green covered the windows. There was a large barn, painted a rusty red, on one side of the house and a ramshackle garage on the other.

Hewitt stopped the car in front of the garage. Overstreet got out of the car and opened the garage door and Hewitt pulled inside and killed the engine.

The car had barely stopped when Shannah flung open the door and started running across the yard. With any luck, she could find a place to hide and then make her way back to town.

"Stop her!" Hewitt's voice cut through the stillness.

Not daring to glance over her shoulder, Shannah kept running. She was certain she could outrun Overstreet.

Hewitt was another matter. She hadn't gotten far before he tackled her. She screamed as his hands closed around her waist, saw stars as her head hit the ground. He landed on top of her, driving the air from her lungs.

She glared up at him. "Get off of me."

Grabbing the handcuff that still dangled from her wrist, he pulled her to her feet and practically dragged her back to the house.

Overstreet grinned at Hewitt. "Nice tackle."

Hewitt grinned. "Thanks. Where's your aunt?" He tugged on the handcuff and Shannah followed him into the house.

"In Boston visiting her sister," Overstreet replied. "She doesn't spend much time here anymore."

"You can tell that just by looking at the place."

Shrugging, Overstreet said, "Yeah, well, it's a good thing, isn't it?"

Hewitt nodded. "Lock the door."

"Right."

Shannah glared at Hewitt. "What do you hope to gain by this?"

"You'll thank us later."

"Thank you for what? Kidnapping me?" She crossed her arms under her breasts and glared at both men. "I want to go home, and I want to go now."

"Listen, Miss Black, Eva . . ."

"My name is Shannah Davis."

Hewitt blinked at her. "So, Black is just a pseudonym? I figured as much."

"Really? Well, figure this. That man you think is a vampire is the romance writer, not me."

Overstreet stared at her, his eyes narrowed. "You're not the author?"

"No."

"Then why were you . . . ?"

"It's a long story," Shannah said imperiously, "and none of your business."

Overstreet slumped into a chair. "Okay, Hewitt, we've got her here. Now what? You've got some kind of plan, right?"

"Plan to do what?" Shannah asked, though she had a terrible feeling she already knew the answer.

"Destroy the monster, of course," Overstreet said. "After I get my interview, although I don't know how the devil we'll get it now." He glared at Hewitt. "Are you sure this guy's a vampire? Who ever heard of a bloodsucker writing romance novels?"

"He's a vampire," Hewitt said. "I've destroyed enough of them to know."

Shannah stared at him. She had known he was a hunter but hearing him admit to killing vampires was unnerving.

"What about you?" she said, speaking to Overstreet. "Are you a vampire hunter, too?"

"No, I'm a freelance reporter, like I said. The interview I did with you appeared in a couple of the magazines I work for. I've also been doing a weekly series on vampires which wasn't going anywhere until I met Jim, here. He promised me an interview with your vampire before he takes his head."

Shannah stared at Overstreet, her stomach churning at the image his words conjured in her mind.

And then she frowned.

And then she laughed. "So, you two plan to capture Ronan and render him helpless, and then you expect him to give you an interview before you kill him?"

She laughed again. "I've never heard of anything so ridiculous. Of course, Overstreet might get a good story out of it before Ronan has the two of you arrested for assault."

Overstreet looked at Hewitt, his expression worried. "Maybe he isn't a vampire."

"Of course he is. You told me so yourself!"

Overstreet shrugged. "Maybe I was wrong."

"Well, I'm not wrong," Hewitt said, bristling. "He's a bloodsucker and I aim to take him out."

Overstreet canted his head to one side. "How many vampires have you killed?"

"What's that got to do with anything?"

"Just answer the question. How many? One? Five? Ten?"

"Twelve. This one will make lucky thirteen."

"So," Overstreet said, looking slightly mollified, "what do we do now?"

"We wait for him to come to us." Hewitt looked at Shannah and grinned. "We've got something he wants."

Ronan woke to a stillness that told him he was alone in the house.

Rising, he showered and changed clothes, then went into his office. Booting up the computer, he wondered where Shannah had gone. Shopping, perhaps, or maybe she had just felt the need to get out of the house for a while. He couldn't expect her to stay in the house twenty-four hours a day. Though they had discussed having her keep his hours, it hadn't worked out too well, though she was going to bed later and sleeping later all the time.

He wrote steadily, his mind focused on his work in progress. It had been days since he had found the time to write and he quickly lost himself in the story, the words flowing almost faster than he could type them. For this moment in time, he was the hero. He was the heroine. He was the villain. The world he had created from his imagination was more real, more tangible, than the solid walls that surrounded him. He finished one chapter and began the next.

It was only when his hunger began to stir that he glanced up at the clock, surprised to find that he had been writing for almost four hours.

When he reached the end of the next chapter, he saved his work and shut down the computer, the first hint of worry rising in his mind when he realized that Shannah had not yet returned home.

Leaving his office, he went into the living room, snarling softly when he caught the scents of Hewitt and Overstreet. Muttering an oath, he took a deep breath. The two men had been in his house recently. Why hadn't he noticed it sooner? He knew the answer even as the question surfaced in his mind. He had been so lost in his work that the house could have gone up in flames and he probably wouldn't have noticed until it was too late.

Opening the front door, he followed Hewitt's scent out to the curb, noting that Shannah's scent was strong here, as well.

He swore again, his anger rising quietly within him. The fools had taken her and for that they would die.

Chapter Twenty-Eight

"Hewitt!" Overstreet called, a hint of panic in his voice. "Hewitt, come here!"

"What's wrong?" Jim Hewitt turned away from the kitchen table where he had been methodically sharpening several stout wooden stakes.

"Come here and take a look at the girl."

"Why? What's wrong with her?"

"I don't know. She looks . . ." Overstreet shook his head. "I think she's . . . dead."

"What?" Knocking his chair over in his haste, Hewitt ran into the living room. He dropped down on one knee in front of the sofa and grabbed Shannah's hand. Turning it over, he pressed his fingertips to her wrist, feeling for her pulse. "Dammit! What did you do to her?"

"I didn't do anything! One minute she was sitting there on the sofa, glaring at me like I was the devil incarnate, and the next she just sort of keeled over."

Hewitt swore again.

"Is she dead?"

"Not yet," Hewitt said, gaining his feet. "She's unconscious, though. Dammit!"

Rising, Overstreet reached for his coat.

"What are you doing?"

"We've got to get her to a hospital."

"In the middle of the night?" Hewitt asked. "Are you completely out of your mind?"

"So, what do you want to do? Just let her die?"

Hewitt raked a hand through his hair. It was time to cut his losses and admit defeat. They could drop the girl off at the nearest hospital and then hightail it out of town.

Returning to the kitchen, he filled his pockets with several vials of holy water, made sure his crucifix was in place and visible, then picked up four of the wooden stakes.

"Bring the girl," he said, striding toward the front door.

Carl Overstreet grunted softly as he lifted Shannah into his arms.

Hewitt snatched the car keys off the table; then, keys in one hand and a stake held firmly in the other, he opened the door, and stopped dead in his tracks.

"What's wrong?" Overstreet asked, coming up behind him.

Hewitt swallowed the bile rising in his throat as he glanced into the distance and saw a pair of blood-red eyes looking back at him. "He's out there."

Overstreet swore and took several hasty steps backward. "What do we do now?"

Hewitt slammed the door and turned the lock. "I wish I knew."

"Hewitt!" The vampire's voice, edged with preternatural power and authority, cut through the night. "Bring her to me."

"Do I look like a fool?" Hewitt shouted.

"You have one chance," the vampire warned. "Bring her to me now."

"Go to hell, you bloodsucker." Hewitt's eyes widened as Carl Overstreet, still carrying Shannah, walked zombie-like toward the door. "Overstreet, what the devil are you doing?"

Overstreet didn't answer, just kept walking toward the door, his eyes glazed over, his mouth slack.

"Overstreet, snap out of it!" Hewitt stepped in front of the newspaperman and slapped him in the face, once, twice. "Carl!"

Overstreet blinked. "What happened?"

"He's playing with your mind. You've got to shut him out."

The vampire's voice rang out in the night. "Bring her to me!"

"Maybe we can make a trade," Overstreet called, a note of desperation in his voice. "The girl for an interview."

"Interview!" Hewitt exclaimed. "Our lives are on the line and you're still worried about that stinkin' interview?"

Overstreet shrugged. Staggering slightly, he returned to the sofa and lowered Shannah onto it.

"What kind of interview?" Ronan asked.

Overstreet and Hewitt exchanged glances as they realized the vampire was on the porch now, with nothing but the door standing between them.

"For one of the magazines I write for," Overstreet replied. "What do you say?"

"Make it quick."

Overstreet grabbed his notebook and a pencil out of his coat pocket, then dragged a kitchen chair close to the front door and sat down. "How long have you been a vampire?"

"Five hundred and thirteen years."

"How many people have you killed in that time?"

"A hundred, maybe more, not counting the two of you."

Overstreet swallowed hard. "How did you become a vampire. Was it voluntary?"

"No. I was brought across by another vampire against my will."

"Are there many vampires in the United States?"

"More than you want to know."

"How about in the rest of the world?"

"We are everywhere," Ronan said curtly. "There have been vampires since the beginning of time."

"Where did the first vampire come from?"

"No one knows for sure. Some say the first man to become a vampire was a man who refused to die. He called up the devil and offered to trade his soul for immortality. Some say the man's name was Vlad Tepes."

"Do you think that's true? That Vlad the Impaler was really a vampire?"

"It's possible."

"This is priceless," Overstreet said, scribbling furiously.

"Is it worth your life?" Hewitt asked dryly. "Because that's what it's going to cost you if she dies before you're through."

But Overstreet wasn't thinking about that now. The reporter in him had taken control. Newspapermen had often sacrificed their lives for a good story, and this was the story of a lifetime. "Have you ever made anyone into a vampire?"

"No."

"Do you know how it's done?"

"Would you like me to show you?"

Overstreet cleared his throat. "She said you're the romance writer. Is that true?"

"I grow weary of your questions, mortal. Bring me the girl."

"And what happens if I do?"

"You should be more worried about what will happen if you don't."

"We think the girl is dying," Hewitt said. "We were going to take her to the hospital, but I'm not coming outside as long as you're here."

"She is ill. Bring her to me now. I will not harm you this night." Ronan forced the words between clenched teeth. "I swear it on her life."

"What about tomorrow night?" Hewitt asked.

"I grow weary of this," Ronan snarled. "Her time is running out. And so is yours."

"Give him the girl," Overstreet urged. "If she dies, he'll hunt us down for sure."

Hewitt swore under his breath. "Back away from the porch and I'll bring her out."

Overstreet peered out the window. "He's gone."

Hewitt snorted as he lifted Shannah into his arms. "Just because you can't see him doesn't mean he's not there."

"Well, it's a chance we're gonna have to take."

"Open the door."

With a hand that trembled, Carl Overstreet unlocked the door, then ducked out of sight, his notebook clutched in his fist.

Hewitt took a deep breath, then stepped across the threshold. Kneeling, he placed Shannah on the porch, then darted back into the house.

Overstreet slammed the door and locked it, then sagged against the jamb. "Do you think he'll keep his word?" he asked, then jumped as Ronan's voice rang out in the night.

"I always keep my word. You are safe. For tonight."

Hewitt slumped against the front door. Damn, that had been a close one.

"That's it for me," Overstreet said, shoving his notebook into his coat pocket. "First thing in the morning, I'm outta here."

"You intend to let him go, just like that?"

"Damn straight! I'm no vampire hunter. I got what I came for. From now on I'm writing about safer topics, like terrorists and serial killers. I don't know about the other vampires you've killed. Maybe they weren't as powerful as this one. Maybe you just got lucky with them, I don't know. But I know one thing, if you go after this guy, you're out of your ever-lovin' mind."

"Then I'm out of my mind."

Overstreet nodded. "I'll be sure to spell your name right when I pen your obituary."

Muttering an oath, Jim Hewitt pushed away from the door. Maybe Overstreet was right. Maybe it was time to quit the field while he still could. He had been hunting vampires his entire adult life and what had it got him? He had a small house he hadn't seen in months, a car with over two hundred thousand miles on it, and a suitcase. No family. No time for a girlfriend. Hell, he couldn't remember the last time he'd been out on a date.

Maybe it was time to give it up. The pay wasn't that great, considering that he put his life on the line every time he went after one of the Undead. He couldn't kill them all. He laughed bitterly. He sure as hell couldn't kill the one he was after now. Not that he had really tried, he admitted sheepishly. And as long as he was being honest with himself, he might as well admit that Ronan scared the crap out of him. It wasn't something he could tell Overstreet, but just thinking about going up against Ronan one-on-one sent cold chills down his spine. There was something about this vampire that frightened him. Maybe it was just the fact that Ronan was so old. Vampires didn't weaken as they aged. Quite the opposite. They grew stronger, faster, more deadly with each passing year.

He blew out a sigh. Dammit, he wasn't a quitter! If he walked away now . . . he shook his head. If he walked away now, he was no more than a coward.

"Is he gone?" Overstreet asked.

Hewitt switched on the porch light, then peered out the window. There was no sign of the girl, or the vampire. "Looks like he's taken her."

"Then let's get the hell out of here while we can," Overstreet said. "I don't want to be here if he comes back tomorrow night."

With a nod, Hewitt unlocked the front door and stepped outside. Overstreet joined him moments later, his eyes wide and scared as he glanced from side to side.

Sliding behind the wheel of his car, Hewitt switched on the engine, wondering if he had completely lost his nerve for the hunt. And what he would do if he had.

Cradling Shannah in his arms, Ronan transported the two of them to his house, materializing inside Shannah's bedroom. He drew back the covers and put her to bed. She was pale, so pale. And cold. He drew the covers over her, stroked a lock of hair from her brow. Her heartbeat was slow and unsteady, her face was deathly pale, her breathing shallow and labored.

Her time had run out.

Kneeling beside her, he lifted her head, then bit into his wrist and held it to her mouth. "Drink, love," he coaxed.

She was too weak to argue.

He spoke to her while she drank, telling her that he loved her, begging her to fight, to tell him what he should do.

He felt the blood flowing out of him, knew she was

taking far more than she ever had before. He waited for her color to improve, for her breathing to return to normal, for her heartbeat to become regular. Waited, and then waited some more, but there was no change, no visible improvement. He recalled telling her that he couldn't keep her alive forever, but he had hoped his blood would prolong her life for years to come instead of just a few months.

"Shannah. Shannah, love, what would you have me do?"

She moaned softly. Her lips moved, as if she was trying to speak, and then she was still once more.

Her heartbeat was faint, so faint that even with his preternatural senses, he could scarcely hear it.

"Shannah!" He was losing her. He could feel her slipping away with each labored breath. "I can't let you go. I can't, and I won't!"

And yet, how could he bring her across? She had told him time and again that she didn't want to be a vampire, that she didn't want to survive by drinking blood.

"Do you want to die?" he asked, knowing she could no longer hear him. "Is that what you want?"

Rising, he paced the floor, his frustration growing with each step he took as her heartbeat grew slower, fainter.

How could he bring her across without her consent?

How could he let her go?

He tried to imagine his existence without her, but it was no use. She had become a part of him, as necessary to his survival as avoiding the sun.

Sitting on the edge of the bed, he drew her into his arms. Tears stung his eyes as he murmured, "Shannah, love, forgive me."

And then he bent his head to her neck, his eyes closing as his fangs pierced the tender flesh of her throat. And all the while, he despised himself for the overwhelming sense of pleasure that spread through him as he drank her life and her memories, her hopes and her dreams. He drank it all, hating himself as he did so, praying as he had not prayed in centuries that she would forgive him.

He gazed down at her, fear striking his heart. She was on the very brink of death now. Had he left her enough to survive the change? With a cry of despair, he savaged his wrist again and pressed the bleeding wound to her lips.

"Drink, Shannah," he urged, his tears dampening her cheeks. "You must drink. Now. Hate me if you must for what I've done, but please, love, don't leave me to walk the earth without you on it."

She lay still and pale in his arms, her heartbeat so faint now it was all but undetectable.

"Drink, Shannah! Dammit, you will do as I say!" he commanded, pleased when, ever so slowly, her mouth closed over his wrist. Smiling faintly, he stroked her hair. "Drink, my love. Drink, and live."

He closed his eyes as she took what she needed. And there was pleasure in the giving, even more so than in the taking. If she needed every drop of his blood to survive, then so be it. He would gladly give up his existence to extend hers. He had lived for hundreds of years. She deserved as much, and more.

He opened his eyes when she pushed his wrist away.

"Shannah?" Her name was a sigh on his lips, a plea, a prayer for forgiveness.

"What happened?" She glanced around, her brow furrowed in confusion. "How did I get here? What happened to Hewitt and Overstreet?" Sitting up, she stared at him a moment, her expression puzzled. "Why can I see your face so clearly when the lights are off?"

"Shannah . . ."

She wrinkled her nose. "What's that smell? And that noise?"

"Shannah, listen to me . . ."

She licked her lips, and grimaced. "And that taste . . ." She looked up at him, her eyes widening. "You gave me your blood again, didn't you?"

"Yes."

"But it's different this time." She frowned thoughtfully for a moment, as if trying to put all the pieces together. "Why is it different? Why are you looking at me like that? Why . . . ?" She clutched her stomach, a groan rising in her throat as she doubled over in pain. "What's happening? I've never felt like this before. I'm dying, aren't I?" She looked up at him, her eyes wide with fright and resignation. "In my room, letters to my parents . . ." She groaned again, an animal-like cry of pain and fear. "Ronan, hold me! Please, hold me. I'm so afraid."

He wrapped his arms around her and held her tight, lightly stroking her cheek and the side of her neck with the backs of his fingers.

"It's all right, love," he murmured. "There's nothing to be afraid of."

"But I am afraid. I don't want to leave you . . . I don't want to die."

He should have told her the truth, but try as he might, he couldn't form the words. She would know the truth soon enough. And she would hate him for it.

He held her all through the night, comforting her as best he could as her body cast off the last vestiges of illness and mortality and began to adjust to its new preternatural state.

At dawn, she went still as the daytime sleep of his kind claimed her. He put her to bed, then went through the house, making sure all the doors and windows were closed and locked. It was then that he saw the broken window in the kitchen. There was no need to wonder who had done it. Cursing softly, he went back upstairs.

He couldn't leave Shannah in the upper part of the house, alone and unprotected, as long as Hewitt and Overstreet were in the area. He didn't credit either of them with enough sense to leave town.

Lifting Shannah into his arms, he carried her down to his lair in the basement. Knowing it would frighten her to awaken in his casket, he lowered her into the chair, then went back upstairs to get the mattress, pillow, and blankets from the bed.

He held her in his arms until the Dark Sleep tugged at him, held her, wondering if he would ever have the chance to hold her in his embrace again once she realized what he had done.

Kissing her tenderly, he put her to bed, then climbed into his own resting place and closed his eyes, truly afraid, for the first time in his life, of what the night would bring.

Chapter Twenty-Nine

Ronan woke an hour or so before the sun began to set. Rising, he immediately went to Shannah's side. His Shannah, now cursed with the Dark Trick because he had been too weak, too selfish, to let her go. Never had she looked more beautiful. Her skin was radiant, her hair more lustrous than ever.

He knew it would be another couple of hours before she woke. Fledglings required a great deal of rest. Only after a hundred years or so did they grow strong enough to rise before the setting of the sun.

Needing to touch her, he brushed a kiss across her brow, laid his hand against her cheek, then drew back.

The thought of facing her filled him with renewed terror. Would she accept what she had become? Would she refuse to accept it and walk out into the sunlight and end her new existence before it had truly begun? Or would she hate him for a thousand years and more?

Too agitated to remain still, he went upstairs where he paced the halls, his senses focused on the woman sleeping below—the barely audible beat of her heart, the lingering scent of her perfume, the remembered taste of her life's nectar on his tongue.

Shannah.

She had been sunlight to his shadow, light to his darkness. She had brought him laughter and a joy in his existence that he had never known before. She had given him her love and her trust, and he had betrayed both in the worst way possible.

The sun had disappeared beneath the horizon when his senses told him she had awakened.

A thought took him to her side. He found her sitting cross-legged on the mattress looking beautiful and bewildered.

"Ronan, what am I doing down here?"

"I didn't feel it was safe for you to be upstairs alone."

"Not safe? Why not?"

"Have you forgotten about Hewitt and Overstreet?"

Her eyes widened as memory of the night before returned. "How did you get me away from them?"

"We made a deal."

"A deal? What kind of a deal?"

"I promised not to kill them if they let you go."

"That was very clever of you," she said, smiling. "But surely you don't think they would try to kidnap me again?"

"I don't know what those two are capable of, but finding out isn't a chance I'm willing to take."

She lifted her arms overhead, stretching her back and shoulders, and then ran her fingers through her hair. "I must look a mess."

"You've never been more beautiful. How do you feel?"

She canted her head to one side, taking mental inventory. "I've never felt better," she declared. "I didn't feel this good even before I got sick. Why is that? And why can I see you in the dark?" Rising, she walked back and forth beside the mattress, her brow furrowed. "I can hear noise from outside. Why? I never could before. And I can smell the grass and the trees, and . . ." She stopped pacing to look at him. "Even you look different, as if I'm seeing you more clearly." She glanced around the room. "Everything looks brighter, clearer, more distinct, even in the dark . . ."

She looked at him once more, her gaze riveted on his face. "What's happened to me, Ronan?" she asked, a tremor in her voice. "What have you done?"

He couldn't sidestep the truth any longer. Expelling a deep breath, he said, "I've given you what you wanted the day you first came to see me."

She digested that a moment, and then she slapped him with all the force at her command. Even though she was a newly made vampire, her strength was considerable.

The sound of flesh meeting flesh echoed like a gunshot in the room. His head snapped back from the force of her blow. He could feel the blood rushing to his face, knew her handprint stood out in vivid relief against his cheek.

"Tell me," she said, her voice rising. "Tell me that you didn't make me what you are."

He stared at her, his silence condemning him.

"Tell me, damn you!"

"I couldn't let you die. Hate me if you wish. Destroy me if it will make you feel any better."

"How could you?" She slapped him again, harder this time. "How could you?" Rage and anger bubbled up inside of her and spewed out in a vitriolic hiss. "You knew how I felt about it. I told you time and again I didn't want to be what you are."

He said nothing. Indeed, what could he say in his defense? Except, "Would you rather be dead?"

"Yes! No! I don't know, I only know I'll never forgive you for what you've done to me. Never!"

"Then may be it a long and healthy hatred."

"I'm going out," she said, striding toward the stairway. "And I don't want you to follow me."

He said nothing, only stared after her as she walked up the stairs. He heard the sound of her footsteps overhead as she moved toward the front door.

He listened as the door opened and then closed.

She was gone, perhaps for good, and he had no one to blame but himself.

Shannah left the house with no destination in mind other than the need to be as far away from him as possible.

She was a vampire. Undead. A creature of the night. Forever lost, forever damned. Nosferatu.

She walked down the street, deaf and blind to her surroundings, her rage and confusion growing with every step. How could he have done such a thing to her? He had known how she felt about becoming a vampire. They had discussed it often enough. She had made it clear that she was dead set against it. She laughed mirthlessly. Dead set. A poor choice of words.

She would never be able to enjoy a summer day at the beach again. She would never be able to have children. Never be able to go shopping with Judy, or out to lunch with her mother. Her mother! How could she ever face her parents again? What could she possibly tell them? The truth was out of the question. She could only imagine their reaction. *Hi, Mom. Hey, guess what? I've decided to come back home. Oh, there's just one thing. I'm a vampire now.* Right.

Maybe she could tell them that the doctor had discovered a cure. *Oh, but there's just one little drawback. I can only be active at night.* She frowned. That just might work. She could tell them her sudden aversion to the sun was a side effect of the cure.

A sudden pain deep in her gut put everything else from her mind. She knew instinctively what it was. It was the need to feed. On blood. Even as the thought was born, her fangs pricked her tongue. Opening her mouth, she explored her teeth with her fingertips. Her new teeth were very sharp indeed!

I am a vampire. I have fangs. What will my dentist think?

A bubble of near-hysterical laughter rose in her throat. *Guess what I'll be next Halloween?*

There was a bar on the corner. Taking a deep breath, she went inside, and almost gagged. The smell of liquor, humanity, perspiration and lust was overpowering, the noise almost beyond bearing. And the blood . . . she could hear it pulsing with the beat of a dozen hearts, smell it, almost taste it on her tongue. She lowered her head, afraid someone would see the bloodlust in her eyes, the way she had seen it in Ronan's.

A young man approached her. "Hey, baby, wanna dance?"

She shook her head and turned away, then practically ran out of the bar.

The pain in her belly grew worse.

She stopped halfway down the block. A man was walking toward her, alone.

She knew Ronan called his prey to him, that he took what he needed and sent his victims on their way, leaving them blissfully unaware of what he had done, but she couldn't do it, didn't want to do it. She didn't want to drink human blood, not now, not ever.

Passing the man by, she walked for miles without tiring or getting out of breath. Amazed by her new powers and abilities, she jumped over a six-foot fence just to see if she could do it, and cleared it with ease. It was like being reborn, she thought, like being Superman. But it wasn't right. It wasn't natural. She was an abomination.

No! She was Shannah Davis.

Vampire.

She walked for hours with no destination in mind, the pain in her insides steadily growing worse, but she refused to give in to it. Gritting her teeth, she walked until a tingling under her skin warned her that it was almost dawn and she realized she had nowhere to hide from the light of day.

For a moment, she thought of waiting for the sun to rise and putting an end to her pain and her new existence. She wondered how long it would take, but the thought of burning to death, whether it happened quickly or not, was more than she could bear and she began to run, not stopping until she found an abandoned building in a town far from North Canyon Creek.

With remarkably little effort, she pulled a board away from one of the first-floor windows and climbed into what had once been a warehouse of some kind. Moving away from the bank of windows, she made her way down a rickety stairway to the next level. Streaks of sunlight filtered through a broken window. She was running now, driven by her fear of the unknown. Spying a dusty canvas tarp on the other side of the room, she dove underneath, hoping it would shelter her from the sun's light.

She huddled in the musty darkness, fearful of the death-like sleep she knew was coming. Tremors wracked her body, her stomach cramped with the sharp pangs of vampiric hunger.

Murmuring, "This can't be happening," she tumbled into the dark sleep of the Undead.

Ronan sat on the mattress in the basement, his face pressed against the blanket that had covered Shannah the night before. He drew a deep breath, inhaling the scent of her hair, her skin, her very essence. They had been parted for one night and it already seemed like a lifetime.

It had taken every ounce of self-control he possessed not to follow her when she left the house, but he had failed her once, he would not fail her again. If she wanted to be alone, he would accept her wishes, even if it meant he would never see her again. And even though she was now far away, he found some small comfort in knowing that she was still alive, that she still walked the earth, even if she no longer walked with him.

Where was she now, he wondered. Would he ever see her again?

Rising, he left the house. Her scent still lingered in the air. Unable to help himself, he followed it, curious to see where she had gone. He followed her scent down the street and into a bar and then into an abandoned warehouse located in another town. It pained him to know her anger had driven her so far away.

He walked around the outside of the warehouse. Her scent was strong but his senses told him she was no longer in the building.

Was she, perchance, on her way back to his house?

Had she fed? He remembered all too clearly the agony he had endured as a fledgling. Unless she fed, the pain would grow steadily worse until it was excruciating.

If only she had stayed, he would have guided her through the transition from mortal to vampire, a change that was often difficult, especially for those who were brought across against their will or without knowing what to expect.

But there was no help for it now.

When his own hunger rose within him, he put Shannah from his mind and prowled the city streets in search of prey. Finding none to his liking, he went into a night club where he found a woman sitting at the bar, alone.

She was a lovely creature, with short blond hair and large brown eyes. She smiled when he sat down beside her.

He returned her smile. "Good evening."

She lifted her drink. "Hi."

He nodded at the dance floor. "Would you like to dance?"

She tossed off her drink. "Sure, why not?"

He took her hand. It was small and soft, warm and pulsing with human life. She went into his arms, easily following his lead. The music was slow and he held her close, wishing all the while that it was Shannah in his arms, Shannah smiling up at him.

"I've never seen you in here before," the woman said.

Her words were slightly slurred, making him wonder how much she'd had to drink.

"I've never been here before."

"I'm Anne."

"Ronan."

"A distinctive name," she remarked.

"A very old name."

His nostrils filled with the scent of her blood, arousing his hunger. It would be easy to take her away from here, he thought, easy to seduce her, but it wouldn't be right, nor would it be fair to the woman, not when he was worried about Shannah. Worried and angry.

But he had no scruples when it came to taking the woman's blood. Mesmerizing her with a look, he took what he needed, there on the dance floor, and then he wiped the memory from her mind and escorted her back to her seat at the bar.

A thought took him out of the night club and back into the darkness of the night. His thoughts immediately turned to Shannah. She had so much to learn; how to dissolve into mist, how to transport herself from one place to another, how to travel with preternatural speed so that her

passing was invisible to mortal eyes, how to block the constant barrage of sights and sounds and smells that he
knew were pummeling her senses every hour of the night.
All that, and so much more he would have taught her if
she had only stayed and given him the chance.

But he could not fault her for shunning his company.
Whatever blame there was lay in him, not her.

Shannah wandered through the city, the ache in her
belly spreading, burning through every nerve in her
body like liquid flame. She had never felt such agonizing
pain before. It was like her blood was on fire, as if her
bones were melting. She needed to feed, and soon, she
thought, before the pain consumed her and there was
nothing left of her at all.

She didn't want to feed off of humans. She didn't want
to consume blood to survive. Perhaps, if she resisted, the
pain would go away. Ah, foolish hope. Even as it crossed
her mind, the hunger clawed at her insides. Her body
screamed with agony until she couldn't bear it any
longer. She needed nourishment, and she needed it now.

Glancing around, she saw that she had traveled far
from the city. Instead of houses and shops, she was surrounded by hayfields and pasturelands. Farmhouses and
barns and corrals lined both sides of the road.

It scared her that she had no memory of how she had
gotten there.

She moved toward the nearest pasture, drawn by the
scent of blood. Several dark shapes were clustered together in the middle of the field. They lifted their heads
as she drew near, their ears twitching, their nostrils flaring.

She called one to her, waited while a small brown
horse trotted toward her. Slipping between the fence
rails, Shannah put her arm around the horse's neck.

"I can do this," she said, and with tears of pain and revulsion coursing down her cheeks, she bit into the horse's jugular and satisfied her hunger. The horse didn't seem to mind. Oddly enough, neither did she.

With the hunger assuaged, she felt content, almost joyful. Quiet power thrummed through her veins. She had never felt better in her life.

Later, at a loss as to what to do to fill the long, lonely hours until dawn, she tried to transport herself across the road, but no matter how hard she concentrated or thought about what she wanted to do, nothing happened. How had Ronan managed it? Maybe zapping from one place to another was something only older vampires could achieve.

Walking back toward the city where she had spent the previous night, it occurred to her that she had no cash and no credit cards. She needed her wallet and a change of clothes. And a shower, she thought, wrinkling her nose. And then she laughed. Of course she smelled. She had been in these same clothes since she died. How long ago had it been? Two nights? Three? She couldn't seem to think straight.

She had almost reached the warehouse when she heard Ronan's voice whisper through her mind.

Shannah, my love, please come home.

The sound of his voice brought hot tears to her eyes. Ronan. In spite of what he had done, she missed him dreadfully. But she couldn't forget how he had betrayed her trust. She could never, ever forgive him for what he had done.

Shannah, are you all right?

She was back in the city now, her senses again flooded with sights and sounds and the scents of those around her. How did Ronan keep from going mad with so much sensory input screaming in his mind?

With a little practice, you can block it all out, love.

She refused to answer. Doing her best to ignore him, she gazed in the shop windows as she passed by, admiring a pretty blue sweater, a black velvet dress, a pair of silver high heels. She felt a sudden lurch in the pit of her stomach when she realized she cast no reflection in the glass. Sickened by the reminder of what she had become, she turned her face away from the shop windows.

Shannah? Answer me, dammit!

She pressed her hands over her ears. *Get out of my head!*

His soft laughter filled her mind. *Come home, Shannah, let me help you.*

Home . . . the very word spoke of solace and belonging. Clinging to her anger, she thrust the thought from her mind. *You've done enough, thank you very much! Now go away and leave me alone!*

I miss you.

Just three small words, but they were filled with love and longing. She swallowed past the lump rising in her throat, then shook her head defiantly. She would not be swayed by the soft yearning in his voice or by the sadness in his words. She had trusted him with her heart and soul, with her very life, and he had betrayed her.

I can feel your confusion, love. Please come home. Let me answer your questions. Let me help you learn how to use and control the powers that are now yours.

It was tempting, oh, so tempting. To see him again, to be in his arms and see his smile, taste his kisses . . . No! With a resolute shake of her head, she continued on down the street. If, as he said, she could block out unwanted sights and sounds, then she could shut him out, too!

You'll have to come back sooner or later, he said, his voice quiet in her mind. *Your belongings are here.*

Drat the man! He was right.

And you belong here, with me.

No, but I do need to come back to your *house to gather my things.* She emphasized "your." *If you care for me at all, you won't be there when I return.*

She felt the pain her words caused him as if it were her own. In her mind's eye, she could see him standing in front of the fireplace in the living room, his hands braced against the mantel, his head bowed, his eyes dark with anguish and regret. She hardened her heart against him, refusing to feel pity or sorrow. He had stolen her mortality, stolen the sun's light from her, turned her into an inhuman monster condemned to exist by partaking of the blood of living beings. She ignored the voice in her head that reminded her that she hadn't wanted to die, that she had gone to his house hoping to find a vampire who could give her immortality. And now she had it. *Be careful what you ask for,* her mother had always said, *lest you get it.* Well, she had asked for it, but she had never expected to find it, nor had she truly wanted to be a vampire. If she was lucky, she might exist for hundreds of years, as Ronan and some of his friends had, but no matter how long she existed, she would die anew each time the sun went down.

It was a frightening thing, tumbling uncontrollably into that abyss that was darker than dark. Last night, hiding in the creaky bowels of the deserted warehouse, she had sensed the blackness creeping up on her, felt herself being dragged down into oblivion. She had fought against it but to no avail. She had told herself there was nothing to fear, that it was normal for her now, but she couldn't stave off the panic that had swept over her as she felt herself sinking into a pool of darkness as deep and wide as eternity. Trapped in oblivion, she had felt nothing at all until the sun went down and she woke from a long and dreamless sleep.

Shannah . . .

I'd like to come for my things tonight, if that's convenient for you.

Very well, love.

Love. The word slipped past her defenses and arrowed straight into her heart. She remembered the night she had asked him if she was truly his love. "*Do you doubt it?*" he had asked, and when she reminded him that he had never said it, he had replied, "No, I never have. I've never said it to any woman, but I love you, Shannah, more than you can imagine."

She thrust the memory away. If he had truly loved her, he would have respected her wishes.

I'll be gone when you get here. Stay the night, if you wish.

Where will you spend the night?

Don't worry about me, I'll find a place.

Thank you.

There was a long silence and then his voice whispered ever so softly and sweetly through her mind again. *I love you.*

Chapter Thirty

Ronan's house was empty, as he had promised, when Shannah arrived later that night. She stood in the middle of the living room, her mind filling with memories of Ronan. His scent was here, so strong in her nostrils that she glanced over her shoulder to see if he had suddenly appeared in the room.

She looked around, somehow expecting to find the house to be as changed as she was. Had it only been two nights ago that her entire life had turned upside down? It seemed an eternity had passed since then. When she had first come here, she had been deathly ill, weak, and afraid. Now, only a few short months later, she was healthy and whole, with the strength of ten mortal women, but she was still afraid. Afraid of what she had become, afraid of the future. How was she to survive? Where would she live? Eternity stretched before her, filled with eons of loneliness and separation from the rest of mankind. Why would anyone want such an existence?

Knowing she couldn't stay here, she wandered through the house, remembering how she had come here that first day, looking for a vampire. Well, not only had she found one, she had become one! She wondered again what her parents would think if they knew. Would they still love her, or would they turn away from her in horror and revulsion? And what of Judy and her other friends back home? Would they notice the difference in her? If she hadn't seen the proof with her own eyes, she would never have guessed that Ronan was a vampire, although now that she knew what he was, it seemed obvious in so many ways.

Climbing the stairs, she went into the bedroom. Pulling her underwear from the dresser, she piled it on top of the bed, thinking that all the beautiful clothing and nightgowns that Ronan had bought for her would never fit in the one suitcase that she owned.

She paused in the act of folding one of her nightgowns. She had no right to take the things he had bought for her . . . she was no longer pretending to be Eva Black, no longer living under his roof, no longer in his employ. Nothing in the house belonged to her. Even the suitcase she had taken from the closet was his.

Everything is yours, love. I bought it all for you. She heard his voice in her mind, saw him smile wistfully as he added, *Anyway, the dresses aren't my size.*

His wry comment made her smile and then, suddenly, she was crying. Sinking down on the bed, she cried for the life she had lost, cried because the man she loved had betrayed her trust and thrust her into a new world that was strange and scary. She cried because she would never marry and have children and grandchildren, never be able to go to the beach and work on her tan. She would never be able to sit and enjoy a Thanksgiving dinner with her family again, or open presents on Christmas morning. Never drink hot chocolate on a cold winter night, never again eat ice cream or drink a thick chocolate malt, or gobble down a double cheeseburger and fries. She refused to listen to the small voice of her conscience that reminded her that in a week or a month, death would have put an end to those things as surely as did her new lifestyle.

She blew out a sigh. So many things she had taken for granted that were forever lost to her.

But there is so much to learn, love. So much to see and explore. A whole new world is out there, waiting for you.

She sniffed back her tears. *I'll find it on my own, thank you.*

Shannah, don't let your anger keep us apart, not now. I'm not asking you to forgive me, only to let me help you until you're ready to be on your own. You don't have any place to go. Stay in the house. Sleep in my lair, if it pleases you, or make one of your own.

I can't stay here. She dried her tears on a corner of the bedspread. *Where will you stay?*

You needn't worry about me. Please, love, keep the house. I've taken everything else from you. Let me give you something in return.

I don't think . . .

Shannah. His voice was stern now, a loving father speaking to a stubborn and rebellious child. *Keep the clothes. Keep the damn house. I don't want it anymore.*

Why not?

It was only a home when you shared it with me. Now it's just a house. I'll find a new lair.

She didn't want to take anything from him, but he was right. She had no place else to stay except that smelly old warehouse, and that wasn't as safe as his basement lair. And she had grown to love the house . . . And darn it, he did owe her something for what he had done.

I'll stay, for a little while, she said. *Thank you.*

Will you let me help you?

She wanted to say no. She didn't want his help. She never wanted to see him again. She was being childish, and she knew it. And, darn him, he was right again. He could make her transition from mortal to vampire so much easier.

Shannah?

All right.

Just say when.

Whenever it's convenient for you.

Tonight? She heard the underlying note of longing in his voice.

No. She didn't want to give him the satisfaction of hurrying right over, didn't want him to think she was anxious to see him or worse, that she missed him. *Tomorrow night will be soon enough.*

All right, Shannah. Have it your way.

She started to answer him, but knew it was useless. He had withdrawn from her mind and closed the door behind him. She tried to slip past his defenses, but he was blocking her thoughts.

She was surprised by how much it hurt to know he was blocking her. She tried not to think of him while she put her underwear and nightgowns back in the dresser, or while she filled the tub with water, or while she relaxed in a hot bubble bath, but it was impossible. She should have known it would be impossible to forget him as long as she stayed here, in his house. It was here that he had sheltered her and cared for her when she was sick, here that he had kissed her. Her toes curled with the memory of his kisses. No mere joining of lips had ever been as tumultuous, as arousing, or as satisfying.

She lifted a hand to her neck. The skin tingled where he had bitten her. Somehow, the thought that he had taken her blood wasn't as repulsive as it had been a few days ago.

And she had taken his. Why didn't the idea disgust her the way it once had? She felt her hunger stir to life at the memory, felt her fangs brush her tongue. Why did she suddenly find herself wanting to taste him again?

"Why, indeed?" she muttered wryly. "Does the word 'vampire' ring a bell?"

Like it or not, her life had changed, she had changed. And she knew it was only the beginning.

She stayed in the tub until the water grew cool. Putting on her nightgown and robe, she went downstairs, plucked one of Ronan's books from the shelf, and curled up on the sofa to read.

The vampire bent over Miranda's neck, his eyes blazing, his fangs gleaming in the light of the full moon.

"Do it," she whispered. "Do it now. I'm not afraid."

"Are you sure?" he asked. "You must be sure."

"As sure as I've ever been about anything in my life," *Miranda said, forcing a brave smile.*

With a nod, the vampire wrapped her in his dark embrace. There was no turning back now for either of them.

She moaned softly as his fangs pierced the tender skin of her throat.

He drank deeply, drank until she hovered between life and death, and then, with a groan, he tore open his own wrist and held it to her lips.

"Drink," he said. "You must drink, quickly."

So, Shannah thought, that was how it was done. That was how she had become a vampire. It wasn't the vampire's bite that made the transformation. He had drained her of blood, taken her to the point of death, and then poured his life into her.

Interesting, she thought, and turned the page.

She dressed with care the following night, choosing a pair of silky black slacks and a dark blue sweater. She brushed her hair until it crackled, spritzed herself with perfume, then looked in the mirror to apply her makeup. She could see the shower behind her, the towels on the rack, the door into the bedroom, and nothing else. How could she have forgotten that she would never see her reflection in a mirror again? It was as if she had been wiped from existence and memory. Shannah was gone and what remained was an abomination.

She stared at the mirror for a long time, her stomach in knots.

It was true. She was a vampire. She had known it before, of course, there was no longer any denying it, but it was suddenly a cold, hard fact, one she felt in the deepest part of her being.

Vampire.

Undead.

She remembered reading somewhere—had it been in one of Ronan's books?—that vampires cast no reflection because they had no soul. Could that be true? Had she lost her soul as well as her humanity?

She felt different, inside and out, there was no doubt of that, but she wasn't a soulless monster, was she? She was still Shannah.

Wasn't she?

Her makeup forgotten, she went downstairs to wait for Ronan.

Ronan paused outside the front door of the house where he had lived for the past seventy years. He hadn't had a case of nerves like this in over five centuries. How could he bear the hatred he was sure to see in her eyes? Maybe he was making a mistake. He'd had no one to ease his way into his preternatural life. He had learned what he needed to know to survive as a vampire on his own. No doubt Shannah could do the same. But he could not abandon Shannah as Rosalyn had so callously abandoned him.

Taking a deep breath, he knocked on the door.

Moments later, Shannah stood before him, looking more lovely than he had ever seen her.

"Come in," she said, her voice cool, aloof.

He followed her into the living room, sat where she indicated.

A taut silence stretched between them.

"You must have questions," he said at last.

"Have I lost my soul, Ronan? Am I damned now?"

"Why would you think that?"

"I looked in a mirror. There was no one there."

It was a frightening experience. He remembered the first time it had happened to him, the sick feeling in his gut, the sense of loss.

"Am I damned, Ronan?"

"I don't know," he replied honestly. "But I don't think so. What have you done to deserve damnation? You didn't ask to be a vampire. If anyone is damned, it's me."

For all that she hated him for what he had done, the thought of his being forever damned distressed her more than it should have.

"Questions," he repeated. "You must have others."

"What? Oh, yes, but I don't know where to start."

"As you already know, your sense of sight and hearing are vastly increased. This holds true for all of your senses. You have many powers," he went on. "Some of them you're already aware of. Others will come to you in time. Some of them, like dissolving into mist, seem impossible or unbelievable, but you can master them all, with practice. You can move so fast as to be virtually invisible to mortal eyes. You can change your shape . . ."

"What do you mean?"

"You can assume the shape of animals."

"Like a bat?" she asked, remembering all the old Dracula movies she had seen.

"A bat?" he asked, obviously amused. "Why would you want to be a bat?"

"I don't know. In the movies . . ."

"Ah, the movies. I don't know if you can turn into a bat. I've never tried. Much easier to turn into something larger, like a wolf. As I was saying, you have many supernatural abilities. You can climb up the side of buildings as easily as a spider, call people to you, mesmerize them with a look, wipe your memory from their minds. If you get hurt, you will heal almost immediately. Few things, save the sun or pure silver, can do you serious harm."

"What about garlic and being unable to enter a church, and stuff like that?"

He shook his head. "Stoker and the Hollywood crowd are responsible for all that nonsense."

"And a stake through the heart?"

"That will destroy you as surely as the sun."

She regarded him a moment. "I want to see you dissolve into mist."

He nodded and then, almost before she could blink, he was gone and in his place there was a shimmering mist of silver-gray motes. She felt her heart skip a beat as the mist moved over her until it surrounded her. Warmth engulfed her and with it, a feeling of pure love. She felt bereft when it floated away, then hovered in the center of the room.

A moment later, Ronan stood before her again.

"Unbelievable is right," she murmured. "But how do you do it?"

"Mind over matter, that's all it is. You think it, believe it, do it."

Closing her eyes, Shannah pictured herself turning into a mist of pale pink motes. At first, she felt nothing and then, abruptly, she felt lighter than air. Looking down, she saw that her body had disappeared and that she was hovering in the air over her chair. She could see and hear, but everything seemed hazy and far away. She willed herself toward Ronan, let herself brush against him. It was an odd sensation. She was aware of sliding over something solid but she had no sense of actually touching him. She drifted around the room, thinking how odd it felt to be weightless and without form, yet able to think and observe. She floated up to the ceiling and stayed there for a few minutes, just because she could. Was this what it felt like to be a ghost, she wondered, or was it perhaps the way one's soul felt when it left the body on its journey toward heaven. Or hell.

Drifting down towards the floor, she was overcome by a sudden fear that she wouldn't be able to assume her own form again, that not only had she lost her soul, but her physical form as well, and that she was now doomed to spend the rest of her existence as some soulless, formless non-entity. Panic flowed through her and she felt herself bouncing aimlessly around the room, careening off the walls, the ceiling, the furniture. She would have screamed, had she been able.

"Shannah, relax!"

Ronan's voice. She turned toward it, her panic growing.

"You must concentrate," he said. "Listen to my voice. There's nothing to be afraid of. Form an image of yourself in your mind, and your body will take on its own shape once again. Yes, yes, that's right."

She landed on her feet on the floor, hard. She blinked at Ronan, then ran her hands over her arms, her face, down her sides, remembering a scene from the remake of *The Fly* where an experiment had gone horribly wrong and the animal had emerged from the chamber inside out. Were all her molecules and atoms back where they belonged?

Deciding that everything seemed to be in place, she breathed a sigh of relief. "I don't think I like that very much."

"It's always frightening the first time."

"Did the vampire who made you teach you how to do it?"

"Rosalyn?" He laughed bitterly. "No, she didn't hang around long enough for anything like that." It was the reason he hadn't wanted Shannah to be left on her own. There was so much to learn, all of it easier to absorb and understand if you had someone to guide you, to tell you what to expect, both the good and the bad.

"Then how did you know you could do it?"

He shrugged. "Trial and error, as I recall. I had heard it was possible and one night I tried it. Other things came easily after that. You can do almost anything you wish, Shannah. You have only to think it, picture it, and do it."

She sat in the chair, one leg tucked beneath her. "But I'll never see myself in a mirror again, will I?"

"No." His gaze moved over her. "You are more beautiful than ever."

"Do I look the same?"

"Yes, you are still Shannah. The changes are subtle. Your skin has a glow it didn't have before. Your eyes shine. Your hair is thicker, more lustrous than before. People who know you will think you look better than ever, but they won't know why. Women will envy you. Men will look at you and want you. Your beauty will mesmerize them as will your words." He paused. "Have you hunted?"

"No."

"You've not fed in three nights?"

"I . . . I drank from a horse."

"It didn't satisfy you, did it?"

"No."

"Animal blood will sustain you, but it will never satisfy you."

"How do I shut out the barrage of sound when I'm outside? All those beating hearts and voices? All that noise! And the smells! Things I never noticed before."

"You can block all the unwanted sensory input. It may take a little practice, but you can do it. You're a strong vampire, Shannah."

"I am? Why?"

"Because I'm an old vampire. Because you're the first person I've ever brought across." The first, he thought, and the last.

"If I go visit my parents, will they notice the differences in me?"

"Perhaps, but I doubt it."

"They'll certainly notice that I don't eat, and that I sleep all day." She shook her head. "It will never work."

"Then go after dark, just for a visit. You're not mama's little girl any more. You don't have to spend the night at home. You can see them as often as you wish, on your own terms."

"Maybe. I don't know."

"You are a vampire now, Shannah. Like everything else in life, you can make the most of it, the best of it, or you can spend the rest of your existence dwelling on what you can't do. The choice is yours."

She nodded. He was right, of course. Attitude was everything. "Thank you for coming."

Knowing he had been dismissed, he bade her good night and left the house.

Outside, he groaned low in his throat. It had been sheer hell to see her, to be close to her, and not touch her. Thanks to the paranormal glamour common to all vampires, she was more beautiful and more desirable than ever.

Quelling the urge to let his frustration rush out in an angry roar, he stormed through the night. But he couldn't outrun the anguish of knowing he had lost her forever.

She was willing to see him again the following night. It was, he thought, both a blessing and a curse to be with her—a blessing to see her, to hear her voice, inhale her sweet fragrance. A curse to know that in her heart she despised him.

"Let me teach you to hunt," he suggested.

"No."

"Shannah, you must learn. You cannot survive on the blood of animals indefinitely." Seeing the refusal in her eyes, he said, "Please, just trust me one more time. I know you think you can't do this, that it will be unpleasant and repulsive, but you're only feeling that way because you think you should. That's mortal thinking, and you're no longer bound by mortal precepts."

"Maybe you're right." She gazed into the fire blazing in the hearth. She had fed on a stray dog earlier. It had eased the hunger but as Ronan had said, it left her feeling unsatisfied. And she was already hungry again, if, indeed, you could call it hunger. It was a pain unlike anything she had ever known, as if dull knives were carving her insides.

"Will you come?" he asked. "Will you trust me one more time?"

With a curt nod, she followed him out into the night. A night that now seemed as bright as day. With her preternatural sight, she could see farther than ever before, penetrate the drifting shadows, discern each individual thread in Ronan's long black coat.

He took her to a distant part of the city. There was less noise here, fewer people, fewer distractions. Most of the businesses had closed for the night save for a couple of small night clubs. One catered to a strictly Goth crowd, the other to an older, more sedate clientele.

Ronan entered the Goth club.

Inside, Shannah looked around. Her first thought was that everyone in the place was a vampire. The men and women milling about were all dressed in black. Some of the patrons wore long black cloaks. The women wore dark makeup, the men wore their hair long. Candles provided the only light in the room. The tables were covered with black cloths. Each table held a slender black vase containing a single blood-red rose. The music was dark and sensual, the heavy beat calling to something primal and earthy deep within her. A handful of couples swayed on the dance floor, their bodies undulating in time with the music, their movements so suggestive that she felt herself blushing.

Ronan found a place at the bar and Shannah sat beside him.

"Open your mind," he said. "Find those who are susceptible to suggestion. When you find someone that appeals to you, call him, or her, to you."

"I don't think I can . . ." Even as she said the words, her mind touched that of a tall young man standing at the end of the bar. As her mind brushed against his, he turned to look at her.

Shannah smiled tentatively. Straightening, he swaggered toward her.

"Exert your power over him," Ronan said quietly.

"But this is so easy!" she exclaimed.

Ronan grinned. "Not for everyone. When he gets here, tell him you want to go outside. When you have him alone, speak to his mind. Tell him what you want, and he will do as you ask, without question."

"Hey, sweet cakes," the young man said squeezing in beside her. "Can I buy you a drink?"

Shannah let her mind merge with the young man's, then imposed her will on his. "Not now," she said, taking him by the hand. "Come with me, won't you?"

"Go with you, yes."

Filled with a sense of power unlike anything she had ever known, she led the young man outside and then around the corner of the building.

Ronan followed the two of them into the shadows under the building's overhang.

"Now what?" she asked.

"Follow your instincts."

"How will I know when to stop? I don't want to hurt him."

"You'll know. When you've finishing feeding, lick the wound to close it."

Shannah stared at Ronan a moment, thinking she should be repulsed by what she was about to do. Instead, she felt a kind of nervous excitement, sort of like the first time she had held a glass of champagne in her hand. She looked at the young man, her gaze drawn to the pulse steadily beating in the hollow of his throat. Her mouth watered. The hunger soared within her, throbbing to the beat of his heart, as if in anticipation of being sated. She brushed her hand over the side of the young man's neck, then lowered her head and followed her instincts, as Ronan had suggested.

It wasn't repulsive. It wasn't disgusting. It was the most natural thing in the world.

She took what she needed, then, looking up at Ronan, she licked her lips. "I did it." The hunger had receded, leaving behind a sense of serenity and euphoria.

He smiled at her. "Was it as bad as you thought it would be?"

"No." She smiled back at him, her eyes glowing. "It was like . . . I don't know, like I've been doing it all my life."

He stifled the urge to say, "I told you so."

"Now what do I do with him?"

"Speak to his mind again. Tell him to go back into the club and forget everything that just happened."

"And he'll do it?"

Ronan nodded.

"Will I have a bond with him now, like the one you and . . . will I have a bond with him?"

"No. That only happens if he drinks your blood in return."

She did as Ronan had said, watched in amazement as the man walked away from her without a backward glance.

"So, that's all there is to it?" Shannah asked incredulously. "I just call them to me?"

"That's it."

"And they'll do whatever I ask?"

He nodded. "Shall we go?"

Side by side, they walked down the street, away from the night clubs.

"Where did you sleep last night?" he asked as they neared the house.

"In the basement."

He looked at her, one brow arched.

"No," she said, "not in your coffin. I just couldn't. I slept on the mattress on the floor."

He nodded. Tomorrow night he would carry the frame down so that she didn't have to sleep on the floor, unless it occurred to her to do it herself. With her preternatural strength, she could easily carry the frame and headboard into the basement. He didn't tell her, though. He wanted to do it for her.

She stopped when they reached the porch. "Thank

you for your help tonight," she said, her voice again cool and polite. And distant.

He took it for the dismissal it was, bowed his head in her direction, and vanished from her sight.

Shannah stared after him, the ache in her heart almost beyond bearing.

He arrived on her doorstep, unsummoned, the following night. "May I come in?"

She shrugged. "It's your house."

He smiled faintly. "I gave it to you, remember?"

"Does that mean you can't come in here unless you're invited now?"

He nodded.

"How does that work, exactly? I mean, what is there to keep you out?"

"The threshold of the house. Thresholds have a supernatural power of their own created by the emotions of those who live within the walls. It can be painful, even fatal, for a vampire to cross one without the owner's permission."

"All thresholds?"

"No, just residences."

She looked thoughtful for a moment, then took a step backward, allowing him access. "Come in."

He followed her into the living room.

"What brings you here tonight?" she asked.

"I thought I'd move the bed frame and headboard into the basement, if it's all right with you."

"Oh." She wondered why she hadn't thought of doing it herself. She started to tell him there was no need, but feared that if she did so, he would leave. And she didn't want him to go. She told herself the only reason she didn't want him to leave was because it was lonely, rattling around in the big old house by herself, and because he was the only one who knew what she had become and didn't care. She recognized both reasons for the lies they were, but she couldn't admit the truth, not to herself, not to him. "Thank you. I'd appreciate that."

She followed him up the stairs, watched the play of muscles in his arms, back and shoulders with feminine appreciation as he dismantled the frame, stacked the pieces one on top of the other, and carried the lot down the stairs to the basement, where he quickly reassembled the thing, then lifted the box spring and mattress into place. The headboard came next.

"Is there anything else I can do for you?" he asked.

"No. I was wondering about your books and your other personal effects. Should I pack them for you?"

"Keep it all or throw it out, whatever you wish." A muscle worked in his jaw. "Do you have any other questions? Anything else you want to know about your new lifestyle?"

She couldn't think of any, nor could she tear her gaze away from his. He loved her. She could see it in his eyes. There was a lingering hurt there, too, and an aching loneliness that was like a physical pain. She felt it as if it were her own, knew how and what he was feeling because she felt the same way. Without Ronan, she felt empty inside, as if a vital part of her very being had been ruthlessly torn out. Was it love that made her feel that way, or merely the blood bond he had forged between them? Was it possible to even separate the two?

Did she really have any reason to be angry with him? He had only given her what she had come looking for. True, he had made her a vampire against her will, but he had done so because he knew she didn't want to die. Because he didn't want her to die. Because he loved her. Would she rather be dead now, never to see him again?

True, she had lost much when he brought her across, but she had also gained much. It was all so confusing!

He stood there, motionless in the way of vampires, watching her, and waiting.

And she wanted him. Right or wrong, she knew she would never be happy in this life or in any other without him.

Desire arced between them, moving through her like a jolt of electricity. She felt it in every nerve and cell of her body, in the sudden intake of her breath, the pounding of her heart, the warmth that suffused her from head to heel.

And still he stood there, watching her, waiting for her to make the first move. When she continued to stand there, mute and unmoving, he whispered her name.

"Shannah."

Just her name, nothing more. Never before had she heard such love, such pain, injected into a single word. It brought a hot rush of tears to her eyes, scalding tears that burned away her anger and turned the last vestiges of her resentment to ashes.

"I'm sorry," she said. "So sorry."

He took a hesitant step toward her, his arms open, and she closed the distance between them in the blink of an eye, her arms wrapping around his waist.

"I missed you," she said. "I missed you every night, so much." She felt the brush of his lips in her hair. "Can you ever forgive me?"

"Hush, love, there's nothing to forgive."

"I've just been so confused. Everything's so new, so different." She made a vague gesture with her hand. "Nothing is as I thought it would be."

"I know." His arms tightened around her, as if he would never let her go. "I know."

She looked up at him. "You'll stay here tonight, won't you?"

"If you want me to."

"Not just tonight, every night."

"Shannah!" Closing his eyes, he rested his brow lightly on the crown of her head. "I was so afraid I'd lost you forever, that you would never forgive me. I worried that you might hate me, that you might hate yourself. That you might destroy yourself."

"I behaved badly."

"No."

He lifted her head and gazed down into her eyes. "Tell me that you forgive me."

"I forgive you, though there's nothing to forgive. I'm glad you brought me across." She smiled up at him. "Like you once said, it isn't a life I would have chosen, but I don't regret it now."

"Ah, Shannah, love!"

"Aren't you going to kiss me?"

"Count on it," he murmured, and lowering his head, he claimed her lips in a kiss that seared her heart and soul, kissed her until she clung to him as the only solid thing in a world that seemed to be spinning out of control.

When she could breathe again, she rested her cheek against his chest. "I love you," she said softly.

"And I you. Will you marry me, Shannah?"

She looked up at him and blinked. "You want to marry me?"

"Very much, if you'll have me."

"Of course I will!" Standing on tiptoe, she pressed her lips to his, thinking she was happier at that moment than she had ever been in her whole life, past or present.

"Can we make it soon?" he asked.

"Are you in a hurry?"

"Most assuredly. I've wanted to make love to you since the moment you first knocked on my door."

"Then why haven't you?"

"Because you're a virgin, my sweet, and I'm an honorable man."

Touched by his old-fashioned chivalry, she rested her head on his chest again and listened to the slow, steady beat of his heart. He wanted to marry her. The thought made her smile anew, and then she raised her head and looked up at him once again. "How long will you love me?"

His knuckles stroked her cheek. "Ah, Shannah, I will love you as long as I draw breath and beyond."

"Will you? People are always telling each other 'I'll love you forever' when they don't have forever. But you and I . . . we could have centuries together. What if you get tired of me?"

"It seems more likely that you'll get tired of me."

"Never! But I keep remembering your friends getting married because they had nothing better to do . . ."

"Believe me, Shannah, that's not why I want to marry you. I think I loved you the moment I saw you. Do you have any idea how difficult it's been for me to hold you and not ravish you?"

"Well, it's your own fault. I've been willing on more than one occasion."

"I know, love, but I'm a product of my time and, as I said, an honorable man. I couldn't defile you, couldn't take your virginity when you didn't know what I was." He glanced past her, his expression suddenly solemn as he murmured, "I have enough sins to atone for."

He really was an honorable man, the most honorable man she had ever known, and she loved him the more for it.

With a sigh, she caressed his cheek, then frowned.

"What about my parents? They'll be so hurt if they aren't at the wedding."

"Then we'll invite them, and anyone else you like."

"Oh, Ronan, you're so good to me!" She showered him with kisses and, abruptly, she drew back, frowning.

"What is it?" he asked. "Have you changed your mind already?"

"No, but don't you think it's time you told me if Ronan is your first name or your last?"

Chapter Thirty-One

Shannah called her parents the next evening to tell them the good news. "Married?" her mother said, sounding somewhat hesitant. "Is that wise? I mean, well, you know, your health . . ."

"I'm much better, Mom. The doctors were wrong about everything. I'm fine now."

"That's all they had to say? They were wrong? All that worry and . . ."

"Mom, I don't want to talk about it. It's over, and I'm getting married next month."

"Next month! Don't you think you're rushing into this a little hastily? I mean, you hardly know this man, not that it won't be wonderful to have a celebrity in the family, but . . ."

"I know all I need to know about him, Mom," Shannah said. "We're planning to get married at home, so you'd better start looking for a dress. And tell Dad to rent a tux."

"How soon will you be here?"

"Not for a couple of weeks. Ronan and I have some things to take care of here first, business, you know. Will you see about the church? We'd like to have an evening ceremony."

"Evening?" Shannah heard the frown in her mother's voice. "Whatever for?"

"It's more romantic, Mom. We aren't planning anything big. Ronan doesn't have any family, so we thought we'd keep it small and intimate."

"Yes, all right, dear. You know, I thought there was something between you two when you were here before."

"I never could hide anything from you," Shannah replied. "Tell Dad I'm sorry I missed him and I'll call him later in the week."

"I will, dear. And be sure to give Ronan my best."

"All right. Good night, Mom, I love you."

"I love you more."

Smiling, Shannah replaced the receiver.

"Your mother didn't sound too thrilled," Ronan remarked.

"Of course she is! You heard her. She thinks it will nice having a celebrity in the family."

"Maybe she's right," he said thoughtfully. "Maybe you are rushing into this."

Shannah frowned, then poked him in the chest with her forefinger. "Are you trying to back out?"

"Of course not."

"Hush, then, and kiss me."

"Working your vampire magic on me, are you?"

"Well, I'm trying!"

"And succeeding," he said, his voice a low growl as he pulled her into his arms.

Jim Hewitt sat in his hotel room, reading Carl Overstreet's most recent column on vampires for the second time.

* * *

And so, dear reader, we come at last to the end of our tale. I searched for a vampire, and I found one. You may not believe me, but I swear by everything I hold dear that it's the truth. I spoke to him briefly, under conditions I would rather not repeat or remember. He told me that he had been a vampire for five hundred and thirteen years and admitted that he had killed "a hundred people, maybe more" in that time.

He said he was made a vampire against his will, that there were many vampires here, in the United States, and many others throughout the world. "More than you want to know" were his exact words.

He said there had been vampires since the beginning of time. When questioned, he said he didn't know where the first vampire had come from, though there were some who believed that Vlad the Impaler was the father of the Undead. Whoever the first vampire was, it's believed that he made a deal with the Devil, trading his soul for immortality.

Our vampire said he had never turned another into a vampire, but that he knew how it was done. Indeed, he even offered to show me. You may be sure that I quickly declined.

At this point, he grew impatient and the interview was over.

As for me, I hope never to see him again.

As someone once said, "Ignorance is bliss." Oh, how I long to be ignorant again.

With a shake of his head, Hewitt threw the magazine across the room. It made a satisfying thump when it hit the wall.

"So," he muttered, "that's the end of that."

He had promised himself he would let this one go. He had told Overstreet the truth when he'd said he had killed twelve vampires. What he hadn't told Overstreet was that the vampires had all been reasonably young in the life. He had never hunted a vampire as old as Ronan, never faced that kind of preternatural power.

Too restless to sit still, Hewitt left the hotel. Getting into his car, he drove through the town, inevitably drawn toward the house with the high fence. Ronan's house.

Exiting the car, he stood in the shadows across the street, trying to summon the nerve to confront the creature in its lair. He had to do it. If he didn't, if he tucked his tail between his legs and ran off like some whipped cur dog, he knew he would never find the nerve to hunt again.

He thought of an old Clint Eastwood movie he had seen years ago. Eastwood had played an outlaw. He remembered one scene in particular when two gunfighters had gone into a saloon to confront him. Eastwood had killed one of the gunmen. The other one had walked outside and then, after a moment, he had turned and gone back into the saloon. His explanation for returning had been because he had to. And he had died for it.

Hewitt stared at the house across the way and wondered if he had the kind of courage the gunfighter in the movie had possessed. And if he would meet the same fate.

Taking a deep breath, he ran his hand over the stake shoved into his belt.

And started across the street.

He paused when he reached the porch, some inner sense of self-preservation screaming that this was not the time or the place.

Feeling like a lily-livered coward, he went back to his car. Maybe he really should look for a new line of work. But to do so was unthinkable. He was a Hewitt. Whenever people asked him why he was a vampire hunter, his standard answer had always been, "because it's what the men in my family do."

With a shake of his head, he slid behind the wheel, then sat there, feeling like he was betraying his father and every male member of his entire family. But as the old saying went, it was better to be a live coward than a dead hero.

He tried to make himself believe it as he drove back to his hotel.

Ronan lifted his head, his nostrils flaring.

"What is it?" Shannah asked, sitting up.

Ronan swore softly. "That damn fool Hewitt is here."

"Here?" she exclaimed, glancing around. "Where?"

"Outside. I've got to remember to keep that gate locked."

"What do you think he wants?"

Ronan lifted one brow. "What do you think?"

She stared at him a moment. "Do you think he knows that I'm . . ." Her eyes widened. "He'll be after me now, too, won't he?"

"Perhaps." He glanced past her, his head canted to one side. "But not tonight. He's changed his mind. Now, let me see. Where were we?" he asked, drawing her back down on the sofa. "Oh, yes, I remember now. I was about to kiss you again."

Shannah smiled up at him, all thought of Jim Hewitt forgotten as Ronan drew her into his arms once more, his hands caressing her back while his mouth explored hers. His tongue slid over her lower lip, then delved inside, dueling with her own, sending shivers of pleasure down her spine. His hands moved over her, ever so softly, ever so deftly, never straying where they shouldn't but arousing her just the same.

She pressed her body to his, feeling his arousal. Sometimes she wished he didn't have such a high moral code because she wanted him more than she wanted anything else in the whole world. She slid her hands under his shirt, ran her fingertips over his back and shoulders, felt him tremble at her touch. It was a heady feeling. She wondered if she could tempt him to make love to her and quickly pushed the thought away. She could do it, she knew she could. After all, he wanted her as much as she wanted him. But it wouldn't be right to tempt him so, because she knew he would feel guilty for it later. He was, after all, an honorable man.

It was a good thing they were getting married soon, she thought, her eyelids fluttering down, because she didn't think she could bear this kind of blissful torture much longer.

Planning for the wedding turned out to be one of the most enjoyable things Shannah had ever done. Ronan told her to spend whatever she wished, to buy whatever she wanted or needed, and she took him at his word.

She bought a white silk wedding gown fit for a princess. It had a fitted bodice studded with crystal beads, a full skirt, a long train, and a matching veil. She bought new shoes, all new underwear, and a white nightgown that was so light and frothy it felt like she was wearing nothing at all. And looked that way, too.

She let her mother take care of ordering the cake and the flowers and arranging for the reception after the ceremony.

Shannah addressed the invitations late one night. Not that there were that many. Counting her friends and family and friends of her parents, the total was right around fifty.

"What about your friends in Las Vegas?" she asked as she addressed the last one. "Wouldn't you like to invite them?"

Ronan shook his head. "Might be tempting fate, don't you think, so many vampires, all in one place?"

Shannah grinned at him. "Maybe you're right."

"We could go there for our honeymoon, if you like."

"I'd rather go some place more romantic, like Paris or Italy." She looked thoughtful. "I suppose you've been to those places already, and lots of others besides."

"Yes, love, but not with you." Moving toward her, he kissed her cheek. "Seeing them with you will be like seeing them for the first time."

"You always say the sweetest things." Putting her pen down, she rose and went into his arms.

He looked at her, his dark eyes hot. "I'm not sure I can wait for our wedding night, love."

"Me, either."

He sat on the sofa, drawing her down into his lap. His tongue laved her neck, just behind her ear. The touch sent a jolt of electricity racing through her.

"What about all that talk about chivalry and being a product of your generation?" she asked, her voice breathless as he pressed his lips to her breast. The heat of his mouth penetrated through her sweater, warming her skin.

"Maybe it's time to put my old-fashioned ways behind me," he said with a low growl, and claimed her lips again.

She couldn't think, not when he was kissing her with such intensity. His mouth was hot and hungry on hers, stealing her breath so that she could scarcely breathe. She clung to him, her hands kneading his back and shoulders, her whole body trembling and aching for his touch.

"Shannah." His voice was a groan, a plea.

"Maybe we should elope," she said, her voice as desperate as his. "Now, tonight."

He laughed hoarsely, then lifted her off his lap. "We've waited this long. Besides, I want that white dress to mean something when you wear it down the aisle."

In the days before the wedding, Ronan continued to help Shannah adjust to her new lifestyle. All the things she had anticipated with dread proved to be unfounded. Drinking blood wasn't disgusting but pleasurable, not only for her, but for those she took it from. She reveled in her new powers, both mental and physical. Every emotion, every sense, was heightened. She saw and heard things more clearly, felt things more deeply. She learned to tune out the barrage of noise that assaulted her on every side.

She threw herself into a fit of redecorating until Ronan declared he didn't recognize the house anymore. He was generous to a fault, never complaining no matter how much money she spent. It was such fun to shop without worrying about the cost, to buy whatever caught her fancy.

With her increased energy, it took her no time at all to repaint every room in the house.

Ronan watched, amused, as his bride-to-be transformed his dreary house into a home. Her taste ran to bright colors—a cheerful yellow for the kitchen that they no longer had any use for, pastel colors for the guestrooms, a deep blue for the bedroom that had been hers. She had decided this would be the room where they kept their clothing. She bought a new bedroom set because, as she said, while she didn't mind sleeping in his lair down in the basement, she wanted this to be the room they used to change clothes and do the other things people usually did in the privacy of their bedroom.

"Like making love?" he had queried.

She had nodded, her cheeks turning a delightful shade of pink.

She bought new carpeting and new furniture for every room in the house, including his lair.

The one thing she was adamant about was sleeping in a casket. She simply refused to consider it.

"I don't care if every vampire ever made slept in one," she declared vehemently. "I won't, and that's all there is to it."

She bought an antique four-poster bed, flowered sheets, and a wine-red comforter and carried it all down into his lair, advising him that he could sleep in his casket if he pleased, but she was sleeping in a bed.

To please her, and because he had no intention of sleeping alone once they were married, he got rid of the coffin that had been his resting place for the last few centuries.

Three days before the wedding, they flew to New York. Ronan had made reservations at the Waldorf and rented a new Cadillac, since they couldn't just materialize in her parents' living room. Shannah's parents had invited them to stay at the house, but Shannah had politely refused, explaining that Ronan had business in the city and that it would be more convenient for them to stay in a hotel.

It grieved Shannah to lie to her parents but there was no other choice.

She was nervous the night they went to visit her parents for the first time since her transformation. What if they noticed the difference in her? She didn't think she would be able to bear it if they turned away from her in horror.

"Relax," Ronan said as they pulled up in front of her parents' house. "It will be all right."

Shannah took a deep breath. "I hope so, but . . ."

He pressed a finger to her lips. "No buts, love. Trust me."

As it turned out, Ronan was right, as usual, and all her worrying was for nothing. Her parents were delighted to see her, naturally overjoyed that the doctors had been wrong in their diagnosis.

"You look wonderful, dear," Verna said. "No one would ever know you'd been sick a day in your life."

"You're going to make a beautiful bride," Mr. Davis said as he embraced his daughter.

"Thanks, Dad."

Davis shook Ronan's hand. "I hope you know what a lucky man you are," he said gruffly.

"Yes, sir, I surely do," Ronan replied. "And don't you worry, I'll take good care of her."

"Well, I just hope the two of you will be as happy as Mother and I have been," Davis said, "and that your marriage will last as long."

Ronan looked over at Shannah and smiled. "You can count on it."

Chapter Thirty-Two

Jim Hewitt sat in a rental car outside the Davis home. It had been sheer luck that he had seen the vampire and the woman leave the vampire's house the night before. But then, sometimes luck was the best thing a man could hope for.

He had called Overstreet, hoping for a little backup, but Carl had adamantly refused to get involved.

"I don't believe in pressing my luck," the newspaperman had said. "And you're a damn fool if you go after that bloodsucker again. He's a mean one."

Hewitt had acknowledged that Overstreet was right, but it hadn't kept him from following the vampire and the woman to the airport. He had managed to get a seat in coach on the same flight they were taking to New York. He had even managed to follow them to their hotel without being seen, obtained a room on the same floor, and made himself at home.

Being a vampire hunter made it easy to keep vampire hours. He slept during the day and rose a couple of hours before sunset. He showered and ate, then took up his post in the lobby where he could keep an eye on the stairs and the elevator.

He had cursed softly when he saw the vampire and the woman exit the elevator earlier that night. One look confirmed that the woman was head over heels in love with the vampire. She clung to him, her eyes filled with obvious adoration as they walked across the lobby, headed for the garage.

Hewitt followed the pair at a safe distance. Getting into his car, he had followed them out of the city, and now he was parked down the street from the girl's house, waiting and watching. And wondering what the devil he was doing there. Not long ago he had been determined to give up the hunt. Yet here he sat, his hands cupped around a mug of black coffee, quietly cursing himself for being the world's biggest fool while he wondered if the girl's parents had any idea what kind of vile creature they had welcomed into their home.

Chapter Thirty-Three

Shannah looked over at Ronan and smiled as he pulled onto the highway. "You were right."

"About what?"

"My parents. They didn't suspect a thing."

"I'm always right," he said with a wink.

"Always?"

He nodded, then swore under his breath when he glanced in the rear-view mirror.

"What's the matter?" Shannah asked, glancing over her shoulder.

"That damn fool's following us again."

"Who?" she asked, then shook her head. "You don't mean Hewitt?"

"He's behind us."

"He is?"

She turned in her seat this time, her gaze scanning the traffic behind them. "I don't see him."

"He's in a black Taurus about six cars back."

With a sigh, she settled in her seat again. "Why doesn't he just go away and leave us alone? We aren't hurting anyone. Oh! You don't think he'll show up at the wedding, do you?"

"I don't know. I sure as hell hope not."

"Maybe we should have eloped, after all."

"I doubt it would have made any difference. The man's as tenacious as a bull dog."

"What if he . . ."

"Shannah, love, stop worrying."

"I can't help it."

He laughed softly. She was quite a worrier, his bride-to-be.

And suddenly the night of the wedding was upon them. They hunted early that evening, quickly deciding on a young couple bound for the movies.

Shannah would have preferred to wait until later, but Ronan assured her that it would be wiser to feed now.

"It will add color to your cheeks," he said with a wink.

Back at the hotel, Shannah was a bundle of nerves as she got ready to go to the church. She had intended to get dressed at the church so that Ronan wouldn't see her in her gown before the ceremony and then, at the last minute, realized that it would never work because, of course, there would most likely be a mirror in the bride's dressing room, and her mother was sure to notice that her daughter didn't cast any reflection in the looking glass.

"If you don't want me to see your gown, you can take the car and I'll meet you at the church," Ronan suggested as Shannah reached for the phone to call her mother.

"No, it's all right. Besides, I'll need you to help me with that long row of hooks up the back of my dress."

Ronan listened while Shannah explained that they were running late and she had decided to get dressed at the hotel.

"I'm sorry, love," Ronan said as Shannah hung up the phone. "Was your mother very disappointed?"

Shannah shrugged. "It can't be helped."

Ronan drew her into his arms and kissed the tip of her nose. "Is there anything I can do?"

"Yes," Shannah said, looking around the room, "help me find my other shoe!"

Ronan stood at the altar alongside Pete Sandoval, who had agreed to be his best man. Organ music filled the air. The light from dozens of long white tapers cast dancing shadows on the walls and the ceiling. There were white satin bows on the ends of the pews, a long white runner graced the center aisle.

Ronan concentrated on blocking the sound of half a hundred beating hearts. The sweet, faintly coppery tang of blood mingled with the fragrance of the flowers that lined the altar. He wondered how Shannah was holding up. Since she had been a vampire, they had avoided crowds in small spaces.

The door to the foyer opened, and there was a sudden sense of anticipation as the organist began to play the Wedding March.

Shannah's maid of honor, Judy, walked down the aisle. Ronan had met her for the first time the night before.

The music swelled and Shannah was there, his bride, looking radiant in a long white gown and gossamer veil. He had seen her in her dress at the hotel but here, with her veil over her face and a bouquet of blood-red roses and baby's breath clasped in her hands, she looked even more beautiful. There was a glow in her cheeks and in her eyes that had nothing to do with her vampire state.

The moment she came into view, he forgot everything else as he watched her glide down the aisle, one hand on her father's arm, a shy smile curving her lips, her eyes alight with love.

Shannah's hand was trembling when her father placed it in Ronan's. She passed her bouquet to Judy and then, clutching Ronan's hand tightly, she faced the minister, who offered the bride and groom a few words of advice on how to have a happy marriage, and then they faced each other to exchange their vows.

Vows they had written themselves. Vows that made no mention of "in sickness and health, until death do us part."

And then, at last, came the words, "I now pronounce you husband and wife. You may kiss your bride."

Lifting Shannah's veil, Ronan drew her into his arms. "Forever, beloved," he murmured, and then he kissed her.

For Ronan, in that moment in time, everything else on earth ceased to exist and he was aware of nothing but the woman in his arms, the sweetness of her mouth, the press of her body against his, the silk of her gown beneath his hand, the musky scent of her perfume. She was his, for now and for always.

He kissed her again, because he couldn't resist the lure of her sweetness, and then, with a smile, he took her hand in his and faced their guests while the minister announced, "Ladies and gentlemen, may I present Mr. and Mrs. Luard Ronan Moss."

Shannah looked up at Ronan, one brow raised as she mouthed, "Luard?"

He shrugged imperceptibly and smiled.

The organist began to play the recessional. Shannah smiled at Judy as she retrieved her bouquet.

People rose as Ronan led Shannah down the aisle, out of the church, and into the waiting limousine. The door had no sooner closed than he had her in his arms again.

"No more waiting," he murmured, his hands stroking her back, her hip, sliding up to caress her breast.

"Ronan!" Shannah cast a frantic glance at the driver. "Not here!"

Grunting softly, Ronan hit the button to raise the window between the front seat and the back. "There," he said. "Happy now?"

"Luard?" she said in mock horror. "No wonder you waited so long to tell me. What kind of name is Luard?"

"English, I believe. It means little wolf. Ronan is my middle name. Now, Mrs. Moss, come here."

"Ronan, don't muss me!"

He growled low in his throat as he reached for her again.

She batted his hands away. "I mean it. I don't want to walk into the reception looking like I just climbed out of bed."

"One kiss?"

Leaning toward him, she kissed him quickly on the lips.

With an exaggerated sigh, he sat back, his arms folded over his chest. "How long do we have to stay at the reception?"

"Not long."

Shannah took Ronan's hand as they walked into the reception. She had planned the wedding to be late enough so that people would already have had dinner. It seemed easier than trying to explain why the bride and groom weren't eating. They had provided food, of course, finger sandwiches, cheese and crackers, fruit salad, and drinks.

Hand in hand, Shannah and Ronan mingled with their guests, accepting their good wishes and congratulations.

Later, they took the floor for the first dance. "What are we going to do about the cake?" Shannah asked as Ronan waltzed her around the floor.

"What about it?"

"The bride and groom always cut the cake and feed each other a piece."

"Ah. Don't worry about it."

"We can't make up some excuse," Shannah said. "Everybody will expect us to do it."

"I'll take care of it."

"How?"

"I'll just plant the idea in their minds that we ate it."

"You can hypnotize the whole room?"

He nodded.

Later, one of Shannah's friends from high school took her aside. "You look fantastic," Leah remarked.

"Thank you."

"I've never seen you look so radiant. What's your secret?"

Shannah looked across the room to where Ronan was conversing with some of their guests, and smiled. "It's Ronan."

"Well, being in love with a handsome man certainly agrees with you."

"He is handsome, isn't he?"

"I'll say. He doesn't have a brother, does he?"

"No, sorry."

Leah looked at Shannah and shook her head. "Are you sure it's just love? You haven't had some work done, have you?"

"No."

"Maybe a little Botox while you were in California? I hear it's all the rage."

"Maybe for movie stars," Shannah said with a laugh. "Come on, it's time to cut the cake."

A crowd gathered around the cake table as Shannah picked up the beribboned knife. She looked at Ronan, wondering if he could really hypnotize the entire room.

At his nod, she cut a slice of cake, speared a piece with a fork, and offered it to him.

He opened his mouth as if to take a bite. She felt a stirring of preternatural power pulsate through the room. She looked askance when he scooped a bit of frosting from the cake and smeared a little of it around his mouth. She understood a moment later when there was a burst of laughter and applause. Smiling at her, Ronan wiped his mouth on a napkin.

He picked up the fork and made as if to feed her a bite. Following his lead, she opened her mouth. Again, a ruffling of power moved through the room. She quickly smeared a bit of frosting around her mouth. Again, their guests laughed and applauded.

Shannah wiped her mouth on a napkin, smiled at their guests, and allowed Ronan to lead her onto the dance floor again while their guests lined up for cake.

"You see?" he said. "Nothing to worry about."

She shook her head. "Do you have any other talents I don't know about?"

His eyes took on a wicked gleam. "Wait and see."

They stayed at the reception for another hour, then Shannah took her parents aside.

"Thank you both," she said, "for everything."

Verna blinked back tears as she hugged her daughter. "Be happy, dear."

"I am, Mom."

Verna hugged Ronan. "Take good care of each other."

"Come on, Mother," Scott said. "Can't you see they're anxious to be alone?"

"Keep in touch, dear," Verna said, hugging her daughter one more time.

"I will, Mom. I love you." She kissed her mother on the cheek, hugged her father. "I love you, too, Dad."

Scott put his arm around his wife's shoulders. "Go

along now," he said, his voice gruff with unshed tears. "Call us when you get home."

With a smile, Shannah took Ronan's arm and they slipped out of the hotel to where the limo was waiting.

The driver opened the door for them, closed it, and climbed behind the wheel.

Ronan slipped his arm around Shannah's waist and drew her into his lap. "You're mine, now," he said, running his knuckles lightly over her cheek. "All mine."

"Yes."

"So it's okay if I muss you a little?"

"You may muss me all you wish, Mr. Luard Ronan Moss. Luard," she said, chuckling. "I can't get over that."

"It was a family name," he said, shrugging. "I always liked it myself."

"Sure you did," she said dryly. "That's why you never told me what it was, you were afraid I wouldn't marry you."

"Ah," he said with mock despair, "you wound me to the quick!"

"Can you turn into a little wolf?"

"Want me to show you?"

"Not here!" she said, casting a frantic glance at the driver.

"You worry too much, do you know that?"

"I can't help it. Now, Mr. Luard Ronan Moss, why don't you stop talking and kiss me?"

"Always my pleasure, madam," he said, and covered her mouth with his own.

His hands moved over her, eager for the time when he could bare her body to his gaze, feel the satin of her skin beneath his hands.

Shannah was on fire when the limo pulled up in front of their hotel. Ronan tipped the driver, then swung her into his arms and carried her swiftly into the hotel. He didn't wait for the elevator but carried her quickly up five flights of stairs, down a long carpeted corridor and into their room.

Kicking the door closed with his foot, he murmured, "Alone at last," as he slowly lowered her feet to the floor. Her body slid intimately against his own.

She leaned into him, nibbling on his chin as his hands moved to unfasten the back of her gown. He pushed it off her shoulders and it fell to the floor to pool at her feet.

His gaze moved over her, hotter than any flame. Her scanty undergarments revealed more than they hid. She was as beautiful as he had known she would be, her body slim and perfect.

His body tensed as she began to undress him, easing his coat from his shoulders, slowly unbuttoning his shirt, unbuckling his belt. The touch of her fingers against his skin was intoxicating.

He shivered with excitement and anticipation as she unfastened his trousers. He toed off his boots. She stepped out of her white satin pumps.

He removed her nylons, his hands bold as they caressed her thighs, slid down her calves. Her skin was smooth and silky beneath his fingertips.

He peeled off his socks, then swung her into his arms and carried her to the king-sized canopied bed. He lowered her gently to the mattress, then dropped down beside her and quickly gathered her into his arms.

Shannah pressed herself against him, loving the feel of his body against hers. Her hands moved over him, eager to explore. She ran her tongue over his skin, over the pulse throbbing in the hollow of his throat. His body was hard, his skin smooth, cool beneath her questing fingertips. He endured her exploration for several minutes and then began an exploration of his own. There was no hesitation in his touch. Each stroke of his hand, each kiss, branded her as his and only his.

He kissed her and caressed her until she writhed beneath him, yearning for the release that only he could give. She was glad now, glad that she had waited for this man, this moment, glad she hadn't squandered her virginity on some other man. This was how it should be, a once in a lifetime moment, and one worth waiting for, just as her mother had promised.

She lifted her hips to receive him, moaned with pleasure as his body became a part of hers. They moved together, slowly at first, and then with greater intensity as the passion between them grew stronger, deeper. She felt his fangs at her throat, cried out as the pleasure of his bite mingled with the pleasure of her release.

He groaned deep in his throat, his body convulsing, his eyes blazing until, sated, he collapsed on top of her, his forehead pressed to hers as he whispered that he loved her.

She clung to him when he would have left her. "Not yet."

"I'm too heavy for you."

"No."

Rising up on his elbows, he gazed down into her face. "Any complaints, Mrs. Moss?"

"Just one."

He lifted one brow. "And that would be . . . ?"

"It was over too soon."

He smiled, looking incredibly pleased with himself. "Then we shall have to do it again."

"Can you?" she asked. "I always heard that men, well, that they had to wait a while before they could . . . you know, do it again?"

"Ah, my lovely wife, you forget, I am not a mortal man."

"Yes," she said, grinning broadly, "I did forget."

He brushed a kiss across her lips. "It will be my pleasure to remind you, and often."

She ran her fingertips down his chest, her nails lightly scraping the skin. "I promise to pay close attention."

"And I promise to never disappoint you."

"Never?" She lifted her hands to his nape, let her fingers sift through his hair. It was thick and silky.

"Never, my love."

He rolled off her, drawing her body against his, his arm holding her close while their bodies cooled and their breathing returned to normal. And then he lifted her in his arms and carried her into the bathroom.

Shannah was somewhat surprised when he put her in the shower, then stepped in beside her and closed the door. He turned on the water, picked up a bar of scented soap, and proceeded to wash her from her neck to her heels.

The touch of his soapy hands moving languidly over her body was the most sensually erotic feeling she had ever known.

Picking up another bar of soap, she decided to treat him to the same and found, to her surprise, that washing Ronan was even more arousing than having him wash her. His body was firm and muscular and beautiful. And aroused.

In minutes, the shower's glass walls were thick with steam and only part of it came from the hot water.

Taking the soap from her hand, he dropped it on the floor and drew her into his arms. His body was wet and slick against her own.

"What are you doing?" she asked breathlessly.

"I'm going to make love to you."

"In here?"

"In here," he said, and easing her back against the shower wall, he showed her that there was more than one way to make love.

* * *

They spent three glorious nights in the Waldorf. Shannah had decided to wait until she had been a vampire a little longer before leaving the country for the first time. Besides, she didn't want to waste time traveling when she could be making love to her husband. They left the hotel only to hunt. Shannah explored her husband's body until she knew it as well as, if not better than, she knew her own.

No matter what else they decided to do, somehow it always ended up in love-making, like the night they decided to watch a movie, and then ended up acting out all the love scenes, and the night they went to the movies and made out like a couple of teenagers in the back row.

This evening, they had gone out on the balcony to dance under the stars and ended up making love on a blanket in the moonlight.

"So," Ronan asked later that night. "Any regrets?"

She considered for a moment. She was strong and healthy. She would always appear to be twenty-four years old. She wouldn't age. She would never get sick. She would never have a child . . .

"Shannah?"

"I'm sorry we can't have children."

He nodded. "That's always been one of my regrets, as well."

"Is there no way?"

"None."

It was a fact she would have to accept. And then she frowned as a new thought occurred to her. "I won't get any older," she said, "but my parents will. Won't they wonder why I don't age? How will I take care of them when they get old?"

"Some people stay young looking for a long time," Ronan said.

"But . . ."

"Shannah, love, let's worry about it when the time comes."

She smiled self-consciously. He was right, of course. There was no point in borrowing trouble.

She trailed her fingertips down his cheek. "Have you always been this wise?"

"Always," he said, stifling a grin.

Her hand trailed down his neck, over his chest, his stomach. "And this handsome?"

He nodded, his eyes growing hot as her fingers caressed him. "Careful, love," he murmured.

She batted her eyelashes at him. "Is something wrong?"

"Not a thing. But you know, there are always consequences to every action."

"Really?" she asked with mock innocence. "What do you think would happen if I did this?" she asked, and trailed her tongue over his chest.

"I can assure you that this would happen." His voice was a low growl as he tucked her body beneath his. "If you wake the tiger, you have to pay the price."

"Nice kitty," she said, and burst out laughing, only to gasp with pleasure as he began to caress her.

"Nice kitty," she said again. Suddenly breathless, she lifted her hips to receive him, held on tight as he moved deep within her, until it seemed she was floating among the stars, her mind and body melded with his, making it impossible to separate her pleasure from his.

The dawn came all too soon. Ronan took the usual precautions. He put wards on the doors and windows so that no one would disturb them. They took another quick shower together. Although he could have stayed up for another hour or two, Ronan got into bed, his arm slipping around Shannah's waist as she slid in beside him. With a little sigh, she snuggled against him, her head pillowed on his shoulder.

"Good night, my love," he whispered.

But she was already asleep.

They returned home the following night. Because of all the wedding gifts and luggage, Ronan had rented a car at the airport.

Shannah glanced at Ronan as he pulled into the driveway. Amazing, how quickly one's life could change, she thought. And how radically it could change. Not so long ago, she had been at death's door. Now she was a married woman, a married vampire, she amended, with all of eternity before her.

"Here we are, love," Ronan murmured as he pulled up in front of the house. "Home sweet home."

She laughed softly, thinking how happy she was to be here, with him.

He opened the car door for her, and she followed him around to the trunk. It was full of wedding gifts, as was the back seat.

He looked at her and shook his head. "What are we going to do with all this stuff?"

Shannah shrugged. She had wondered that herself. They really had no need for a toaster or a mixer or for any of the dishes and pots and pans they had received.

"At least we can use the blankets and the sheets," she said. "And the quilt my mother made us."

Ronan nodded.

"We can give the rest of the stuff to the Salvation Army, or maybe donate it to a women's shelter," Shannah suggested.

"Let's leave it here for now," he said, closing the trunk. "We can decide what to do with it tomorrow . . ." His voice trailed off and he spun around, peering into the darkness.

"What is it?" she asked anxiously.

"Get in the . . ." His words ended in a groan.

Shannah gasped as something hot stung her cheek. "Ronan!"

Her eyes widened in horror when he turned toward her. One side of his face and neck were raw, as though he had been burned with acid.

"Get inside!" he roared. "Now!"

She started to ask him what had happened when she saw a movement out of the corner of her eye. Turning her head, she let out a cry of alarm when Jim Hewitt lunged forward, a long wooden stake in one hand, an empty bottle in the other. A bottle she knew must have been filled with holy water.

She screamed as Hewitt drove the stake into Ronan's back.

"Run, Shannah," Hewitt cried. "My car's at the end of the driveway."

"Stop it!" she screamed. "You'll kill him!"

Hewitt's teeth flashed in a wolfish grin as he twisted the stake in Ronan's back.

With a grunt of pain, Ronan dropped to his hands and knees.

The scent of fresh hot blood wafted through the night.

With a scream of rage, Shannah grabbed Hewitt by the arm. Startled, he glanced at her. "What are you doing?"

"Stopping you." She pulled his hand away from the stake, her fingers curling around his wrist.

"Are you crazy?" Hewitt exclaimed. "He's a vampire!"

"Yes," she said, baring her fangs. "And so am I."

Hewitt's face paled. And then he lashed out at her.

Shannah laughed as he struggled in vain to free himself from her hold. And then she caught his gaze with hers.

"Stop fighting me," she commanded, somewhat surprised when his arms fell limply to his sides. "Stay there."

Letting him go, she dropped down beside Ronan. "Are you all right?"

"Pull it out," he said, his voice raw and edged with pain.

"Out?" Revulsion made her stomach clench when she looked at the stake protruding from his back.

"Pull it out or push it through," he said, panting. "Just get the damn thing out of me!"

Grasping the stake firmly in one hand, she pulled it from his back. A torrent of dark red blood flowed from the nasty wound. The scent of it filled the air.

Unable to help herself, Shannah licked her lips. So much blood. How could he survive after losing so much? Ripping a strip of cloth from his shirt tail, she stuffed it into the wound to stop the bleeding.

"Ronan? Are you all right?"

Grunting softly, he dropped into a sitting position.

"Your poor face," Shannah said. She started to stroke his cheek, then drew her hand away, afraid her touch would only make it hurt worse. "And your neck. Does it hurt dreadfully?"

"Like sin." His gaze moved over her. "Looks like he got you, too."

She lifted a hand to her cheek, flinched when she touched the place where the holy water had splashed her skin. She had only been sprayed by a drop or two but it stung like the devil. She couldn't imagine the pain Ronan must be in.

"Are you going to be all right?" she asked.

He nodded. "The burns will heal, in time."

"But . . . your back."

"He missed my heart. The wound's already healing. Bring him to me."

"You're not . . . are you going to . . . ?"

Ronan looked over to where Hewitt stood, held fast by Shannah's will. "Kill him? I haven't decided."

"I guess I wouldn't blame you if you did."

Rising, Shannah grabbed Hewitt by the arm. Dragging him toward Ronan, she ordered him to sit down.

"Release him from your spell," Ronan said. "I want him to know what's happening."

Shannah did as bidden, then stood back, her teeth worrying her lower lip as she waited to see what Ronan intended to do with the man who had tried to kill him.

Hewitt's face went deathly pale when he roused and saw himself looking into the vampire's blood-red eyes.

Ronan drew back his lips, exposing his fangs. "I warned you," he said. "You should have listened."

Hewitt swallowed hard.

Shannah shook off a rush of pity for the man as Ronan pulled him closer. Whatever happened to Jim Hewitt, it was his own fault.

The stink of Hewitt's fear stung her nostrils. His terror was a palpable thing as he struggled helplessly in Ronan's grasp.

Her mouth watered as Ronan sank his fangs into the vampire hunter's throat.

Knowing it would help to ease the pain of his wounds and speed his recovery, Shannah had expected Ronan to drink deeply, but he continued to drink long after she expected him to stop. He drank until Hewitt's heartbeat fluttered faintly, and then he drank some more.

"Ronan . . ."

He lifted his gaze to hers, his eyes red.

She feared he was going to kill the man. She couldn't

find it in her heart to fault his decision, and yet . . . it seemed wrong somehow.

When Ronan lifted his head, Hewitt lay white-faced and limp in his grasp.

She looked at her husband and knew he was going to drain Jim Hewitt dry.

And then Ronan spoke.

"Hewitt! Listen to me. You have only a few minutes to make up your mind. Do you want to live or die?"

Hewitt's eyelids fluttered open, his gaze unfocused, and then he stared into Ronan's face. He didn't speak, but it was evident from his expression that he knew what the vampire was asking.

Shannah glanced from one man to the other. What would Hewitt decide? Would he choose death? Or would he choose to become what he hated? What he had spent his life hunting?

Though it seemed impossible, Hewitt seemed to grow paler, weaker. Had he chosen death?

She looked at Ronan. He was all vampire now. His fangs gleamed whitely in the light of the moon. His eyes glowed with a pure red flame. She saw death in those eyes, a burning desire to destroy the mortal who had attacked him viciously and without provocation.

"Your time is running out," Ronan said curtly. "Make your choice!"

"Live." The word seemed torn from the very depths of Hewitt's soul. "I want . . . to live."

With a feral cry, Ronan bit into his own wrist. "Then drink," he said, and his voice was like sandpaper over steel.

Hewitt grimaced as blood dripped from Ronan's wrist into his mouth. He choked down the first taste and then he clutched the vampire's arm in both hands.

"Damn you!" Hewitt said hoarsely, and then he pulled

Ronan's wrist to his mouth and took his first step into another life.

Preternatural power stirred on the wings of the night.

Shannah watched in mingled horror and fascination as the color returned to Hewitt's face. His breathing returned to normal, his heartbeat grew stronger.

Moment's later, Ronan jerked his arm from Hewitt's grasp. "Enough!"

Sitting up, Hewitt dragged the back of his hand across his mouth. He stared at the crimson stain on his hand as if he had never seen blood before, and then he looked at Ronan. "Now what?"

Ronan licked the wound in his wrist, sealing it, and then gained his feet. "Tonight you'll die . . ."

"What?" Hewitt scrambled to his feet, his eyes wide with panic. "I thought that you . . ."

Ronan silenced him with a look. "When you wake tomorrow night, you'll be one of us." Unlocking the front door, Ronan swung Shannah into his arms and carried her inside. "Enjoy your new life, vampire," he told Hewitt, and slammed the door.

Chapter Thirty-Four

"That was cruel," Shannah said. "To bring him across and then leave him without telling him what to do, what to expect."

They were sitting in the living room in front of a roaring fire. Earlier, they had carried their luggage and the useless wedding presents inside. The gifts were now housed in one of the upstairs bedrooms.

"Cruel?" Ronan muttered. "I could have killed him. I should have killed him. But he's one of us now."

"Born under a dark moon," Shannah murmured. "Just like me. How will he get by, with no one to help him?"

"The man's been hunting vampires for years. He, more than most mortals, should know what to do."

"I guess so," Shannah murmured somewhat dubiously. Then, with a sigh, she snuggled closer to his side. "I hope he'll be as happy as I am, but I don't know how he could be, since he doesn't have you."

Ronan lifted one brow, and then he laughed. "Ah, Shannah, whatever did I do without you in my life?"

"I don't know," she replied seriously. "But you'll never be without me again."

Taking her into his arms, he slid down onto the floor,

his hands divesting her of her clothing while he rained kisses over each inch of exposed flesh.

He lay back, a faint smile curving his lips when she straddled his hips and began to undress him.

"All's fair in love and war," she said, grinning.

"And what is this?" he asked, then grunted when she punched him in the arm.

"Don't you know?" she asked with mock ferocity.

"Love," he said, pulling her down on top of him. "Definitely love."

"Yes," she murmured as he claimed her lips with his. "Oh, yes!"

It was definitely love, she thought as he lifted her into his arms. He carried her up the stairs to their bedroom where he made slow, sweet love to her until the sun came up.

Later, her head pillowed on his shoulder, she wondered why she had fought against becoming a vampire when it was really quite wonderful.

She smiled a sleepy smile when Ronan whispered that he loved her.

"I love you more," she murmured.

With a sigh, she closed her eyes, secure in his dark embrace and in the knowledge that she would wake at his side on the morrow and for all the tomorrows of her life.

Dear Reader:

Once again, we come to the end of the journey. I hope you enjoyed Shannah's story as much as I did.

Once again, I want to thank Joseph Walsh for allowing me to use his poetry, and I want to thank my editor, Kate Duffy, for her help and encouragement along the way.

I recently finished a sequel to *Night's Touch*, which will hopefully be out later this year. At the moment, I'm working on a new book.

I hope life is being kind to you, and that you stop often to voice your love for those you hold dear, and always remember to count your blessings.

God bless you,
Amanda
www.amandaashley.com
DarkWritr@aol.com

If you loved this Amanda Ashley book,
then you won't want to miss any of
her other fabulous vampire stories
from Zebra Books!
Following is a sneak peak . . .

NIGHT'S TOUCH

Cara DeLongpre wandered into the mysterious Nocturne club looking for a fleeting diversion from her sheltered life. Instead she found a dark, seductive stranger whose touch entices her beyond the safety she's always known and into a heady carnal bliss . . .

A year ago, Vincent Cordova believed that vampires existed only in bad movies and bogeyman stories. That was before a chance encounter left him with unimaginable powers, a hellish thirst, and an aching loneliness he's sure will never end . . . until the night he meets Cara DeLongpre. Cara's beauty and bewitching innocence call to his mind, his heart . . . his blood. For Vincent senses the Dark Gift shared by Cara's parents, and the lurking threat from an ancient and powerful foe. And he knows that the only thing more dangerous than the enemy waiting to seek its vengeance is the secret carried by those Cara trusts the most . . .

Cara Aideen Delongpre sipped her drink, too preoccupied with her own thoughts to pay any attention to the crowd and the noise that surrounded her. She had grown up knowing her mother and father weren't like other parents. Once she had started going to school, she had discovered a whole new world. Other kids went on vacation with their parents when school was out. They went out to dinner and to the zoo and to Disneyland and Sea World. They had birthday parties at Chuck E. Cheese's. Other kids had brothers and sisters, aunts and uncles, and cousins and grandparents. When Cara asked why she didn't have brothers or sisters or aunts and uncles, her father had explained that her mother couldn't have children, and that he and her mother didn't have any siblings, and that her grandparents had all passed away.

It was a perfectly logical explanation, but it didn't make her feel any less lonely. It would have been nice to have a sister she could share confidences with.

What wasn't logical was the fact that, in over twenty years, her parents hadn't changed at all. She told herself she was being foolish, that she was overreacting, imagining things. But there was no arguing with the proof of her own eyes. They both looked exactly the way they had when Cara was a little girl. Her mother never gained or lost an ounce. Her face was as smooth and clear as it had always been. The same was true of her father. Roshan DeLongpre looked like a man in his mid-thirties, and he had looked that way for as long as Cara could remember. He had taken her to the movies one night last week and they had run into a couple of Cara's acquaintances. Before she could introduce her father, her friend, Cindy, had taken her aside and asked how long she had been dating that "good looking older man."

Cara stared into her drink, wishing she had the nerve to ask her parents why Di Giorgio aged and they didn't, why their lifestyle was so different from everyone else's. She knew about their aversion to the sun and their liquid diet, but why did that keep them from other normal activities? Why did they encourage her to make friends, but discourage her from bringing them home? And why did they keep the door to their bedroom locked during the day? What were they doing in there?

She looked up as a man sat down beside her. He smiled, then pointed with his chin at her drink. "Can I buy you another?"

"No, thank you."

He lifted a hand. "Hey, no problem. You just looked a little down. I thought you might like some company."

He had a nice voice, blond hair, and dark brown eyes. What harm could it do to share a drink with him?

"Are you sure you won't change your mind?" he coaxed, as if sensing her indecision.

"Well, I would like another."

"What are you drinking?" he asked, signaling for the bartender.

"A virgin pineapple daiquiri."

He ordered her drink and a scotch and water for himself, then held out his hand. "I'm Anton."

"Cara." She hesitated a moment before taking his hand. Though she had been on her share of dates, she tended to be shy around strangers. She wasn't sure why. Maybe because she had never forgotten her father's warning that he had "ruthless enemies." Still, she told herself there was nothing to worry about. Frank was here.

Anton's grip was firm, his skin warm. "Do you come here often?"

"No, this is my first time. I was just passing by and I heard the music and . . ." She shrugged. "I thought it might cheer me up."

"If you tell me what's got you feeling so blue, I might be able to help."

"I don't think so, but thanks for offering."

Cara glanced out at the dance floor as the lights dimmed. The music, which had been upbeat, changed to something slow and sensual with a dark, sexual undertone. It called to something earthy deep within her.

"Would you like to dance?" Anton asked.

Again, she hesitated a moment before agreeing.

Anton took her by the hand and led her out onto the floor. "So," he said, taking her in his arms. "Tell me about yourself."

"What do you want to know?"

"Let's see. What do you like to do for fun? Do you work, or are you an heiress? Who's your favorite singer? And, most important of all, are you a chocoholic like every other woman I've ever met?"

She laughed. "Guilty on the chocolate," she said, and then frowned as she realized she had never seen her mother eat or drink anything chocolate. Even the most rigid dieters cheated every now and then.

"Did I say something wrong?" he asked.

"No. I work at the library, and I don't really have a favorite singer." She didn't tell him that she was, in fact, an heiress. After all, he was a stranger and she wasn't a fool. Not that she had anything to worry about, not with Frank Di Giorgio sitting at the far end of the bar watching her like a hawk.

"You're a librarian?" Anton exclaimed.

"Is something wrong with that?"

"No, no, but . . . well, you're a knock-out. I sort of thought you might be a model or an actress."

Cara smiled, flattered in spite of herself. "Disappointed?"

"Not at all."

When the music ended, he escorted her back to their seats. Their drinks were waiting for them. Cara sipped hers, thinking how glad she was she had stopped in here tonight. Di Girorgio had tried to dissuade her, but she had insisted. Once inside, she almost hadn't stayed, it was such a strange place. For one thing, she was the only one in the place who wasn't wearing black. Voodoo masks and ancient Indian burial masks decorated the walls. Tall black candles flickered in wrought iron sconces, casting eerie shadows over the faces of the patrons; a good number of them wore long black cloaks or capes with hoods.

"So," Anton said, "what do you think of the Nocturne?"

"I'm not sure. Why is everyone wearing black?"

"This is a Goth hangout."

"Oh! Silly me, I should have guessed."

He grinned at her. "I take it you're not into the Goth scene."

"Not really," she replied, and then frowned, thinking that her father would be right at home in a place like this. He had an affinity for dark clothing, and he had a long black cloak. But it was more than that. From time to time, she had sensed a darkness in her father that she couldn't explain and didn't understand.

Cara finished her drink, then looked at her watch, surprised to find it was so late. "I should be going," she said reluctantly. "My folks will be worried."

"Don't tell me you still live at home with mom and dad!"

Cara shrugged. "I like it there." And she did, although sometimes, especially when the days were long and the nights were short, it was like living alone.

"One more dance?" he coaxed.

"I don't think so. I really need to go," she said, and then wondered why she had to be home before midnight. She wasn't a child anymore. Why did she still have a curfew? Lately, she'd had so many questions about the way she lived. Why did she still live at home? Why did she still need a bodyguard? She was twenty-two years old and no one had ever tried to kidnap her or molest her or so much as given her a dirty look. Of course, Di Giorgio was probably responsible for that. A man would have to be crazy to try anything with The Hulk lurking in the background. Still, maybe it was time to sit her folks down and ask the questions that had been plaguing her more and more in the last few months.

"Thank you for the drink and the dance," she said, rising.

"Any chance you'll be here tomorrow night about this time?" he asked.

She tilted her head to the side, considering it, and then smiled. "I'd say the odds were good."

"Great. I'll see you then."

Leaning back against the bar, Anton Bouchard watched his enemy's daughter leave the bar, followed by a big bear of a man who looked as if he could easily take on every other man in the place without breaking a sweat.

Anton grunted softly, thinking how pleased his mother would be when he told her he had put the first part of her plan into operation.

DEAD SEXY

The city in in a panic. In the still of the night,
a vicious killer is leaving a trail of
mutilated bodies drained of blood.
A chilling M.O. that puts ex-vampire hunter
Reagan Delaney on the case,
her gun clip packed with silver bullets,
her instinctss edgy.

But the victims are both human and Undead,
and the clues are as confusing as the
vampire who may be her best ally—she hopes . . .

They called it You Bet Your Life Park, because that's what you were doing if you lingered inside the park after sundown, betting your life that you'd get out again. It had been a nice quiet neighborhood once upon a time, and it still was, during the day. Modern, high-rise condos enclosed the park on three sides. Visitors to the city often remarked on the fact that most of the buildings didn't have any windows. A large outdoor pool was located in the middle of the park. The local kids went swimming there in the summertime. There was also a pizza parlor, a video game arcade, and a couple of small stores that sold groceries, ice, and gas to those who had need of such things.

Large signs were posted at regular intervals throughout the park warning visitors to vacate the premises well before sunset. Smart people paid attention to the signs. Dumb ones were rarely heard from again, because the condos and apartments that encompassed You Bet Your Life Park were a sanctuary for the Undead. A supernaturally charged force field surrounded the outer perimeter of the apartment complex and the park, thereby preventing the vampires from leaving the area and wandering through the city.

Regan Delaney didn't have any idea how the force field worked or what it was made of. All she knew was that it kept the vamps inside but had no negative effect on humans. It was against the law to destroy vampires these days, unless you found one outside the park, but the force field made that impossible. Any vampire who wished to leave the park and move to a protected area in another part of the country had to apply for a permit and be transported, by day, by a company equipped to handle that kind of thing. What Regan found the hardest to accept was that vampires were now considered an endangered species, like tigers, elephants, and marine turtles, and as such, they had to be protected from human predators. The very thought was ludicrous!

It hadn't always been so, of course. In her grandfather's day, vampires had been looked upon as vermin, the scum of the earth. Bounties had been placed on them and they had been hunted ruthlessly. Many of the known vampires had been destroyed. Then, about five years ago, the bleeding hearts had started crying about how sad it was to kill all those poor misunderstood creatures of the night. After all, the bleeding hearts argued, even vampires had rights. Besides, they were also human beings and deserved to be treated with respect. To Regan's astonishment, sympathy for the vampires had grown and vampires had been given immunity, of a sort, and put into protective custody in places like You Bet Your Life Park. And since the Undead could no longer hunt in the city, the law had decided to put the vampires to good use. For a brief period of time, criminals sentenced to death had been given to the vampires.

The thought still made Regan cringe. Though she had no love for murderers, rapists, or child molesters, she couldn't, in good conscience, condone throwing them to the vamps. She didn't have to worry for long. In less than a year, the same bleeding-heart liberals who had felt sorry for the poor, misunderstood vampires began feeling sorry for the poor unfortunate criminals who had become their prey, and so a new law had been passed and criminals were again disposed of more humanely, by lethal injection.

Unfortunately, the new law had left the Undead with no ready food supply. In order to appease their hunger and keep them from killing each other, blood banks had agreed to donate whole blood to the vampire community until synthetic plasma could be developed. In a few months, Locke Pharmaceuticals invented something called Synthetic Type O that was reported to taste and smell the same as the real thing. A variety of blood types soon followed, though Type O remained the most popular.

Taking a deep breath, Regan shook off thoughts of the past and stared at the lifeless body sprawled at her feet. Apparently, one of the vampires had tired of surviving on Synthetic Type O. She felt a wave of pity for the dead man. In life, he had been a middle-aged man with sandy brown hair and a trim mustache. He might even have been handsome. Now his face was set in a rictus of horror. His heart, throat, and liver had been savagely ripped away, and there wasn't enough blood left in his body to fill an eyedropper. The corpse had been found under a bush by a couple who had been leaving the Park just before sunset. From the looks of it, the victim had been killed the night before.

"Hey, Reggie."

Regan looked away from the body and into the deep gray eyes of Sergeant Michael Flynn. Flynn was a good cop, honest, hardworking, and straightforward, a rarity in this day and age. He was a handsome man in his mid-thirties, with a shock of dark red hair and a dimple in his left cheek. She had gone out on a number of dates with

Mike in the last few months. He was fun to be with and she enjoyed his company. She knew Mike was eager to take their relationship to the next level, but she wasn't ready for that, not yet. She cared for him. She admired him. She loved him, but she wasn't in love with him. It was because he was the best friend she had in the city that she didn't want to complicate their friendship, or worse, jeopardize it, by going to bed with him. She had seen it happen all too often, a perfectly good friendship ruined when two people decided to sleep together.

"So," Flynn said, "definitely a vampire kill, right?"

"Looks that way," Regan agreed, but she wasn't sure. She had seen vampire kills before. The complete lack of blood pointed to a vampire, but the fact that the victim's heart, throat, and liver had been ripped out disturbed her. She had never known a vampire to take anything but blood from its prey.

"So, you about through here?" Flynn asked.

"What? Oh, sure." She wasn't a cop and she had no real authority on the scene, but in the past, whenever the department received a call about a suspected vampire killing, they had asked her to come out and take a look. She had been a vampire hunter in those days, and a darn good one, but that had been back in the good old days, before vampires became "protected" and put her out of a job. Fortunately, she had a tidy little inheritance from her grandfather, though it wouldn't last much longer if she didn't find another job soon.

"I'll call you next week," Flynn said with a wink.

Regan nodded, then moved away from the scene so the forensic boys could get to work. It gave her an edgy feeling, being in the park after the sun went down, though she supposed there were enough cops in the area to keep her reasonably safe from the monsters. At any rate, it felt good to be part of a criminal investigation again, good to feel needed. Still, she couldn't help feeling guilty that she would be out of work in a heartbeat as soon as they caught the killer.

She remembered the first time the department had requested her expertise. Even now, years later, the thought made her wince with embarrassment. After all the classes she had taken at the Police Academy, she had been convinced she was prepared for anything, but no amount of training could have prepared her for the reality of seeing that first fresh vampire kill. At the Academy, the bodies had been dummies and, while they had been realistic, they hadn't come close to the real thing. Regan had turned away and covered her mouth, trying in vain to keep her dinner down. It had been Michael who had come to her aid, who had offered her a handkerchief and assured her that it happened to everyone sooner or later. They had been friends from that night forward.

Now, she stood in the shadows, watching two men wearing masks and gloves slip the body into a black plastic bag for the trip to the morgue while the forensic team tagged and bagged possible evidence from the scene. Maybe they would get lucky downtown, but she didn't think so. She had a hunch that whoever had perpetrated the crime knew exactly what he was doing and that whatever evidence he had left behind, if any, would be useless.

Regan watched the ambulance pull away from the curb. Once the body had been thoroughly examined, the medical examiner would take the necessary steps to ensure that the corpse didn't rise as a new vampire tomorrow night. She didn't envy him the job, but if there was one thing the city didn't need, it was another vampire.

Regan was jotting down a few notes when she felt a shiver run down her spine. Not the "gee, it's cold outside" kind of shiver but the "you'd better be careful, there's a monster close by" kind.

Making a slow turn, she peered into the darkness as every instinct for self-preservation that she possessed screamed a warning.

If he hadn't moved, she never would have seen him.

He emerged from the shadowy darkness on cat-silent feet. "Do not be afraid," he said. "I mean you no harm."

His voice was like thick molasses covered in dark chocolate, so deep and sinfully rich, she could feel herself gaining weight just listening to him speak.

"Right." She slipped her hand into the pocket of her jacket, her fingers curling around the trigger of a snub-nosed pistol. She never left home without it. The gun was loaded with five silver bullets that had been dipped in holy water. The hammer rested on an empty chamber. "That's why you're sneaking up on me."

The corner of his sensual mouth lifted in a lazy half-smile. "If I wanted you dead, my lovely one, you would be dead."

Regan believed him. He spoke with the kind of calm assurance that left no room for doubt.

DESIRE AFTER DARK

Cursed to an eternity of darkness,
Antonio Battista has wandered the earth,
satisfying his hunger with countless women,
letting none find a place in his heart.
But Victoria Cavendish is different.

"You wish something?" he asked.

She shook her head. "No. Good night."

She started past him only to be stayed by the light touch of his hand on her shoulder. She could have walked on by. He wasn't holding her, but she stopped, her heart rate accelerating when she looked up and met his gaze.

Time slowed, could have ceased to exist for all she knew or cared. She was aware of nothing but the man standing beside her. His dark blue gaze melded with hers, igniting a flame that started deep within her and spread with all the rapidity of a wildfire fanned by a high wind.

Heart pounding, she looked at him, and waited.

He didn't make her wait too long.

He murmured to her softly in a language she didn't understand, then swept her into his arms and kissed her, a long searing kiss that burned away the memory of every other man she had ever known, until she knew only him, saw only him. Wanted only him.

He deepened the kiss, his tongue teasing her lips, sending flames along every nerve, igniting a need so primal, so volatile, she thought she might explode. She pressed her body to his, hating the layers of cloth that separated his flesh from hers. She had never reacted to a man's kisses like this before, never felt such an overwhelming need to touch and be touched. A distant part of her mind questioned her ill-conceived desire for a man she hardly knew, but she paid no heed. Nothing mattered now but his arms holding her close, his mouth on hers.

Battista groaned low in his throat. He had to stop this now, while he could, before his lust for blood overcame his desire for her sweet flesh. The two were closely interwoven, the one fueling the other. He knew he should let her go before it was too late, before his hunger overcame his good sense, before he succumbed to the need burning through him. He could scarcely remember the last time he had embraced a woman he had not regarded as prey. But this woman was more than mere sustenance. Her body fit his perfectly, her voice sang to his soul, her gaze warmed the cold dark places in his heart, shone like the sun in the depths of his hell-bound spirit.

He felt his fangs lengthen, his body tense as the hunger surged through him, a relentless thirst that would not long be denied.

Battista tore his mouth from hers. Turning his head away, he took several slow, deep breaths until he had regained control of the beast that dwelled within him.

"Antonio?" Vicki asked breathlessly. "Is something wrong?"

He took another deep breath before he replied, "No, my sweet." Summoning every ounce of willpower he possessed, he put her away from him. "It has been a long night. You should get some sleep."

She looked up at him, her eyes filled with confusion. He expected her to sleep, now?

He forced a smile. "Go to bed, my sweet one."

Vicki stared at him a moment; then, with a nod, she

left the room. That was the second time he had kissed her and then backed away. Was there something wrong with the way she kissed? But no, he had been as caught up in the moment as she. She couldn't have been mistaken about that.

She closed the bedroom door behind her, then stood there, trying to sort out her feelings. She knew very little about Mr. Antonio Battista. She had no idea where he came from, who he was, if he had a family or friends, or what he did for a living. But one thing she did know: no other man had ever affected her the way he did, intrigued her the way he did, made her want him the way he did.

Tomorrow morning, she thought. Tomorrow morning she would find out more about the mysterious Mr. Battista.

A WHISPER OF ETERNITY

When artist Tracy Warner purchases
the rambling seaside house
built above Dominic St. John's hidden lair,
he recognizes in her spirit the woman he has
loved countless times over the centuries.

She wasn't surprised when Dominic appeared in the doorway. He wore a long black cloak over a black shirt and black trousers. His feet were encased in soft black leather boots. Though she had refused to admit it, she had known, on some deep level of awareness, that this was his house.

He inclined his head in her direction. "Good evening. I trust you found everything you needed."

"Yes." Her fingers clenched around the brush. It was hard to speak past the lump of fear in her throat. "Thank you." Though why she should thank him was beyond her. He had brought her here without her consent, after all.

He took a step into the room.

She took a step back.

He lifted one brow. "Are you afraid of me now?"

"How did I get here? Why am I here?"

"I brought you here because I wanted you here."

"Why didn't I wake up?"

"Because I did not wish you to."

The fear in her throat moved downward and congealed in her stomach. She started to ask another question, but before she could form the words, he was standing in front of her, only inches away. She gasped, startled. She hadn't seen him move.

"I will not hurt you, my best beloved one."

"Where are we?"

"This is my house."

"But where are we?"

"Ah. We are in a distant corner of Maine."

"So, I'm your prisoner now."

"You are my guest."

"A guest who can't leave. Sounds like prison to me."

"We need time to get to know each other again. I will not be shut out of your life this time. I will not share you with another. This time, you will believe. This time, you will be mine."

"So you're going to keep me locked up inside this house?" She stared down at her hands, noticing, for the first time, that she was holding the brush so tightly, her knuckles were white. "And what if I believe and I still don't want you? Still don't want to be what you say you are?"

"Then I will let you go."

AFTER SUNDOWN

Edward Ramsey has spent his life hunting vampires.
Now he is one of them.
Yet Edward's human conscience—and his heart—
compel him to save beautiful Kelly Anderson.

After dinner, they drove to the beach and walked bare-foot along the shore. It was a calm, clear night. The moon painted ever-changing silver shadows on the water.

After a while, they stopped to watch the waves. Ramsey's gaze moved over Kelly. She looked beautiful standing there with the ocean behind her. Moonlight shimmered like molten silver in her hair; her skin looked soft and oh, so touchable. He wished, not for the first time, that he possessed a little of Chiavari's easy charm with women.

"Kelly?" He took a deep breath, the need to kiss her stronger than his need for blood. He knew he should turn away, afraid that one kiss would not be enough. Afraid that a taste of her lips would ignite his hellish thirst. But she was looking up at him, her brown eyes shining in the moonlight, her lips slightly parted, moist, inviting. He cleared his throat. The kisses they had shared at the movies had been much in his mind, but he had lacked the courage to kiss her again, afraid of being rebuffed. "I was thinking about the other night, at the movies. . . ."

"Were you? So was I."

"What were you thinking?" he asked.

"I was thinking maybe we should kiss again—you know, to see if it was as wonderful as I remember."

"Kelly . . ." He swept her into his arms, a part of him still expecting her to push him away or slap his face or laugh out loud, but she did none of those things. Instead, she leaned into him, her head tilting up, her eyelids fluttering down.

And he kissed her, there in the moonlight. Kissed her, and it wasn't enough. He wanted to inhale her, to drink her essence, to absorb her very soul into his own. She was sweet, so sweet. Heat sizzled between them, hotter than the sun he would never see again. Why had he waited so long?

"Oh, Edward . . ."

She looked up a him, breathless. She was soft and warm and willing. He covered her face with kisses, whispered praises to her beauty as he adored her with his hands and his lips. He closed his eyes, and desire rose up within him, hot and swift, and with it the overpowering urge to feed. He fought against it. He had fed well before coming here, yet the Hunger rose up within him, gnawing at his vitals, urging him to take what he wanted.

"This is crazy," she murmured breathlessly. "We hardly know each other."

"Crazy," he agreed. Her scent surrounded him. The rapid beat of her heart called to the beast within him. He deepened the kiss, at war with himself, felt his fangs lengthen in response to his growing hunger.

Romantic Suspense from
Lisa Jackson

See How She Dies
0-8217-7605-3 $6.99US/$9.99CAN

The Morning After
0-8217-7295-3 $6.99US/$9.99CAN

The Night Before
0-8217-6936-7 $6.99US/$9.99CAN

Cold Blooded
0-8217-6934-0 $6.99US/$9.99CAN

Hot Blooded
0-8217-6841-7 $6.99US/$8.99CAN

If She Only Knew
0-8217-6708-9 $6.50US/$8.50CAN

Unspoken
0-8217-6402-0 $6.50US/$8.50CAN

Twice Kissed
0-8217-6038-6 $5.99US/$6.99CAN

Whispers
0-8217-7603-7 $6.99US/$9.99CAN

Wishes
0-8217-6309-1 $5.99US/$6.99CAN

Deep Freeze
0-8217-7296-1 $7.99US/$10.99CAN

Final Scream
0-8217-7712-2 $7.99US/$10.99CAN

Fatal Burn
0-8217-7577-4 $7.99US/$10.99CAN

Shiver
0-8217-7578-2 $7.99US/$10.99CAN

Available Wherever Books Are Sold!
Visit our website at www.kensingtonbooks.com

Discover the Romances of
Hannah Howell

Nail-Biting Romantic Suspense from Your Favorite Authors